A Collection of Romantic Stories
Where Seclusion and Love Collide

Tammy Goodwin . Angie Jones . Charlie Jules
Denise Wells . Kayla Maya . Billie Parsons . Rachel Radner
Rene Folsom . Anna-Marie Lopez . Sam Trathen
Nikki Lynn Archambault . J. C. Smoak . Tina Gallagher

Parsons Publishing LLC

CONTENTS

ZERO: CADENCE

BY RENE FOLSOM

Cardinem.

...that moment in time when everything suddenly changes. An unseen force of nature forever transforms your world, as if your life is spinning on an axis that centers around one pivotal moment in time.

When the clock reaches zero.

USA TODAY BESTSELLING AUTHOR

RENE FOLSOM

THE COUNTDOWN SERIES

To all those who have loved and lost—know that there is hope and never let others make decisions when your heart is what hangs in the balance.

00:00:02:04:16:59

Ducking beneath the pipes and dodging various obstacles, I run as fast as I can, desperate to distance myself from him. A burning sensation in my legs causes me to slow, but I know I have to push on. My breath huffs from my lungs in pace with my stride, and my heart thrums in my chest, hard, rapid, like it is bound to leap out at any moment.

Just a little bit further. My shoes pound against the hard steel decks, echoing off the barren bulkheads, as I sprint down the long passageway. The muted green surface seems dingy under the scrutiny of the weak, florescent lights above—paint chipping from the metal surfaces and pipes that line the ceilings.

"Cadence Jane! I will find you," he hollers. It seems like his voice is coming from every direction, echoing off every surface, yet I still keep pushing toward my goal.

I know this particular passageway is a dead end. He is bound to catch me eventually if I go this way in the now-vacant base level of the station we are on. But that doesn't mean the chase isn't tons of fun. After all, there's not a whole lot to do to stay entertained on this hunk of metal anyway.

Approaching the end of the hall, I slow my pace, coming to a measured walk and peeking around the corners of various empty rooms and bends along the way. My heart continues to pound, blood whooshing through my ears, as I listen for signs of his advance.

Just when I think I've lost him, a pair of strong arms wrap around me, snatching me off the deck and making me squeal in surprise.

"Gotcha!" he cheers. "Thought you could get away?"

"Okay, I give up," I beg. "You win... again. Now put me down!" With surprising ease, he turns me around in his arms so I'm facing him. Pushing against his chest doesn't seem to help much, but I am not going to relinquish control that easily.

Then, looking into his blue eyes, I lose all the fight I have left. Despite no longer running, my breathing quickens along with my heart rate.

"When are you going to learn that I will always catch you?" he whispers, our stares locking. His chest rises and falls with heavy breaths while our bodies press close.

So close.

The feel of him is always so exquisite.

"Never," I respond with a shy smile.

Wrapping my arms around his neck, I give in to temptation and inch my lips toward his. Easing me down his body, he never allows any distance between us as he sets my feet on the metal surface of the deck.

With his mouth precariously close to mine, he whispers, "You know what this means, right?"

"No. What?" I ask, a crease to my brow. Our noses nearly touch, making his intentions clear as crystal.

"I win." With those two words, he dives in for the kiss. A sudden gasp of breath is all I can manage before our lips meet in a heated embrace.

His one hand tangles in my hair while his other pushes into the small of my back, holding me to him like I am his only oxygen source in the sea of stars surrounding us. Our tongues touch and tangle together as his chest presses hot and hard against mine. Struggling for air, I can't seem to pull away. He consumes me, and I love it.

His mouth probes at mine. First nipping with his teeth, he soothes my upper lip with his tongue before moving to the corner of my mouth. His touch, his kiss, his very essence, surrounds my soul, filling me with a sense of bliss I have only dreamed of.

Snaking his hand beneath my ass, he lifts me, causing me to straddle his hips while he carries me into the room at the end of the hall. We'd found this unit a few months back and enjoy the privacy of the abandoned sector hidden in the bowels of the space station. The far room has several bunks that are no longer used—perfect for two lovers needing to escape the reality of controlling worlds and relish in the confinements of the single room.

As he carries me toward a mattress we placed on the deck, I can feel his excitement pressing into my center through his pants.

Reaching for him, I glide my fingers through his silky, dark hair at the nape of his neck and pull him closer. With my arms still wrapped around him, I begin moving my hips slightly, uncontrollably, against his body.

Normally we use this space to talk, maybe make out a little, and ultimately escape the judgmental eyes of our parents and the rest of the station's civilians. It's like our own little shelter—a way to confine ourselves from the world and enjoy the solidarity of each other.

Not today though. Today, I want more from the man who currently holds me so passionately in his arms.

His strong hands brace the middle of my back as he sets me down onto the plush surface. I loll my head to the side, offering my neck as he trails kisses down my jaw. Throwing my head back gently, I willingly offer more of myself to him.

His kisses trail down the neckline of my rather busty top. The wet sensation of his tongue tracing the swell of my breasts make a moan escape my mouth in a sound of pure ecstasy.

He slowly pecks and licks his way back up to my mouth, devouring me again and laving at me with his tongue.

His strong fingers caress my cheek and the side of my head as he begins to pull away. Our breaths are short and erratic. Our foreheads are pressed together, the tension between us exploding like a rocket, sizzling through our bodies.

I want you, Mason," I whisper between panting breaths, my lips still within an inch of his and tingling in the aftermath of his touch. "I want you now."

He pulls back and looks at me with a bewildered expression on his face. Mason Delancy—my best friend since our teen years—is no longer the infuriating boy who teased me and expressed himself with immaturity. Now he is a man—a strong, handsome man—and I know I can't hold my desires back any longer.

"CJ, I don't know..." His rejection puts a pout on my face I know damn well he can't ignore. "It's not that I don't want to. God, you know I want to. But, we... we just can't." With the rebuff still hanging in the air, he stretches out on the mattress beside me and pulls me to him, allowing me to lay my head on his chest and listen to his heart beating wildly.

Yeah, I know why he is hesitating—although I don't agree—and it has nothing to do with how much, or how little, he desires me.

The thing that brought us together could be the very thing that will tear us apart.

Cardinem.

The timers embedded in our wrists seal our fates. Each time the number flips, it counts down to the moment we will finally meet our soul mate. It's the universe saying we are predestined to be with one person... the only other person in the cosmos who share our second in time.

Mason's clock ticks in rhythm with mine, nearly identical in every way, except for one number.

Our fate is off by *one* second.

Still, I am, and always will be, certain it's a fluke—a minor discrepancy that can't possibly change the way we feel about each other, or the outcome of our destiny.

Even though I am determined to be with Mason for eternity, I can't help the nagging question that constantly barrels around in my mind. If we are truly destined to be soul mates, then why did we meet so many years before our timers would reach zero?

"Mason?" I ask, glancing up toward his face.

"Hmm?" he responds as he reaches out and grabs my hand, lacing his fingers with mine.

"Let's come down here for our *Cardinem*. I want to be with you, and you only, when they stop."

"Are you that confident we're one another's match?" he asks, sitting up slightly to meet my eyes. "Because, I've been doing the research, and there hasn't been a single case of soul mates who didn't have identical times, down to the millisecond."

"All I know is that I can't stand the thought of being with anyone but you," I say with honesty as I lean in and peck him on the nose. "Please, Mason?"

Sighing, he agrees. "Anything for you." His words spark the memory of why I brought him down here in the first place.

"Anything?" I ask, arching my brow and curious if he'll take the bait.

"Of course. Anything," he agrees with a kiss to my forehead.

Pushing at his chest, I force him to lie flat on his back and climb on top of him, straddling him with my legs. My long, blonde hair falls into a curtain around us as I brace my elbows on either side of his head.

With our lips nearly touching, I softly say, "Make love to me."

"CJ, you know we're not even supposed to be kissing, let alone anything more."

"We're two consenting adults. I don't see how this stupid *Cardinem* should stop us from showing what we mean to each other." Placing seductive pecks along his jaw, I finally murmur, "I want to feel you inside me."

A groan emanates from his chest, making his frustration obvious.

Without a response from him, I sit up on my knees and unfasten the front of my shirt. I know if I don't do it now, it will never happen. I didn't seclude us deep in the body of this ship to puss out when things finally got heated. My happiness is on the line.

All Mason can do is watch, with shock and fascination on his face, as my soft, small fingers flick each latch on my shirt. Soon, my top is splayed open, showing the sexiest lace bra I own—hell, the *only* lace bra I own.

Boldly, I grab his hands and lead them up my torso, between my breasts, and to my shoulders, directing him to remove the scrap of vinyl from my body. He does as instructed and slowly pushes the shirt down my arms. Within moments, I unclasp my bra and toss it to the side.

Mason stares at my nakedness, his mouth agape and expression void of any reaction. Doubt tickles the back of my mind with worry that he won't approve of me. I never even thought about being self-conscious around him before—he has always made me feel desirable. Not wanting me isn't something I even consider until this moment as I sit above him, partially nude and vulnerable.

Just as I am about to change my mind, he speaks.

"God, Cadence. You're so damn beautiful." His fingers dig into my hips as his eyes rake over my upper body.

Without wavering from my plan, I grab one of his hands and coax him to touch me. I want to feel more than his eyes adoring me. Just as his hand is about to make contact with my breast, he tries to pull away marginally, like he's hesitant to even touch me.

"What's wrong?" I ask, lacing my fingers with his and placing a light kiss to his knuckles, hoping to ease the tension he holds tight in his muscles.

"If I touch you, I'm worried I won't be able to stop." His hand trembles at the mere mention of the sensual act. I know just as much as he does that society takes *Cardinem* very seriously. A man and a woman who aren't predestined to be together shouldn't even consider acts of the sexual nature. It is unheard of for two people to engage in sexual activity before their timers reach zero.

"I know," I whisper. "But I need to feel your hands on me. Please, Mason."

"Come," he says with conviction, coaxing me off his lap and onto my back. "Lie down."

Hesitant at first, I finally concede and follow his orders. As soon as I am settled onto my back, he props his head up with one arm and uses his other hand to trace the line of my jaw.

With delicate attentiveness, he continues his fingered assault down my neck and over my collarbones, until he reaches the juncture between my breasts. My breath shudders at the nearness of his hands against my sensitive peaks. One quick thrust of my chest and I can close the distance between us, effectively relieving me of this delicious torment.

"So beautiful," he whispers again as his eyes watch his fingers trace lazy circles on my skin. His hand slowly trails down my cleavage and comes back around to cup my breast.

I suck in a ragged breath and roll my eyes at the feel of his fingers grazing my nipple. Just that one simple touch is more pleasure than I could have ever imagined. Yes, I've touched myself before, but it never felt as good as it does now with his fingers tracing over my sensitive skin.

A moan escapes my lips before I ever have a chance to think otherwise, filling the void around us with my sounds of desire.

"Does that feel good?" Mason asks against my ear.

"God, yes," I breathe, thrusting my chest upward to encourage him for more. Fluttering my eyes shut, I take the moment to enjoy the exquisite feeling of his sensual touch.

With my breast still cupped gently in his palm, he closes his mouth over my nipple.

An intake of air hisses through my teeth as pleasure explodes through my body.

"God, I love your breasts," he murmurs, switching to the other nipple and begins his tantalizing assault with his tongue.

Twining my fingers into his hair, I hold him tighter against me, relishing the feel of his hot breath against my skin.

Breaking away, he looks at me, his gaze blazing through me like fire, and says, "You're so beautiful. I can't seem to get enough of you." He speaks soothing words that make me feel special as he fully climbs on top of me and settles between the juncture of my thighs.

"I love it when you tell me I'm beautiful." My voice is nearly a whisper in the dark, yet sounds so loud as it bounces off the void of the vacant rooms.

I clutch his biceps, wanting nothing more than to feel his power. Touching the fabric of his sleeves, I snake my arms to his waist and begin tugging his shirt up his body. In one swift movement, he grabs the back of his tee and pulls it over his head, discarding it across the room with a thump.

With steady fingers, I trail my hands down the front of his gorgeous, toned chest. The dim glow from the timer embedded in my wrist barely illuminates the curves of his strength. His muscles aren't large and bulky.

Instead, he is perfect—cut and defined at a size just large enough for me to grab hold of.

He slowly begins his descent again, causing my skin to erupt in a constant flurry of crackling warmth. My back arches, seeking more of his attention.

I suck in another quick breath of air when his lips close around my nipple again, and his tongue toys with my peak. He nips at the bud, grazing my puckered skin with his teeth.

The sharp, tantalizing feel of his mouth on me causes me to moan—loudly. My sounds of ecstasy echo off the metal bulkheads, making him smile against my skin.

With warm fingers, he traces my side and makes his way down my body—down to the depths of my soul. With a tormenting measure, he finally makes it to the waist of my pants.

My heart picks up its pace at just the thought of Mason touching me... down there. We've never gone this far together and, I am sure as the starlit sky is black, I won't last long if he continues with his delicious tirade.

With the same arm that holds his timer, he begins to toy with the latch on my pants and lifts his head to see what he is doing. The loss of his mouth on my breasts is barely discernible with the growing anticipation of what is yet to come.

After releasing the latch, he sits up on his knees and tugs at the waist of my pants. I lift my butt to help, amazed at how comfortable and excited I am with my clothes being removed by him.

He gets rid of my pants and panties with one rapid movement before staring down at my naked form. His gaze bores through me, touching the very core of me, as if I am the most beautiful thing he has ever laid his eyes on. Just the look on his face has heat pooling between my legs.

Lying along my side, Mason leans forward and takes my mouth with a furious force. Just the potency of his kiss is enough to take my breath away.

With an abrupt halt to our passionate kiss, he pulls back and whispers against my lips. "CJ, no matter what happens for our *Cardinem*, I want you to know something."

I can barely think with the feel of his warm breath tickling my skin and his hard body pressing against my side. Realizing he is waiting for a response, I touch his cheek and look into his eyes, before saying, "And what's that?"

"That you're my girl. No matter what happens, or how our supposed fate is determined, you will always be a part of me."

His words, while touching and oh so real, seems more like a farewell instead of what he probably means them to be. I notice my mind wandering to dangerous places in regard to our future, so I stuff the bleak possibilities in the back of my brain and focus on the present.

"Mason?"

"Yeah?"

"Shut up and kiss me."

A sexy grin is the only answer I need as he dives in for the kill. His hand finds my breast once more as his tongue dances in my mouth with enchanting torment.

Slowly, and even more gingerly than before, he draws his hand down the center of my body. His warm fingers tickle over the small triangle of curls just above my wetness, causing me to thrive beneath his provocative assault.

As if he knows one touch will surely do me in, he lifts his head and gazes into my eyes. Within moments, his finger drives between my slick folds and makes contact.

As I tense and tighten my grip in his hair, he thrusts his finger against me, causing me to let out a strangled cry. I tremble uncontrollably, my legs shaking, my mouth dry, and my senses screaming for reprieve.

I moan helplessly as my orgasm starts to build and swell. I quiver as waves of pleasure ripple through me like an incoming tidal wave. Exquisite indulgence bombards me and rains down over my body.

My sob echoes over the room and I fight for breath as gratification overtakes me, robbing my sense of reality.

I know if he touches me I won't last long, but the magnitude of pleasure is unfathomable, especially since I am aware his eyes are on me—watching me come apart beneath him.

Looking up into his face, I feel the sudden need to apologize for coming so quickly. Surely, he was expecting more from me than that.

"I'm sorry, Mason. I couldn't hel—" His lips cut off my explanation with a quick, yet scorching kiss.

"Shh. No need to be sorry. That was, by far, the hottest thing I have ever witnessed." His acceptance makes me feel marginally better. "Come, I'll help you get dressed so you don't get chilly."

"Wait," I say, grasping at the back of his neck so he won't, can't, get up. "Where are you going?"

"CJ... damn it." He sighs as he places his hand on my cheek—the same one that so skillfully made me climax and break into a million pieces mere moments before. "I want so badly to bury myself deep inside you and watch you tremble beneath me until you scream my name. You have no idea what a struggle it is to control myself and not take you, right here, right now. But, we just can't. The trouble you could get into just isn't worth it."

All I can hear out of his mouth is the word *worth*. "I'm not worth it?"

"No, that's not what I said."

Knowing I don't want to be the broken girl or the damsel in distress, I decide to take matters into my own hands and rip his self-control apart at the seams. Reaching down, I grasp his length through his pants. Before he can react, I begin to rub up and down, soliciting a rather masculine grunt from him as his eyes roll to the back of his head.

"Mason. Our *Cardinem* is only a few days away. I want... no, I *need* to feel you, even if it's just this once. I desperately need you inside me. You have been my everything for the past seven years. Ever since we were thirteen, you have been all I can think about." I pause to make sure he is paying close attention to the words leaving my mouth. "I love you. And I want to show you just how much before it's too late."

With those three important words spilling from my lips, Mason squints his eyes shut as if in pain. Not quite crying, but obviously filled with gut-wrenching emotion, he opens them and says, "I love you too, Cadence. Always have. Always will. Which is why I'm going to put my foot down and say no. If anyone finds out we've gone as far as we have—God, I don't even want to think of the consequences. I care way too much for you to let my dick make the decisions."

My heart aches—shatters into a million pieces—first because of his refusal, and then because I know he's right. Deep down, I know it's a stupid move to have sex before our *Cardinem*. But what if I will never be able to feel him in my arms again?

"Say something, CJ. Anything," he begs, obviously concerned with my silence.

Sitting up and curling my arms and legs around my naked body, I respond, "I don't know what to say, Mason. Even though I know you're right, it doesn't change the fact that I still—" My words are cut off with emotion... emotion I am determined not to show in front of him, no matter the issue. I am dead set on keeping the tears at bay, at least until I get to my private unit and seclude myself.

I push myself up off the mattress and make quick work with dressing, never asking for a response from him. While placing his shirt back over his head, I notice he is watching me like a hawk, as if every move I make will somehow change our fate.

Sliding my shoes back on and fastening my shirt, I become increasingly angry. My fury seems to grow with each latch I fasten until I am shaking.

Strong arms reach for me. Bringing me close, he holds me against his chest. He always knows how to read my emotions and discerns I need his comfort even when I am falsely projecting my fear and anger toward him.

I drop my hands from the latches of my shirt and meld myself to his strong, protective body. Tears I was attempting to hold back suddenly burst forth unbidden. My shoulders shake as my best friend holds me, comforts me, and makes me feel somewhat whole.

Lifting my head, I open my mouth to say something and am suddenly interrupted by an intense quake. The metal surfaces shake beneath our feet, causing the items surrounding us to come to life with movement.

Within moments, a loud siren begins to wail through the long passageways. A sea of red light surrounds us as another rumble shakes us to our core.

If it weren't for Mason's strong arms wrapped securely around me, I would've surely fallen from the forceful tremors.

"Something's wrong," he says, stating the obvious. "C'mon. We need to get out of here... now!"

Grasping my hand with a protective force I've never experienced from him, Mason drags me out of the room and hurries to ascend back up to the main level. The sheer speed with which we run quickly dries my tears before we reach the main deck of the station.

My lungs feel like they have been set on fire when I push my way through the final doorway and into utter pandemonium. Mason holds me tightly as we snake our way through the chaos. Where people are running to is beyond me. It isn't like there is an *outside* to escape to unless we want to die in the vast darkness that surrounds the vessel.

The *Mira* Station is one of the largest human space stations in existence, as far as I know. Being self-sufficient—growing our own foods and purifying our plentiful water supply—makes the small community one that many across the universe stand in line for. And, unlike other space stations, *Mira* orbits the sun as if it were its own planet in the small solar system.

So, evacuating a space station that holds over ten thousand people doesn't sound very plausible, or fun for that matter. Even though so many live on this hunk of metal, we still live in confinement, sequestered away from the rest of the worlds that also play ring-around-the-rosie with the sun.

Peace guards stand strong, their droid-like facades masking their true human forms. They are obviously trying to keep people calm as they wait for further instruction.

Mira's chancellor finally makes her appearance—her face lighting up the large bulkhead of the main deck in a holographic display. She definitely isn't a pretty woman, but her words often calm even the most panicked masses.

"As you may have noticed by the severe tremors, *Mira* has been struck by unknown space debris. The entire *Omicron* Sector has been damaged and parts of the *Pi* and *Rho* Sectors have also been affected. For your protection, the damaged sectors have been temporarily sealed off from the vacuum that surrounds us. Since the *Omicron* Sector stores our oxygen replenishing supplies, we will need to make swift decisions regarding evacuation until our engineers can assess and repair the damages. It is of the utmost importance that you listen to the directions supplied by the guard when it comes time to evacuate your sectors. Every being should return to their units until each sector is called for evacuation..."

Mira is a large sphere divided into twenty-four sectors total, eight of which are filled with residential units. The core of *Mira* is off-limits to the common human. Only the employees, engineers, and occasional droids are allowed in the lower levels. The commotion that continues around us ensures the guards are too preoccupied to notice that Mason and I just emerged from one of the prohibited tunnels.

Chancellor Aldric continues with her evacuation instructions, but the words about separate sector evacuations keeps swimming in my head, drowning all other thoughts in their wake.

Looking up at Mason, I blurt out my biggest fear. "We're going to be separated."

Without drawing too much attention to our embrace, he hugs me and places a soft kiss to my forehead.

00:00:01:11:46:44

Boarding one of the many zeppelins—the only transport airship I've ever ridden on—I can't help the panic that rises in my throat. My mother must have noticed me tremble, because she pats the top of my hand in a soothing gesture and whispers her assurance that everything will be okay.

The evacuation isn't what makes my head spin with uncertainty and fear. Being separated from Mason during my *Cardinem* is what makes my nerves spike to full attention. Hell, being separated from Mason at all has apprehension clawing at my insides. Glancing down at the numbers embedded in my wrist, I hold my breath and watch as they continue to count down—a newfound dread reaching my heart with each tick of the timer.

"Everything happens for a reason, Cadence," my mother, Em, says as she places her hand over my timer, effectively covering up the feared evidence of my fate. My mother's face is twisted in a combined expression of sadness and resolve.

Despite the fact that my mom usually turns a blind eye to my obsession, she knows how much Mason means to me. Ever since my father passed, my mother's compassion and understanding for companionship increased. She must miss him terribly, even though she chooses not to talk about it much. She is all about concentrating only on happy memories, but I can still see the occasional sadness in her eyes.

My mom hugs my shoulder, making me hope for at least a bit of solace in this unforeseen turn of events. It doesn't matter that I am twenty Earth-years old. My mother's comforting embrace will always make the fear fade, even if only for a few moments.

Heading back toward Earth—a planet I haven't stepped foot on since I was a child visiting—I have an overwhelming feeling I'll never be the same. The evidence is clear. I will meet my soul mate in a little less than thirty-six hours. And, with the slow pace of *Mira's* evacuation, I have a strong sense that Mason won't be there in time.

The realization coats my emotions with nothingness, making me numb. I suddenly feel like I am just going through the motions in solidarity, being herded like mindless droids as a quarter of the humans from my sector are shooed off the zeppelin's platform. The ride to Earth is a relatively short one, but in my distracted and anxious state, it seems to fly by in an instant. I barely even notice the intensity of Earth's gravity until I am forced to stand.

Keeping close to my mother, I maintain my passive gaze with my head down as I watch my feet shuffle along the dirty concrete. My steps feel weighted, sluggish, as if it takes more effort just to make a few meager strides. I'm not sure if it is the increase in gravity that my body needs to get used to, or if it's my state of mind making something as simple as walking a dire feat. There is simulated gravity on *Mira*, but the difference between the space station and Earth is suddenly obvious—and heavy.

The sun beats down on my shoulders—a sensation I don't remember but suddenly enjoy. The warmth reminds me of Mason. It seems like everything is a constant reminder he's still stuck back at *Mira* until his sector will be rescued.

Our instructions are to keep together until news is received regarding *Mira's* condition. The fear we will have to stay on Earth indefinitely seems to be lost on us all. Everyone is taking this change with an eerie calm that frightens me a bit, as if we are used to someone higher up making decisions for us without question.

Thankfully, this section of North America has upgraded their accommodations since I last stepped foot on the once-dilapidated planet. Earth's occupants seemed to have bounced back and rebuilt nicely after the devastating effects of World War V in 2401, which is surprising considering it was only a mere thirteen years ago.

I might be young, but I don't remember Earth being quite so beautiful and bright. The greens and blues being animated by the sun's rays are a stark contrast to the usual steel and white colors of *Mira*. Yes, the space station has gardens and foliage in certain areas, but the simulated light sources don't quite do them justice. The holographic scenes displayed in various sectors definitely don't compare to the real thing.

The experience is bittersweet because all I can think of is how much I wish Mason was here to enjoy the view with me. I am so used to sharing every aspect of my day with him. So, for him to be ripped from my everyday routine is more difficult to grasp than leaving the only thing I've ever called my home.

In reality, *Mason* is my home, not some space station. *Mira* is simply a hunk of metal floating through a vacuum. My friend is the only home I know.

The occupants of my sector are invited to stay at the Dara Colony, which is located in an area once known as California. I notice the beach first. Oceanic waves are something I've never experienced before and paled in comparison to the photos and holograms I've seen in class and throughout *Mira's* historical sectors.

Pulling my transmitter from my pocket, I sit at one of the benches on the boardwalk and try to pick up a signal. I know Earth's occupants use a somewhat primitive cellular phone system still, but I'm not sure if my transmitter works the same or not. I remember some of my friends communicating with family members on Earth using their transmitters, so the idea seems plausible.

"It won't work while we're down on this godforsaken rock," a girl's voice says, causing me to jump.

I look up, peering into a pair of female eyes and frown. I don't know Haden well, other than she is about two or three years older and works opposite shifts at the same café on *Mira*. I watch as Haden sits beside me on the bench.

"I figured it wouldn't, but—"

"Yeah, I know. My best friend is in the last sector to be evacuated. What kills me is the unknown. I'm not sure if she'll make it off *Mira* in time, and I heard in passing that they're placing us in different colonies."

"Wait, what?" Panic rises like poison in my throat. "They're not placing us all near each other?"

"There's no way they can. Earth is overpopulated as it is. They're placing us in various colonies, but I don't know which colony is accepting her sector." Haden shakes her head and looks away, disappointment clear on her face.

"Do you happen to know where they're placing the *Lambda* Sector?"

She shakes her head again, this time more adamantly than before causing her dark curls to swirl messily in her face from the ocean's breeze.

"I'm guessing that's Mason's sector?" She doesn't dare look at me while the question barrels out of her pretty little mouth. Everyone who knows me, even a little, knows Mason and I are inseparable.

"Yeah," I answer, glancing down at the timer in my wrist. Haden must notice the direction of my thoughts though, because her voice lowers in volume.

"He's not your match, you know," she whispers. It isn't a question. She is clearly stating the obvious. "If he were, you two wouldn't have met yet."

I don't answer. Instead, I just stare at the waves in the distance. My plans to seclude myself in a room with my best friend, the love of my life, during my *Cardinem*, begins to crumble—the alternative eating away at my resolve.

Sitting next to an acquaintance from my sector, an almost stranger, I let myself go and start to cry.

00:00:00:17:55:26

That night, while sharing a bed with my mother, I try to settle my mind. The idea of the entire world shutting down in order to sleep is foreign to me. We have schedules on *Mira*, but there is no moment in time where things go dark across the entire sphere.

Day and night aren't a factor, or even something we think about in a society entirely simulated. Seasons are a thing I've only experienced when reading classic novels or perusing the historical sectors.

Now, lying next to my mother in a restless state of frustration, I am hot, and obviously not used to summers on Earth.

Ripping the covers from my body, I look over at my mom to make sure I'm not going to wake her. My transmitter is never going to get a signal, it's dead in the water, and I don't have any idea what time it is. The uncertainty bothers me, not to mention the lack of music and media. I am clearly beginning to go through sensory withdrawals.

A few other citizens from *Mira* are bunking in the same room, so I try with all my might to stay as quiet as possible while I ease out of the warm unit. Thankfully, the buildings of the Dara Colony all look to have wraparound balconies that overlook the ocean. The view of the moon and stars hovering precariously over the water is one thing I will never forget.

An audible sigh works its way through my lungs as I breathe in the salty air, relishing in the feel of the wind coursing through my hair and refreshing my face. The difference between the stifling air inside the room and the ocean breeze outside is invigorating to say the least.

Sadness descends on my heart once more, worry tickling my spine with the idea that Mason is still stuck on the damaged space station so far away. Looking up into the star-filled sky, I wonder what is going through his mind. Is he still hurting? Is he already on transport to Earth? Is he still waiting for the next zeppelin to arrive?

Is he thinking of me?

I shake my head, attempting to rid my thoughts of the nagging dread that keeps me awake on this dark night. If I were on *Mira* right now, there'd be all kinds of things to do in order to occupy my mind. The theater would be active—classic twenty-first century films all the rage. The library is always thrumming with activity, and I can forever get lost in a book—if only my transmitter had a dang signal.

The thought of the library brings back a wonderfully delicious memory of Mason.

It was my eighteenth birthday, and Mason had asked me what I wanted to do for the special day. Hating to be the center of attention, I insisted we spend several hours in the library. I was searching for a particular paperback book and craved the seclusion of the archives.

Of course, the library was known to be a place of social activity rather than the literary resource it was once utilized as in previous centuries. With the use of tablets and media transmitters, there was no real need for shelves and shelves of books. Most of Mira's *citizens didn't even know the archives existed.*

There was one level completely filled with historical paperbacks that occasional citizens of Mira *brought with them from Earth over the past several decades. Since no one really saw the need for such archaic items, the filing system was practically nonexistent and the treasured items were placed haphazardly on the shelves. Finding a certain book was basically a hit or miss.*

The fact Mason was willing to spend his time helping me find a particular book made my heart swell for the man. It was the first time I saw him as more than just a friend, wanted him for more, and made my desires known.

When we finally found the paperback copy of the book we'd been hunting for, I squealed all too loudly as I tackle-hugged Mason, successfully pushing him to the deck and hovering over him. Too excited to hold back, I placed messy kisses all over his face until he laughed freely.

The sound of his laughter was heartwarming.

Things suddenly turned serious, the sexual tension finally becoming a tangible thing between us as I continued to stare into Mason's eyes. Frozen in place, I held my breath and couldn't bring myself to look away.

Reaching his hand up to cup my cheek, he regarded me adoringly and said, "I love watching you smile."

Of course, my response was to widen my smile as nerves fluttered in my stomach with his compliment. I wanted so badly for him to kiss me, our bodies pulsing with the need to close the gap between our lips.

Looking at the arm he still extended toward my face, I caught sight of his timer and was reminded of why our current embrace was a mistake. Mason noticed where my thoughts went and reluctantly released me.

Pulling away, I sat near him on the deck of the historical section and crossed my legs as I flipped through the thick papers, inhaling the musty scent like it was a beautiful bouquet of flowers.

My eyes fluttered shut—the sound of the pages flicking across my fingers was like a sweet lullaby to my ears.

"What do you find so fascinating about these books? You could have read it on your tablet within a few minutes, or even listened to it on your transmitter. Why go through all this trouble?" Mason asked, his voice full of sincere curiosity at my captivation.

"I've already read the entire series from this author on my tablet. So, it's not just reading the story." I hesitated, wondering how to explain so he would understand. "There's just something about holding it in my hand. Almost like it's truly real—something tangible to see, feel, smell..."

He propped himself up on one arm and grinned at my enthusiasm.

"I know, I sound stupid," I scoffed.

"Not stupid. Charming. Passionate." His words made me blush. "Why this particular book though?"

"Well, the author's mind fascinates me, mainly because of when it was written. Her speculations of our future at the time were so detailed and romantic, especially the progression of our social cultures and..." I paused, holding up my arm as evidence. "I enjoy the fantasy of it all, especially the fact she was amorous enough to never anticipate something like this coming."

"Like what? Our Cardinem *clocks?"*

"Yeah. I am intrigued by the notion that love was once a choice. The adventure of falling in love, finding your soul mate amongst billions of people around the Earth, seems so much more realistic than being told who you're meant to be with for eternity. I feel like I would much rather go through loss and heartache in order to find my true match, instead of being told by a stupid internal timer when my soul will finally be complete. Not to mention sex should be a choice as well, instead of being forced to wait until this damn thing reaches zero." I sulked for a moment before shaking my head and chuckling to hide my discomfort at my rambling. "I can't help but feel like these timers were placed here on purpose to control us rather than allowing us to make mistakes for ourselves."

"Wait, you don't think they always existed? I thought..." He hesitated. "We were taught that humans used to just ignore their timers, which is what caused all kinds of havoc with divorce, unwanted babies, and sexually motivated crimes. You don't think that's true?"

"I have a hard time believing that. I won't ever say it to anyone else but you because it's only my speculation, but why would humans go so many centuries ignoring something they see every single day? No. History shows that humans suddenly became aware of their Cardinem *timers after the collapse and reformation of society. I find it too convenient to be coincidental. Suddenly, we're a society free of indecision when it comes to love. It's almost as if love has given up and all that's left is our preassigned mate."*

He looked up at me, confusion crinkling his brow.

"I just don't understand the concept that a silly timer we're born with determines the love of our life," I said, hugging the book close to my chest and tugging at the sleeve of my shirt. "It doesn't seem realistic to me. It's not a concept I can grasp. Now, this," I added, gesturing between Mason and my own body. "I get this. This is real. This feels right. I..."

I hesitated, doubt flitting across my face, worried I was saying too much.

Sitting up, Mason reached for me and wrapped his hand securely around mine. He didn't say anything at first. He just sat, staring at our fingers intertwined with each other.

"Mason," I said softly. "I want it to be you."

Suddenly, his head popped up, and his intense gaze burned through me like fire. Bringing himself to his knees, he grabbed my face gently and leaned in... close. Pressing his forehead to mine, he whispered, "I know."

That was the first time Mason ever kissed me. I vividly remember the feel of his soft lips and the intensity behind his actions. It's like he'd been waiting a thousand years for just a taste of me, and suddenly all his tension melted when our souls finally touched.

"Can't sleep?" a voice says, startling me and interrupting the memories of my first kiss and all things Mason. Turning my back to the ocean, I meet Haden's stare.

"The whole concept that this entire colony shuts down for sleep is just bizarre. It's giving me the creeps," I respond honestly, making my shiver visible. "I'm going stir crazy with the fact there's nothing to do."

"Yeah, I know. Some dude in my unit is snoring so loudly, there's no way I can even think of sleeping," Haden jokes. "I wish our transmitters would at least pick up some music. But a local kid told me we would need a satellite subscription here on Earth for it to work."

"I know what you mean. My thoughts are just a little too loud for me to sleep. Music would definitely dumb things down a bit for me." I pause, wishing I didn't break down in front of Haden earlier that day. "Listen, I'm sorry about earlier. I lost my cool and that doesn't happen often. It's just been a very emotional and shocking few days."

"Shit, don't worry about it," Haden replies with a flick of her wrist. "To be honest, the fact you were showing some human emotion was refreshing. So many people around here act like cyborgs with their rock-hard resolve."

She has a point. Everyone is acting like *Mira's* accident is just par for the course and doesn't really affect our lives much. They seemed so calm after they safely landed on Earth. Don't any of them have someone they worry about they had to leave behind? Aren't they concerned they may never return to the space station they call home?

"How much time do you have left?" Haden blurts out, pointing toward my wrist with a single nod.

Glancing at my timer, I quickly cover it with my hand, an act of shame I've never felt before. "Just under eighteen hours." My head drops with the realization.

"I still have a little over seven months, and my nerves are standing on end with just the thought."

Looking over at Haden, I am forced to remember I'm not the first one to go through something like this—and I definitely won't be the last.

"I feel sick to my stomach," I admit. "I wanted Mason to be the one standing next to me as we watched all the numbers reach zero. His timer being nearly identical to mine made me want to at least experience it with him, even if he's not the one my numbers are meant for. Having him next to me would just feel... well, normal."

"Yeah, but from what I've seen, it all happens for a reason," she says, causing me to glare at her with annoyance. I am sick of people saying everything happens for a reason. The whole destiny shit is grating at my last, ever-loving nerve. I open my mouth to speak, but the other girl continues, "I'm sorry, but it's true. You're on Earth for a reason. You've been separated from Mason for a reason. And you'll meet your soul mate here for a reason."

"I just can't even imagine..." I cut myself off before I say too much. "I feel like I'm not allowed to make my own choices. The decision has been made *for* me, and I'm forced to grin and be happy about it."

"I know. I've done so much research on it, desperately trying to figure out how it works. How it *knows*. How we are somehow fated to a specific day, time, place, and person," Haden rambles. "The only assurance I have found is everyone, every single person, praises the success of their *Cardinem*. They truly love their matches. I don't think I ran across a single case study that wasn't happy with their soul mate. I can only hope it's true."

I nod, completely understanding where Haden is coming from, yet wondering if unhappy stories have been redacted for some reason. Leaning against the railing, we stare at the ocean—the waves making the scene come alive with power.

00:00:00:11:23:47

The bright sun shining through the plethora of windows has me awake before I deem comfortable.

"Ugh. Don't these windows have tinted shades?" I whine, covering my face with a pillow.

"I'm sure they have a holographic tinting system built in, but who would want to cover up that beautiful view?" my mom says beside me.

Cracking one eye open, I force my eyes to adjust to the brightness and finally focus on the stunning ocean view. It truly *is* breathtaking. Too bad Mason isn't here to enjoy it.

"Mom, has anyone heard anything about *Mira's* evacuation or where they placed Mason's sector?" I ask as we both lay there watching the waves crash against the impossibly white sand.

"Not that I know of, but we'll try to get some information today. Someone has to at least know where they've been relocated," she assures. "I'm going to see what there is for breakfast. Don't seclude yourself for long."

Smiling, she rises from the bed and gracefully exits the room.

I can't help but glance at the damn numbers scrawled across my wrist. Just over eleven hours. My stomach lurches at the thought.

"Christ, Mason. Where are you when I need you?" I whisper. Thankfully, the room is empty, except for a little boy sleeping soundly across the way. Closing my eyes, I try to remember the first time I met the infuriating Mason Delaney.

A new group of humans were brought from Earth to settle on Mira. *I was seething when my physics teacher sat this lanky boy next to me because I was rather enjoying the open space. Being a bratty teenager, I was rude and standoffish. I didn't bother looking in his direction or introducing myself to the new boy in class.*

It wasn't until I was forced to look in his direction that I noticed his timer. With a second glance, I watched helplessly as the numbers continued ticking, counting down to an eerily similar goal.

With several jerks of my head back and forth, I realized our Cardinem *had a mere second difference.*

"What are you staring at?" he asked coldheartedly, but was cut off when he also noticed the similarity. "Huh. Well, that's interesting."

Before I could control my reaction, I looked into his eyes and lost all sense of myself. The blue gaze that stared back at me couldn't possibly be real. I'd never seen a color so vibrant, so full of life.

The fact he made me feel flustered caught me off guard and caused my defenses to falter. I wanted so badly to tell him to go away, but something about him drew me in. I wanted to know more about the boy with blue eyes, and the thought scared me a little.

While my attraction toward him seemed almost instantaneous, I knew he would never feel the same way. Nor should he—it wasn't like our timers matched anyway, even though they were dangerously similar.

"I'm Mason," he said, holding his hand out formally. Manners were hard to come by in a young man, and the action surprised me. Staring at the foreign gesture and back at his face, I finally gave in and extended my hand to meet his.

"CJ," I said, my face flushing with embarrassment at the crack in my voice.

"CJ. Is that short for something?" he asked, a tight smile playing on his boyish features.

"Ahh, yeah. Cadence Jane. But, it's a mouthful, and I prefer CJ."

"That's actually pretty," he complimented. I wondered what his game was or whether he was being genuine.

We were supposed to be working on our lab at the time, but I couldn't keep myself from staring, stealing glances equally between his eyes and the timer on his wrist.

As the years passed by, we became closer—even though Mason continually picked on me. The attention was both infuriating and addictive. I didn't understand at the time, but I came to appreciate that any attention from him was better than none at all.

"Cadence," a maternal voice whispers, breaking through my daydream and back to reality. My mom motions for me to follow her out into the hall.

As soon as the door to the room shut, my mom starts talking and walking at the same time. "So, there hasn't been any news about the specific sectors or where they've been relocated, but I just found out *Mira* was running low on oxygen and there's no confirmation that all the sectors were successfully evacuated."

I stop walking, my feet feeling like they're glued to the floor. I suddenly feel like someone kicked me in the gut. What is my mother telling me?

"Cadence, don't get upset yet. Mason's sector wasn't the last in line, so it's very possible he's fine, and we'll find out soon enough where he is," she says in an attempt to placate me.

My hands fly to my mouth, an unwelcome, audible sob leaving my throat. I can't help but get upset. There is no other option when it comes to Mason's safety.

"Don't cry," she coos, pulling me to her and cradling my head in an attempt to comfort me.

I feel the sudden need to harden my heart. Show no fear. Pretend there's nothing wrong when everything feels like it's falling apart around me.

"I'm going to go take a shower," I tell my mom, ignoring her continuous attempts to calm me. Instead, I steel my emotions and walk away. If anything, I know I can cry inconspicuously in the shower and no one will know about the gaping hole in my heart.

00:00:00:00:13:19

Walking barefoot on the beaches of the Dara Colony, I struggle to ignore the timer in my wrist. I know the numbers continue to dwindle, and it takes every ounce of courage for me to stand strong. I want so badly to hide, bury myself in a hole in an attempt to avoid the inevitable. I have witnessed enough *Cardinems* to know how nerve-wracking the whole experience can be.

The Earth's evening air is just cool enough to make the grains of sand chilly as they squish between my toes. The ocean breeze causes a curtain of hair to swirl around my head while I continue to amble along the coastline, deep in thought and consumed by emotional turmoil.

Sitting on the shore and looking out into the ocean water as it shimmers like glitter beneath the late evening sunset, I feel secluded from the rest of the Earth—lost in my own little world where dictators of love don't exist. Closing my eyes, I take a deep, refreshing breath and think of him.

Dark hair, just long enough to grab onto... Strong, protective arms, just solid enough to wrap around me and make me feel secure... Deep blue eyes, just light enough to match the Earth's bright blue atmosphere and cause a girl to get lost in their depths... A masculine voice, filled with just enough promise to send a thrill through her core...

Brushing my fingertip along my trembling lips, I remembered what it felt like for him to kiss me. The passionate feel of his mouth crushing against mine is one I will never want to forget.

Keeping my eyes closed, I block out all the sensations around me and try to remember the last moments I spent with Mason.

The chancellor's orders were to go back to our private units and wait for further instruction. Knowing we would be going in order, my sector would ultimately go before Mason's.

With some begging, I convinced Mason to try and stay with me. Maybe in the mess of chaotic confusion, the guard wouldn't scan our identities to make sure we were properly placed.

Mason opened a holographic chat on his transmitter with his mother, letting her know where he was and that he would meet her in their unit if the guards wouldn't allow him to stow away with me. I was grateful my mom allowed him to stay, knowing that our sector would be one of the first to board the transport.

Mason wanted his mom and dad to join him, but she declined, saying, "The guards are already stopping people from leaving their units. There's no way we can come to you. Just stay put. If you step foot out of Em's unit, they're definitely going to relocate you to your proper sector. So, just stay where you are, please."

Her begging broke my heart. I could hear the fear in her voice and knew there was a danger with being one of the last sectors to evacuate.

To get our minds off the mayhem while we waited for our sector to be called forth, I brought several movies up on my transmitter. The transmitter's movies were smaller, but the three-dimensional hologram still made it enjoyable, not to mention it gave us a reason to stay close to each other. The distractions successfully passed the time.

After almost twelve hours of waiting, I snuggled beneath Mason's arm, breathing in his scent and burning the feeling of his embrace into my memory.

"Are you sniffing me?" he asked, humor laced in his tone.

"Maybe," I admitted shyly.

"Well, then," he mumbled against my head before taking a large whiff of my hair. I was suddenly thankful I had used my new gardenia-scented shampoo. He finished off his playfulness with a kiss to my forehead. A thrill coursed through my veins at the contact, and I knew only a man who truly cherished me could ever make me feel that way.

The hours of waiting were spent comfortably, and I couldn't help but feel like it was just the calm before the storm. I wondered just how long Mira *could last with the oxygen-replenishing supplies damaged.*

Determined to spend this time in a carefree state with my best friend, I pushed the stressful thoughts from my mind and focused on Mason. A low rumble rose from his chest when I let him lay his head on my lap and rubbed my fingernails through his hair. The sound of his pleasure made me smile. I knew I wanted to spend the rest of my existence making him happy.

All the media channels in my unit were suddenly interrupted by the chancellor's voice announcing it was our sector's turn to evacuate. Dutifully and quickly, we grabbed our few bags and exited the unit, prepared to fall in line where necessary.

"Mason Delaney," a gruff voice said almost immediately after stepping out into the hall. My heart leapt into my throat with the instant dread that surged through me. "You cannot be here. Your instructions were to remain in your own sector until called upon. Please step back so you can be escorted to your unit by a guard."

The motherfuckers scanned him and now he was going to be sent to the back of the line like a child who misbehaved. Anger poured over me, and my eyes immediately glazed over with a red haze.

"He's with me," I seethed, grasping Mason's hand and holding on for dear life. Upon my defiance, the guard raised his Taser rod to the ready and prepared himself for a confrontation.

"No!" Mason warned, holding his hand out toward the guard and placing his body between the weapon and me. "I'll talk to her."

The guard backed off, but still kept his hand on his weapon, seeming ready and willing to use it if I dared defy him again. Violence wasn't common on Mira*, but no one ever really had something to defend. I thought now was as good a time as any, and Mason was definitely worth defending, no matter what the consequences.*

Turning toward me, Mason bent so he was face to face with me.

"Cadence Jane, for Christ's sake, you need to go with your mom. Just do as they say. I'll be fine. I'll be right behind you," he assured me as he grabbed both sides of my face and forced me to look into his eyes.

"There's no reason why you can't come with us, Mason. I can't just walk away from you. You have to stay with me," I begged. I knew I was about to lose my cool and forced the tears to stay hidden. My eyes burned with the salty liquid threatening to spill over.

"Please, don't make this harder than it is," he said, his tone full of emotion. "If you will listen to me, just this once... go."

Without warning or a care for who could be watching, Mason's lips crushed against mine—harsh, painful, urgent. With strength that took my breath away, he squeezed my body against his and deepened the forceful kiss. Both love and fear emanated from his actions, causing my heart to fray at the edges.

The passionate farewell was cut off all too soon by his face twisting in agonizing pain. The guard's Taser rod brought Mason to his knees at my feet. His body was arched with tension while his head tilted upward, obviously biting back a scream. His grimace was followed by a tormented growl, his teeth grinding together with such force I could almost feel his agony. The vision of his pain hit my chest like a sledgehammer.

"STOP! Stop, please! Stop hurting him!" I screamed as several pairs of arms grabbed me and pulled me away. My incoherent sobs echoed through the halls as I watched them drag his limp body into the darkness. My heart—my sole reason for existing—was gone in an instant.

Through the chaos, I heard him call out my name. The sound of his voice gave me hope that he was okay, but I still fought the arms that bound me and kept me from running to his aid. The glass doors of the lift stifled any noise I could still hear from him as my mom held me tight and we descended to the transport sector.

The memory of my last moments with Mason weighs heavy on my heart. Before the zeppelin departed, Mason's mother messaged mine to let her know Mason was with her—shaken up, but otherwise fine. The fact he went through any pain for me, all because of my stupid actions, still makes my head spin and my stomach twist with regret.

Taking a few deep breaths, I attempt to calm my erratic heart. As much as I want to distract my mind from my *Cardinem*, I don't want to remember Mason's face riddled with pain.

Instead, I clear my mind and try once more to picture his handsome face as a happy one. I loved when he looked at me with adoration in his eyes, as if I were the only girl in the universe meant for him. I think of his myriad of expressions when he would laugh at me, as he often did. His joy was infectious.

And I need to stop thinking of Mason in the past tense. I will see him again, no matter what the cost.

The sun descends further beneath the horizon, causing the glow from my timer to illuminate my face, a stark contrast to the approaching darkness of the night. Despite my attempts to ignore the numbers, I can't help but notice the seconds ticking by. *If only Mason were here...*

18...

The nearness of my *Cardinem* has me looking around the sandy shore in an attempt to find another being. No one is around. Confusion begins to overpower my fear and anxiousness. *If only Mason were here...*

15...

14...

13...

I keep still as the breeze from the Pacific Ocean continues to swirl around my head and fill the air with activity. How can there not be anyone around? *If only Mason were here...*

9...

8...

7...

My heart rate is surprisingly calm now that I breathed through my anxiety, especially considering I have waited twenty years, two hundred and sixty four days, nineteen hours, forty-seven minutes, and fifty-two seconds for this very moment to arrive. Every breath I have taken in my lifetime has come to this very moment. *If only Mason were here...*

4...

Memories of him still continue to flood my mind.

3...

Mason's passionate personality.

2...

His heart beating against my ear as he held me.

1...

His lips pressed against my forehead during the last moments we spent together.

ZERO...

The soft chime of my timer as it disintegrates beneath my skin forces me to open my eyes. Without the dim glow coming from my wrist, the surrounding night is surprisingly dark. I've never experienced such darkness, both visibly and in my heart.

On shaky legs, I stand and look up into the starlit sky, allowing the wind to whip around me with a vengeance. I brush the sand from my clothes and turn in circles. Confusion at how alone I am blocks the previous void that filled my chest. The research I've done told me just how accurate these soul-sucking timers are. So, the fact I am now walking toward the boardwalk alone has me at a loss for words.

As I make my way through the thick sand, my feet begin to stumble. I am grateful no one is around to witness me falling face-first, grains of grit covering my face and embedding into my hair. A strong arm catching me startles me and makes me realize that I'm not really alone at all.

"Are you okay?" a velvety voice next to me asks, causing a startled cry to escape my chest. His hand tightens its grip, grasping my elbow in order to help me up from the ground.

"Thanks," I mumble, never looking at my rescuer.

"No problem. I'll always be here to catch you," the voice responds, bringing fond memories of Mason and his overwhelming need to be there for me—to protect me.

Shaking my head of the eerily similar recollection, I look over at the man who has hold of my arm.

Blue eyes, dancing like crystals in the moonlight, stare back at me, making me gasp with surprise and robbing me of oxygen.

When the timer hits zero, fate takes over. And fate is a fickle bitch.

This has been *ZERO: Cadence*, Episode One in the Countdown Series. Stay tuned for a preview of ZERO: Rhys, Episode Two, coming to all retailers Winter 2021.

A SNEAK PEEK OF ZERO: RHYS

EPISODE TWO IN THE COUNTDOWN SERIES

Without warning, I feel the world slip beneath my feet as I stare into her eyes, shock evident in her gaze. She is breathtakingly beautiful—more than I could have ever imagined she would be. Just when I thought the adrenaline surge from my timer reaching zero would pass, she literally fell into my arms, making my heart pick up speed once again.

Jerking out from my grasp, she backs away and holds her hand out, pointing her finger in defiance. "Who the hell are you?" Her words are harsh, cruel, like I somehow betrayed her without realizing it. My stomach drops at the realization she won't want me.

"I'm sorry. I was just getting a breath of fresh air when..." Well, I am reluctant to admit I was out here to avoid contact with any other human, but fate clearly has other plans.

Cocking her brow, she waits for me to provide an answer to her question.

"My name is Rhys. And you are?" I ask, keeping my hands tucked neatly into my pockets. She already seems skittish enough. I don't want to reach out and give her another reason to be scared.

"Did your timer just stop?" she asks with a shaky voice, backing away further and crossing her arms over her chest in defiance. With her heels still embedded in the plush sand, she begins to trip again, her arms flailing outward to catch her balance.

Without a second thought, I reach for her again, catching her by the waist and pressing her against my chest. My breath pulls from my lungs in waves as my blood continues to pump through my veins like a motherfucking freight train. It has to be a reaction of her near demise, not the fact this girl has any affect on me. If she is going to act affronted by my presence, I am damn sure to respond with the same.

Well, fuck. The desperate look in her gaze has the thought leaving my mind as quickly as it popped in, the sudden need to protect her overriding any other emotion fathomable.

Pushing at my chest, she begins to fight. But one look into one another's eyes has her nearly breaking down into tears. The sudden change in emotion is one that both confuses me and has me curious about this silly girl.

"Please let me go," she begs in a near whisper. With a gentle slowness, I release my hold around her body, making sure she can stand upright before I step away. She looks down, obviously embarrassed with the intense way we are staring at each other.

"Yes," I answer with a rough, gravelly sound to my voice, unable to hide how she manages to leave me breathless with just one look.

"What?" she gasps, jerking her head back in my direction, clearly catching the change in my tone.

"Yes, my timer just stopped." I know hers had too, and the answers coming from my mouth apparently upset her. My emotions are torn—the need to comfort her warring with the hurt from her reaction.

Nodding her head, she doesn't say a word as a tear slowly trickles down her cheek.

"Hey," I whisper, stepping to her again. "Don't cry." Without hesitation, and forgetting my damned ego for an instant, I lift my hand to her face and wipe the stray tear, wanting nothing more than to take her sorrow away, even if just for a moment.

"My name is CJ," she mumbles. "I'm sorry about acting all weird. I just... it's just been a long few days."

"Hey, I get it. I came out here to hopefully clear my head and avoid anyone."

She shrugged, and then sniffs. "But you got stuck with me instead."

"Obviously a bonus," I say with a smile.

She responds to my comment with a shy grin, mirroring the expression on my face. Looking back into my eyes, her brow furrows, confusion filling the slight joy that was once there.

"You look so familiar," she says in a near whisper, her voice so quiet, it's almost lost over the pounding waves. "...like someone I know."

She starts to look back down at her feet, but I don't want to lose connection with those beautiful greens again. Hooking her chin with my finger, I hold her gaze steady.

"He must have been one good looking guy," I say jokingly, hoping she'd grace me with that gorgeous smile of hers once more.

The light giggle that leaves her mouth is quickly stifled by sorrow. "He was... is. He is very handsome."

I don't know what has happened to make her feel such sadness. The powerful need to comfort her is confusing, but also feels oh so right. Then again, words are lost in a sea of thought and indecision. I have no idea what to say.

"I'm sorry. I know you were probably looking forward to this moment. The last thing you need is a whiny girl as your..." CJ hesitates, the word *match* hanging in the air like a forbidden thought. "I just..."

"I know. Trust me, I know how you feel," I say, interrupting her and hoping my understanding was enough to make her feel a bit more comfortable with me. Backing away, I offer my hand, an invitation for her to grab hold. "C'mon. You look like you could use some normalcy. Let's just grab a bite to eat and talk, okay?"

Hesitant at first, several foreign emotions cross her face before she finally nods and grasps my outstretched hand. I know my imagination is running rampant, yet I can't completely ignore the sudden surge of power and warmth that seems to have enveloped our touch. I wonder if it has anything to do with the timers that have magically disintegrated beneath our skin. Have they really just disappeared or is there some sort of electrical surge that continues to pump through our veins? Even though my head tries to come up with a rational explanation, my heart seems to have a mind of its own, and I consider the fact that we truly have some sort of powerful connection making me feel so euphoric.

Walking up the sandy steps toward the street, the wind picks up, whipping around us and causing her hair to cascade around her head, mimicking the waves of the ocean and filling the air around us with a scent I don't quite recognize but suddenly can't get enough of.

She lets go of my hand and begins swiping at the blonde locks, taming them into submission until the gust of wind finally died down. Continuing to pad down the boardwalk toward the street full of shops and restaurants, CJ holds her arm out and clasps her other hand around where her timer had once been.

"So weird," she whispers, tracing her fingers along her skin, marveling at the completely unmarred surface—evidence of the ticking time bomb completely gone. “Almost twenty-one years of a constant nuisance attached to me, and now…” she trails off.

I am about to say something profound and whimsical when a yell caught my attention.

“Cadence Jane!” the weak holler says again.

“Shit,” she whispers. “Over here, Mom!” With a pause, she looks at Rhys with guilt riddling her pretty face and says, “I apologize in advance for what is about to happen.”

“Cadence J— Oh,” her mother says with a gasp as she catches sight of me. I can't hold back my laughter at the look on her face and imagine what my mom would say in this same situation.

After a light jog, she stops in front of them and says, “I was wondering where you went.”

“Sorry. I just needed some time to myself to think,” CJ says while biting her lip and seemingly attempting to hide her embarrassment. “Mom, this is Rhys. I met him on the beach a few minutes ago. Rhys, this is my mother, Em.”

Shaking her hand, I feel a tickle of self-consciousness under her probing stare. “Nice to meet you. I was just going to take CJ to grab a bite to eat so we could get better acquainted.” While inviting her would be the polite thing to do, I feel now is not the time for family get-togethers.

“Oh my,” Em gasps.

“Mom, please,” CJ nearly begs.

I stand dumbfounded by the exchange, unsure of how to respond in the moment.

“I'm sorry,” the woman says. “He's just… you guys… your…” She stumbles over her words, clearly more rattled by the *Cardinem* situation than both CJ and I combined.

“Yes,” CJ interrupts, and the fact she understands her mother's rambling is a bit comical, because I am completely lost. “We're just going to grab a bite to eat. I'll be back later.”

“Okay,” Em says with bewilderment. “But your transmitter isn't working here. How—”

“Don't worry. I'll stay in the area,” CJ promises.

Em nods, obviously realizing her daughter wants her to stop worrying. The dismissal in CJ's tone is faint, but evident nonetheless.

“Well, it was nice to meet you, Rhys. I'm sure we'll be seeing each other soon,” she says before turning and making her way back toward a large building shrouded in shadows.

“It was nice meeting you too. I promise to bring her back safely.” I only receive a meek wave from CJ's mother in response as she continues walking away.

"So, Cadence, huh?" I say, looking down at her face flushing with discomfort over the whole situation.

"Yeah, it's a mouthful," she mumbles, shaking her head and taking a few steps in the direction we were originally going.

I like how her name feels on my tongue, and my mind twists around the fact that I am looking forward to all the opportunities I will have to say it in the future. "I think it's very pretty." The compliment has her cheeks blushing again, and I can't help the satisfaction that soars through me at the sight.

We walk in silence for another block, reaching a small restaurant that is well known for their classic pizza cuisine.

"Oh, thank Christ," CJ breathes.

"What?" I ask, bewildered at her reaction to the place.

"I'm so sick of the processed food and nutrition pellets they've been feeding us at the shelter," she explains with a roll to her eyes. The action is so freaking adorable, and it takes all the control I can muster not to laugh at her excitement. Wait, did she say—

"You've been staying at a shelter? But why?" Usually only families who are involved in catastrophes or suffer the death of a family member have to stay in shelters, at least until they get back on their feet. Shelters are very rarely used anymore after society adjusted its economics, nearly eliminating the homeless and hungry.

"I'm only staying here at the Dara Colony temporarily. It's a long story," she briefs as we approach the restaurant's entrance.

Allowing her to enter through the automatic doors first, I hold my hand out and say, "Well, I'd love to hear all ab—"

"Rhys Delaney!" a female voice shouts, breaking my concentration on the lovely CJ. Looking around, my eyes land on the hostess.

"Stella," I chime, recognizing the girl I went to school with several years ago. Her hair has been dyed a silvery color with rhinestone implants adorning the side of her face and making her shimmer in the dim restaurant lighting.

"Well, how the hell have you been?" Stella asks, smiling and adjusting her posture to a more confident stance.

"Can't complain. Stella, this is Cadence," I introduce, reaching beside me and gesturing to... an empty space? Darting my eyes around the foyer, I finally find CJ standing by the door with a look of utter shock on her face. "CJ, what's—"

"What did she say your last name was?" she asks, her voice laced with terror and her eyes near tears.

"Delaney. My name is Rhys Delaney."

My approach didn't go unnoticed as she holds her hand out and yells, "Stop! Don't come any closer."

Visibly shaking, CJ never takes her eyes off me as she pounds the button that forces the doors back ajar. As soon as the panels whoosh open, she runs.

ABOUT RENE FOLSOM

Rene Folsom, USA Today Bestselling Author of contemporary and paranormal romance, lives in Florida with her husband and three kids. She has officially diagnosed herself with creative ADD and often has a million and one writing projects going at once. In addition to writing, she is also a graphic artist who enjoys creating custom book covers for indie authors. She is definitely an artist at heart and would love nothing more than to be elbow deep in clay during her waking hours.

Rene believes that all fiction is based on some form of reality—otherwise we would never have the inspiration or knowledge to dream up the realistic situations we portray with our words. She is proud to say that her personal experiences have been inspirational, though perhaps not always identical to that of her fictional characters. Where reality and fantasy diverge, however, must remain her little secret...

www.ReneFolsom.com

Follow Rene by signing up for her newsletter at www.ReneFolsom.com/newsletter. Not only will you receive a free book, but you will also stay up to date on any new releases in the Countdown Series!

amazon.com/author/renefolsom
facebook.com/renefolsom
twitter.com/renefolsom
instagram.com/renefolsom
bookbub.com/authors/rene-folsom
youtube.com/renefolsom

PORTAL ON THE EDGE OF FOREVER

BY RACHEL RADNER

A prince who sticks to his own limiting beliefs.

An Earthling woman who belongs to an extinct race.

The mystical portal which will forever change their fates.

Océana never imagined being stuck aboard a ship with the Izarkian Prince Kodee. Ordinarily, Izarkians and humans don't come into such close contact. It's forbidden. But she's en route to handle the most important mission of her life--and the swoon-worthy prince might just be the death of her.

Upon arrival at the portal, the one that will reverse time and save her people, Océana's reality is thrown into a reverse orbit. Nothing goes as planned, and the two of them wind up trapped inside the portal.

Stuck together in between worlds, Océana and Prince Kodee come to terms with their differences--and face the prejudices they have of one another. As they're confined in a tight space, which they assume will also serve as their grave, they touch on the heaviest subjects. Society. Freedom. Revolution. Even... love.

While the rest of the universe carries on outside of the portal, Prince Kodee and Océana's hearts begin to open to one another. And Océana finally recognizes that in order to secure her future, she'll have to let go of the past she's clung on to for most of her life.

1

The portal kissed the darkest reaches of space, floating amidst distant moons and planets. A wrought iron stairwell stretched into the expanse and spiraled upward toward the base. On the landing, a hazy golden hue illuminated the oval screen at the epicenter—beckoning me closer.

Somehow, I knew this would be the start of all the changes to come.

My mouth hung open in awe as I silently studied the portal through the ship's front glass window. As the vessel neared, the engines hummed more loudly. A warm vibration danced over my skin, lulling me into a euphoric dream-like state. If what I'd read during my research turned out to be true, portal traveling could be manipulated in such a way as to traverse *all* time and space.

Returning to the past. Saving people from dying. Both possibilities.

Father would be proud.

"You don't see one of these every day," Prince Kodee's tone drawled out ironically, breaking me from my reverie. A little huff accompanied the end of his statement. He rested against the back of the co-pilot seat in his navy, double-breasted officer's suit. An arm dangled over the chair's rest.

Even in the darkness, Prince Kodee's powder-blue Izarkian complexion bloomed with a healthy shine. Appearing especially supple next to my calloused, pasty self. I was an Earthling, a species on the verge of extinction. And the color of my skin never allowed me the benefit of forgetting my origins.

I was marked. Different. Unworthy.

A refugee taken in by Izark and constantly reminded of this fact. By everyone.

Prince Kodee shifted in his seat and let out a faux yawn. "We're here. You've seen your portal. Now, it's time to go."

"Those are not the orders from the Queen." I plugged our coordinates into the flight system, marking our location and sending it back to headquarters on Izark as a safety precaution. Then, I pressed the acceleration button to move us along more quickly. The ship coasted forward, inching toward the portal. "We're here on peaceful reconnaissance. We need to see this through."

Prince Kodee snorted. "Right. Peaceful reconnaissance. Collect data. Report back. Do you want to know what I think about all that?"

He wagged his finger in my direction.

"What was that Earthling expression?" he asked. "Oh, yes. Those orders are nothing but a shitty horse."

"Horse shit."

"What?"

"The expression is horse shit. As in... shit. Not that the horse is shitty. The idiom is comparing fecal matter from a horse to whatever it is you're saying is terrible."

His brows furrowed; finger still outstretched toward me. A deep crease formed across his forehead, and his eyes burned with little gleaming darts of anger. My skin tightened, and I thought of how hard I'd worked to get to this position—and how quickly I could lose everything from one careless statement to a prince.

No. Not just a prince. *The* prince. The man who would one day rule Alpha Federation. The prince who belonged to the family of the monarchy funding my research.

On Izark, one behaved appropriately around royalty—or suffered the consequences. One did not speak back to any of the anointed family members. One did not so much as glance at them in a funny manner.

Correcting Izarkian royalty? This was punishable by hanging. Even if they were without a doubt wrong.

"You're lucky I've always liked you," Prince Kodee hissed. He jammed his finger into the de-accelerator, and the ship slowed. I dared not speak. He added, "This is how we're going to do this. You're going to wait until I give the command to move forward. Once we reach the portal, I'm going to wait here on the ship. You'll go and take care of your duties, whatever they are, and you'll do it as quickly as possible. We get back to Izark promptly, and I can return to my own business instead of serving as chaperon. Is this understood?"

A rush of anger shot through my bones.

"Queen Taree wouldn't agree," I mumbled through gritted teeth. "She ordered you to accompany me for protection, yes. But she granted me as much time as I needed. There are things I'm trying to uncover with my research."

"Yes, well, Mother will not always be the ruling party. When I'm in charge, we will spend our money on better suited things for Izark and the Federation."

"Everything I'm researching *is* for Izark and the Federation," I breathed, careful not to push too much. Besides, what I'd said wasn't entirely true.

I had other reasons for being here.

"Studying portals for Izark?" Prince Kodee asked. "This is what they teach the younglings in school before they're ready to move on to more advanced study. Not even the *iggy* continue to study portals."

Iggy was Izarkian for *teen girl*. On Izark, young children were separated by sex once they reached age twelve—the year girls became iggies. Boys became *izars*—the Izarkian equivalent for *young man*. The izars from the richer classes studied to become leaders and military officers or to aid the royal council in some way. Meanwhile, the poorer males concentrated on technical subjects such as machine repair or trash collection operation for the cities.

Izark lumped all the iggies, whether rich or poor, into the same classes.

Where they were essentially taught how to be good breeders.

Being an Earthling had its advantages. No true Izarkian had ever considered breeding with me—nor would they ever—and this freed me from the typical female obligation. Instead, I'd lived a life of poverty, crawling my way through the dredges of Izarkian society. Never knowing where or when I'd get my next meal.

Until a chance encounter with Queen Taree.

She saved me. Gave me hope. And clued me in on how I might reverse what had happened to the people of Earth.

My use of the portal was a secret between only me and the Queen. She'd given me a set of very specific instructions, warned me of how portal travel might permanently alter my mental state, and set me on my journey with hope.

No being had ever tried what I was about to do.

And, for some reason, Queen Taree had insisted on sending her son to go with me.

"The Queen will be upset if we don't complete this mission," I urged, hoping Prince Kodee would accept this as a logical answer and allow us to continue forward. Queen Taree would not have aided me only to have her son sabotage the mission, so I wondered what his true purpose for being here was.

Queen Taree must've known something about him that I didn't.

Prince Kodee rolled his eyes. "You should start concerning yourself with more important matters, Océana. Before this meaningless research swallows you whole. And, by the by, I'm formally adopting the phrase *shitty horse* into our vernacular once we get back to HQ. I rather like the sound of it."

My blood boiled, and I clenched my fists. I *hated* being talked to like this. Especially by an entitled male. I'd spent a good ten years in the slums of Izark—enough time to learn how to kick anyone's ass. Enough time that I'd learned how to talk back—and talk back fast.

I wanted to put Prince Kodee in his place.

But I'd also learned when to keep my mouth shut. Unfortunately, some of my battles had to be fought silently. Or, in this case, until I reached that portal. My key to potentially fixing everything.

Little did portal-hating Prince Kodee know.

Holding my tongue, I hovered a finger over the acceleration button, waiting for Prince Kodee to give the order for us to move forward, just as he had commanded. An awkward beat passed between the two of us. I looked down at the ship navigation dashboard. Then back to Prince Kodee. Then back to the dashboard. He uttered not one word.

Prince Kodee's expressionless eyes remained locked on mine, and his body stiffened. The tight position of our seating on this vessel brought us so close together I smelled the scent of his body wash.

This intimate thought of his smell gave way to a more uncomfortable memory, and my cheeks warmed. The other day, after finishing a shift in the lab, I'd accidentally turned the wrong corner in the High Imperial Castle and passed Prince Kodee's open chamber. Izarkians of all classes did not bother with doors.

Three male servants had dressed him down from his daywear, a navy tunic with beads, and prepared to change him into the dinner wear, the usual officer's suit. I caught a glimpse of him completely naked and couldn't stop from taking in his muscular legs and arms. For the first time since I'd been on the planet, I discovered that the anatomy of an Izarkian appeared strangely human. Including a certain male part. For the rest of the evening, I envisioned Prince Kodee's broad shoulders and defined abdominals. But, even more puzzling, I found myself wondering what it might be like... to actually be with someone and feel their physical touch on my body. To be with an Izarkian, yes... but, also, to be with anyone period.

Passing into the dining hall that night, toward a table at the very back reserved for the few humans in attendance, my eyes fell over Prince Kodee in his evening attire. He'd nodded his head in my direction with a smile, and I'd simply blushed and sped away.

Even now, I couldn't stop thinking about his muscular build. His uniform made it difficult to tell, but Prince Kodee had the body akin to that of a U.S. Marine back on Earth.

Despite myself, and despite his awful attitude toward me, I quite liked the look of him—naked or clothed. And I hadn't stopped thinking about what it might be like to feel his body on mine.

Why did it seem to be a universal truth that all assholes were hot?

Clearing my throat, I returned my attention back to the task at hand.

"Well?" I finally worked up the courage to ask.

"Well what?"

"I'm waiting for your command, Your Highness." I spat out the title, hoping the facetious underlying meaning remained inconspicuous.

"Oh... ah... yes. You may proceed." His eyes glinted with power and command.

Once again, I pressed on the accelerator, and the ship lurched forward. In a few minutes, we reached the very edge of the portal, and I glided the ship toward the base, landing it in front of the doorway to another dimension.

The engines churned more loudly, and the vibration over my arms spread throughout my entire body. A buzzing noise sounded in my ears, increasingly louder as we neared the portal. The golden hue carried over to the ship, and everything inside the cabin glowed in a yellow tone.

"What happens now?" Prince Kodee asked.

"I'm supposed to suit up and go out there," I said. "And run some typical diagnostics."

I patted my pocket and felt my electronic device known as a DigiBook—a square object with grooves over the surface no larger than a cigarette lighter back on Earth. While most Izarkians, and a few humans, had their own DigiBook—our way of accessing the Izarkian net the way an Earthling once used a phone or tablet—the Queen had sworn me to secrecy about the texts she'd sent me over an encrypted transfer. She explained that the books contained far more information than anyone else had ever seen before. That she alone had the literal command string to manipulate time.

No one was supposed to know I had these.

Not even Prince Kodee.

"As you wish, then. You have my blessing. Just be quick about it." Prince Kodee bowed his head, gesturing toward the back of the ship with a storage unit containing two spacesuits. I twisted in my seat, accidentally brushing up against Prince Kodee's arm as I reached behind to grab the gear.

At our touch, Prince Kodee's blank expression morphed into a look of concern.

"Sorry," I breathed. "I'm not trying to touch you or anything."

"No need to apologize. It's of no concern that we briefly touched."

"Then why the look of fear?"

"Look of fear? No. You're mistaking my outward appearance for something other than what it truly is."

I dared not ask him what his appearance actually meant, if it wasn't fear. It could only be something worse. Like disgust.

I let out an *oomph* as I dug around the container and started pulling out the spacesuit. The material caught on something. No matter how hard I tugged, the suit wouldn't give and remained stuck in the storage space. It hadn't even dawned on me how much of a challenge it would be to not only get this thing out but then also put it on in such a narrow space.

And do so in front of Prince Kodee.

"Here. Let me help," he said.

With one yank, Prince Kodee lifted the entire suit out of the container and placed it in my lap. Then, he reached into storage once more and produced a sleek helmet with a breathing apparatus which I'd attach to the ship's oxygen tank.

"Thanks." I gazed down at the suit in my lap meant to keep me from freezing in deep space. Fortunately, the suit would be large enough to fit over the clothing I wore, including the knapsack of rations I carried around my waist. No need for Prince Kodee to see me naked.

As I started to slide the material over my legs, the ship rattled.

"Look!" Prince Kodee placed a hand over my bare arm, and I froze. Both from his touch and the sight in front of us through the glass window.

Little tufts of smoke billowed wildly across the oval screen. The stairwell and base shook, knocking the ship—and us—to and fro. The vessel bounced around. Prince Kodee and I slammed against the right side of the ship; his frame the only thing protecting me from a collision against metal.

He groaned.

"Are you alright?" I asked, gazing up at him. A gash formed across the top of his head.

"I'll be fine."

The ship moved again, and we slammed to the left. This time, my body crunched against the siding, and something sharp sliced into the back of my leg. Prince Kodee's body squeezed against mine as if we were two sardines crammed into a can.

"Fucking hell!" I cursed, feeling the warmth of blood trickle down my calf.

Prince Kodee jerked back and returned to his seat.

"We need to leave!" he cried.

"No. We can't leave."

"Shitty horse, we can't! Get us out of here! That's an order!"

"No. I mean, we physically can't leave. The portal's locked onto us."

"Then tell it to unlock!"

"It doesn't work like that."

As the foundation rumbled beneath the vessel, I did the only thing I could do. I continued sliding the spacesuit up and over my body, ignoring the throbbing of my leg and the tightness overtaking my body.

I rushed out the words, "I gotta get out there so that I'm close enough in range to hook up my DigiBook and deactivate the lock on us. That's the only way."

"You can't go out there!"

"Watch me."

Prince Kodee's eyes flashed with anger yet again, but I no longer concerned myself with his fragile emotions. If I didn't get out there, we were as good as dead. From what I'd read, the portal would trap us inside of it, without a clear destination, and we'd be stuck in there for the rest of our lives.

As I finished suiting up, a flash of lightning cracked directly above the portal. The screen erupted with even more activity; squiggly lines like a photograph taken with a low aperture rate danced across the portal. The energy aimed toward us. My pulse quickened. Every cell in my body vibrated at an alarming rate.

I could feel my body being called to the portal.

Next to me, Prince Kodee held out his arms. I watched with horror as his hands crumbled into tiny particles which then drifted through the ship and floated toward the portal. The rest of his body followed suit. His arms. Legs. Torso. Upper body. He was disintegrating before my very eyes.

"Océana... what's... what's happening to me?"

I lifted my own arms to see the same thing occurring. The world began to darken.

Shaking my head, I said the only thing that came to mind, preparing to die as the rest of Prince Kodee's body disappeared into nothing.

"Fucking shitty horse," I spat.

My body crumbled into ash.

2

"Océana! Océana!"

Father's voice echoed through my mind. Whispers of the past chanted into the ethers... haunting my present.

"Océana!" Father again with his gentle voice. "I've always been here. I've always been home."

A droplet of water dripped from the ceiling and plunked against the floor.

I sprang to life with a jolt, gulping for air. "What the fuck!"

"Nice of you to finally awaken." Prince Kodee sounded calm and collected. Too relaxed for someone who I'd just seen disintegrate into ash moments ago.

"Where are we?" Twisting from my position on the ground, I gazed at Prince Kodee. He huddled over in the corner of our damp and dark confined space. Head cocked over his shoulder as he flashed me a look of annoyance. A ceiling light in the middle of the space provided our only source of illumination.

The only proof of what we'd just been through remained in the form of a cut on Prince Kodee's forehead; a scrape close to being fully healed thanks to the organic regeneration cells in Izarkian DNA.

"Aren't *you* the one with all the answers?" Prince Kodee raised a brow. "Why don't you tell us where we are and how we get back to the ship?"

As my eyes adjusted to the light—or the lack thereof—I took in our current environment. Four stone walls surrounded us in a room hardly large enough for two people. Water pooled at every corner on the floor.

A draft sent a shudder through my body. I realized that, somehow in the transference, my spacesuit had fallen off my body and landed in the corner.

"I don't know where we are or how to get out." My answer sounded monotone. I really didn't have the answers. None of this made any sense. Those DigiFiles Queen Taree had secretly transferred to my DigiBook to help me during my research process... none of them explained what'd happened to us back there.

I'd failed. Had all the information handed to me on a silver platter. And had either misinterpreted what I'd been given... or somehow missed some key piece of information.

This was all my fault. I'd gotten so close to the portal that could save the fate of my people. Somehow, the portal had sucked us in. We might be stuck here for the rest of our lives.

And now my ignorance had cost Earth its last hope.

"Fuck me," I breathed.

"Fuck me?" Kodee's ears seemed to perk up. "This is an Earthling expression I've not yet heard. Doesn't fuck mean to... fornicate? Are you saying—"

"No!" I cried. "Sorry, but no. That's not what I meant at all."

"Then please enlighten me. I'm always open to learning more about your culture and manners of speaking."

I laughed, assuming he was being facetious. If he expected an honest answer, he didn't press me for one. Instead, he simply continued staring. Watching. Studying me for god knows what purpose.

I gazed down to avoid eye contact.

It was then that I realized my bare feet were pressed against Prince Kodee's leg, and a flush worked its way through my body. As I adjusted so that we wouldn't touch, I noticed blue cloth wrapped around my bare leg. Now it dawned on me that Prince Kodee must've been the reason my spacesuit ended up off my body. He'd presumably undressed me while I was unconscious. Every hair stood on end, and my heart pounded in my chest. I was reminded all too well of the nights in the streets. If you slept too long, or slept in the wrong place, bad things happened to you.

I inched back against the wall defensively. "You had no business undressing me."

A cross expression flashed over Prince Kodee's face. "Excuse me?"

I swallowed, giving my heart a beat to settle. This was Prince Kodee. A jackass. But... a harmless jackass.

"Your leg was bleeding badly, so I folded up your pant leg," Prince Kodee said. "I applied cloth around the gash until the bleeding stopped... then wrapped your leg to hopefully prevent outside bacteria from causing an infection."

I eyed the blue cloth once more. Then gazed over at his own exposed leg with little tufts of dark blue hair. A piece of fabric from his pants had been ripped off.

"You used your pants over mine?" I scrunched my nose.

"Is that a problem?"

"No. I'm just..."

"Surprised that the prince who will one day lead Alpha Federation would help one of his citizens?" He smirked. "Don't look so shocked. I'm supposed to perform acts of bravery."

"Bravery... right, yes, okay." I wanted to roll my eyes, but I refrained. In the event that we got out of this *dungeon*, wherever this was, I didn't need an angry prince ordering my execution.

"You don't agree that it was a brave act?"

"Oh, sure. Of course it was, Your Highness." I dipped my head.

Prince Kodee crossed his arms and dipped his chin. "It may be of the popular opinion that royalty can't understand the average Izarkian, but I assure you I'm seeing right through you."

I swallowed the lump in my throat.

"Speak, Océana," he urged. "Tell me what's on your mind. Your prince orders you to do so."

I shook my head, unwilling to offer my candid thoughts. Every bone in my body begged me to speak up, to say what I truly believed, but I didn't dare. Instead, I offered him nothing but a canned response. "You know, I'd never want to say anything against you or your family. For as long as I'm living on Izark, I will never be anything but your loyal servant."

"Quite the pragmatist, I see."

"I try."

"Yes, well. We're stuck here for now. You've sent the coordinates of our location back to Izark. Smart move. After a certain time, they will come for us, and surely discover what has happened and will send a rescue crew."

"So, you're not worried at all?" I asked.

"Not in the slightest. I didn't realize this before we were transported, but I've had hours to think while waiting for you to awaken. I now recall from my days as a youngling that when a portal locks onto a foreign vessel seen as a threat, the beings inside the ship are transported to a holding cell. You clearly inputted the wrong string before our journey. Izark will have our coordinates and come for us once they realize we've been gone too long."

I raised a brow. "Uh, what? No. From what I've read, the portal locked onto us and sent us into unknown coordinates. Forgive me for saying this, but we might be shit outta luck. No one's coming."

"What on Earth are you saying? Portals don't just randomly send organic matter out into nowhere. It doesn't work this way. There's always a plan. And a purpose. In this case, we activated the portal's alerting system by not properly traveling through the correct channels."

"My books never mentioned anything about seeing certain vessels as threats."

"Before we left Izark, did you double-check that you entered the correct configuration into the nav system?"

"Of course. I did everything exactly the way the DigiBooks specified."

A line formed across his forehead. "Then... I don't understand. Why would the portal see us as a threat? Are you *sure* you followed the exact instructions?"

"Yes, I'm sure. Look. I'll prove it."

From my pocket, I produced the DigiBook and ran my thumb over the tiny square object, feeling the grooves on the surface. I rested it on the ground between us. For a split second, I reconsidered what I was about to do.

The Queen had sworn me to secrecy about these texts.

How could I betray her trust?

Swallowing, I hit the power button, and an image of a book on a podium projected from the device. I raised from the floor and stood in front of the faux podium, using my finger to flick through the pages of the book hologram.

Prince Kodee joined me. I cautiously tabbed through the text, throat tightening at the idea of betraying Queen Taree's confidences.

"It's in here somewhere," I said. "I'll show you the key I added to the coordinates since you don't trust me."

"It's not that I don't trust you. I simply know your information is wrong."

"I mean, there was nothing in here about portals taking prisoners—"

"We're not prisoners. We're simply being held in a neutral zone. We'll be stuck here until another Izarkian crew arrives to unlock us from the outside."

"Yeah, okay. Whatever you want to call it. There was nothing in any of my books about this cell we're in, let alone it needing to be unlocked."

I quickly paged through, searching for the section on space travel. When I found the chapter, I tapped on the book. "There! See? This is exactly what I typed into the nav."

A rush of relief washed over me. At least I hadn't fucked *this* part up. I clearly remembered inputting this into the nav two days ago—the night before we left.

Prince Kodee rested a finger to his lips. "This... this doesn't appear to be right. Something's off with this key. Where did you get this DigiFile?"

"Uh, there's nothing wrong with it."

"I'm telling you there is." Prince Kodee produced his own DigiBook and powered it up. A moment later, a second podium appeared with a book that butted up against my own. As he thumbed through the pages, similar words stared back at me. The two books nearly looked identical.

Nearly.

His contained chapters I had never seen before. A few times, he paused just long enough for me to catch a piece of information entirely contradicting what I knew I'd read in my own book.

"What is this?" I asked.

"The portal manual sanctioned by the Royal Izarkian Council. This is the text they use to teach the younglings." He stopped on the page in the book allegedly equivalent to mine—the navigational input for travel to the portal. Hovering his finger directly below the string, his eyes darted back and forth between his copy and mine. "Your key is missing the oooZark portion. No wonder this happened. That's our computer's way of telling the portal we're on an Izarkian Royal Council ship. Like a passcode or a computational handshake."

"So, it still got us to the portal... because the rest of the command was correct. Just sans password."

"Exactly." His nose crinkled and eyes bore into mine. He paused a moment. Bit his lip. Then asked, "Océana, did you say the Queen gave you this book?"

"I didn't say that, no."

"Did she?"

Like on the ship, he placed his hand on my arm. A tingle shot down my spine.

"Your Highness, I can't—"

"Please," he begged. "I need you to trust me for once."

A heavy pull tugged inside my chest. I regarded the prince before me, raking over every feature in his face. Those same green eyes which had cast me down so many times now appeared softer. He was pleading with me, ready to take my word, when he'd never given the information I contained such weight ever before.

Despite these subtle differences in his expression, this was still the male who made it clear to me time and again he held power over me, and he always needed to be right even when he was in the wrong. He was asking me to trust him?

How could I do that without betraying every logical and intuitive thought?

Plus, this might all be a trick. One word betraying the Queen spelled doom.

"I didn't get the texts from her," I answered.

"You're lying," he said. "You realize this is a punishable crime, yes?"

Heat raced to my face and words of anger rushed out. "Betraying royalty is punishable by death. What would you have me do? I'm damned either way."

"Ah. So, she did give you the books."

Shit.

Prince Kodee took two steps back until he banged up against the stone wall. He brought his hands over his face. Distorted chuckling noises erupted from him, and he shook his head within the palms of his hands. Though our space was dimly lit, I watched his blue complexion turn a few shades lighter.

"Shitty fucking horse," he said as he moved his hands away. "Shitty, shitty fucking horse."

"Can you tell me what's going on? What do you know?"

"Oh, I'm not sure you'll understand. Only the son of the Queen would get it. It turns out, you were correct in your statement earlier. No one's coming for us. This will be our prison, it seems." He gazed up at the ceiling and shouted, "Well played, Mother! Well played!"

He slid down to the ground. His body shook as he started laughing again.

"You think Queen Taree did this on purpose? Gave me the wrong codes? To what... trap us here?"

"Yes. Exactly."

"She would never do that. Especially not to her son. You're the heir of Alpha Federation!"

"Exactly. I'm the heir. Well, *was* the heir. The only child to a corrupt queen who needed to ensure her own reign would last."

My breathing sped up at his accusations; heart pounding in my chest.

Suddenly, a hazy episodic memory flashed through my brain. I was back in the slums of Izark, scraped and cut all over after losing a fight for the last scrap of food in the trash. We, the poor, always hung around the City Capital Commerce building in hopes of procuring the best trash. A distant time I would never forget. Lying there in the mud, exposed to the elements of the urban cityscape, I thought I'd die right there beside the commerce building. Male Izarkians, all dressed in their fanciest business suits, passed me without a second thought.

Until one hand with polished purple fingernails reached out to help me up.

Queen Taree pulled me out of the garbage—and had guided me toward the light.

No. I wouldn't give into this horse shit about the Queen.

"You're wrong. There's been some kind of mistake," I said. "Maybe I input something wrong. Queen Taree sent me here. She promised me she'd let me help my people by reversing what happened to Earth. That's why I'm here. She's a benevolent queen... she would never do what you're claiming she's done."

Prince Kodee eyed me suspiciously. "She said you'd be able to reverse something from the past? That isn't how portals work." He let out another laugh. "I was such a fool! Following an Earthling girl blindly!"

Face flushed with anger, I pointed a finger in his direction. "Oh, you're a fool alright! But it isn't because you listened to me."

Once more, I saw the darts flicker in his eyes. "You insubordinate—"

"When we get out of here, we'll see how the Queen reacts to the discovery of her only child's disloyalty."

Prince Kodee curled his fists and jumped back up.

"You're so sure of the Queen's benevolence? Let me show you what your queen is doing for Izark." He accessed a few sites from his DigiSphere—the Izarkian's version of the World Wide Web—sites he'd clearly already visited and were therefore cached to his device without access to their Internet. He perused through a few until he landed on a page with a video of the Queen.

She appeared to be attending a fancy dinner at some party. Surrounded by male Izarkians in their finest suits and the females dressed to the nines in gowns. Fancy chinaware spread across each table, and the Queen stood at the head, on a stage, with a microphone held out to her by a human in server attire. I didn't balk at seeing a human server, because I'd grown accustomed to seeing the few human survivors working in the lower ends of society.

Besides, Queen Taree had always promised me she would do something about that.

Eventually.

The Queen spoke into the mic, her voice regal and steady. "I present to you... the next phase of our Earthling Refugee Workers program." She smiled with sparking white teeth, motioning to a screen behind her that splashed the animated title of the aforementioned program, Earthling Refugee Workers. She nodded her head, and the presentation began to switch through different screens. Showing various pictures of human beings. I squinted my eyes to get a better view.

"Let me enlarge it for you." Prince Kodee pinched his fingers together and then expanded, zooming in on the presentation. I watched in horror as I realized these were pictures of human beings in labor camps, performing hard work for the Izarkians. Most of them were covered in mud, working mechanical equipment, and moving together to the same beat in a field created for heavy labor.

"What..." I murmured.

The Queen's speech continued. "Within twenty years, we will have a new type of worker. Sparing our own people from the more tedious tasks of society. We've got to prepare for when war comes from the Gamma Federation. While we all hope this never comes to pass, I recognize this is wishful thinking."

War with the Gamma Federation? Making humans do all the manual work?

"We haven't been at war with Beta or Gamma in over fifty star years," Prince Kodee said, and I quickly converted star years in my head to its Earth equivalent of seventy-five years. He continued, "Yet Mother is going to build an army of human workers, freeing up the lower class of Izarkians for the military. She means to start a war." He paused the video. "Do you see now that she is not someone to put your trust in?"

I froze. This video couldn't be real. Not the kind woman who had lifted me up from the dirt and given me a place to live in the Royal Imperial Castle. For five years, I'd lived in the castle. Always with food to eat and a place to sleep—even if that place was no bigger than a utility closet. She visited me often in the lab and had spoken so gently to me. Almost with love.

"I was sorry when I learned of what happened to your father," she had told me during one of our conversations, a gentle smile on her face. "No one should ever have to lose a parent. Especially not someone as important as your father."

Shaking my head, I stepped back from Prince Kodee. "This is a lie.

Someone's tampered with this video. Just like they used to do back on Earth."

Except we both knew that wasn't something that logically happened on Izark. Unlike Earth, only authorized individuals from the Royal Council posted anything on the DigiSphere. It was therefore safe to assume this footage to be accurate. At least, sanctioned by the council.

Prince Kodee swiped the video away and went into his own personal photos. He'd been to the fields. Taken photographs. Saw with his own eyes what they did at these camps.

This was all true.

"You've been there?" I asked.

He said nothing.

"How could she do this to me?" I spoke the words softly, voice dripping with hate. "How could *you* be a part of something like this?"

Prince Kodee scoffed. "You know not what you're saying. Things are not always what they seem to be."

"Oh yeah? Then tell me... since I'm obviously so clueless."

"Look what she's done to her own son. I'm not on her side, and she's not on mine. No one's coming for us, don't you see? She's tricked us into coming here. You... a dispensable Earthling... and me... the threat to the throne."

"Earthlings aren't dispensable." My tone contained more venom than I'd ever known. "Even now, after what you've shown me, you still sit here and say something so ludicrous? And here I was... thinking you were just another asshole! You're more than an asshole!"

He gazed away.

"I should've taken a more honorable death a long time ago," I breathed.

Prince Kodee shut off his DigiBook and slammed it against the wall. "Fucking shitty horse!"

"Fucking shitty horse is right."

He dropped to the ground and screamed.

"So, what, this is it? There's no loophole?" I asked. "Nothing in your DigiBook... you know, the one you just probably broke after you threw it against the wall? Really no way out?"

He glared at me. Then let out a loud groan and turned away. I shut off my DigiBook and punched the wall behind, instantly retracting as a surge of pain throbbed around my knuckles. I lowered and rested on my back, shaking my head. A cutting sadness sat along the ridge of my head, and I blinked back a few tears.

How could I have been so careless?

"We don't know what we'll find in space," Father had told me the day we boarded the plane which would take us from Earth forever. Because of who he was, we'd been the first people to leave during the evacuation. After all, Father had been the one who engineered the space shuttles.

"There will be strange creatures out there," Father had said. "Maybe some good. Maybe some bad. We need to take extra care of who we trust."

I had been reckless.

Prince Kodee and I stayed in silence for what seemed like forever. Every so often, he groaned or yelled or cursed in his native Izarkian language, which I'd never been able to truly learn. One thing to know about Izarkians: they were almost all polyglots and spoke to humans exclusively in English.

Eventually, Prince Kodee reached for his DigiBook and began to shuffle through the files. He hadn't damaged it, as it had turned out. After a futile effort to send a message out into the DigiSphere, Prince Kodee threw the device against the wall once more—this time cracking it in half—and he stormed around in a tiny circle before dropping back down to the ground.

Eventually, I heard him shifting in his seat, and I turned to see him rummaging through his own supply bag.

"What do you have in terms of rations?" he asked surprisingly calmly.

"I brought two weeks' worth with me."

"Then, between the two of us, we've got six weeks' worth of food and hydration. Meaning, if we split the rations evenly, we can survive for another three weeks before we begin to starve."

I shot him a look. "Don't you mean, you've got six weeks' of rations for yourself? I'm assuming you're going to try and fight me for mine. Well, be prepared. I'll put up a fight... even if you do end up killing me."

He smirked, rubbing a hand over his perfectly shaved chin which just started to show signs of a five o'clock shadow. "Don't be silly. What was that Earthling word you used? Only an *asshole* would do something like kill someone for their rations."

With that, he reached into his bag and held out a hydration pill for me. I hesitated a second, wondering if it was a trap, if he was baiting me only to make his attack more entertaining.

But then I snatched up the pill and quickly swallowed it down. Before he changed his mind.

He reached into the bag and popped a hydration pill into his mouth.

"Truly wish this were something stronger," he mumbled. But then he laid back against the floor and shut his eyes.

We were silent after that; nothing but the *plunk* of water droplets splaying across the floor every so often... serenading us into the dismal night.

3

On the seventh day of confinement, a droplet of water splattered across my forehead, and I cracked open an eye.

Little snores escaped Prince Kodee. He lay facing me, and I watched him breathing, a full-grown beard formed around his mouth and upper neck. Since it'd started to grow in, I marveled at the deep, royal blue color of the hairs.

Enough time in a cell alone with someone, and you tended to notice the little things.

Like the way he cried out in his sleep.

Prince Kodee let out a sharp yelp, twitching in between gasped breaths.

"Hey," I said, nudging him. He didn't move. Whacking him across the chest, I added, "Hey, *Sir Asshole*. Are you still alive?"

"Must you always wake me, *Earthling*?" He grumbled as he sat up.

Since our containment, I'd taken to calling him sir asshole, and he'd started responding by calling me Earthling. Pet names we'd accidentally established from our first night here.

Funny how things changed the moment we both realized he no longer had any power over me. When a person didn't have control over whether you lived or died, they tended to lose that power.

"Oh, I'm sorry," I said. "Did I ruin your precious beauty sleep?"

While he rummaged through his knapsack, I stood and walked over to the side of the wall filled with our markings. I used the sharp edge from one of the broken pieces of his DigiBook and carved out another line on the wall.

One week to the day.

Though, in all honesty, one week of being trapped in a tiny space with someone tended to feel like a lifetime. We'd spent the first three days trying to figure out a way out of here... we had no tool sharp or strong enough to get through the stone, my DigiBook wouldn't get us connected to the network, and we had no other means of reaching the outside world.

On the fourth day of trying to escape our confinement, we each threw in the towel and recognized something very important.

We were fucked.

We would die here.

The last person either of us would talk to would be each other.

"Happy anniversary," I remarked ironically, joining him on the floor for breakfast.

His nose crinkled as he tossed me a hydration pill and a packet of food rations.

"Happy anniversary?" Prince Kodee poured his food ration into his mouth and swallowed, making a slight face. "This isn't an expression I've ever heard before."

I popped the pill. "Oh. It means... uh... well, usually when two people are commemorating something together. I mean, it's typically used for a relationship of some sort. But it can also be a work anniversary, too. Like, if a person worked for the same company for two years."

"Earthlings celebrated things like this?" Prince Kodee asked.

"Yeah, we did. We do... for those of us still alive." My chest grew heavy, thinking of all those people—the very few humans left—forced into labor camps.

Before my emotions had a chance to run rampant, I closed them off and tried to think of something else.

I poured the food rations down my throat—a powdery substance that almost tasted like nutmeg. The instant the dust hit the back of my throat, I recalled holiday dinners back home—at my house on Earth—and the way Father poured extra nutmeg on the frothy milk drinks he served. He loved to hold his annual Christmas party. Father was a workaholic, yes, but when it came to the holidays, he insisted on closing the office until we had rung in the new year.

"How can you actually enjoy eating this abomination?" Prince Kodee asked.

"Huh?"

"That smile on your face. You look happy. We're withering away in here, and you seem positively joyful."

"I… uh…" Suddenly, I realized the way my lips were curled into an undeniable smile. I dropped my mouth into a neutral expression. "Sorry."

"Why are you sorry? At least one of us is happy with our sullen circumstances."

"I mean, I'm just used to shit, I guess. This doesn't seem that bad."

Especially compared to the slums of Izark.

Sure, in the last Earth year since Queen Taree had pulled me off the streets, I'd grown accustomed to opulent food fed to those in the Royal Castle—something Prince Kodee had most likely experienced his entire life. Lavish meals with three courses, spirits, and lively chatter. In the upper echelon of Izarkian society, they celebrated each mealtime as if it were a major event.

Food rations like the ones we had now were for those who needed to travel light through space and nothing more. Even the poor found more substantial scraps lingering around or in the trash.

But I'd still seen worse. Even a fed belly didn't prevent someone from experiencing the fear of being out on the slums of Izark—where you always had to be at the ready in case of an attack by other famished souls fighting off their competition.

I placed a hand over my stomach and suddenly wondered about the humans in those camps. Prince Kodee had only shown me the one clip and refused to show me anymore. This made me think there were far more terrors than what he wanted me to see.

"I can't believe those labor camps exist," I said.

I crossed my arms and shot him a sharp look, even though I recognized the camps weren't Prince Kodee's fault exactly. He was still a part of the Izarkian society doing this to humans, and I therefore held him partially responsible.

He gazed away, just as he did every time this subject came up. Which was every day multiple times a day. I knew it made him uncomfortable—and I was glad about it. Even if I couldn't do anything to help the remaining humans who were out there on Izark somewhere being forced to suffer. Even if I couldn't go back in time and prevent the near extinction of human beings.

I could make him feel uncomfortable.

And, somehow, that made me feel at least a smidgeon better.

Prince Kodee let out a slow breath. I assumed he would do that thing he always did. Huff and puff and then never say a word.

This time, he surprised me.

"I never believed in labor camps," he murmured, "or what Mother was doing."

"But you never tried to stop it, did you? What, was it just easier to let it happen? What did you care? You thought the throne was yours to inherit."

"I told you the first day we were here, and I'll say it again: you are speaking on matters you do not understand."

"So make me understand."

"What would be the purpose of that? We're going to die. There's no way out. Everything I ever believed in or fought for has been nullified. Why does anything matter?"

"It always matters."

"No." He let out a drawn-out sigh. "Maybe you've retained your own personal meaning in this madness, but I have lost all my purpose. There is no longer meaning to my life, and I will spend these final weeks with you, an Earthling, doing nothing but withering away. I'm a prince without a nation to lead... without anything to fight for. I'm already dead."

He rolled into a ball on the floor. Squeezing his eyes shut, he mumbled a few more words. "Just let me die. Take the remaining rations for yourself. Enjoy the extra few weeks of life. I'm done."

Maybe it was the human in me, or the fact I'd spent so many years surviving, but I wasn't ready to give up hope yet. And, as much as I didn't like Prince Kodee, I couldn't sit by and watch anyone wither away. He'd told me twice I didn't understand his involvement on Izark. Despite his bad behavior, he'd done enough to show me there was something more to him. Like wrapping up my leg... and insisting that we share our rations even though he had much more than I did.

And not trying to kill me for his own benefit.

Any other Izark might've killed me for the meat. Not that I'd ever heard of an Izarkian eating a human being. It just seemed like something an Izarkian would do in this specific situation.

Based on Prince Kodee's kind actions, and the fact he'd left me alive, I therefore guessed that when he told me I didn't understand, this meant he'd been doing more behind the scenes to speak out against his mother than what anyone knew.

I wanted to hold onto this hope until he told me otherwise.

So, I smacked him across the back to get his attention. To keep him from losing his spirits completely.

He twisted his neck to look at me, glaring with those angry, gleaming eyes.

"You can't die yet," I said. "There's still meaning in all this. You're just not seeing it yet."

"Just let me sleep, Océana."

"We just woke up."

He untwisted and returned to his fetal position; clearly his way of answering me.

"Fine. Be that way then," I said. "I'm going to make better use of our time."

Standing, I decided to resort to what I did best in times of crisis when I had some downtime: stretching and my stationary exercises. I crossed an arm over my chest, moving into the stretch and feeling that good kind of pain. My mind always jumped back to those days as a kid, sitting in the living room and watching cardio dance games. Father worked in his study most of the time, playing with one of his many gadgets, and so I kept busy in the summers by entertaining myself with interactive gaming. By age ten, the year Father and I left Earth, I'd done some of the same fitness workouts so many times I had them memorized.

A fact I only completely realized once I forced myself to recall them from memory in the darkest hours of my life. After I'd ended up in the Izarkian slums and had nothing left, exercise gave me something to hold onto.

Now, in this cramped cell, all the moves rushed into my head. I jumped back and forth, careful to keep within my confined space and not kick a certain prince in the head. Movement kept my mind busy. Kept me from the anxiety which would eat me alive if I curled into a ball like Prince Kodee. I wouldn't allow that to happen.

I was a survivor.

I kept on living. That was what I did.

So, I moved.

"Not this again," Prince Kodee grumbled, scrunching against the wall.

"Why don't you join me?" I asked as I began my knee raises.

"Join you in what? Making a fool of yourself?"

"Keeping sane."

"No, thank you."

"Alright then."

I'd show him what *making a fool of yourself* really meant.

Without a second thought, I paused and reached for my DigiBook. Turning it on, I scrolled through my own personal content. I had photo albums, videos, and music playlists from the one hard drive I'd managed to grab before Father and I fled our home and headed for the ship which would bring us away from Earth forever. Once she found me, Queen Taree gave me my own DigiBook and provided a transfer adapter, allowing me to import the data on my hard drive to the Izarkian device.

Another stab of sadness dug into me.

I still didn't want to believe what I'd learned about her.

But I existed in a world where you had no choice but to believe it when you found out someone had screwed you over.

Inside the music section on my DigiBook, I discovered my exercise playlist. Workout Beats 2k86 I'd labeled it. Little did I know, 2086 would be the final year of Earth as a planet. Trying not to dwell on things, I landed on one of the songs on the playlist, selected shuffle, and pressed on play.

A beat later, one of my favorite workout songs from childhood blasted through the cell.

"What is that *klingar*?" Prince Kodee groaned, muttering the Izarkian word translating to "noise trash."

"Cardio hits from Earth." I was jumping again. Moving through the workout I had burned into my mind. Though I was crammed into a tiny space with stone walls on every side, I was suddenly back in the living room of my home. A house with a yard and a dog and a place where I had my own room. It'd always just been Father and me. Well, Father and me and whoever he was dating. A few women had come and gone, so I never grew very attached to any of them. I quite liked it that way, honestly. Being a small family in a house where I was free to run around and play on my own.

We had a swing set in the yard. Sometimes, even now, I smelled the freshly cut lawn and heard the crickets singing their song at night. In the warmth of the summer, the fireflies blinked in little spurts, glowing in the dark. Sometimes, I still saw all of it.

"Is that how all Earthlings dance?" Prince Kodee rested on his butt, staring up at me from the floor. A crooked smile formed over his lips.

"Huh?" I said a little breathily. "This isn't dancing."

"You're moving to what you consider music. Isn't that by very definition... *dancing*?"

"No."

"Well, whatever it is you're doing... you seem to be doing it poorly."

I kicked a foot in the air, narrowly missing his head. "You telling me my moves are off, hotshot? If you're so good, you better get up here and show me how it's done then."

He scrunched his nose together. "No, I think it's best I don't."

I kicked another foot over his head. This time grazing his nose. Prince Kodee hopped up.

"On second thought," he said, "before you kick me in the head with your wild moves, I best get up and join you."

"Good answer."

The current song ended, and another fast-paced beat entered the space. I started jumping along, twisting to the rhythm of the music.

"You up for a dance off?" I asked.

"A what?"

"A dance off. I'll show you the moves. You shadow me. Once you get the hang of it, if you do get the hang of it, that is... then we can see who's doing it better."

"That's hardly fair. These are your moves. They already look ridiculous. And how would we even judge who did it better?"

"Just follow along, Sir Asshole." I nudged him on purpose before planting my feet on the ground.

"I've never heard more eloquent words, Earthling."

"Okay, so... watch, okay?" I briefly showed him a portion of one of the dances. The one where you lifted a knee up and twisted toward the knee with your chest and opposite hand. I brought up my left knee twice. Then the right. And alternated. I performed the moves slowly, so he could see. After a few times, I added, "And... now... your turn."

I stepped back and crossed my arms, giving myself a full view of the spectacle that I knew I was about to watch. Prince Kodee clunkily lifted up his knee, barely making it to his chest, and flailed his opposite hand around like a drunk person. In his officer's suit, he looked especially ridiculous.

"You know, you haven't taken that thing off once since we've been here," I remarked.

He smirked, gazing down at his jacket as he stumbled around.

Perhaps I'd distracted him. He hopped on the left leg, lost his balance, and tumbled into the wall.

Clapping my hands, I laughed so loud I snorted. "Still think I'm performing the moves poorly?"

"What sort of barbarism is this madness?" he scoffed.

"Some people call it jazzercise... others refer to it as a cardio dance workout. Why don't you try it again?"

"No."

"Okay." I kicked up a leg in the air, nearly coming into contact with his face.

"Good hell! I'll try it again!"

"Good hell?" I started laughing even louder. "Where'd you get that expression from?"

He rolled his eyes, ignoring me. He lifted up a knee a little higher than his last attempt but instantly lost his balance. This time, he fell toward me, and I held out my arms to catch him.

"You're stronger than you look," he said.

"Yeah. I know."

Prince Kodee regained his balance and started again. I joined him, and together we jumped up and down, bringing our knees up twice, switching sides, and then alternating. We danced along to the beat of the music for the rest of the song... and then the next two that followed. Every so often, I peered over at him. A small grin formed on his face. Near the end of the dancing, his grin had turned into a smile.

"Please, I need a second to catch my breath," he said at the end of the song.

"No problem. Take some time to breath."

"This is nothing like the way we dance on Izark." He held a hand against the wall, panting as he spoke.

"Oh yeah?"

"Yes."

"I mean, do *you* have any dance moves to show me? That'd make this fairer. I can't be the only one expecting you to learn my moves... and I've never seen an Izarkian dance, so I'd love to learn."

He shook his head. "Me showing you dance moves may not be appropriate."

"Why's that?" I asked playfully.

"Izarkians don't dance solo. We dance with a partner."

The lightness in the air faded away. I understood what he meant instantly. On Izark, an intimate relation between an Izarkian and a human would be an especially taboo thing. This went for any Izarkian—lower and upper class.

Even before I'd learned of the labor camps, I had understood not to ever involve myself in that way with any Izarkian. If caught, a human being was put on trial for misbehavior—and it typically resulted in life imprisonment.

A royal member of the family and a human being having an affair of this nature? It would be an outrage.

Not that any of this mattered now.

Prince Kodee's brows furrowed. "I didn't say that for the reason you're thinking. I just meant... it might not be appropriate."

"If it isn't about me being a human, then what else could it be about?"

"You being a female dancing in a confined space with a male. I would feel as though I'm taking advantage."

"Umm, what? How is that taking advantage?"

"Typically, after younglings reach the age when they're separated in school, a male and a female only dance with one another if they're intended to mate."

"Oh... I see. And you can't just dance without it meaning something more?"

"I'm sure one could... but..." His words trailed away.

"...but that isn't normally how things are done."

"Precisely."

"Well, I'm a human female. We're not allowed to *do* those things, so it really isn't the same thing, is it?"

"Er... you do have a point..."

I held out my arms. "I'll tell you what, I won't tell anyone about this dance, if you don't. Show me some moves."

He cocked his head to the side. "But I just said..."

"We're both going to die once the rations run out. Whether we're trapped here, or we're back on Izark, there's no world where we would've ever done the dirty. So, you might as well just dance with me while we have the chance. If I didn't feel comfortable, I wouldn't have my arms out."

He nodded his head. "Yes. Okay. Fine. Just... it's... I'm a little warm."

Indicating toward his jacket, I understood. He unbuttoned the front and slipped it off, revealing a black undershirt exposing his arms and some hair on his chest. As I'd seen the day the servants undressed him, sculpted muscles shaped his upper arms. The undershirt clung to his upper body, exposing his defined abs and muscular form.

"What?" he asked.

"Umm. Nothing."

Prince Kodee slowly inched forward. "Alright... you'll need to put on a slow song, yes?"

"Right." Backing out of the workout playlist, I found a selection of slow pop songs and selected shuffle. A soft melody drifted through the room. I held out my arms again.

Prince Kodee lay one arm on top of mine and placed the other right below. "You step with your partner. The timing has to be exact. Once to the left... then the right. This is the first part of a traditional Izarkian dance."

As I moved to my left, he moved to his left, and then we stepped away from each other.

He chuckled. Little crinkles formed beneath his eyes.

"You said move to the left," I said.

"The male's left. The female adjusts her direction according to him."

"Oh, I see. So, once again, the man dominates."

"I'm not a man. I'm an Izarkian." He glared. "Do you want to learn the dance, or not?"

"Yes, I do."

"Let's try again."

Once more, he rested one arm on top of mine, and one below. The warmth of his skin sent a soothing sensation through my body. We moved in sync to his left, then his right, and followed the musical beat.

"The next move is a twist," he said. Gently, he glided our arms to the center, pulled back until just our fingertips touched, and then he returned, maneuvering me in a circle beneath his arm. Taking such care and being so delicate. At the end of my rotation, he glided me in closely and cupped his arms around my back.

The tip of his nose touched mine, and I swallowed sharply.

"This is the first part of a traditional Izarkian dance." His breath landed against my mouth and left an almost ghostly kiss on my lips. I'd never been kissed—*that's what happens when you leave Earth at age ten*—and so this was the closest thing I'd ever experienced to actually having lips on mine.

I found myself wondering what it might be like to experience the real thing.

We swayed back and forth to the music. My hands naturally glided to the back of his undershirt as we danced. The pulse in his arms beat against mine, and his warm skin pressed against mine. Izarkians and humans really weren't too dissimilar from one another. Each species had a beating heart pushing blood through their veins. Recognizing the similarities, I somehow experienced a deeper tie to Prince Kodee. As different as our cultures were, we were also the same, too.

Here, in this moment, recognizing my connection to Prince Kodee... there was something comforting in knowing I wasn't alone.

There was something soothing in being able to touch him this way.

"Did you dance a lot on Izark?" I asked softly. "I mean..."

"You mean was I ever intended for someone?" The right side of his mouth curled. "Yes, naturally. I had a few females I danced with and courted at different times of my life."

Unlike any royal family I'd ever heard of on Earth, an Izarkian male of noble blood always picked his own bride after extensive meetings with her to determine if she was the right fit for him.

From what I remembered on the Earth reality TV shows, it was like watching an episode of *The Bachelor*. Except the male could order your execution if he didn't find you pleasing.

"Order anyone's execution?" I spat out.

He gave me a look. "What do you think?"

"You don't strike me as the love 'em and guillotine 'em type."

He snorted, shaking his head with a smirk. "Were all Earthlings like this?"

"I mean... no. I don't think so, anyway. I left Earth a long time ago."

"Right, well. To put you at ease. I'm not a royal who wants to sentence anyone to death. Instead, I typically found other suitors for the females who crossed my path."

"No one you actually liked, huh?" I asked.

"I'm a picky Izaree," he said, using the Izarkian equivalent of the word man. Unlike the Izarkian words for female and young boys, the first letter of Izaree was always capitalized. He shrugged as he added, "Most of the dances I attended were during my classes as a youngling."

"They taught you dancing in classes?"

"Yes. Was that not done on Earth?"

"I mean, I only got through the fifth grade before we had to flee. From what I remember, we did have dancing in gym class. Sometimes. Never ballroom dancing at my school though."

"Ballroom?"

"Yeah. It's the most similar name for what we're doing now. Where you have a dancing partner. We don't have those moves you showed me in the beginning. Well, kind of the twisting thing."

"That's too bad you didn't have *ballroom* in your studies back on Earth. Some youngling would've been lucky to have you as his dance partner."

My cheeks flushed. "You don't have to say that just to be nice."

"That's not the Izarkian way. We're taught to always speak our truth."

"Yeah, uh huh. Okay."

"I'm being honest. You would've made the most attractive mate for someone on Earth, I'm sure."

At his mention of *most attractive mate*, I raised a brow, instantly assuming *mate* was code for *excellent breeder*. That was how Izarkians viewed women, anyway.

I let out an irritated, "Really?"

"What did I say wrong? It was meant as a compliment."

"And I understand that on Izark it might be a kind thing to say. But, with all due respect, Izarkians have a way of doing things I don't agree with. Females are not just meant for breeding purposes."

He bit his lip and gazed down. "I meant no offense."

"I know... but sometimes a statement meant inoffensively still hurts."

Prince Kodee nodded. "I won't tell you that I understand, because I don't. What I can offer is a promise to try to understand... with the time we have left."

"I can live with that." I leaned into his chest.

He smiled, head naturally tilting down to rest on mine. "We may have just become the first Izarkian and human being to reach a compromise."

"That wasn't so hard, was it?"

"Not at all."

A rush of natural euphoria worked its way through my body at this closeness. We gently swayed to the music, dancing to the soft tune which continued playing in our space.

"Are there any other moves?" I asked through my drunken tranquility.

"Yes. Though I'm not sure we should do them."

"Try me."

Spinning me around once more, he stopped me halfway during the rotation and pushed my back flush against his chest.

"Izarkian dancing isn't so bad, huh?" he whispered into my ear.

"I actually like it," I said softly, tilting my head back and up. My cheek brushed against his. I watched as his eyes shut.

Maybe it was the dance—a dance meant for two who intended to mate. Or maybe it was the way his bare arms wrapped over my body. I drew toward his lips and fluttered my mouth over his. Softly. Gently. No more than a butterfly kiss. A little jolt worked its way down my body.

Prince Kodee stood like a statue.

"This is why I didn't want to do this," he murmured, his lips resting up against mine. His heart beat rapidly, and I could feel the pulse in his arms. He gripped me more tightly, and I let out a breath I'd been holding in.

Slowly, I twisted against him, and returned to the place where we had been earlier, with my chest against his, and his arms wrapped behind my back. He walked us back against one of the walls and cupped his hands over my face.

"I thought you were a picky Izaree," I breathed.

"I am."

He pressed his mouth to my mouth, and I captured his lips in mine.

This kiss landed more deeply than the first one. Every part of my body tingled, and my hands rested at the base of his shirt, a hand slipping through the material and feeling his bare chest. He let out a deep breath at my touch.

We froze together, our lips locked in place with his forehead resting against mine.

Suddenly, Prince Kodee's eyes snapped open. He cleared his throat and abruptly broke away.

"I need to lie down and... and... I just need to lie down," he insisted.

I waited in the place where he left me. Partially feeling like a fool.

And partially wondering what I'd done wrong.

4

"Océana!" Father said with his gentle voice. "I've always been here. I've always been home."

"Father?" I asked softly.

I hovered above a dark, winding pathway. At the edge of my line of sight, at the edge of the portal, a cutting light sliced across the horizon. I saw the Alpha Federation ship in which Prince Kodee and I had arrived. Near the brightest spot at the end of the pathway.

My body floated, separate from the physical, yet I remained a part of all space and time.

Gazing behind, I noticed a brick wall. I had the ability to see through it. On the other side, two sleeping bodies rested—one of them the blue shape of Prince Kodee. The other my own body. It was us. I was looking at us inside our confined space, and my spirit had somehow separated, split, and reached the outside of our jail.

I swallowed down a lump of anxiety at the idea of being separate from myself. As I let out a deep breath, a rush of calm and serenity washed over me. Wherever I was, I knew I was safe.

"Océana, hope isn't lost." Father's words echoed into the ethers. I spun in every direction, searching for the source of his voice. Though no matter where I turned, I could not see him.

"Father?" I asked. "Where are you?"

"Hope isn't lost," Father repeated. "You're more capable than you realize. There are things... powers... you must use them. You must be the one who saves you both."

"Father... I don't know how. Tell me how..."

I reached out a hand toward nothing. Helplessly searching. Searching, searching, searching...

Prince Kodee's whimpers roused me from a deep slumber.

A heavy fog clouded my brain, and I slowly opened up my eyes. Two weeks of being stuck here, and it still took me a second to recalibrate. The dreams had been getting worse.

Next to me, Prince Kodee's eyes were clamped shut. He shook in his sleep. Sobs escaped him, and his movements were filled with little tremors.

"Prince Kodee," I whispered, reaching out a hand.

The spasms continued.

I slid a little closer to him.

"Prince Kodee." I spoke the words a little more firmly, pressing my fingers to his face. The full-grown beard prickled at the touch.

His eyes fluttered open, tears rushing down his cheeks. In an instant, he became aware of his surroundings—and my fingers on his face—and he jerked away.

"Sorry," he mumbled in between sobs. "I... you shouldn't see me like this."

"Like what?"

"I'm a grown Izaree! Crying!" He curled into a ball facing away, shaking in little fits. I paused for a second, taking a breath in order to consider the best course of action. I didn't want to violate his space. If he needed to cry alone, I wanted to give that to him. But, also, in good conscience I couldn't just sit here ignoring him.

In the last week that we'd been here, his crying in the middle of dreams had only gotten worse. I'd been too afraid of crossing a boundary, but today I would do something more. We had such little time left, and if it was anything I understood especially well, it was regretting the things you didn't do in the time you had left.

Slowly, I curled up from behind and wrapped him in a hug.

His body tensed under my touch for a split moment, but then I felt him let out a huge breath, almost a sigh of relief, and he loosened.

"What... what are you doing?" he sobbed.

"Showing you that you're not alone."

He twisted around. In the process, my arms wrapped over his back, and his hands pulled me in more tightly. Our chests pressed together, and my knees curled up against his torso. My insides fluttered, and I bowed my head. Just two weeks ago, I could've been jailed for touching the prince in this manner.

But inside this cell, our titles had been stripped from us. No societal labels remained. We were simply two beings stuck together in the same place.

"We're going to die here," he said. More tears slid down his face. "I'm not ready to die... and... I'm..." His voice lowered to a level barely audible. "I'm afraid."

I brushed away some of his tears. He shut his eyes. As I traced a finger over his face, I marveled at the structure of his eyes... and how a species from a planet in another galaxy could look so similar to a human. Minus the shade of his skin, his eyelids appeared the same as any person's.

"We've got another week of rations left," I said, summoning up the small amount of hope remaining. "Who's to say we won't get out of here?"

I thought of my dream. Of the hope still residing in my subconscious mind.

He shook his head. "We're not getting out. We're trapped. We're going to die. It's going to be a slow, painful death..."

"Not necessarily. One of us could eat the other." I smirked, hoping the joke would land.

He let out a small laugh. "She's going to eat me. The truth comes out."

"No. Something tells me you'd be the one to eat me first, if it came down to that."

"I'm not going to eat you, Earthling. Who would be around to annoy me with her silly, fast-paced dancing, if I were to do that?"

"You, Sir Asshole, seem to enjoy the dancing."

"Yeah... maybe I do enjoy it," he murmured. His gaze turned more serious. "Would that be such a bad thing?"

"No." I wiped a few more stray tears escaping his eyes.

"Why didn't they ever show us this on Izark?"

"Show you what? Human dancing?"

"No, not the dancing. This compassion you humans have. This hope. I've never met any Izarkian who behaved like you. Who held onto hope even when you were in a situation comparable to one shitty horse."

I shrugged. "Hope and compassion don't have to be something only one species has. Look at you. You're changing. I bet I can correct your use of horse shit now without worrying you might order my execution over it."

He let out another laugh. "I wouldn't have ordered your execution."

"You didn't see the look in your eyes that day, Sir Asshole."

He paused. A quizzical look passed over his features.

"Was I that bad?" he asked.

"I mean... yeah."

"Why didn't you say something to me then?"

I narrowed my eyes. "Really? Insult Prince Kodee... the heir to the Alpha Federation... the Izaree who hissed out the words telling me to be glad he liked me as a retort to one correction? I wasn't about to take my chances on a premature death. Hell, on second thought, maybe if I had at least one of us would've lived."

"You shouldn't speak that way."

"It's true. You're here because I trusted the wrong person."

He gripped my hand in his and shook his head. "No. It's as you said our first night here. What choice did you have?"

"I don't know."

"You believed you found an opportunity to save Earth, and you took it. You're sitting in a cell with a grown Izaree who is crying, yet your spirit remains unscathed. You're the bravest being I've ever met."

With that, he leaned inward and planted a soft kiss across my forehead. I shut my eyes, enjoying this intimate moment for what it was.

"Thank you for showing me how to be better," he whispered in my ear. "And... I'm sorry for how I treated you before we came here."

"Prince Kodee..." I started to say, using his name respectfully for the first time since I'd ever uttered it.

He planted another kiss on my forehead. "You don't have to call me that."

"What should I call you?"

"Just call me Kodee."

"Kodee." The words rolled off my lips with ease. "I was just going to say, you don't have to be worried about crying in front of me. Crying doesn't mean you're weak. It means... you're human."

"I'm Izarkian."

"It's an expression. When you're telling someone that they're normal for their feelings. Besides, you're as human as anyone else I've ever met. That term doesn't have to apply only to my species."

I curled up into his arms, and he wrapped me up in the safest embrace. We drifted to sleep together; his face buried against mine.

For the first time ever, my soul found a place to rest—a place to call home.

5

"I'm begging you to take them both." Kodee placed the final set of rations onto his palm and reached his hand toward me. He'd been begging me to take his rations for the last week, ever since we'd fallen to sleep together. We were on week three. The final week. The one we'd been dreading since landing here in this prison.

"We've been over this. If you don't eat yours, I'm not eating mine. You pick."

"Océana..."

"Kodee. Eat."

I clasped my hand over his and pushed his arm back toward his body. He hesitated for a long moment, but then he swallowed both the hydration pill and the food ration. I waited to be sure he'd done it and hadn't tried to trick me—that'd happened three days ago, and he claimed he only broke his Izarkian code of honesty because it was a matter of putting a life over his.

I watched his Adam's apple bob up and down.

"Open your mouth," I demanded. "I want to be sure."

"I promise you I took it." He held out his hands. One was empty. The other contained the final food ration and hydration pill meant for me.

Kodee offered them out.

Slowly, I took them in my hands. One after the other, I plopped them into my mouth and swallowed.

"Well, that's that then." I gazed down at my empty hands. An unnerving emotion crawled along my spine, but I burrowed it, as I buried most feelings of fear and panic.

"Yes, that's that."

"Not so bad, huh? All that anxiety and we're still here." A lump formed in my throat. *For now.* This would be the hard part. Dying. "At least we aren't going to be alone, huh?"

His forehead crinkled, and he let out a sigh.

"What is it?" I asked.

"I will most likely die first."

I laughed. "Is that some kind of joke? You're Izarkian. Your species has a much stronger body constitution than any human."

"While we may have naturally stronger muscles and a greater endurance than a human, we also require fuel more than you do. In all probability, your human body will outlast mine."

"By how long?"

"Izarkians can only last a couple days without water. Isn't it weeks for humans?"

"I think the average human can go a week without water." I gave a noncommittal shrug. "I know my own personal limit... I've gone close to two weeks without food or water before on Izark. It wasn't pretty. But I survived."

"Two weeks?"

"Two weeks."

"Goodness. That's... that's madness." He reached out a hand and cupped mine in his. They fit together perfectly. Like two meant to be one. His firm yet protective grip sent a calming sensation over my body, and I naturally scooted closer to him.

I rested my head against his shoulder. "You know, sometimes I wonder if landing in the slums was supposed to happen to me. As a wakeup call."

He scrunched his nose. "I couldn't imagine *you* needing a wake-up call."

"Have you ever asked yourself why only a select few Earthlings got off planet? It wasn't inhabitable anymore. Oxygen levels weren't high enough. Yet Father and I were one of the first families to escape."

Eventually, some people with less financial means got out, too. But no more than a million Earthlings in total made it out in time. At least, that was the total number of Earth Refugees once listed in a report I found in my DigiBook.

"Were you of the royal class back on Earth?" Kodee asked.

I snorted. "No. I mean, not the way Izarkians classify royalty, anyway."

"Your father was wealthy."

"He was extremely wealthy. One of the wealthiest people at that time.

And we had so many advantages because of it. I took a lot of things for granted, and I finally learned the hard way what it meant to struggle for simple things... like food and water."

"So, we're the same. Two individuals who have experienced extreme opulence... and extreme poverty."

"You, Sir Asshole, have been in poverty for only a hot second," I joked.

"Enough time to understand a little bit more. That no one deserves to struggle like this. Whether you've lived a life of privilege or not."

"That's right," I said. "No one deserves to struggle."

My words lingered in the air, a thick mass of energy neither of us could tangibly grasp. Here we were. A former prince. And the daughter of a former American billionaire. You wouldn't know it from our ragged looks, our dirty clothes and spirits, and the desperation in the words we exchanged. But we'd both come from something once, and we now each had nothing.

Except each other.

"What happened to your father?" Kodee asked softly.

"The vaccine."

"Oh." Kodee's voice cracked as he said the word, a sadness to the timber.

As the Izarkians had started bringing humans to their planet, they quickly realized a bacterium in the air—not found in The Milky Way galaxy—was toxic for humans to breathe. While Father and I had been one of the first families to leave Earth, we'd been fortunate, or so we thought, that the Izarkians had not found us until they'd already discovered what their atmosphere was doing to human beings.

To combat this, Izarkian scientists developed the vaccine. It created antibodies in a human's lungs that would prevent the sickness brought on by the bacteria.

The only problem? Some human bodies rejected the vaccine. Many died after taking the injection.

"I told Father I wouldn't let him take it first," I explained to Kodee. "So, on the Izarkian Royal Ship that was transporting us to Izark, I jumped ahead in line and got the vaccine first. When I was fine, we thought he'd be okay, too. But... that wasn't the case. He died in my arms."

"I'm... I'm so sorry."

"It isn't your fault. The vaccine isn't even Izark's fault, as far as I know. Still. That's how I arrived on your planet. Alone. Dumped into a strange place with nowhere to go... and a language I didn't speak."

"You were ten in Earth years."

"Yes. With nothing but a hard drive full of memories, and a debit card to an account I'd never be able to access. Father'd given me some cash, too, before we left Earth. It's just... no one on Izark cared for the strange paper bills in my bag. Or that I was a little human girl without any help."

Kodee's thumb traced circles around my knuckle. "If we somehow get out of this..."

"I know," I said, finishing his thought.

"You'll help me, yes?"

I eyed him suspiciously. "You want me, an Earthling, to help you appeal to the Izarkian citizens regarding social justice?"

"Not just that," he breathed. "I want you to help me lead the revolution."

"Me? What am I going to do? I'm just a person."

"Wrong. You're *the* person. Let me show you something I haven't ever shown anyone."

He lifted from the ground and walked over to his DigiBook. Though two pieces had chipped off, the device still powered on—apparently. Kodee rested it in the middle of our space, scrolling through blurry images on his personal drive. Clearly, something in the processing board had been damaged after he'd flung his DigiBook at the wall that second time.

He reached an album tucked away within the pictures, and he scanned his finger in order to pass onto the encrypted folder.

"Do you remember a few weeks ago when I showed you the footage of that dinner?" he asked. "You asked me why I didn't try to stop the labor camps."

As he flicked through his device, I squinted my eyes, attempting to understand the words on the screen—all written in Izarkian. These weren't photographs. They appeared to be nothing more than bullet-pointed lists.

And *plans.*

"What is this?" I asked.

Before he had a chance to answer, we reached images with English words. The message became quite clear. Each slide mentioned enlisting the help of the Izarkian Royal Guard to overthrow Queen Taree.

"You were going to steal the throne," I breathed.

"Yes. But not for the reasons you might be thinking."

The next set of images were maps. Listing the different labor camps... and how Kodee planned on evacuating the people from each site.

"I may not have shared the same views as the humans or even understood them," Kodee admitted. "But I understood the wrongs committed by Mother. Not just the labor camps. She's done a lot of terrible things even to her own people. And she always does it with a kind smile. Fooling everyone."

Eventually, Kodee neared the end of the album. He gave me a beat to process, and then he shut off the device.

"Now you know what could have been." He sighed.

I walked over to him and wrapped him up in a hug, squeezing him so tightly I worried I might suffocate him. Loosening a bit, I gazed up at him as his soft eyes reached down to meet mine.

"It would've been a dream leading the revolution with you," I said.

He smiled sadly. "In another life, perhaps?"

"In another life."

Kodee leaned down to my ear, and he whispered something in Izarkian, speaking to me in a tongue he knew I wouldn't understand.

I rubbed my nose against his face. "What are you saying?"

"I'll tell you another time." He brushed a lock of hair behind my ear.

"*Time*. We might not have too much of that left."

"I'll tell you before ours runs out. I promise you."

He cupped my chin in his hands and spoke a few more foreign words straight to my face. Though more statements in the Izarkian language, his eyes narrowed in a way that told me he was making me some sort of vow. He spoke especially quickly, yet still with that same softness in his tone, so that the few words I might've picked up on would've escaped my comprehension.

At the end of his speech, I leaned into his chest and shut my eyes. We swayed together to the beat of our own song, a gentle tune carrying us away.

Though death would not be a pleasant thing, our journey toward the end had been the most magical.

6

"Océana! Océana!"

Father's voice echoed through my mind. Whispers of the past chanted into the ethers... haunting my present.

"Océana!" Father's voice echoed through my mind, whispering to me to find him. "I've always been here. Come and find me... I'm on the other side of these walls. You have the power. Use it. Get out. This is a portal... the rules of physics don't apply."

"*Father?*"

My eyes fluttered open. Every limb was weighed down by weakness. Five days without food and water, withering away in a cell, and my body suffered. I shifted in my place on the floor, pressing my nose into Kodee's chest. His arms wrapped around me tightly, as if he never planned on letting go.

Kodee's eyes were clamped shut.

"Hey," I mumbled weakly, stroking a finger over his cheek. A pit formed in my stomach.

What if he didn't wake up this time?

"Hmm?" Kodee asked, sending a rush of relief straight to my heart.

"Thank god you're still alive."

"Yeah." He smiled, voice sounding raspier than I'd ever heard it.

"Talk to me. Tell me anything."

"I think…" He took a breath. "I think it may be time… for me to sleep… now."

"It's not time for you to sleep. Not yet."

He slowly cracked open his eyes. They looked tired. Glazed over. A duller green.

"No, aore," he said softly. Slowly. "It may be my time."

Aore.

Love.

"I promised you I'd tell you what I said the other day… before our time was up," he added. "What I told you… was that I found my meaning. In you."

Tear leaked from my eyes, and the world became a cloudy haze. He kissed my face where the tears fell, whispering words in English this time. "I promised to always love you, no matter where the afterlife takes me. If there is still a world where my soul exists, I will find you again." He kissed me a few more times. "And I will never forget… the person who showed me the real meaning of life."

He leaned his chin downward, eyes searching mine with hesitation. I moved in to meet his lips, and our mouths met in the middle. I tasted full, sweet lips, and he tasted mine. After one single kiss, he pulled back with his eyes shut and smiled with the widest smile, the most joy, a look of contentment covering his expression.

A second later, he drooped against the floor.

"Kodee?"

I rested my head against his heart. Still beating. Still a pulse.

But he remained lumped over without a sound.

"Kodee." My voice squeaked. "Get up, Sir Asshole."

I nudged him, but he wasn't budging.

Crawling into his arms once more, I shut my eyes, tears still falling from my eyes. Sobbing into his chest, I thought of all the things that could've been between the two of us, and all the things I'd never gotten to say to him. He was going to die, and I'd be next.

And if there was nothing beyond this world, it'd be like none of this ever happened.

Like none of it had ever mattered.

I'd come to this portal in search of the past—and instead, I'd found a way to return to the present.

For a few minutes, I cried with wild abandon, letting everything out I'd been holding in for years. I cursed up at nothing, swore about how unfair life had been, and finally resolved to let myself go. To follow Kodee into the unknown.

As my mind quieted, I took a few deep breaths. Tried to reach a mellow place of nirvana. If I could relax my soul, perhaps I'd drift away more quickly; be rid of the pain of a dying, malnourished body.

I took another big breath.

Océana, I heard Father's voice inside my head. *Come and find me... I'm on the other side of these walls.*

I shut out his voice. There was no sense in listening to a hallucination. Father had died. I'd watched him die. And nothing would get us out of here.

Océana, Father pushed through. *You're not dead yet. There's still hope. Go to one of the walls. Break through.*

I opened my eyes.

"We can't break through, Father!" I yelled out, exasperated. "We've tried. We've got nothing to get out of here!"

No object will set you free, Father said in my brain. *You've got to use your mind.*

I gazed around, meekly trying to find out where the voice was coming from, or if I had reached a point of psychosis, due to the lack of nutrients going into my body, that I couldn't distinguish fact from fiction.

Afraid the voice in my head wouldn't shut up—Father had been haunting me in my dreams ever since we'd arrived here—I stood on wobbly legs and fell forward into one of the walls. The stone felt cool beneath my palms.

Your mind will set you free, Father said.

I shut my eyes once more. Pressing my palms into the wall, I took another deep breath. Nothing happened. The material firmly remained beneath my touch. What had I expected to happen?

"I feel like a fool," I breathed.

Try again, Father sent.

I swallowed. Inhaling one final time, I felt the weight of the stone beginning to disintegrate. Little particles of energy melting under my fingers and dissipating into nothing. Rumbling sounded from the structure. Everything began to shake.

"What's happening?" I shrieked.

No response.

I gazed back down at Kodee. He hadn't moved.

In front of me, the wall crumbled into nothing, and an elongated path—that of darkness—the one from my dreams—stretched out toward the other end, a beacon of light, with our ship resting at the edge.

"Kodee," I said, my mouth wide. "Kodee!"

I bent down, practically falling into his arms.

"Our ship!" I cried. "We're free. We can go."

"Mmm?" he mumbled.

"Come on," I said, reaching for our DigiBooks on the floor. We'd need these—especially his—if we were to follow through with everything he'd planned.

The revolution was about to begin.

As I lifted with Kodee, my weak body crumbled to the ground. My knees locked, and a heaviness surrounded my head and blurred my vision.

No, no, no, no.

Pulling on every last ounce of strength in my body, I gritted my teeth together and raised Kodee up with me. Every muscle burned. The room shook, the walls deteriorating before us, and we bobbed from side to side as I moved us toward our exit.

"Océana?" Kodee's eyes opened in slits. "What..."

"I'll explain once we're out of here. Can you walk with my support?"

"Barely."

"Then that's barely enough for us to get out of here."

I guided us out onto the bridge, leery we'd simply fall into the unknown space inside this portal. To my surprise, our feet planted firmly against the dark space beneath us, and I moved us along as quickly as possible, despite the weakness in my limbs.

I couldn't stop now. Had to muster up every final piece of strength left.

Our ship, lit up and bright with joy for weary eyes, beckoned us nearer.

As we stepped, voices blasted into my ears and visions into my mind—a time of past, present, and future. Real visions—real memories—formed across the environment around us. Father taking care of me as a child. The slums of Izark.

A young Izarkian male—I assumed Kodee—being yelled at by a younger version of Queen Taree.

An even younger boy—a boy who looked like an Earthling, but who I did not know—being whipped by another man.

And then a young girl taking the steps leading to the royal castle on Izark. Someone else I did not recognize.

Yet... when she reached the throne room, she bowed her head two people I knew very well.

"No need to bow," Kodee of the Future said. "We're all equals here."

"What brings you here today?" I saw and heard Future Océana ask.

"I've come for your help," the young girl said.

The images faded away. As I neared the ship, my brows crossed.

What in the hell had I just seen?

Reaching the ship, I opened the doors and helped Kodee inside. He slumped against the passenger seat.

"Hang on, Kodee," I said, starting up the engine of the ship. Above us, I noticed the source of the light. A window which appeared to serve as the door for how we'd entered. How the portal had transported our ship here, or where we even were, I still couldn't even begin to understand.

That and so many other things were questions for another day.

Right now, I needed to fly us somewhere, anywhere, to restock on food and supplies. I needed to get us out of here.

I twisted to see Kodee staring at me.

"Can you hang on for a little bit longer?" I asked.

He leaned over and wrapped his arms around me, nodding his head.

"Good." I kissed him on the lips once more as our ship lifted up and out and into space. "Because... I sort of have a revolution to win with the person I love."

I wasn't sure where I was headed. Just that I knew we needed to survive.

As the portal trailed away behind us, I took it in one last time.

During my time here, I'd learned that a portal couldn't change the past.

But it certainly had changed my future.

MORE BY RACHEL RADNER

Standalones Novels:

A Setting Sun Can't Save My Soul

Prometheus Burning

Anthologies:

Summer Sizzle

Help Desk Heat (novella part of The Girl Power Collective)

Summer With You

ABOUT RACHEL RADNER

Rachel Radner lives in Los Angeles, CA with her husband and two furry Golden Retrievers (*cough* children *cough*). When she isn't writing, she can be seen drinking coffee or tea... and probably watching something geeky on the internet. Or one of her favorite movies like Casablanca. Oh yeah, and she also has an unhealthy obsession with history and learning languages like Latin, French, and German.

Rachel has been writing since the first grade when her teacher handed her a journal and instructed her to write about her day. Since then she's continued journaling... though she spends most of her time writing fictional stories. There's always another idea that comes to her randomly. You should see the notes on her phone. Seriously.

Join my mailing list:
www.mailchi.mp/e6e3b7ed625f/rachelradner

Rachel Radner's Romantics Group:
www.facebook.com/groups/rachelradner

facebook.com/rachelradner
twitter.com/rachelradner
instagram.com/rachelradnerauthor

KISS OF TOMORROW

BY BILLIE PARSONS

When Paige's vacation is interrupted by a ghost from her past feelings that she never let go start to rise again.

Nicholas is looking to hide away while on leave. Instead the not so little girl from his hometown claim not only his home but his heart.

It's been a long time since they walked away from each other. Five years to be exact. Now Nicholas and Paige get stuck in the storm full of forgotten feelings.

To all of those who never gave up on their love story and to those who are not afraid to try again.

1

PAIGE

Five Years Ago

"Paige. We're going off to college in a couple of weeks. This cannot be our last summer together," Jessie says.

"Let's make a pact," I offer, and Jessie looks at me in question.

"No matter what, we come back every summer." I suggest.

"We always stay in touch. You can't replace me as your B.F.F.," Jessie adds.

Present

We made those promises five years ago and we have never followed through. We stayed in touch here and there and would text each other during the holidays. Both of us always had an excuse for why we couldn't make it to the beach house, either because I was working or she had a boyfriend that she didn't want to leave.

This year will be different. I am done with school and ready to go back home.

2

PAIGE

"Yes, sir. I'm packing up the rest of my belongings now and will be at the airport within thirty minutes." I tell my new boss.

"Great. Great. We are so happy to have you come back and teach at the school you went to, Paige. I mean, Ms. Hansen," he says.

"I'll see you this fall, Mr. Evergreen." I say before I hang up.

I finish packing the last of my belongings and hand over the keys to my sweet little New York apartment. I send a quick text message to Jessie, letting her know that I am driving to the airport and will be landing in Florida in about three hours. Without a response from her, I put my phone in my carry-on and head out.

Four and a half hours later, I am pulling up to the beach house. There's not a car in sight. Hell, there's not even a single person around. Jessie was supposed to pick me up at the airport, but she never showed. I tried calling her a few times to no avail. Luckily, I have a key for the place, otherwise I would be stuck out on the driveway.

I drop my bag in the room that has always been designated as mine and find myself walking out onto the white, sandy beach After lying on the private beach for a couple of hours, I am woken by a car door slamming.

I jump up, excited to see my friend again. As I dash to the house, I see the backside of a very large man. His jeans flex with every movement he makes and they stretch across his tight ass as he bends over to pick up a can of chewing tobacco that fell out of his truck. His dark grey t-shirt hugs his arms and shoulders, and I watch as his muscles bunch while he reaches over the edge of the bed of his large, black truck to grab a large green duffle bag. When he turns to walk back to the house, my heart flutters.

"Pidge?" The man uses my nickname.

"Nicky?" I almost cry.

"Well, how the hell are you bird?" Nicholas asks. He drops his bag as soon as he reaches me, immediately wrapping me in his arms.

"I'm good, Nicky. How are you? When did you get home? What are you doing here?" I ask quickly.

Before answering, he picks up his bag and gestures for me to lead the way inside.

"I'm alright. Home on leave right now. I go back in three weeks. I wasn't planning on seeing anyone. You guys haven't come home in years, so I thought this would be a good place to hide out." Nicholas answers.

"Oh, I thought Jessie told you we were going to be here." I admit.

"I just got off the phone with Jessie. She said she was still in Texas." he says with a sympathetic look.

"Are you serious? She was supposed to pick me up at the airport this morning and she never answered my phone calls. Damn her. I say with frustration. I reach for my cell phone, but Nicholas stops me.

"Here, let me piss her off," he says before he grabs his cell phone, throws an arm around my shoulder, and takes a quick photo of us. My heart beats hard as he sends the photo to her, typing only god knows what. His arm lingers a second longer than we both know it should.

"Come on Nicky, let's get inside. It looks like a storm might be brewing," I say while looking up at the cloud-darkened sky.

3

NICHOLAS

It's been a long time since I have seen little Paige Hansen. The last time I saw her, she was a sophomore in high school. She has clearly shot up overnight, becoming a woman in a blink of an eye. One day, I see my bratty little sister's best friend, and then the next, I have to stop myself from committing a crime. Two weeks later, I was deployed to Iraq. Now here she is, standing in front of me in little white shorts and a light green, skintight tank top. Her blonde hair is in a loose braid that falls to the middle of her back. I had forgotten that I tower over her at six and a half feet tall while she stands at a measly five foot four.

"Damn, Pidge. Have you grown at all since I last saw you?" I joke.

"Very funny, Nicky. In fact, I've grown two inches since my sophomore year." Paige replies.

"Oh, and you know the exact time we saw each other last?" I question.

She looks away and doesn't reply. Instead, she walks back out onto the patio. I don't understand what I said to piss her off, but I decide to give her space while I put my shit in the bedroom.

PAIGE

Of course, he doesn't remember. It was so many years ago. I'm not sure why it still bothers me so much. Maybe it will be best to leave in the morning and go to my new home in a familiar town.

I quickly scratch that idea because I promised myself that I would be here this year. Even if Jessie doesn't show up, I'm here doing what I said I would.

I wake up the next morning to the smell of rain and bacon in the air. I roll out of bed and instantly regret that I didn't close the window before going to bed. I am wearing nothing but an oversized t-shirt and underwear. As soon as I go to close the window, a huge gust of wind and rain whips in, causing me to step back and slip on the already wet floor. I can't hold back my curses as I hit the ground with a thud.

"Pidge! Are you okay?" Nicholas runs into the room. He stops in his tracks, staring at my prone body for just a moment before he is at my side, one hand instinctively grabbing the back of my head to check for injury.

"Damn it, Nick. Could you at least put a shirt on?" I gripe.

"Could you at least wear pants?" he throws back. I feel my cheeks heat and look away from him while he helps me up from the floor.

"Are you sure you're okay?" he asks again.

"Other than dying of embarrassment, yeah, I'm fine." I answer.

"I was just kidding about the pants. You can go without them anytime." He flirts.

I walk to my bag and pull on a pair of shorts.

"I made breakfast," he says as he leaves the room. I turn around to try and close the window again and notice he already closed it for me.

I follow the smell of bacon to the kitchen and see Nicholas flipping eggs on the stove. For just a moment, I can picture a future with a man like him—hard in all the right ways, soft in others. While literally shaking my head to clear those thoughts, I grab the orange juice from the fridge and pour us both a glass. I hand him one before I turn on the news to try and see when the weather is supposed to clear up.

"Here you go, Pidge," Nicholas says as he slides a plate to me.

BREAKING NEWS

The outer bands of Hurricane Twin have begun to batter the west coast of southern Florida. The roadways leading inland are majorly

congested, so all residents are advised to stay put and take immediate shelter. Please be safe and stay tuned for continuous weather updates as the storm progresses across the panhandle.

"Looks like we are stuck inside then," Nicholas says.

"We're stuck. Let's play nice," I tell him.

"What the hell is that supposed to mean?" he asks.

"Just be nice, Nick," I say before walking back to my room.

4

NICHOLAS

Paige keeps hinting that I am a bad guy or that I did something wrong. I haven't seen her in seven years, yet I have thought about her almost every day. What the hell did I do wrong?

Seven years Ago

I finally finished packing the last of what I need to ship out. After being stationed a couple of towns over, I came home for a short period of time before my deployment orders to Iraq came. I told my parents right away and left in twenty minutes to go back to my base to prepare. My sister took it hard. She hasn't really talked to me since I told her, but just in case I don't make it home, I have to make this right.

"Jess? Where are you?" I call down the hallway.

"Nicky!" Paige yells while running through the front door.

"Whoa, Pidge, are you okay?" I ask.

"Yes. I just wanted to see you before you left," she says before throwing her arms around my waist. When she does, I can feel the swell of her newly developed breasts pressing against my chest, and I inhale the sweet peach smell of her hair. She pulls away from me, causing me to look down at her. I am met with a beautiful face, and the lone tear trickling down her cheek breaks my heart.

"Oh, hun. Don't cry. I'll be alright," I say to try and console her.

"I just... I wanted to tell... you something," she says around small sobs.

I tuck her hair behind her ear and brush away her tears.

"Go ahead then, Pidge," I tell her.

She takes a moment to get herself together before she starts to speak. "I was going to tell you before, but I was scared. I have to say it though."

I don't respond yet. No need to interrupt her.

"Nick, I am in love with you."

"Paige. No, you aren't," I tell her

"Yes. I think of you when I wake up. I dream of you in my sleep. My love for you is more than just bone deep. I feel my love for you in my soul." Paige confesses.

"Listen to me, Paige. You're so young. You'll find someone your age and fall in love—real love. I'm not the guy for you," I explain.

"This is real love, Nick," she says as tears start again.

"Pidge. I have to leave soon. Please stop crying. I don't want this for you," I say sweetly.

We are interrupted by Jessie then. "You do not get to love MY brother. It isn't fair!"

A full-on sophomore girl fight breaks out and my parents are breaking them up as I pull out of the driveway.

Is she still mad at me for that? For not saying goodbye? For not telling her that I loved her back? How was a twenty-year-old man supposed to tell a sixteen-year-old girl that he had feelings for her without sounding like a complete pedophile? I did the only thing I could do in the moment and walked away from her.

Little does she know I will not walk away now.

Determined to make this right, I turn the stove off and follow her down the hallway.

"Paige?" I knock on her bedroom door. "Can I come in please?"

"What do you want, Nick?" She says, her voice muffled.

"Look. Can we just talk about it?" I plead.

I'm momentarily startled when Paige opens the door, now dressed in jeans and a tight t-shirt. She deliberately avoids eye contact as she pushes past me.

"I don't want to talk about it. Can you just help me prep the house? Your parents have the *hurricane kit* in the garage," she asks.

I answer, "Sure. Let me change really quick."

It's getting late, so after placing the last of the sandbags along the lower parts of the home, I make my way back inside and see Paige curled up on the couch sleeping. I walk up quietly, take the blanket from the back of the couch, and drape it over her. My touch makes her stir slightly before she settles back in.

About forty-five minutes later, a thunderclap startles her awake.

"What was that?" she says with some panic.

"It's just the storm, Pidge. You're okay," I answer from the recliner.

PAIGE

I wake up to a loud rumble from the storm and look to see Nick's face as he talks to me from the recliner; beer in one hand, remote in the other. The news is playing quietly on the television and producing the only light in the room.

I shiver not because I'm cold, but because of the man looking at me. Even though Nicholas didn't want to listen to me all those years ago, what I said back then still rings true.

I am in love with Nicholas Moore.

5

PAIGE

I sit up on the edge of the couch and stare at Nicholas for a moment before he starts to move. He lowers the leg rest and leans forward to rest his elbows on his knees.

"What's going on in that pretty head of yours, Pidge?" he asks. I feel the heat in my cheeks and readjust myself in my seat.

"Are you finally ready to listen to me, Nicholas?" Using his full name gets his attention and he sits a little taller. He doesn't answer me, so I start anyway. "Seven years ago, you walked away from me after I poured my heart out to you," I state.

"Paige. Are we really doing this?" he asks—not angry, not frustrated, but with more of a lustful tone to his voice.

"Why would I bring up one of the hardest moments of my life other than to talk about it?" I ask more as a question than I wanted to.

"I'm not sure, Pidge. That was a long time ago. Things have changed," he answers.

"Maybe they've changed for you. Not for me," I choke back tears. "I told you that I was in love with you. Not that I had a crush on you. I'm way past that point."

"Am?" he asks.

"Damn, you are an arrogant ass! Do I need to spell it out for you?" I half yell. Again, he doesn't answer. "I. Am. In. Love. With. You. Nicholas. Moore." A tear escapes and I realize that I am now standing in front of him. "Best friend's brother be damned!" I finish.

Nicholas stands up and reaches for me. Within seconds, his lips are on mine; hard and needy. I wrap my arms around him, and he pulls me in closer—so close our bodies align perfectly, just the way they were meant to be. One of his hands twists in my hair while he pushes my mouth against his harder. His tongue begs for entrance and when I finally give in, I relish the taste of him. He tastes like beer and man.

He pulls away slightly, rests his forehead on mine, and says, "There hasn't been a day that I haven't thought about you saying those words to me again." He finishes by placing another kiss on my lips before pulling his body away completely.

"Paige. If we do this... I need to let you know that I'm more trouble than the average guy," he starts. "I re-enlisted for four more years. I am only home for R&R for two weeks, then I leave again. I will not let you be a hometown fling while I'm passing through. That isn't fair to you or me," he rambles on.

"Okay, so we have two weeks to figure it out," I tell him.

"You don't get it. When it comes to you and me... it is all or nothing," he admits.

"All," I answer. He looks at me crookedly.

"'All means that you will wait for me to come home. That means no other men in your bed. That means possibly moving when I get stationed stateside. That means our children will grow up surrounded by military brats," he explains.

"I get it. I think you forget that my brother enlisted and died over there. I know how it works," I remind him. Nicholas bows his head slightly in remembrance of his friend and my brother.

Just as he takes a step towards me again, thunder crashes above us and lightning flashes outside. Then we are cloaked in darkness as the power goes out. I jump at the sudden blackness, but Nicholas grabs my hand and leads me to the kitchen where we left the candles and flashlights.

6

NICHOLAS

For the last twenty-four hours, I have watched Paige. I watched her walk through the dark house, lit only by candles. I watched her nap on the sofa. I watched her watch me. I have tried to give her time to explore her feelings and the commitment that we both would be taking if we do anything.

As I rest my head on the back of the sofa, eyes closed, legs slightly spread; I hear Paige approach, but I stay still. I feel her legs brush against my knees, and she crawls on top of me, straddling my hips and placing her cool hands against my bare chest. I move my hands to her hips and tighten my grip just a bit when I feel more skin than clothing. I dare myself not to look at her. I know that I might lose my control if I do. I feel her weight shift as she leans forward and caresses my unshaved cheek before grazing her lips against mine.

"Paige," I say under my breath.

PAIGE

I am a chance taker, but when it comes to Nicholas, I double-check myself every time. He is the only thing in my life I am one hundred percent sure of, but for some reason, I still question my moves. This time though, I am going with my gut and letting my body lead the way.

With light brushes of my lips against his, our kiss deepens. Nicholas whispers my name and squeezes my hips tighter while sliding his hands up under my ribcage. Our tongues tangle, each push and pull at war with each other, as he sits up so his chest almost meets mine. Finally, he opens his eyes, staring into mine just long enough to inhale some much-needed breath. Not another moment passes before his lips are on mine again, harder than what I gave him. I arch my back a little bit so I can brush my chest against his, knowing he will be able to feel my nipples through my thin tank top. Teasing him is definitely my goal.

He groans deep in his chest and crushes me to him, kissing and nibbling down the soft length of my throat. Nicholas reaches a hand between us to brush his thumb across my nipple, causing me to shiver in his arms. I smile as I feel his cock getting harder and lengthening underneath his sweatpants.

"Take me to bed, Nicholas," I say. He doesn't say a word as he lifts me in his arms. I wrap my legs and arms around him, devouring his mouth as he walks. I barely notice him laying me on the bed, his lips a welcomed distraction, before spreading himself above me.

He stops kissing me and looks at my face as if he is making sure this is what I want. He must see my answer because he slips a hand into my top, across my stomach, and up my chest. He squeezes my breast slightly as he kisses across my hip line and then starts to lift my shirt off.

He smiles crookedly before looking me in the eyes for a moment and then down at my chest. He quickly pulls my boy shorts off and bends down to kiss me, making his way up from my knee, over my thigh, and to my core. His mouth is on me feverishly for just a moment before he gets up and stands long enough to shed his sweats and boxers, allowing me to sneak a quick peek at his manhood. I thought I had a pretty good idea on his size when I was sitting on his lap, but I clearly underestimated him. He crawls on top of me again, a hand beside my head to push himself partway off me, and the other touching my cheek.

"Do you know how incredibly beautiful you are?" he asks. I only blush in response because no one has said that to me. Everyone else I have ever been with says I am sexy and hot. Being told I am beautiful is much nicer to hear.

Nicholas kisses my forehead and across my face, down my throat, and across my breasts. I feel his arm slide between us again, his hand finding my core. A finger brushes through my folds before entering me.

I gasp faintly at the intrusion, but it quickly turns into a moan.

He presses in more, with more force and my chest lifts to him. He captures a nipple between his teeth. He uses his knee to separate my legs further so he can add another finger inside of me. I am on the edge of an orgasm when he pulls his fingers away.

"I want you to come around me, not my fingers," he whispers in my ear as he places himself at my entrance. I nod my head against him, and he slowly, punishingly pushes inside of me.

"Fuck," he moans. "You are so tight."

"Please, Nick?" I plead.

"What do you want, baby?" he asks.

"Make love to me," I beg.

He starts to pump in and out of me, all the while kissing my whole body and fondling my breasts. After what seems like a lifetime, I reach that edge again.

"Come for me," Nicholas demands against my neck. My body starts to tighten in release, and just as I do, he bites my throat, throwing me into an abyss of an orgasm. I feel him start to move again, gently, and slowly in a way to bring me down.

"Still with me, baby?" he questions. My hands tingle from the orgasm that continues to ripple through my body. I throw my still sensitive hands onto his back to pull him towards me and use my legs to encourage him to keep going. He starts to move faster and harder. Lifting himself onto his knees, he holds my hips up so he can pound into me. Nicholas groans and thrusts a couple more times before growling out his release. He collapses against me and I can feel him getting softer as his length rests inside me. I rub a hand over his shoulders, and he moans in pleasure.

"If you keep that up, I will fall asleep. It feels so sweet," he mumbles into the mattress.

"That's okay," I smile. He leans up and kisses me hard before pulling himself free and cleaning us both up.

He lays next to me in the bed and pulls me close. After a few minutes, he starts to snore.

7

NICHOLAS

I wake up to the loud crashing of thunder above us. Rain pelts the windows and the wind howls around the house. Paige squeezes closer to me and throws a leg over my waist in her sleep. I listen to the storm above us and Paige's sweet snores.

Just when I fall back asleep, my cell phone rings with an extreme weather alert. Paige jolts awake and rubs the sleep from her eyes.

"Was that a storm alarm?"

"Yeah. I think so. Get dressed real quick. I'll go check it out." I look through the glass door off the kitchen and see the hurricane warning flags ripping in the harsh winds as I scan the beach. Waves crash into the abandoned lifeguard towers, almost pushing them over. Lightning and thunder continue to crash around us.

"Paige?" I holler down the hallway.

"Yeah?"

"We have to go. The storm is getting pretty nasty out there."

"The news said to stay indoors," she reminds.

"Screw the news."

As Paige finishes packing everything, I go outside to start the truck and I get assaulted by the rain. The bullet-sized raindrops crash against my skin and splash off the ground beneath me. I jump in the driver's seat, turn the truck on, and twist the volume dial on the radio.

"*...the hurricane has been reclassified as a category five in the last twenty-four hours. Many people are without power. Others are still stuck on the coastline. I* *want to add that if any of the listeners are still in their homes on the beaches, as horrible as it sounds, stay there. The roads are all closed due to flooding, power lines are down, and there are no emergency crews able to reach you."*

"Damn it!" I turn the truck off and run back inside to relay the message to Paige.

"So, what? Are we just supposed to stay here as the storm gets worse?" she asks.

"I guess that's what we are going to do."

"Nick, stop acting like a soldier. No one is ordering you to stay put."

"This has nothing to do with me being a soldier!" I yell. "This is about me keeping you safe."

"You don't have to protect me, Nicholas." She screams back.

I start to say something when the front door slams open. Jessie and another man bounce into the room and stare blankly at me; water soaks their clothes and creates puddles at their feet. The color drains from Paige's face when she sees the man.

PAIGE

First, Jessie doesn't show up; no call or text, even after Nicholas sent the picture of us. Then she shows up with *him*. What is wrong with her?

"Jessica," Nicholas calls.

"Hey, Nick. How are you?" she questions. "What are you doing here?"

"Did you get my messages?" he asks.

"I lost my phone at the airport in Dallas," Jessie says.

"What are you doing here?" I ask the man.

He looks around the room briefly before he steps towards me and holds out a hand. "Can we just talk in private, P?" I flinch away from his touch and Nicholas must notice.

"Do you two know each other?" Nicholas asks.

"Are you seriously asking if I know my wife?" he says.

Nicholas' shoulders bunch up and his fists ball. He looks between the two of us and I interject. "Ex-wife, Nick." He doesn't seem to care about that though.

"Who are you and what the hell do you want?" Nicholas asks.

"Drew. Andrew. I am Paige's husband. And you are?"

I slide in front of Nicholas and ask, "Drew, what are you doing here? It has been almost a year since our divorce."

"I reached out to Jessie a few months ago and asked her to help me see you. I miss you, P." He takes a step towards me again, and I back into Nicholas who stands completely still behind me. "I know I messed up, but I've changed. I am not the same man I was a year ago."

"Jessie. What the hell? Why would you help him?" I ask.

"He said he's different. Give him a chance," Jessie begs. I have to walk away from her before I start to scream. Nicholas follows me to the room we slept in together last night and he watches me pace the room.

"I hate to ask but..." he starts.

"He is my ex, Nick," I interrupt.

"He's your ex-husband. That's different than saying he is just an ex." I stop my pacing and look over at Nicholas. "Look. You want to be mad that I tried to move on. Fine. You want to hate me. Fine. You do not get to be mad that he is the one I chose. I was wrong and I almost lost my life because of it." I blurt out.

Nicholas stands and gets very close to me, "Did he hurt you, Paige? Did I force you into an abusive man's arms?"

"Nick, you don't even know him. We hadn't even talked for three years when I met Drew. How the hell would you have forced me to him?"

He grabs my hands and looks me in my eyes before asking again. "Did he hurt you?" He must see the pain in my face because he kisses my forehead and walks out of the room. I follow behind him slowly and when I hear Jessie yell, I pick up my speed.

I walk in the living room and notice Jessie is still soaked from being outside in the storm. Nicholas stands over Drew who is lying on the ground, grabbing his bleeding nose. Drew tries to stand but Nicholas grabs him by his shirt, throws him up to the wall, and starts to scream in his face. "If you ever touch Paige or any other woman again, I will destroy you and no one will ever find your body."

"Nick! Get off him!" Jessie yells. Nicholas lets Drew's body fall to the floor in a heap after slamming him against the wall again. He doesn't say anything before turning and walking away from us all.

I help Jessie get Drew to one of the spare bedrooms before I find Nicholas in the bathroom. He sits on the side of the tub, hands folded together, looking at the floor.

"I don't do that. That is not me."

"What do you mean, Nick?" I ask.

"I don't just beat people up. He does not get to hurt you. Not anymore!" Nicholas rubs his hands together harder and faster in frustration.

"I want to believe you. But Nick. You could have really hurt him."

"What do you care?" Nicholas shouts.

"Stop making me the bad guy, Nick. That is not fair." I try to hold my shoulders back so I do not look as defeated as I am. "Look, they can't leave. They are stuck here too. Can you play nice? Just for a little while?"

Nicholas growls under his breath and pushes past me to the bedroom.

8

NICHOLAS

It's been two god-awful days with Drew. He walks around the house like he owns the place. Looks at Paige like he owns her and is constantly begging her to talk in private. He won't let us be alone for more than two minutes. Hell, Drew even had Jessie switch rooms so that the girls would share. I might just kill him.

Getting stranded in a beach house with Paige is a dream come true. I can finally touch her the way I want to; tell her my feelings that I kept hidden for so long. Then Drew shows up and ruins it all.

I lay in bed when I hear the door creak open. Turning slightly, I squint my eyes to make out the figure approaching me. Paige.

"Nicky? Are you awake?" she whispers.

I answer by reaching out for her hand and she crawls into bed next to me.

"I miss you."

Again, I answer with my actions rather than my words and I slant my lips over hers to draw her breath into my lungs. She presses her body against me harder. As I reach down to her pajama shorts, light floods the room from outside. My Navy brothers choose now to pick us up.

Jessie barges into the room. "They are here to get us. Pack up."

I see the panic in Paige's eyes. "Nothing has to change, Pidge." She barely acknowledges my statement. Instead, she rolls out of the bed and follows Jessie from the room.

Paige stands in the middle of the living room when I bring my bags out. Tears run down her porcelain cheek. “What’s wrong, Pidge?”

“I… What if? What about?” She stutters but never finishes. I wipe away a few tears and cup her face.

“Honey. You need to take a couple of deep breaths and start over.”

She lets a few more tears slip free before she takes a deep breath and tries again. “What if I screw this up?”

“Screw what up?” I ask.

She gestures between us. “This.”

I pull her into my arms and kiss the top of her head.

“Just always tell me the truth and tell me how you feel, and we will be fine.”

One of the crew members walks in the house and shouts, “It’s time to go. We are in the eye of the storm,”

9

NICHOLAS

Four years later

I am finally going home for good. I will no longer have to report to anyone. As of five minutes ago, I am no longer an active-duty soldier and am back on American land. Pulling up to the beach house that created so many memories for me—a house that started and ended something so important to me.

That day we left in the middle of the hurricane was the last day I saw Paige. We talked for a few months off and on when I returned to base, but it has been radio silence ever since.

I walk through the house and hear giggling coming from the backyard. I stand at the open glass door and see the woman of my dreams playing in the sand with a small boy.

"Paige?"

She turns to look at me, before standing and wiping the sand off her hands.

Paige rocks on her heels. "Hey, Nicky. Been a while."

"What are you doing here, Paige?" I ask.

"Nathan! Come here, sweetheart. There is someone I want you to meet," she hollers at the child.

He bounces over and looks at me. I know what she will say before she is able to open her mouth. I know it because I see it.

"I'm his father." It wasn't a question, but Paige answers anyway.

"Nicholas, this is your son, our son, Nathan."

The little boy reaches his hand out to shake mine. "Hello, mister. My name is Nathanial Nicholas Moore. Nice to meet you."

Finish the story in
Kiss of Yesterday
Coming Soon

ABOUT BILLIE PARSONS

Lover of everything books

Born and raised Oregonian.

Billie resides in her home state of Oregon and spends most of her time going to college, reading, writing, and other things normal people try and do.

Ever since she was a young girl, she knew that books would also be a part of her life. Being able to tell stories from her point of view and hope that someone else will fall in love with her characters and their stories as much as she does is all she can ask for.

Check out Billie's website at
www.billieparsons.com

Join her Facebook Reader Group: Billie's Book Babes

facebook.com/billieparsonsauthor
instagram.com/billieparsons_author
goodreads.com/billieparsonsauthor

CAUGHT IN THE CROSSFIRE

BY CHARLIE JULES

Five years ago, these guys ruined me. They should have made sure I stayed down. Now I'm back and I'm not sure any of us are ready for the consequences of our actions.

Quarantine is nothing new in my world. Thanks to an experiment gone wrong, a deadly strain of bacteria now lives among us. The winds can change any minute of any day. When it happens, we have to be ready to shut our doors.

What definitely is new is unexpectedly ending up quarantined with four men, the same men who happen to be my former best friends.

Nick's devastating blue eyes still rip my soul apart when they meet mine. Alex still feels like home when he looks at me, Connor is so handsome, but so cruel. And Jax? He's the best, and the worst, of them all.

I haven't seen them since they turned their backs on my family, but we're forced to join forces again; to expose the truth and uncover lies.

For old times sake.

For humanity's sake.

No creepy underground tunnels or secret labs will stop me from doing just that.

Caught in the CROSSFIRE

1

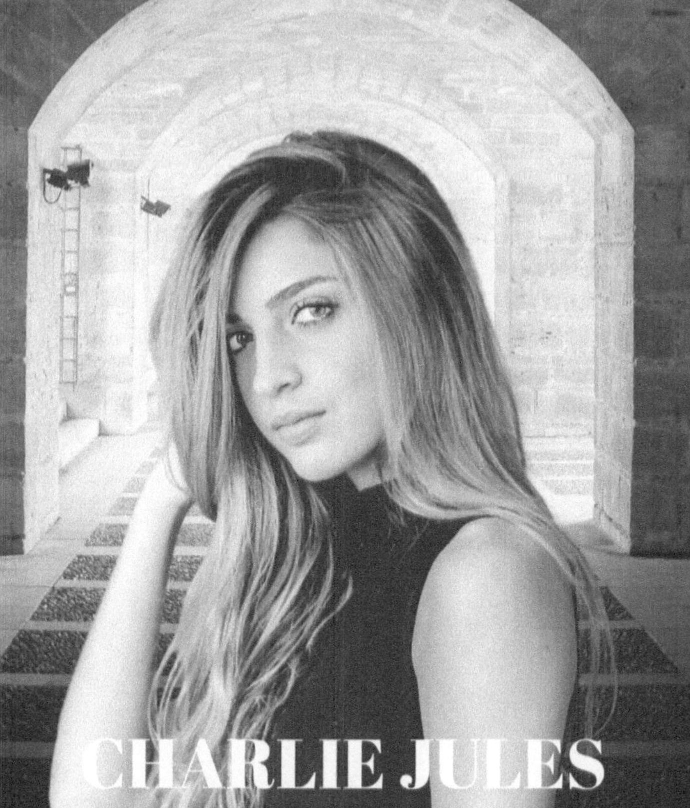

To everyone having a tough time right now.
To everyone whose lives turned out differently than they wanted them to.
To everyone who picks up a book by an Indie authors and decides to give it a go.
Last but not least, ever, thank you to my husband. It's soppy, but the fact this thing exists is your fault. I see you. I appreciate you. I love you.

AUTHOR'S NOTE

This book is the first of a trilogy and has a cliffhanger at the end. But don't worry, I won't leave you hanging for very long. It is also a why choose story, meaning that our heroine won't have to choose between her different possible love interests and she will end up with more than one of them. There is swearing contained in these pages as well as some sexual scenes, but the heat level will pick up as the series progresses.

1

ARCHER

Sirens warned of danger.

The distinctive wail was something I'd gotten used to over the last few years but that didn't mean it wasn't a bone-jarring shock every time.

I stopped in my tracks as the sound pierced the cool night air. All around me other pedestrians did the same. As if we were operating on a collective hive mind, our heads dropped back and our gazes peered toward the cloudless sky.

One minute there were only stars above, the next: bedlam. The towers holding the sirens shot blinding red lights into the universe like beacons calling for help-- only no help was coming. People all around the world were trying, sure, but for now, this was all we had. If there was someone or something out in the great black sky, they hadn't come to our aid yet and I doubted they would.

An early warning system that the winds had changed was all we had and probably the best we'd ever have.

My fellow pedestrians wasted no more time; their limbs kicked into gear and suddenly, the leisurely pace of the evening changed. No longer strolling hand-in-hand or talking on phones or waiting on the packed sidewalk to be seated at a bistro in the upmarket area of town.There was only scurrying and hurrying and all kinds of frenzied, urgent movement.

"Fuck!" I cursed under my breath, tightening my grip on my paper grocery bags as I moved my shoulder to dodge a woman built like a linebacker who rushed at me. I forced my feet to move just as the mandatory announcement came over the loudspeakers placed on every corner of Main Street and every few blocks throughout the town.

"Attention citizens," the nasally, disembodied voice of a long-dead leader announced. "A level five alert has been issued for the town of Winterton."

I groaned but picked up my pace as I was swept into the current of people trying to get the hell out of dodge. No one would be allowed across the town's borders, but we needed to clear the streets.

Mentally doing the math as my sneakers hit the paved sidewalk, I figured I had time to get to Aunt Maeve's, drop her supplies and get home before the lockdown period started. If push came to shove, I could always hunker down with her for a few days.

Tucking my chin into the scarf around my neck, I flipped my hood up and lowered my head. My breath came out in misty puffs as I navigated my way through the throng, narrowly avoiding running into people while at the same time trying to cover as much ground as possible.

Aunt Maeve would kick my ass up and down these streets if I didn't get these groceries to her on time. Not even the imminent threat of death if I got infected by the spores heading our way would grant me pardon.

It was still sometimes difficult to believe this was my life. I lived in the same town where I'd been born, but everything had changed. Hell, the only time I was even allowed close to the people and the neighborhood I had known all my life was when I had to make a grocery run for my aunt.

Bitterness crept into my very soul when I let myself think of the life that had been stolen from me. By who, I wasn't sure, but if I ever found out, there'd be hell to pay.

I didn't miss the luxury of the gated community where I used to live. I didn't even miss having a warm bed in winter or the security of knowing where my next meal came from. At the very least, my aunt could be trusted to find a way to make a small deposit into my bank account for those things from time-to-time.

What I missed was the feeling of home. It was the smell of onions sizzling when Mom tried to cook and the weight of Dad's arms when he hugged me. I had no idea where my mom and dad even were or if they were still breathing; given their line of work, it was unlikely that air still graced their lungs.

I refused to dwell on it, though. God knew it got me nowhere to cry or scream or speculate, so I kept moving. I didn't have time to be tripped up by the past. Especially not when I only had one hour to get home.

In the meantime, the sirens continued. The sky remained awash with that awful blood-red light that cast a glow worthy of a horror movie on my quaint town and the disembodied voice kept reminding people of what they already knew.

"The law states that citizens must return home immediately and remain confined there until further notice. Isolation is mandatory. Anyone caught disobeying these orders will be arrested and liable for a fine, imprisonment, or both."

"Yeah, yeah," I muttered to nobody but myself. Speaking to myself wasn't anything new. I'd only been doing it for five years. I was all I had now, so I had to make do with my own company. *A lone girl trying to navigate this terrifying new world.*

The gates to Aunt Maeve's neighborhood were open and the guardhouse empty. I frowned as I passed it. Bill was supposed to be on duty tonight. I knew because I made sure to do my aunt's monthly drop off when it'd be him on duty. The other guards didn't trust my family enough to let us in after what had happened. Even the newer ones were wary of me; they'd heard the stories, of course. The whole fucking town had.

There'd even been a few reality show producers that had contacted us in the early days, wanting to do a series on the mighty Maxwells' spectacular fall from grace. I snorted at the thought but an intense sense of nostalgia hit me after passing the vacant guardhouse.

Still making sure my nose and mouth were covered, I lifted my head a little to see the tall oak trees that lined the wide, clean streets. There was no one around but that didn't exactly come as a surprise. People around here took the early warning system seriously. It made sense, considering they were the ones who'd developed it. The entire neighborhood consisted of only a few houses that were reserved for the best and brightest scientists and doctors around-- all of whom worked for one corporation.

I tried my best to keep my eyes on the road and my mind on reaching my aunt's house but light streaming into the street caught my attention. Most of the other estates were dark but not the Kents'.

No, it had to be theirs that was lit up like the Fourth of fucking July. I scowled as I tore my gaze away from the familiar facade of the stone-built mansion that used to be like my second home.

Seriously, the place looked like a Gothic castle from the outside: black, slate stone, arched entrance ways, and wide square windows. Seeing it from the street, I couldn't imagine an actual family living inside. It seemed better suited for Count Dracula and his victims. Then again, the Kents were bloodsucking vampires in their own right, as far as I was concerned. Blood might not have been their snack of choice for consumption but they sure as hell didn't mind spilling it.

Maybe their choice in architecture was an ironic embodiment of that.

Icy air stung my throat and lungs as I sucked in a deep breath. I couldn't think about the Kents without thinking about their son and I couldn't think about their son without thinking about three other boys who lived around here.

I also couldn't think about any of *them* without feeling the intense need to sever someone's genitals with a blunt butter knife. If I was given a choice, Nicolas Kent's genitals would be first on the chopping block. But I didn't have a choice, I hadn't had a fucking choice in any of this. So, I tucked my head close to my chest again and kept right on going.

Aunt Maeve's house was next to the Kents'.

Fun fact: My aunt's house used to be mine. Well, ours.

I'd grown up in the Tuscan-style mansion in front of me. The brittle, dry lawn on either side of me, as I crunched up the gravel drive, used to be my playground. It never used to be brittle and dry. It used to be bright green and the hedges used to be trimmed.

I huffed out a breath and shook my head at the state of it now. Untended, overgrown in places and dying in others. Truth be told, it was a little like a visual representation of my life.

I knocked on the wide double doors at the top of the stairs and one swung open from the wrap of my knuckles against the wood.

"Hello?" I called out into the dark foyer. "Aunt Maeve? It's Archer. I have your stuff."

Silence greeted me, but a sliver of light shone through from the dining room. I sighed softly and made my way inside.

Even without that single sliver of light, I wouldn't have bumped into anything. I knew this place better than the back of my hand and I'd done my fair share of sneaking in and out back in the day. My rubber soles barely made a sound as I crossed the marble floors, paper bags still clutched in my hands. I was so intently focused on dropping them off and running to make it back to my place that I didn't hear the moans at first. They registered vaguely but it was only once I'd rammed my shoulder into the door and burst into the room that the reason behind them became clear.

Bile rose in my throat at the same time that my cheeks flushed with embarrassed heat.

My aunt was lying spread eagle on the expansive mahogany table my mother had imported, every inch of her skin on display. Between the garter belts on her thighs, a man sat in the seat *I* had occupied for every family dinner of my first seventeen years on this planet.

They both noticed my intrusion at the same time and an almost agonized cry left Maeve's lips when her head popped up. "Archer? What the *fuck* are you doing here?"

Her usually perfectly-styled red hair was wild, the matching lipstick on her mouth smeared. She didn't wait for my horrified brain to formulate an answer before her expression contorted into one of rage and she jabbed a finger at the door.

"No matter. Get out, girl. We're not done yet. Wait for me outside."

My eyebrows lifted but I didn't argue with her. Clearly, she didn't know about the alert and I wasn't going to let her in on it, either. Call me crazy, but interfering with one's mean-girl aunt while she was having her lady bits serviced just didn't seem like a good idea.

I slammed the door, dropped the bags and took off as fast as my feet could carry me. Fuck hunkering down with her for a few days, I wasn't about to get quarantined with my horny aunt and whoever her gentleman suitor was.

I'd caught a glimpse of him when he lifted his head. He looked faintly familiar, but I couldn't put my finger on where I'd seen him before. I also didn't want to think about putting my finger on anything right now because *gross*.

I was almost at the gates when a tall figure stepped out of the guardhouse; even shrouded in shadow, I still knew who he was. Every inch of Nick was seared into my brain like a brand but instead of raised welts on my skin, I had thousands of memories that would never leave me.

Five-year-old Nick smiling at me and taking my hand when I was too scared to jump into the lake. Always encouraging, always protecting me.

Ten-year-old Nick looking at me with adoration shining in his eyes at our elementary school graduation when I'd won a prize for math. Always cheering, always by my side.

And all the small, secretive smiles he kept shooting at me over his shoulder in high school classes, almost like he couldn't bear to let me out of his sight for even an hour. Always a heart-throb, always a flirt.

Of course, I couldn't think back on those memories of *him* without being barraged by those of the others, too. But I couldn't afford to dwell on them now, not when I had to deal with Nick blocking my exit.

Even so, so many memories crashed into me as Nick stared me down that my knees almost buckled. The memories, and hell, even the love we had once shared had been so damn powerful that it made the hurt and hate in their place now twice as strong.

My breath stuck in my lungs and my feet planted themselves on the pavement. I didn't have a blunt butter knife on me, but I'd make do with my bare hands if *he* got in my way.

"Nick," I said, my voice a low warning that thankfully didn't betray the pounding of my heart. "I don't want any trouble. I just came to bring Maeve some food."

Leanly muscled arms crossed over his chest as he stepped into the lamp light outside Bill's post. Dark lines of script were visible on his skin, even from this distance and in the low light. Or maybe it was just because I knew the tattoos were there.

"That's nice, Archer," he said in that beautiful silk-wrapped-in-gravel voice he'd developed at thirteen years old. Now that he was older, it was more like smoke wrapped in smooth, expensive whiskey but just as familiar. "But it doesn't matter what you were doing here, you're stuck with us now."

2

NICK

Well, this is just fucking inconvenient. Of all the places in all the world where Archer Maxwell could've been tonight, why the hell did it have to be here?

Every fiber in my body reacted to her: my heart nearly imploded, the tiny hairs on the back of my neck stood up, and my muscles braced like I was preparing for impact.

In a way, I was. Archer, or Max as we used to affectionately call her, was the impact that could finally destroy me and she didn't even know it. *Probably*.

Her strawberry blonde hair billowed around her head in the potentially deadly breeze, her chest rising and falling beneath her ratty hoodie. Her dainty chin rose in defiance as her eyes narrowed to the barest of slits.

"I still have at least thirty-two minutes to make it home," she said, taking three steps closer to me. "Just let me leave and we can both forget we even saw each other."

A chuckle rumbled deep in my chest but there was no humor in the sound. I hated this girl, or at least I'd convinced myself that I hated her. And yet, I could never forget I'd seen her. No matter what I did or ever would do, Max's shadow was always there.

"I'm afraid that's not going to happen," I said, lifting my chin to meet her silent challenge. "Go back to Maeve's. No one in or out until the alert order's lifted."

She took another step forward, landing at the outer edges of the orange light from the nearest streetlamp. Even though a gray scarf with white skulls and crossbones all over it covered half her face, she was just as beautiful as I remembered.

Eyes I knew were the color of the summer sky at dusk were obscured by the shadow of her hood but I could feel the piercing glare she was sending me. "I'm not staying with Maeve, Nicolas. It's not an option. Let me go and I won't start screaming."

I cocked an eyebrow, though I knew she probably couldn't see it. "Scream away, Maxi. No one's going to hear you." Throwing my arms out to my sides, I smirked and turned in a slow circle. "Even if they do, it's not like they're going to help you. Everyone's locking themselves away nice and tight to avoid getting the infection."

She took another step forward and this time, with more light illuminating her gorgeous features, I saw her eyes darting from one side to the other. *Too bad for her-- there were no exit routes.*

Fuck knew, I wanted her in my house as much as she wanted to be there, which was *not at all.*

Regardless, I couldn't help but laugh at her predicament. It was cruel but oh-so-fucking-just. "Don't try to run, Max. It's miles to town. You'll never make it to civilization before I catch you."

"Why would you try to catch me?" Her voice rose an octave or two as she clenched her fists. "I still have time, Nick. I can get home before the hour runs out."

"No, you can't." I tightened my jaw and tried not to think about the implications of this decision. "It's like I said, no one in or out after right now."

"You're a fucking psychopath," she mumbled, loud enough for me to hear. "If you think I'm going to stay just because you said so, you're even more deluded than I thought."

"I'm deluded now, am I?" I swore my teeth would crack from how hard they clenched. I advanced on her like the fucking predator I was, my gaze zeroed in on hers. "You and I both know I'm not the deluded one. Don't make this any more difficult than it needs to be."

The heavy metal gates to the estate slammed closed behind me and Max let out a loud growl. "Open them. Right now, Nick! I'm not playing with you. I just want to get home."

"Sorry, Max. I can't do that. I wouldn't even if I could. If you wanted to go home so badly, you should've gone when you had the chance. You know how seriously we take the alerts around here."

Especially now, but she didn't know that. She didn't have to know, either.

God, the guys were going to be pissed as fuck about this but I didn't have a choice. "If you don't want to go to Maeve's, you'll come with me."

The movement of her scarf told me her jaw had dropped. "No. Nope. That's not going to happen."

She shook her head like that might change the outcome. "Who knows how many days it'll be until the wind turns? I'm not staying with you until then."

"Then go to Maeve's," I said, pivoting on my heels with a crunch of loose stones on the asphalt beneath them. I turned to look at her over my shoulder. "My offer was a gift. A gift I sure as fuck don't owe you. Have fun with your deranged aunt."

Without waiting for her answer, I started toward my house. There were preparations to be made to keep the people I actually liked safe and trying to reason with her wasn't going to help, anyway. Archer Maxwell was beyond reason. The girl who'd been my precious Max was gone and, in her place, there was only a conniving, lying woman desperate to keep herself off a stage at a strip club to make a living.

Yeah, I knew where she'd ended up and I didn't have the least bit of pity for her. *Or at least that's what I wanted to believe.*

With any luck, none of my chosen brothers would ever have to know she'd been here tonight; they'd write my mood off as a result of the fight we were gearing up for and no one would ever be the wiser.

The soft thud of footsteps behind me told me I wouldn't be that lucky--not that it came as any surprise. My luck had run out the same day her family had been booted from the estate; the day that had eviscerated my heart. Losing her had broken me in ways I wasn't sure I could recover from.

"You can't lock me in here, asshole," her raspy voice came a second before her small hand hit my shoulder. "If you enable the override now, I can get home before I face jail time for trying to get there."

I released a frustrated breath through my nostrils, stopping so abruptly that she smacked into my back. I didn't bother trying to break her fall.

When I spun around, her ass hit the pavement. "If I could've let you go, I would have. Unfortunately, while I'd happily let the spores climb into you and devour you until the apocalypse comes, I can't risk the safety of thousands of people for you. It figures you'd ask me to, though."

A feral sounding scream ripped from her lips as her tiny fists hit the ground beside her. "Are you even listening to yourself? Everyone has one hour after the alert to get home. I'm part of everyone. I wouldn't be risking anyone's safety but my own."

I stared down at her compact form sitting on my driveway. She never used to look at me with such hatred burning in her eyes. Her expression had always been soft and open with me. I was sure the same could've been said for me with her.

Even now, my hands ached to reach out to her, but my brain knew better. If I touched her, I'd be done for.

"Yeah, that would've been true," I taunted. "Except for the fact that we got the alert before anyone else did. There was a glitch in the system. There was never an hour this time. We have about five minutes to get our asses into that house and the entrances sealed or our brains will be feasted on by bacteria until somebody collects our bodies to burn them."

For once in her miserable life, Archer was speechless. She stared up at me for a long moment and for just that one moment, I let my guard fall and felt that familiar buzzing electricity passing between us.

It fizzed out of existence when she nodded and looked away. "Fine. You win. I'll hole up with you this time, but don't even try to talk to me."

"Suits me like an orgy on a tropical island would've right around now," I retorted as I started back up the drive. "I'm sure you remember the way to your room. When we get inside, just go up there. The TV's still connected and I'll be sure to bring meals up to you, if I remember."

"My room?" The scuff of her shoes let me know she was getting up, her breaths heavy behind me. "What do you mean the TV is still connected?"

"Jesus," I muttered as I made my way up the cold stone steps to our front door. "The words are pretty self-explanatory, aren't they? I mean that the television in the room my mother set up for you a decade ago is still linked to all our accounts."

"Why?" she questioned behind me, confusion deepening her voice. "I haven't been here for more than half that time."

I threw my hands up as I entered the house. "Don't fucking ask me. I don't know. Mom refused to change anything in it. Fair warning, though: I've used it as a fuck pad for me and the guys. You might want to change the sheets."

Archer's answering growl was music to my ears, but I didn't turn back as I made my way to the study. The generosity of letting her stay was as far as I was willing to go.

Besides, I had to go let the guys know Max was back. Having her here was already going to royally screw with our plans. I didn't need them jumping all over each other to see who I'd brought home with me.

I also didn't need her walking into the study with me and distracting them. I doubted Archer knew how much power she still had over us all.

Although we made a point of not talking about her anymore, I knew they still missed her as much as I did. *Every fucking day.*

Jax still had a picture of all of us in his wallet. Alex wore a thin golden chain he'd found in her room after she left around his wrist. And Connor still whispered her name in his sleep. As for me? She was never far from my mind, either.

But we needed our wits, energy and focus on what lay ahead of us. Not on the girl who'd nearly been our undoing.

3

ARCHER

Nicolas could go fuck himself if he thought I was going to hide in my room. God, that room hadn't even been mine for years.

Mrs. Kent had always been whimsical and weird, but knowing that she'd kept it there for me without ever offering to take me in after my parents' disappearance just added another layer of weird. I also had no doubt about Nick's claim that he and the others had been defiling said room at every opportunity, so going to it hardly seemed like entering the same place it'd been all those years ago.

My sanctuary had been turned into a room where there were probably condoms in the drawers and sex things on the floor. What kinds of sex things? I didn't know, but sex things.

Mrs. Kent probably wouldn't have let them install a mirror on her pressed ceilings, but anything other than that would've been fair game. I knew these guys; they'd been my family once and they went balls to the wall on everything. *Probably* literally, *in this case.*

A shiver passed through me. Turning my former bedroom into a palace of carnal desire wouldn't have held them back; if anything, it'd probably spurred them on. I wouldn't be surprised if they'd come on my pillow, and stuffed the mattress with their used condoms in case I ever came back.

Tears stung the backs of my eyes at the thought, but I didn't let them fall. It'd been years since I cried and I wouldn't let my dry spell be broken by the same boys who'd caused the waterfalls in the first place.

I waited in the foyer instead. Nick carried his perfectly toned form toward his father's study, raking a hand through his jet-black hair as he went.

Twenty-three-year-olds had no right carrying themselves with that kind of haughty poise. Every movement was graceful, calculated. He radiated power, charm, and authority in a way that suggested he'd had many decades of practice.

Even those cerulean blue eyes carried more depth than they should've. Nick was just... *that* guy. He always had been.

When he should've been a snot-nosed know-it-all in fifth grade, with tears in his eyes from being wronged, he never had been. Nicolas Kent didn't seem to manufacture snot and his eyes never had tears in them. For as far back as I could remember, he'd had this mantle of something almost otherworldly about him; like he was above everything that worried mere mortals. He was always one step ahead.

It sounded like he had a deplorable character when I thought about him like that, but the truth was that he was the furthest thing from deplorable. At his core, he was a caring, passionate, loving guy. When he let his guard down, like he had just a minute ago and so often used to, letting me see that secret part of him, his eyes lit up like the ocean after a storm did under the dawning sun.

He was also the only person who could make a jaded, cynical soul like mine wax poetic about his eyes.

Sadly, despite knowing those things about him, I didn't feel like I really knew him at all. Once upon a time, I'd thought I knew him better than anyone in the world. I'd thought no one would ever know him the way I did.

Nick had been my first best friend, first crush, first kiss, and first of so many things that I'd believed our souls had become fused somewhere along the way. Imagine my surprise when he'd also been the first to publicly denounce me, the first to stand beside his parents to accuse mine of the unthinkable, the ungodly and the treasonous.

All those memories played like a bad movie in my head as I crept closer to the door of his father's study. I didn't know why he'd insisted I stay here with them but I was determined to find out.

The brains of the people behind these gates might've designed that early warning system, but they didn't get earlier warnings than any of the rest of the population. The system had been designed that way by my father. Every person had equal opportunity to make their way indoors before the spores hit. There'd been a near-uprising when he'd programmed the system that way, but he'd stuck to his guns. No community within the danger zone of an outbreak would receive advance notice. As soon as there was a threat, the public safety sirens sounded, and everyone had the same amount of time Ato avoid getting sick.

After the initial outbreak of the bacterial infection that nearly brought humanity to its knees, places of safety had been made available to the homeless and the vulnerable-- also, at Dad's behest.

Nick's claim that they'd had earlier notice of this alert made no sense and, if they had, I needed to find out why. I was no hero or whistle-blower, but what little remained of my father's integrity and honor was mine to protect. There was no one else to do it.

Nick hadn't closed the door fully when he'd stormed into his Dad's study; the lock lay harmless on top of the latch, as if he'd expected it to catch. Several voices spoke at the same time from beyond the door, each of them like a dagger to my heart.

"... the fuck were you thinking, Nick?" Alex said. "You can't believe it was a coincidence that she turned up here tonight, of all fucking nights?"

My brow furrowed at that one. Out of everyone, Alex had been most like a brother to me. I'd trusted him implicitly and thought it was mutual. Apparently, the sad downturn of his mouth when Nick's family had banished mine had been an act. Or maybe time had convinced him of our guilt.

"There's still a couple minutes," Jax insisted. "Let's send her to the Devil's Spawn and get it over with."

His description of Maeve wasn't wrong. In fact, we'd come up with the nickname together. My father's sister was too ambitious for her own good and always had been. The Devil's Spawn, she'd been named, and the Devil's Spawn she remained.

I rolled my eyes anyway because given the choice between the Devil's Spawn and the boys who'd become devils themselves, I'd rather take the enemy I knew. Which was them. At least no one had been eating them out when I'd arrived.

"Fuck that," Connor sneered. "I say we kick her out and let her take her chances with the fucking spores. With any luck, the bacteria will do the job for us."

Blood rushed in my ears. Knowing what they thought of me and hearing him say I should take my chances with the disease that had wiped out nearly half the damn world were two entirely different things.

My vision blurred and the next thing I knew, I was barging into their little meeting. "Listen to me, you fuck-faced ass-turds. If any of you try to boot me out that door before the quarantine ends, I'll hang around outside until the spores get me and then I'll eat all your motherfucking faces the second you step foot outside."

Okay, so, I had no idea whether I'd have the mental faculties to stalk anyone if I became infected. The evidence said I wouldn't.

In the last five years since the first outbreak, none of the infected had targeted a specific person. So, it stood to reason that within an hour or so after the spores took hold of your brain and before you died, your memory evaporated. Otherwise, the rate of attacks on the teachers, spouses, and bosses of the victims would be significantly higher.

Given the seriousness of the threat that faced me if they went with Connor's boneheaded idea, though, I wasn't above ludicrous threats.

Nick's bright blue eyes, Alex's forest green, and Connor's ebony had met mine as I barged into the room. Only Jax's soft hazel was missing.

Just as it had when I'd seen Nick, my brain attacked me with hundreds of memories.

Alex's eyes lighting up when he laughed at one of our many inside jokes, his arm around my shoulders as he glanced down at me.

Hours spent studying in the library with Jax, figuring out our homework together; the way he never left until I was ready to leave as well.

Connor threatening my first date with bodily harm if he hurt me. How he'd stuck to my side that time I'd fallen out of a tree and hurt my arm. He'd waited on me hand and foot for a week until the swelling went down.

Jax was sitting at a conference table facing me, but his hands were in his light brown hair and his head faced the table. As with the rest of them, he'd grown since I'd last seen him. The jade green shirt he wore stretched across shoulders that never used to be so broad, and new muscles rippled beneath the fabric.

It was Alex who caught my eye first, though. He crossed his muscular arms tightly across his chest and squinted at me from behind thick black-framed glasses. "You shouldn't be here, Archer. We have enough to deal with."

The mere audacity of his apparent belief that I *wanted* to be here made me throw my hands out to my sides. "Take that up with your pompous leader, then. Nick pretty much kidnapped me. I was almost out of the compound but he refused to let me leave."

Connor's menacing form took a step forward. The funny thing was that despite being almost seven feet tall, having eyes the color of onyx, and the build of a refrigerator, he was actually the biggest softie of the bunch.

Unfortunately, he only showed that part of himself to his inner circle. I'd most definitely fallen out of that circle. And to those unlucky people beyond the circle, he was a fucking terror.

Gone was the fierce protectiveness he used to look at me with; in its place, there was nothing but ice. As his gaze locked onto mine, I realized that there was something beneath the ice. *Something that looked a hell of a lot like hurt.*

I frowned, feeling echoes of his pain in my chest. It had always been that way with us. If one of us was in pain, we all hurt. I wondered if they still felt it, too; if they had been feeling it for all these years. But before I could ask, Connor spoke.

"If Nick told you to stay, it was because it was too late for you to leave," he said simply, in that trench deep voice of his. "But if you make trouble for us, I'll dispose of you myself."

Anyone else might've felt chills running down their spines at those words. I wasn't anyone else, though. I was the girl who used to share my teddy bears with him when he was scared at night, the one who packed his night light on camping trips and claimed it was my own.

I took two steps closer to my giant bear and softened my tone. "I'm not going to cause trouble for you, Con. I was only around to bring Maeve her food. I'd have stayed with her if some old man hadn't been eating her out at my dining room table."

Alex groaned, but I caught the edge of his smile before he scrubbed his hands over his face. "Seriously? You walked in on that shit?"

"Yep," I said, trying to catch each of their eyes. It didn't work. No one would look directly at me.

Except for Nick, whose penetrating blue eyes were boring into my brain. "I told you to go to your room."

I scoffed. "The same room you told me you'd turned into your sex haven and ordered me to like I was a fucking child? Yeah. No, thank you."

The tips of Jax's ears turned red but he still didn't look up. "Yeah, if you're going to be staying here, you might want to change the sheets."

His declaration was like a punch to my gut, even if Nick had warned me. "I've been told, but seriously? All of you?"

"Uh," Alex made a non-committal noise but then straightened up to his full, now rather impressive height. He shoved one hand into his blond hair and slammed the other fist onto the table. "What did you expect us to do in there, Archer? Use the Cali king bed to braid each other's hair while we cried and tried to smell you on the sheets when you weren't there anymore?"

Honest to God, my jaw slackened as I gaped at him. "You're blaming me for not being around anymore? How's it my fault that you turned my room into some kind of sex dungeon just because I wasn't around?"

Nick cleared his throat, an infuriating smirk on his lips as those sparkling blue eyes lit up like cold fire. "We needed somewhere to go, Maxi. You left us high and dry, after all. You never even chose between us. We figured if you could use that bed for all kinds of fun, you wouldn't mind if we did the same."

My throat closed up as he spoke.

Anger, humiliation, betrayal? Name it, I felt it. I tucked my arms under my breasts as armor. It didn't work as well as Victoria's Secret but I had a secret of my own. "That's what you think? You think I slept with all of you? You think using my room as a place of depravity will make your egos less bruised?"

"I don't think, Maxi; I know," Nick sneered. "Betrayal's in your DNA. Your parents sold the company out and you just took us all along for the ride."

"You mean the company my father started?" I went toe-to-toe with him, which meant I had to tip my head back to keep my eyes on his. He positively dwarfed me but my rage was big enough to take him on. "It was my father's company to do with what he liked, asshole. Even if he sold it out, it was his right to do it."

Alex's head reared back, rage burning bright in the mossy green depths of his eyes. I never thought I'd see that kind of rage from him, not aimed at me. Not when I was used to seeing so much love there that I still got choked up thinking about it sometimes.

"*Even* if he sold it out? *Of course*, he fucking sold us all out. He's working in a lab not even an hour away from here right now. Except he's not working on a cure, Archer. He's building a fucking weapon."

"What?" I stumbled back, blinking like I'd been sprayed with mace. If he'd hit me, it would've been more welcome and expected than his words had been. "You're lying. There's no way he's been only an hour away all this time and there's no way what you're saying is true."

Jax finally lifted his head and the fight melted right out of Connor. He held up his arms as if he expected me to fall and was going to catch me. I guess that instinct to protect me was still somewhere in there, after all.

It was the darkening pity in Nick's eyes that got to me, though. The way he studied my expression and suddenly deflated as his arms opened up convinced me, like he just couldn't help it and was about to hug me despite everything.

My parents, or at the very least my father, was alive and less than an hour away. For the past five years, I'd believed they were gone.

It was easier than to accept the alternative.

If they'd died, it meant they hadn't abandoned their only child when times had gotten tough.

It meant when they'd said they were leaving to help fix their mistakes, they'd lied.

It meant my parents, who'd once been accused of being murderers, might be exactly that.

I'd never fainted before but as my vision started swimming and black closed in around the edges, I had a pretty good idea of what was happening. I was going down and it was up to four boys who hated me because of how much they used to love me to keep my head from cracking open on the ridiculously expensive tile.

4

NICK

"I really think she doesn't know," Jax said. He'd run his hands through his light brown hair so many times during the night that it was greasy and standing up in all directions. His wide eyes met mine, an imploring look in them as he shook his head. "It's possible, Nick. Think about it. I know we've operated on the assumption that she knew everything but I don't believe that anymore."

Alex scoffed into his coffee, making steam scatter from the surface as he lifted his face into the early morning sun where we sat on the enclosed deck. His wide green eyes shone like emeralds before he closed them.

"We haven't slept. That's why you're feeling confused. I want to believe she doesn't know anything either but look at the facts," he said, but I heard the regret in his voice. Even if what he was about to say was true, he still wished it wasn't.

With his eyes still closed, he sipped his hot drink, wrapping his fingers around the mug. "The underground lab was found in her house. Archer isn't stupid. She had to have known it was there. All the evidence suggests human trials were conducted in those labs but she never complained about hearing anything. What was done down there was fucking barbaric. No way she didn't know, see, or hear anything."

Connor sighed into his mug. The big guy never said much, but we could all read him like he was an open book that had been written in bold, capital letters. "We never knew."

I pinned him with a glare. "Does that mean you believe her now, too?"

"No." He shrugged his giant shoulders. "Alex said to look at the facts. The facts are that her house wasn't the only one with tunnels into those labs and *we* never knew."

Out of everyone, I wasn't surprised it was Connor speaking in her defense first. He'd always called shit like he saw it, but having Archer back was messing with his vision. If there was anyone who was a blind spot for us all, it was her.

"Exactly." Jax's open palms hit the coffee table on the deck. "We've known her all our lives. She had her own room in this very house, for God's sake. All because the moms wanted to keep her safe from us when our hormones kicked in. But until that day, she was in bunk beds with us almost every night. That makes it very possible that she hadn't known anything."

Alex interjected again, eyes flashing as his blond hair glinted in the early morning sun. "What if it was because our moms already suspected sabotage to the experiments? That'd explain why they made her share with us to begin with, so we could keep an eye on her."

Jax snorted, letting his hazel eyes do a long once-over of Alex's body. "Please. Let's not forget who offered to share *her* in the first place."

My eyes nearly bulged out of my head. Archer wasn't mine by any stretch of the imagination but in my head, she'd always been exactly that. "What the fuck are you talking about?"

"Stand down, Captain Growl," Connor said, a hint of a grin at the corners of his mouth. "It was a different time. We all liked her. The possibility came up one day."

"Where was I when it came up?" Because it sure as shit wouldn't have come up if I'd been around. Last night, I'd only given her shit for doing stuff with all of us in her bed because I was a jealous, possessive asshole who needed to make sure that she kept hating me. If she didn't, if she started looking at me like she used to again, I didn't know if I'd be strong enough to resist her.

Connor's lips continued their upward trajectory. The bastard had always had a sick sense of humor. "I believe at the time, you may have been *coming up* in her."

My stomach plummeted. Despite what I may have led them to believe, I'd never actually slept with Archer. We'd gotten pretty close and we'd been each other's firsts at just about everything else but we'd never taken that final plunge.

"That's not up for discussion," I snapped. "The point is no one's sharing her with anyone because none of us have her."

"And if we did?" Alex asked, turning away from the reinforced glass that came down around this area when there was an alert in place. His eyes widened as they landed somewhere behind me but only for a moment before he schooled his expression. "How long have you been standing there?"

"Long enough to hear that you were considering passing me around like a goddamn pencil," Archer's indigent voice replied. "Where was *I* in this decision? Because I sure as hell don't recall being consulted in our free-love relationship."

To my surprise, Jax recovered first. So far, when it came to Max, he'd been the utmost gentleman. He'd even been the one to volunteer to take her shoes off after she'd fainted last night so he could 'defend her honor' from us.

He still had a soft spot the size of a continent for her, but it'd been years since he'd really been the good guy.

Five years, to be exact. Same as the rest of us.

He smirked at her as he propped his ankle on his knee. "We didn't consult you because it never became necessary, baby. You seemed perfectly happy kissing one or all of us. It didn't seem like the right thing to do to burst your bubble. Before any of us had to make any decisions, you were off trying to kill the world."

God fucking damn it. I wanted to strangle both of them.

No, *all* of them.

Archer had been mine all those years ago. Or at least, I'd thought she was. Now I had to find out that, on top of all the other betrayals, she'd kissed my best fucking friends? *Was it possible that my snide comment last night had been true?*

The thought made me sick to my stomach.

Archer's face turned several shades of red in quick succession but, before I could question her, she snapped a finger at Jax. "You kissed me. We were thirteen. Get the fuck over it. Surely you've had better kisses than that."

From the look on his face, he hadn't gotten over it. He also hadn't had better kisses. Unless I was very much mistaken, which I didn't think I was, she'd really hurt him with that comment.

She turned her attention on Connor next and the big guy actually took a step back. "I love you, Con, but I've never loved you like that and you know it. We never even kissed. You held my jaw and grunted out that you thought we should kiss."

He shrugged, but his jaw tightened in a way that told me she'd gotten to him, too. His gaze flicked to the side, and the muscles in his throat worked like he was struggling to swallow a reply.

Venom burst from her eyes as she faced Alex, her voice reduced to little more than a hiss. "You were like a brother to me. All of you were. Why would you lie about this?"

Alex looked sufficiently chagrined for me to know it wasn't true. But the guilt in his eyes when he caught my gaze sure as fuck made it look like he wanted it to be. He wanted to have kissed her then, and I'd have bet the house he still wanted it now.

As she turned to me, I folded my arms and leaned against the wall. "Are you done with your journey to the past yet? None of it matters, Max. Don't you get that? Whatever we had or didn't have died the day your parents agreed to work for Boplex."

Her eyes flared wide before they narrowed then she was in my space, her index finger poking my chest. "That's not true. They were never spies for Boplex and they never worked for them. Why would they turn their backs on their own company, on saving the world from bacteria we've never seen before, when they'd put everything they had into it?"

I glanced down at her hand on my pec and removed it, dropping it gingerly once it was free of my body. Touching her or having her touch me in even such a small way wouldn't be good for my resolve. Even though it had only been her fingertip touching me, I still felt its absence so acutely it was like I'd lost a limb. *Get a fucking grip, Kent.*

"I don't know, Max. All I know is our systems were upgraded and your Dad's signature was on the code. Next thing we hear, all systems are capable of this upgrade but no one else gets it. Then there are the reports that we were the only ones to get the upgrade because your Dad was running some kind of experiment."

"That's ridiculous," Archer scoffed, rolling her eyes as she hopped onto a stool at the bar. She propped her elbow on the hardwood countertop and rested her cheek in her palm. "If that was true, why wouldn't the area we moved to have been upgraded? Why would he have left the only neighborhood with the upgraded, superior alert system and taken his family with him?"

"Because," I moved in on her, enjoying the way her pupils still dilated when I got close, "it would throw us off his track. Besides, how long did he stay in that new neighborhood before he disappeared?"

"Two weeks," she choked up as she said the words, averting her gaze from mine. Her eyes hit the deck but her voice was strong. "That doesn't mean he's a traitor, though. There are so many other explanations."

"None that make sense." I stated it as fact because the guys and I had spent the last five years trying to come up with an alternate version of events. I took the opportunity to crowd her, to pin her to the railing and waited for her to lift that defiant glare to mine. "Face it, Archer. You're stuck with us for now. This quarantine could last much longer than the others. The town's running out of space for mass graves to bury the bodies far enough away, but that's not even really the issue. They're using this quarantine to buy time."

"Buy time? What for?" Her cheeks paled. "How much time?"

"Good questions. Tell us what you know and we might make it fun for you to be here. You might even get that sharing thing you wanted." The sharing I didn't know how to feel about even if it'd never happened. "Fuck, it's not like we have any other options. Sure, maybe your father synthesized a species of the bacteria that took millions of lives, but pussy's pussy. And yours is the only one here right now."

In case anyone was wondering, I knew I was being a Grade-A Dickhead. But I needed to be. I needed her to be stronger than I was. She might think this was going to be like any of the other periods of quarantine that we'd endured, but it wasn't.

This wouldn't be the standard seventy-two hours after the winds changed to see if a person developed symptoms from the grave spores latching onto them. It wouldn't even be the required ninety-four hours for people who'd been in contact with a person who'd tested positive.

Thanks to Alex's superior, uh, Internet skills, we knew this was going to be a long one. We also knew the disease was changing, though we didn't know how or why.

"I don't know anything and even if I did, the last thing I'd do with the information is pass it along to you." Archer flipped me off and propped one hand on her hip, then slapped me across the face with the other. "Also, the sharing thing *I* wanted? I *just* found out about it. But you're right, it doesn't matter anymore. If your hand can't keep you satisfied for a few fucking days, I suggest you order some new lube or practice your wrist movements. Pussy might be pussy, but mine ain't available to any of you."

5

ARCHER

"Archer," Jax's voice followed a soft knock on my bedroom door, "are you awake?"

I groaned, rolling over in bed. After our fight earlier, I didn't really feel like talking to any of them.

"Go away," I called out, shutting my eyes. "I'm not in the mood to argue more right now."

"That's not what I'm here for," he said, the door creaking quietly as he pushed it open. "I came to apologize, actually."

I frowned and sat up, bringing my gaze to his. It was dark in the room, but the bathroom light was on and the ambient light it provided was enough that I could see him.

He scratched the side of his jaw and walked further into the room, shutting the door behind him. "What I said downstairs was stupid."

I sighed when he took a few more steps and sat down on the bed uninvited, but I didn't chase him out. To be honest, I knew I should, I just didn't have it in me to do it.

Jax wasn't looking at me like I was the enemy right now; he was looking at me more like he used to, like he really was afraid he'd hurt my feelings and wouldn't be able to sleep until he got this off his chest.

As much as I wasn't about to melt into an instant puddle of forgiveness, I *did* want to hear him out. He used to be one of my best friends, my study buddy, and the guy whose patience was the reason I'd ever passed science. Among so many other things.

If I could get that camaraderie back, the comfort of having him in my corner, even if it was just for a few minutes, I'd take it. I missed him. I missed them all. I missed *us*.

With all the chaos in the world, I didn't even feel bad about just wanting that feeling of *us* back. I'd weathered so many storms on my own, both literal and metaphorical, that I just wanted that calm back for one fucking night. Jax used to be a rock to me, a place of quiet and understanding when nothing else made sense.

"You called me '*baby*,' Jackson. Why?" I asked, not proud of how small my voice was or how that was the only part I focused on out of every hateful thing he'd said.

He hung his head, shaking it slowly from side-to-side. "Maybe I just missed you."

My teeth sank into the back of my lower lip as I took in the figure he cut sitting there at the foot of my bed. His shoulders were slumped, and when he lifted his head again, he looked exhausted. Seeing him like that made my heart ache in my chest. It also made me itch to get answers.

"I know you all blame me and you're hurt. But don't you think I'm just as hurt, if not more? Why lash out?"

He gave me a sad smile. "You wouldn't. Can you at least understand why it would have been embarrassing for us to have you walking in on that particular conversation?"

"Yeah, I guess." What I didn't understand was why I couldn't stop thinking about the sharing thing now that it had come up. It wasn't like it had ever happened, or like I'd ever even thought about it before, but I couldn't help but wonder what it might have been like. "Why didn't you ever speak to me about it, though? Before that day, I mean. Obviously, I understand why you didn't bring it up to me that day."

In the darkness it was difficult to be sure, but I swore his cheeks flushed. "We didn't bring it up because it was never anything more than a fantasy, Max. It's not like you would've gone for it, and it's not like any of us were mature enough to make that kind of decision back then."

"Fair enough. I don't even know how something like that would work." But that didn't make it any less intriguing.

This time I was sure his cheeks flushed, but he held my gaze steadily. "I do. I looked it up after Alex made a comment in passing about it once."

"You did?" I pulled my head back. "You were that serious about it?"

"No." He grinned. "But knowledge is power. You know I can't just let something go if I hear about it but don't understand it."

"True." The corners of my lips inched up and I found myself leaning toward him. It was like Jax had a gravitational field around him and I had just gotten sucked into it. "Are you still like that?"

"Do you really want to know?" He seemed strangely hesitant, his eyes moving from one of mine to the other as he searched them. "Why?"

"Why?" I repeated, my eyebrows lifting as I held his gaze. "How about because I'm curious to know if my friend is still in there somewhere underneath all your new muscles?"

Falling into old habits was too easy. Teasing Jax came so naturally that it'd happened before I could even think about it.

He smirked, raising an arm to curl it and show off his admittedly impressive bicep. "I'm glad you noticed. Connor and Nick have been slave drivers about the gym. It's good to know it's paying off."

"Are you really fishing for compliments from me right now?" *Damn it. Stop teasing him. He's not your friend anymore.*

As if he'd read my thoughts, his expression darkened again. "You're right. I shouldn't even be talking to you. I just came to apologize. Being surprised or embarrassed doesn't justify having treated you like that."

"Thank you." My hand moved toward his like it remembered the way we used to offer each other comforting touches all the time. I only just caught myself before my fingers wrapped around his.

Jax noticed the movement, obviously, and glanced down at my hand. A part of me wondered if he would laugh, ridicule me, or snap at me again. But he didn't.

Instead, he slowly reached out his own hand and gently placed his palm against mine, letting out an almost relieved breath as his skin touched mine. Both of us stared at our point of contact, neither of us moving away.

"I'm glad you're back, Max," he said in a voice so quiet it was barely more than a whisper. "Even if I don't know anymore what's true and what isn't, it just didn't feel like home without you here."

My throat tightened and tears welled up in my eyes, but again I didn't let them fall. "Yeah, for some reason, I'm glad I'm back, too."

He smiled, but then sighed and withdrew his hand, wiping it on his jeans as he stood up. "I should go. Get some sleep, okay?"

"I'll try." But it probably wasn't going to happen, especially not after this conversation and all the weird feelings it stirred up. "You too."

"Yeah, I'll try." The look he gave me told me he wasn't convinced it would happen for him, either. With another soft smile, he nodded and headed out.

When the door closed with a soft click behind him, I sank back on the bed and tried to make sense of what had just happened. It felt like there had been a shift in the house after this morning, but I wasn't sure what it meant yet. Or whether it would last.

Five days later, seven whole days since Nick had basically taken me hostage, the alert still hadn't lifted. I groaned as I rolled over in bed, pressing a pillow over my head to stifle my scream.

A clean pillow. Grabbed from a clean bed.

I hadn't trusted anything once I'd woken up after my fainting incident that first night. Fresh linens had been packed away in my closet, but I'd washed everything again.

And then again, just for good measure.

I'd also scrubbed every inch of the en-suite bathroom with bleach, vacuumed the immaculate carpets, and emptied out the drawers. Contrary to what I'd been promised, I hadn't found any condoms.

Everything seemed exactly as I'd left it instead. No sex toys had come out of my nightstand except for the small purple vibrator Nick bought me years ago. My books, notebooks, pens, and odds and ends had still been inside all my drawers.

Even my high school textbooks from when I still believed I'd be going to college were on my desk. The guys had all gone off to some form of higher education and were only holed up at Nick's because they'd known the alert was coming.

I sensed there was more to it, but our relationship was cold at best. It hurt to be this close to them and not be part of them but I wouldn't let it show.

So far, everything was good. Relatively speaking anyway, by which I meant we were all still breathing. I'd also been right about the mood in the house changing, but it still wasn't exactly warm and welcoming. There had been less and less hostility as time went on. We'd also talked a bit, but the comments about my parents were wearing me down. And since no one had been able to produce credible evidence one way or another, we were at something of an impasse.

When I rolled over in bed again, I realized the blankets were tight around my feet. I felt myself pale at the implications then hurled the pillow at whoever was pinning me down.

"Holy penguin, Max. Get a fucking grip," an amused voice said.

I sat up slowly, narrowing my eyes at Alex's playful green ones. I drew my knees up to my chest to hide my skimpy pajamas and looped my arms around them.

"I'll get a fucking grip once someone starts being honest with me about what's really going on instead of just making snide remarks," I said, tightening my arms.

Apparently, the motion had the effect of enhancing my cleavage because Alex suddenly winced and looked away. "Put those things away, will you? I don't want to be thinking about your boobs and I really don't want Nick knocking my teeth out for thinking about them."

"Nick doesn't have the right to knock anyone's teeth out for thinking anything about me," I replied, but I raised the sheet higher, anyway. "I would've put them away but I can't. The only clothes I have here are those that fit me when I was seventeen. Just talk to me, Alex. Tell me what's going on."

He hesitated but then stretched his big body across the foot of the bed again and propped his cheek on his palm as he peered at me. For the first time in a long time, those gorgeous green eyes of his were unguarded when they met mine.

"Events have unfolded. They exonerate you from foul play, since you've been here with us."

My head dropped to the side, my eyebrows pulling together as tight as they could. "You mean to tell me that I've been living basically on the streets for years and all it takes is a week to convince you I'm innocent of whatever you've been thinking?"

He had the decency to flinch, pain shooting through him before he buried his blond head in his arms. "You've really been on the streets? Nick said something, but I thought he was exaggerating."

"Why the fuck would I have exaggerated that?" Nick's voice came from the doorway.

When I whipped my head up to face him, he was leaning on the jamb with a tray on his hand. I practically salivated at the idea of being fed breakfast in bed by the hottie delivering it but I quickly got a grip on my stupid fantasies.

Nick was the type who was fed, not the type who did the feeding. He surprised me by coming to sit on the bed with us instead of just leaving the tray like usual.

His expression turned serious when he looked at me, his head cocked to the right. "Was living mostly on the streets a front?"

I sneered and tried to turn away from him but he caught my chin and brought my eyes back to his. "Why the fuck would I have been pretending to live on the streets?"

He didn't fall for my snide sarcasm. His fingers cupped my face in a firm but tender grip, making sure my gaze never left his. "If that's true, why didn't you come to us for help?"

"For help?" I couldn't help it, I let out a derisive laugh right in his face. "You hate me. You blocked my number and refused to talk to me. Why the fuck would I have come to you for help?"

I felt Alex's body sagging and, though Nick still held my face, I turned so I could see our friend's. "What, Alex? Or should I call you Mr. Montgomery now? Obviously, none of the parents are around and you all seem to have slotted into their personas just perfectly."

Alex moaned and rolled onto his back, shoving his hands in his hair. "No, Max. You've got us all wrong. We're trying to figure out what they're doing. We're-"

"Enough." Nick's authoritative hand slashed through the air as he scowled in his best friend's direction. "What are you doing? Inducting her to the inner circle without a vote?"

"Last I checked, I was born into the inner circle." I grabbed the pillow from underneath my head and whacked Nick upside the head with the goose down. "I was born two-and-a-half hours before you, Mister Monster. I think it's time you remember that."

For a long minute, I thought I might've crossed a line. Nick looked at me like I was a ghost, didn't say anything then pointed at the door. "Get the fuck out, Alex."

Alex grumbled but I felt the bed shift again and then he was gone. Nick was still looking at me like I was some kind of miracle. "You've hardly changed at all."

"Oh, I've changed." I snorted. "Why did you banish Alex?"

Banishing was what we used to call it when we ordered someone out. It was usually because something embarrassing had happened or because we just needed to talk to one person at a time. Eventually, all of us found out the issue anyway but it was less intimidating this way.

Especially for me, being the only girl pea in the pod. For the longest time, I hadn't even noticed and neither had they. Until one day when I was thirteen, Mrs. Kent had brought me out of *our* room and taken me to *mine*.

"Darlin'," she'd said, her arm around my shoulders and a twinkle in her eyes. *"Now I know you're going to have better options in life than these scoundrels but they* are *scoundrels. Or at least they're about to be."*

She'd winked at me even as I frowned at her.

I'd liked sleeping in a bunk with Nick, even when he'd gotten so big that I was squished all the time. To this day, I only ever occupied one side of the bed; it was like even my subconscious still wanted there to be space for him in case he ever wanted to come back.

"Your mama and I talked about it and, since our work ain't gonna change soon, we figured you needed this." She'd swung open the door to a room roughly the size of a basketball court. It'd been done up in dove gray and white with pink and purple accents.

I'd felt super awkward about it, until Mrs. Kent smiled down at me again. *"Your mama and I picked out everything together. We want you to be comfortable here, sweetheart. Soon, things are going to start happening that we won't always be here for and we want you to have someplace safe to go."*

They'd been right, of course. My period had started and they'd been in Indonesia studying some medical anomaly. I developed feelings for the boy I'd been sleeping next to for years and they'd been tracking bacterial growth at an African chicken farm.

Our caretaker had turned a blind eye somewhere along the way. Left to our own devices, we attended school, did well enough not to have our parents called back and pretty much did our own thing.

Nick's fingers brushed along my cheek and his forehead fell to mine. "I fucking hate you, Archer. You know that?"

My hands had found a comfortable spot on his chest but I pushed him away. "What?"

"I hate you." He grabbed my hands, keeping them in a vice grip at my sides. All sorts of emotions flickered in his eyes, but I couldn't understand why so many of them clashed with his words. "You fucking ruined me, and for what?"

"I ruined you?" I challenged, barely managing to get one of my wrists free so I could gesture wildly at the room we were in. "What do you think happened to me, Nick? What? I ruined this room for you? I made it hard for you to get it up when you were in here? All while I went days without fucking eating? I'm sorry for ruining one room in a house with seven others."

I wiggled out from underneath him, my eyes wide and probably a little crazy as my heart raced. The next thing I knew, admissions I'd never planned on making to him tumbled out of my mouth.

"I heard those sirens wail and found a homeless shelter, hoping the one I'd found had been properly maintained. I passed by the graves and prayed the wind wouldn't change at that moment."

His nostrils flared, horror flashing in those azure eyes. "You went close to the graves?"

"I didn't have a choice. You know they auction off their stuff there. I bought what I could and used the money from selling it to survive."

"But the graves..." Nick trailed off, bringing both hands to my cheeks, "...the graves are so shallow, Max. The spores could've reached you even if there wasn't a fresh body nearby. How could you be so reckless?"

Anger leaped into my chest. I swatted his hands away and bulged my eyes at him. "Have you ever been hungry, Nick? Yes, I could've caught the bacteria from being so close to the bodies but I didn't care."

"But Maeve--"

I cut him off. "Maeve doesn't look out for anyone but herself. She deposits small sums of money into my bank account every couple of months. In return, I bring her groceries. The amount I get out of it is negligible."

"What about your trust fund?" he asked, eyes stretching almost impossibly wide as he wrapped his hands around my hips.

"It's gone," I said. "I don't know how, but Maeve said my parents' bills ate it up. I don't even care, Nicky. But don't judge me for the things I've had to do to stay alive."

"What else have you had to do?" he asked darkly, resting his head on my shoulder.

"A lot of stuff. Why do you even care? I ruined you, remember?"

Nick shook his head against my skin, burrowing his face deeper. "I'm ruined and it's because of you, but I don't think it's by you, Max."

I sighed into the relative darkness of the room, glad Alex hadn't opened the curtains when he'd come in earlier. "Not that you have any right or reason to know but I've waited tables, I've stripped, I've tried my hand at more but I could never bring myself to give a blow--"

"No," he moaned into my neck. "God, no. Maxi."

"I'm not your Maxi anymore, Nick." I shoved his head away from me and sat back, my eyes flashing with hatred as I remembered the reason I'd had to do those things. *Why have I been softening toward them after all that?* "Stay the fuck away from me."

I ripped the blankets off my body and took off for the shower, scrubbing myself until I was pink. I had to stay strong no matter how tempting it was to let them back in; no matter how much I wanted what we used to have. If I was being completely honest with myself, I knew I wanted what we used to have back.

But that couldn't happen. What I'd been through wasn't necessarily their fault, but they'd *abandoned* me when I needed them most. I couldn't forget that.

When I stepped out and wrapped an impossibly large and fluffy towel around my body, Nick was still sitting on my bed. It didn't look like he'd moved a muscle but his head swung slowly to me.

"I can't." His voice came out as a croaked whisper. "I can't stay away from you. I've tried, Max. Archer."

He scrubbed his fingers over the light stubble on his chin as silence fell between us for a moment. "I fucking tried, but my private detective never told me it was that bad. I knew about the stripping, but I thought it was all part of the act."

My mind spun out at his words. "Your private fucking *what*?"

"Detective," he said, his smile sheepish while not at all apologetic. "I've been keeping tabs on you. You can't think I left you out there by yourself? Who the hell do you take me for?"

I was just about to lose every ounce of shit I'd ever had when Connor stuck in his head in the door. "Mr. and Mrs. Melodrama, we have something that urgently requires your attention. You can fight later. For now, we need to go down into the tunnels."

6

NICK

"You have tunnels in your fucking house," Archer hissed as we descended the staircase from my father's study. "Hidden behind your father's bookshelf? That's insane, Nick."

I shrugged because I didn't have any answers. I'd known about the secret passage beyond the bookshelf, but I had no idea why something we'd discovered a year ago had interrupted one of the most important conversations I'd ever had.

Archer was still shooting me angry, questioning glances. Obviously, she wasn't happy that I'd had a P.I. on her. I hoped it would count in my favor if she found out that my instructions had been to bring her back before she did anything too outlandish.

Not that I thought it would; there was no way. She was going to be angrier than a hornet in a kicked nest. To be honest, I kind of got how she was feeling right now.

Kind of.

I'd asked the P.I, to stay on her, hoping she'd lead us to her parents or their associates. Personal details about her were supposed to be spared unless it could be related to them, but some stuff had slipped through in reports.

But I'd put my foot in it and now my Max was pissed off with a capital P. "Your fucking P.I., Nick? What exactly did he tell you about me? Was he spying on me in my bedroom when I took my vibrator for a stroll? Was he listening to the fast-food orders I took? Or, wait, did he take free videos for you when my clothes started flying before I showered? That must be the kicker, right?"

"No," I gritted out, trying to restrain myself. When she looked at me over her shoulder on the next step down and huffed out a breath, though, I decided enough was enough.

I grabbed her wrist roughly and pinned her against the damp wall. "I asked him to keep an eye on you." When she sagged against the hard rock, I moved even closer. "I know you think I was spying on you. I was and I wasn't. I thought I was protecting my loved ones from you, I thought-"

I thought I was protecting you.

"I don't give a fuck what you thought." She lifted her hands to my chest and pushed hard. "All I care about is this being over."

"It won't be over, though," I replied, my breathing ragged at the sense of urgency I felt to make her understand. "It'll never be over."

She scowled but didn't push me again. "All I want is to be free of this. Free of you."

"Then why the fuck are you coming into the dungeons with us right now?" I stepped closer to her. "Why is it that you ended up back here with us just when we were on the cusp of finding out what's down there?"

"I'm here because you forced me to stay, idiot," she hissed. "I'd have been at my own place right now if you hadn't."

My brows rose. "I've seen pictures of the dump you call home now. You're safer here."

"It might be a dump, but at least it's mine. It took me years to afford it and I'm damn proud of having it."

The raw pain in her voice ripped me to shreds. Desperation swelled like a beast inside my chest. "Why didn't you come to me? If not me, why didn't you reach out to any of the others?"

She slumped against the wall, but her head was held high. "You wouldn't have helped me. You hate me, remember? So do they."

Silence filled the space between us for a second as I shook my head. "There's a fine line between love and hate. I wouldn't have turned you away, and neither would they."

She glanced at the receding forms in the tunnel ahead of us and swallowed hard. "You made them hate me. They would never have gone against you, not with their loyalty to you."

"Is that why you're so much angrier with me?" I asked, finally starting to understand the answer to the question that had been haunting me for days.

I'd seen her with the others. Every once in a while, they'd joke and laugh like in old times. It never lasted long, but it also never included me. The knowledge had made my insides twist more than once.

"Yes," she whispered, but even that sounded defiant. "I loved you, Nick."

She'd loved me? I swore even my blood stopped flowing in that moment. *How the fuck had I* not *known that?*

"Yet you were the first to turn your back on me." Daggers flew from her eyes and pierced my very soul. "Do you have any idea how much that hurt?"

"Yes, I do. Believe it or not, you weren't the only one who got your heart ripped out." Even the memories of that time made it hard to breathe sometimes. I still woke up at night drenched in sweat from the nightmares.

Archer looked up at me with disbelief clouding her eyes. "If you felt anything for me at all, you would've talked to me about it."

"I was a kid!" I groaned. "A scared, hurt kid. You have no idea how much I wanted to reach out to you."

"But you didn't." There was a hint of finality in her voice. "That's all there is, isn't it? Even now, just a week ago, you wouldn't have pissed on me if I was on fire."

"Bullshit. I don't believe in chance or coincidence, Archer. I caught you at those gates that night for a reason. I took you in, but you can't blame me for being suspicious." I closed the distance between us, her chest against mine. "This was the first time we had advanced warning. It was also the first time the spores were headed right toward town."

"Let me guess." She licked her lips and let her head fall back, looking into my eyes with such openness the guards around my heart almost shattered. "You thought me being here had something to do with it?"

"Let's review what we know, shall we?" I crowded her against the wall, placing my palms on either side of her face and hating that I was close enough to kiss her but couldn't. "Your parents picked up and left in the middle of the night."

"We never heard from you again," Alex's voice came from the side, penning her in from the left. "Our best friend was suddenly gone. As was the girl we all loved."

Archer's soft gray eyes darted between Alex's and mine. "I wasn't gone. I went to school, I--"

Connor's voice joined in next but he was looking at me instead of staring down at Archer. "Is Max finally putting the fuck out or can we move on?"

"We're moving along swiftly," she said, shoving at my shoulder with one hand and Alex's with the other. "What was so urgent, Connor? Or are you dragging us all down here for ghost stories?"

Archer scoffed but Connor's black eyes glinted into mine in the tunnel's darkness. "Jackson and I heard something."

"Thanks to your bickering, there's nothing left now," Jax barked from the front. "We'd be lucky to find a dead fucking rat down he--"

He cut himself off when he reached what I knew was the end of the tunnel. We'd been down here exploring a million times.

Except tonight, there was a glow illuminating his form where there should've been solid rock. The light was barely there but the ends of Jax's hair shone gold around his head before he rushed forward.

"Holy shit, guys. There's someone down here," he called out in a harsh whisper, then he was gone. He disappeared around a corner that shouldn't have been there.

I didn't make anyone wait on me. Shoving past Connor and Alex, I took off down the tunnel in search of the answers we'd been after since Max had disappeared. Archer Maxwell had been such an integral part of us that no one had accepted she'd just leave after her parents picked up and left.

But then she'd made her appearance at our high school just days later and pretended like nothing had changed. She'd even tried to get us to believe that her parents were innocent.

They weren't.

Only so many people had access to the lab where they'd worked, the one where the so-called zombie spores had originated. The spores were bacterial; the disease should've been treatable by antibiotics, but it wasn't.

Instead, those little motherfuckers clung to your brain and about fifty minutes later, turned you into the undead. For all of about five minutes, anyway. After that, you were dead, dead.

There was still no cure. All any of us knew was it came from an outbreak out of Machax Labs and Machax belonged to Archer's parents. Well, not anymore; it belonged to all our parents, now.

Maxwell, Kent, Montgomery, Stone and Cant.

Blame had been rampant when the bugs first got free. Everyone, worldwide, had hated the company but no one could understand how their little experiment got loose. Until one day, Archer's dad stepped up and confirmed the truth behind the suspicions and accusations.

They'd moved out of the complex, resigned their positions on our board. We'd thought the worst was behind us.

It hadn't been. Not by a long shot.

The first evidence I'd seen that Archer herself was innocent had been the look in her eyes when we'd straight-up asked her. The second was all the movement on the dark web while she'd been here. Something big was happening and there was no way she could be involved. The third, and most compelling piece, was when she stumbled into the antechamber at the end of the tunnel right after me, with no hesitation.

The guys were close on her heels but I couldn't hear their footsteps. Blood pounded in my ears, and the only sound I could make out above it was the gurgling sounds of the man strapped to the chair in the center of the chamber.

I'd seen the chair before. Theoretical designs of it, anyway. It was a prototype being tested by my father but this sure as fuck wasn't what it'd been tested for.

7

ARCHER

The guy strapped to the thing in the middle of the room was clearly in agony. Fluorescent lights hummed above him in the sterile, laboratory like place. A chill raced down my spine at the thought that this was right below the houses we'd grown up in.

In the second it took to look out from behind Nick's back, I realized the contraption they'd tied dark-haired guy to bore similarities to a chair.

In its present use, however, it was a torture device. I didn't know how it worked, only that the guy sitting in it had some kind of futuristic ring around his head and he was tied down at his wrists and ankles.

I didn't know what the thing on his head was doing but it couldn't have been good. His body would go still for a moment, then his face would turn into a grotesque, contorted mask of pain before it went back to normal. I'd seen faces like his before but never in anyone who'd returned to themselves.

"What the fuck?" Connor roared as he burst into the chamber. The poor guy hooked up to the machine tensed again and Connor threw his arms out in front of us. "Get the fuck back, you two. He's infected, turning."

Turning into what? No one knew. The best guess so far was a human-shaped thingamabob that liked to eat human flesh for the few minutes it had before it finally succumbed. It was sad, really. Everyone had always assumed that the zombie apocalypse would be much more impressive than it had actually turned out to be.

All we knew was that it was a bacterial infection that affected the brain. No one knew how or why but they dropped dead within an hour of being turned. There were two fundamental problems: the bacteria didn't die with the host, and people could become infected without any symptoms until up to three days later.

Jax grabbed Connor's arm. "Don't tell them to get back. He can't fucking bite them. In fact, he still seems mostly human."

Alex followed Jax into the chamber where nightmares came true, both appearing driven by scientific curiosity. The man in the chair still screamed periodically but neither Alex nor Jax seemed to notice anymore.

"Do you see this?" Alex asked, circling the chair and pushing his glasses up to the bridge of his nose. He frowned at the man. "He can focus on us. His eyes are following me."

Jax was beside him in a flash, leaning over until his face was only inches away from the stranger's. A strangled scream ripped out of his throat and he whipped his head back to glance between Connor and Nick in a panic.

"Help me. We have to get him out," Jax barked. "Now! Guys, it's Evan."

Nick stiffened and rushed forward while Connor sprang into action; he sprinted for a wall with electronic panels in it that I hadn't noticed.

"Who's Evan?" I asked, moving forward to see what I could do to help. "And if he's infected, why are we freeing him?"

"Because he's immune," Jax replied, with concentration marring his forehead. His voice was calm, though. Then again, he was used to having to explain stuff to the rest of us in layman's terms. "He's a technician for our parents. About three years ago, he got infected but nothing happened. He's also not a carrier, somehow."

My brows climbed up on my forehead. "If that's true, why's he in so much pain?"

"Because an experiment's being conducted on him," Alex gritted out. His hands were flying to check Evan's vitals while Nick worked on the bindings and Connor kept muttering to himself as he inspected the panels. "I'm not sure how yet but it's the only explanation."

"Your father hasn't been in these tunnels for years," Nick said quietly, glancing up at me with an apology in his eyes for the first time. "We thought the labs belonged to him. We haven't been able to get into them since but this was one of the labs he used for his experiments."

"So, it wasn't him," I said, feeling both lighter and a ton heavier. "Why did he confess? I mean, I knew he was innocent but I've never understood why he'd admit to something he hadn't done. He never answered any of my questions about it, either. This proves it wasn't him."

"Technically, the only thing it proves is it isn't him now," Jax said. His tone was even and non-judgmental. He was just saying things the way he saw them, but that didn't make it hurt any less. "Who else do we know of that could be doing this?"

At that moment, Connor tripped some switch and Evan's body sagged as the light in the ring around his head went out. The humming sound in the room disappeared.

Without Evan straining against them, Nick managed to undo the bindings while Alex frowned and brought his ear closer to Evan's mouth. I could see his lips moving but only ever so slightly.

Alex, apparently, heard whatever it was he said. His eyes flashed and grew so wide I saw the whites all around them. All the color drained from his face as he looked at me. "Maeve. Maeve and..."

He trailed off as he glanced down at Evan whose eyes fluttered closed.

Nick cursed. "Maeve and what, Alex?" he demanded, working with Connor to lift Evan's weight from the chair. "We need to get him upstairs before whoever is responsible for this comes back. Jax, go up ahead of us. Clear a space for him and get the first aid kit. It's the best we can do."

"On it," Jax said, turning around and loping out of the room.

Alex seemed frozen to his spot. When his gaze came back to mine, there was a dazed look in his eyes. "Maeve and my father."

As soon as he said the words, the flicker of recognition I'd had at Maeve's house made sense. My hands flew up to clamp over my mouth. "Oh, God. Your Dad. He's the one I saw with her that first night."

"That doesn't make sense," he replied, his focus only on me. "They're all out of state at some conference to discuss developments in the disease and new methods of fighting it."

"He's not out of state. I've only ever seen your Dad once or twice in my life, but it was him." I was absolutely sure of it. "If you want, we can look at some pictures when we get back upstairs. But it was him. Evan confirmed it."

Nick and Connor each had one of Evan's arms around their shoulders and they moved to the door. Nick grabbed my hand with his free one as he passed me, tugging me toward him. "We have to get out of here. We'll figure it out, but it doesn't need to be here."

I nodded. When Alex still didn't move, I grabbed his arm and dragged him out of the room with me. I could've sworn I heard footsteps echoing from somewhere inside the chamber of death.

The two of us moved as fast as we could but our pace was set by the others. As we walked out, I realized I had to try to seal up the bizzaro lab. Releasing my grip on Alex, I went to inspect the door.

From this side it looked like a slab of stone but on the inside, it was made of sleek metal. Alex came out of his haze long enough to help me slide it back then locked the door at the top of the stairs after we stepped back into the study.

Once the bookshelf was back in place, he collapsed onto a stuffed armchair. Jax hovered over Evan, who was lying down on a couch in the corner while Connor and Nick stood over them with their arms folded across their powerful chests.

"What does this mean?" Nick asked no one in particular. The two of them standing side-by-side with their inky hair, tattoos and bulging biceps looked like avenging angels. Dark avenging angels, but still.

Looking at them now, there were only tiny hints of the boys I used to know hiding inside the men they'd become. I wanted so badly to know who those men were, but I just didn't.

Nausea swirled in my stomach. My life had been snatched away from me because of those accusations against my father. I'd always sworn I'd track down whoever was responsible and make them pay.

There was no way I wanted to make Alex pay, though. *If his father was involved, that was on him. Not on his son.*

Despite how they'd treated me when this same information had come out about my family, I wasn't about to react the same way. Walking over to the chair he sat on, I lowered myself onto the armrest and lifted my hand to his hair, running my fingertips repeatedly through his blond locks. He kept it longer on top than at the sides now and the contrast between the sharp ends there and the longer, softer hair at the top somehow kept me in the here and now.

"It means Maeve has always been involved," I said, being the first one to break the heavy silence in the room.

The only other sounds were the fire cracking in the fireplace on the other end of the study and Evan's deep breathing. "Maeve and Alex's dad are obviously having an affair but I don't know how she even met him. He was almost always traveling when we were growing up. So much so that even *I* don't really know him. How does she?"

"Singapore," Jax muttered, only sparing a glance at us before going back to the guy lying prone in front of him. "Just before the first outbreak, Maeve attended a conference in Singapore. Alex's Dad was attending on behalf of the company. Maeve said your father had sent her to observe, Archer."

"How do you know all this?" I asked, keeping up my stroking through Alex's hair. It seemed to be relaxing him. He was leaning into my side with his head resting on my shoulder. It brought back so many childhood memories of being with him like this but I couldn't afford to focus on those right now. I'd waited too long for any information to let this opportunity pass me by.

Jax looked up at me. "I've been looking into any company records I could gain access to going back as far as possible. The board escaped accountability because of everything they've done to counteract the disease, developing the warning systems and all that. But someone needs to figure out what the hell happened."

"That's what you've been doing all this time?" I asked, already knowing the answer. "That's why you had a P.I. on me, too, isn't it?"

Nick blinked at my question but then gave me a tight nod. The ink on his skin rippled as he shook out his arms and moved away from Connor's side to take the chair across from Alex's.

"Yes." Scooting forward until he was so close to me that I could see the darker blue crystals in his eyes, he rested his elbows on his knees and swiped at his mouth with the back of his hand. "I saw your reactions down there. You've never seen any of those labs before, have you?"

"No." I held his gaze, even though the intensity of it practically burned my retinas. "I've told you before and I'll say it again" I don't now nor have I ever known what's really been going on. I'm intent on finding out, though. I'll do anything to get to the truth."

"We're all on the same page about that, then." He tore his eyes away from mine and looked to each of his friends in turn. "What do you say, do we trust her?"

"I don't think we have much of a choice," Connor said. "We're all holed up in here together and after what just went down, you can bet your ass the fight will be coming to us. And soon. Keeping secrets isn't going to help anyone when that happens."

"Thanks for the vote of confidence," I snapped, narrowing my eyes at him. "Pretend like you have a choice. Do you trust me?"

I studied Connor's eyes. For a long minute, they were almost perfectly expressionless. Just before I lost hope, the corners softened and he nodded. "Yeah, Max. I trust you. I'm sorry about before."

"I'm not accepting any apologies right now." I made sure to make eye contact with each of them. "We can work together because, despite everything, I do still trust you all."

Nick opened his mouth, a slight smirk already tugging at it. I shook my head at him. "None of that means I can forgive you for what you did to me. I won't forgive you, not that easily and maybe not at all. There's a lot of work to be done before that might happen."

Alex was the first to nod his agreement. A loud sigh came out of him and his shoulders slumped. "I get it. For now, we work together. We'll work on all of us later."

"I can do that," Jax agreed. "For the record, the sedative I just gave Evan will keep him knocked out for a while. Unless anyone's too tired, should we just get right into it?"

"You have sedatives that strong in your first aid kit?" I asked, standing up and stretching out my arms. Every eye in the room focused on the sliver of skin that was suddenly exposed below my belly button. "Stop looking at me like that. I'm not too tired to get to it, but I need something to eat. Who's with me?"

Nick's eyes were the last to leave me but he nodded. Jax opted to stay with Evan and asked Nick to stay with him. Connor declared that he needed a shower and went upstairs without looking back, leaving me and Alex to get the food.

"You okay?" I asked as we walked into the palatial but somehow still cozy kitchen. Copper pots and pans hung from a rack above the stove, a large, family style table took up the center of the room and pictures of us as kids were stuck on the fridge.

My heart clenched when I saw them. In almost every one, I was in the middle. Nick and Alex flanked my one side and Connor and Jax had the other. That was the way it'd always been; the way I thought it would always be.

Alex followed my gaze, nodding as he rubbed his eyes. "Yeah, I'll be fine. Eventually, anyway. This isn't the time to dwell in it."

"Dwell if you want to, Lex." I walked over to the freezer and opened it up, examining our options for dinner while also painfully aware that his eyes never left me. "Trust me, I know how big a shock it is."

"Yeah, but the difference is that you were close to your Dad. I never have been. You know that."

I stilled before I shook my head and reached for a box at the top. "Do I? Know that, I mean. For all I know you've gotten closer to him over the last few years."

"I didn't." He sighed and raked his hands through his hair, coming over to stand next to me. When I looked up at him, he reached out to place his hand gently on the side of my neck. "I know you're not accepting any apologies right now, but I need to say that I'm sorry, anyway."

I caught a glint of gold on his arm, sucking in a sharp breath when I recognized the delicate chain. "Is that..."

A shy smile ghosted across his lips, his eyes intent on mine as he dipped his head in a tiny nod. "I found it in your room two days after you left."

"Why are you wearing it?" I frowned, the same sense of confusion that I'd felt with Jax the other night creeping in. It felt like Alex's skin was electrified where it touched mine, a faint tingle traveling through me at the feel of it.

I shouldn't have been feeling anything with any of them, but it wasn't like I could stop it. His thumb stroked me softly as his expression grew thoughtful. "I'm wearing it now because I haven't taken it off in five years. If you're asking why I'm wearing it in general, the answer is a little more complicated."

Complicated wasn't good, but I also couldn't let it go. "I can handle complicated."

Something sparked in the depths of Alex's green eyes, but he shook his head. "No, you can't. Not this and not now."

Our eyes remained locked for another beat, his chest so close to mine that I felt his heart hammering against it. He lowered his head so slowly that I would've had time to run a lap around the entire estate, but I couldn't move.

When our lips were so close together I could practically taste them, he paused and lifted his gaze back to mine. Whatever he saw in them was the answer he'd been waiting for because he finally moved to close the last bit of distance between us and brushed the softest of kisses to the side of my mouth, a whisper quiet moan catching in the back of his throat before he took a step back. Reluctantly, judging by the way his hand lingered. "We'll get there, Max. I promise I'll explain to you sometime, but now isn't that time."

I nodded, trying to make sense of the tingling that had now traveled to my lips, the pounding of my heart and why the hell I wanted him to do that again. *This is insane. I couldn't have feelings for three, possibly four, different boys. Especially not* these *boys.*

"Let's make some food, then. It might not be time for that conversation, but it *is* time for a different one."

"Yeah, I know." He took another step back but before he turned away, he focused his attention on me again. "But Archer? We *are* going to talk about this. Maybe it'll be complicated, but I'm not letting you go again until you've heard me out. Maybe not even then."

With that utterly confusing statement, he gave me a playful smirk, winked and went for the fridge.

Twenty minutes later, we were all assembled in the cozy lounge next to the theater room in the basement. The ceiling was low; the lights dim.

Another fire had been lit in here and we each settled on the enormous sofas with plates of cheesy quesadillas.

"Where's Evan?" I asked after swallowing my first big bite. "Is he going to be okay while we're all down here?"

"He's fine. We've taken him to one of the guestrooms," Jax said. "To answer your earlier question, yes, I do have sedatives that strong in the first aid kit. They're hardly the harmless little kits they used to be. We've got stuff to treat just about anything in ours. You never know what you're going to have to deal with or how long you're going to be inside."

I sat back, pain searing through my veins as if it was traveling in my blood. Our lives had become so damn different. There were so many secrets, so many lies between us, but it was their indifference to having medication like that so easily accessible that felt like the best example of real rift between us right now.

"You have all of this," I said, motioning around the room, "enough frozen food to feed an army, medical supplies that'd put most emergency rooms to shame. Do you even realize how many people don't have even a fraction of that?"

Connor nodded, his dark eyes never leaving mine. "We do know, Max. We can't save the world but we're trying to do what we can."

"That's why we're investigating our own parents," Nick said, his voice strained. "It hasn't been easy, but they're all specialists in their fields. There's no way they could've been working on something like this and had an *accidental* outbreak happen."

Alex jerked his head in a nod, his skin still pale as he pulled his glasses off his face to clean them on his t-shirt. "I've gotten pretty good at hacking. There was no evidence of them working on something this dangerous. If they were, it was top-secret, which means they'd have needed very special equipment to ensure containment."

"There's no record of anything like that being ordered either," Jax said. From the look in his eyes, I knew he was dying to recap to us what kind of equipment they'd have needed but he held himself back. "Well, *almost* none of it was ordered but some was."

"By who?" I asked, regretting the question almost immediately. The guys exchanged a glance and what was left of my heart shattered before I'd even gotten an answer.

Eventually, it was Nick who confirmed my suspicion. "Your mother, Max. All the evidence we've found in the last five years points at no one but your parents."

8

JACKSON

Our group's dynamic had always fascinated me. Four guys and one girl should never have worked, but it always had. Just not in any romantic sense.

The one time we'd talked about it and wondered whether to even suggest it to Archer, we'd been interrupted. It hadn't been a small interruption, either.

It'd been the interruption that changed the course of our lives. With that day in mind, I sat forward. "I think it'll be useful to start at the beginning."

"Yeah, let's do that," Archer said, her tone dry. "After all, one day you were my best friends and the next you accused me of being part of some plot that killed half the world's population."

Nick's jaw flexed as he ground his teeth; he was barely keeping it together. Unfortunately, Nick's style was confrontational. He didn't like what she'd just said and he wanted to make some snide comment about it.

I loved the guy, but he wasn't the right one to handle this. Alex caught my gaze and tapped his chest with his thumb. Leaning back, I motioned for him to take over. It had been obvious to me the second they'd walked into the room that something had happened between them in the kitchen, but I would have to wait for my answers.

After my moment with Archer the other night, I'd have expected the knowledge of something between her and one of my best friends would bother me but it didn't. In fact, it did the complete opposite.

I'd never admit it to anyone but it was a turn on. The thought of watching the two of them together was intriguing, and now that Archer was back in our lives, I had to wonder whether I'd ever get to see it for real.

Over the years, I'd thought about it a lot. I'd read up on relationships involving more than two people and yeah, I'd gotten off to imagining her with all of us like that. Alex and I had talked about it a few times, too.

Even when it'd seemed impossible that it might happen, neither of us had been able to let the thought go. Every once in a while, especially when the drinks had been flowing, we'd end up there. There'd never been another girl we'd considered it with, though.

The truth was no matter how many different girls we fucked, there was no one else but her. No one else we wanted. No one else we wanted to experience it with. The reason was the beautiful, gray eyed girl watching Alex with an expectant expression on her gorgeous face.

"We thought that because it's what our parents told us," he started. "Connor's mom called, then mine, then Jax's. They all said pretty much the same thing. It had been confirmed that the bacteria had been synthesized in our labs, an investigation had been conducted and your dad was about to be arrested."

"He was never arrested, though," she said. "I got a call that afternoon, too. Mom said to come home immediately. They didn't tell me anything before I went to sleep, but I woke up in the middle of the night. My parents were packing, but all they said was that we were in danger and needed to disappear."

Finally getting to hear her side of the story was like having poison slowly drained out of my system. Alex relaxed for what seemed like the first time in years, so I guessed he felt the same.

"Right. That's why you were gone by the time we showed up?" he asked, understanding flickering in the forest green of his eyes.

"You showed up?" She frowned. "I never knew that."

Nick shrugged, the only one who still looked like he was struggling with the truth. I was pretty sure he *knew* by now she was telling the truth, but setting aside all the rage and hurt would be difficult for him.

"Of course we fucking showed up," he said, harshly. "Jesus. I was in love with you, Max. I'm pretty sure all these other assholes were, too. We didn't just believe what they said when we were all sat down that night and got told you'd had a hand in mass murder."

"But you were already gone by the time we got there," Connor said succinctly, not denying Nick's assertion that we'd all been in love with her. "Our parents discovered we were gone, ordered us to come back and then showed us some of the *evidence* they had."

Alex flinched when he remembered that part of the night. "It seemed pretty iron-clad to a bunch of seventeen-year-olds. We were also told that if we didn't distance ourselves from you immediately, people would think we'd known and been complicit."

"So that's it, huh?" she asked flatly. "You came to my house and when we weren't there, you assumed I was guilty just because you were shown some stuff?"

"It wasn't just stuff, Max," I said. "It was security footage, emails, signed documents. It was only later that we started questioning the authenticity of it all and even then, it took a long time before we started smelling a rat."

"Why were you all so pissed off at me when I got here on the first night, then?" she asked. "If you already knew something else was going on, why didn't any of you ever reach out to me?"

"Because we still didn't know at first why you'd shown up again. You could've been a spy for Boplex. You have to at least try to see it from our side. You showing up here less than ten minutes before the start of the longest quarantine we've had in years after we hadn't seen you for five? It's suspicious."

"Why did you really invite me in, then?" she asked Nick, fixing her eyes to the side of his head. "The truth, this time. Not all the vague lines you spewed down in the tunnels."

He didn't turn towards her. "Because even if you were a spy for them, I didn't want you to *die*."

I reached over to clasp his shoulder.

"Even if you were a spy, I would prefer fighting you to losing you," he said.

I was proud of him for having made that decision and for saying it without sounding like he was blaming her for something.

Archer frowned but then shook her head. "Okay, let's table that part for now. We agreed to come back to the personal stuff later."

"Right." I nodded at Alex.

He slid his glasses back onto his face and sighed. His blond hair shifted with the movement, a lock of it falling across his face before he shoved it back. "Those are the highlights between then and now. When was the last time you saw your parents?"

"Two weeks after the last time you did," she said, her eyes clouding over. "Why do you think they're working with Boplex?"

"They've always been our biggest rival. We suspect there was a mole within our company," I said when Alex didn't answer her question. As the most analytical one of us, I guess it was easier for me to discuss it without getting emotional. "We think that person, whoever they were, was responsible for dispersing the bacteria that first time. None of us believe it happened by accident."

"Why would anyone do that?" Archer set her plate down on the coffee table and leaned back, folding her arms over her stomach like she was feeling sick. I didn't blame her. "Why would anyone want to release something that would kill so many people?"

"We think it was an experiment gone wrong. We know Boplex is working on weaponizing the bacteria but we don't know why. Alex only managed to get into their systems for a few minutes."

"You saw my dad?" she asked him, leaning back against the sofa as she tightened her grip on herself.

He hesitated before nodding, running his hands over the top of his hair as he bounced his knee. "He's definitely one of the scientists working on it. We think they're responsible for altering the disease, as well."

"Given his skill set as a biologist, it would make sense," she agreed, but her voice broke at the end of the sentence. Her jaw set and I knew she was fighting back tears.

"Yeah," I cleared my throat. "That's what we thought, too. If it helps, we didn't see your mom there."

She sighed but didn't say anything. Connor shifted closer to her, then slung a thick arm over her shoulders, pulling her into his side. Surprisingly, she didn't fight his silent offer of comfort. Not surprisingly, Nick looked at him with murder flashing in his eyes.

Connor met his gaze unwaveringly and I nodded at Alex to continue. This wasn't the time for these squabbles.

"This latest alert was the first time the upgraded system was used," Nick said, drawing in a deep breath as he took over from Connor. "That's how we knew we were in for a longer period of quarantine. Communications we intercepted indicated that was what would happen. We sent the guards home, too. No one should stay in a tiny hut for that amount of time."

"That's why Bill wasn't there that night? I wouldn't have expected you to send him home for this." Archer sat up slightly but remained snugly under Connor's arm.

Seeing them like that made me want to touch her just like Connor was. If even I had a hard time keeping my distance from her, it must've been killing Nick to sit there, away from her warmth.

But we had to get over it. Regardless of my fantasies or how much I wanted her back in our lives, as ours and us hers, permanently, she didn't belong to us.

She'd made that pretty clear and we'd all respect her wishes. No matter how much we all still wanted her. I knew my best friends well enough to know it was true. They all wanted her in their beds. So did I, but Nick was the only one who'd had her there and that probably wouldn't change.

He looked up at her. "You're surprised that we have hearts?"

She shrugged. "You're surprised that I wouldn't have guessed it?"

The two of them locked eyes and Alex heaved out a breath. "Not now, guys. Let's just get through this."

Another tense minute passed, then Archer flicked her gaze to mine again. "It also makes sense why you were taking the alert level so much more seriously. You knew the system had been upgraded but why did the announcement in town still give people the usual hour?"

My heart plummeted. "It did?"

"Yeah." She frowned. "You didn't know that?"

"No, but there's nothing we can do about it now," Connor said finally, though he was practically vibrating with fury. "We'll have to see what the fallout was once the order's lifted."

This latest realization caught everyone off-guard. Archer slapped her palms down on her thighs and shot up off the sofa.

"And that's about the extent of the terrifying, depressing, shocking and downright devastating information I can handle for one night. If I learn one more thing, my brain's going to explode."

"I agree with Max," I said. "I'll check on Evan and we can talk more in the morning."

No one looked particularly happy, but everyone eventually nodded and went in their separate directions. I looked up at the clock, it was just before midnight now, and a sliver of apprehension rolled through me.

We'd gotten into and out of that lab way too easily. Evan should've been guarded; someone should've checked on him by now and would've seen he wasn't there.

The system of tunnels, as far as we could tell, linked to every house within our neighborhood but didn't lead outside. Maeve and Alex's dad had to know Evan was somewhere inside these gates and they would come for him.

That was the best-case scenario.

The worst-case scenario was that they didn't come only for him but for us all. When they did, we'd better be ready because they wouldn't leave without a fight.

9

ARCHER

"Max," Connor called out from behind me when I hit the staircase, "wait up."

I squeezed my eyes shut. I couldn't take much more tonight. Information overload was a real thing and I was dangerously close to it. I'm so done with doubting everything. So tired of trying to comprehend what's right and what's a lie. I was so sick of hearing about how my parents betrayed everyone. If he stuck into me about them, I wouldn't be held accountable to my actions.

"What is it?" My voice was weary. "I meant it when I said I needed to go to bed."

"I know." He came up beside me, nudging my shoulder with his arm. When I dipped my head back to look at him there was a strange and unfamiliar longing in his eyes. "I won't keep you. I just want to walk with you."

"Why?" I gripped the railing as we headed up the stairs together.

He surprised me by letting out a low chuckle. "I just want to walk you."

"Why?" I repeated, suddenly supremely aware of how large he was by my side and the heat of having him there. I had a momentary flash of wondering what it would feel like to have him on top of me instead of next to me, what those eyes that used to look at me with such love would look like in the heat of the moment.

He released a long breath through his nostrils. "Do I need a reason?"

"Yes." I wasn't trying to be bitchy about it, I was just really fucking confused about absolutely *everything* in my life.

Connor shrugged, sliding his hands into the pockets of his jeans and straightening his thick, colorful arms. "I've missed having your back, is all. Is that a crime?"

"No. I guess not." We hit the landing and he suddenly reached for me, circling his long fingers around my wrist. I was so surprised that I gasped, frowning up at him. "What are you doing?"

Instead of answering me, he tugged me closer and enveloped me in one of his bear hugs. The guy had to be the best hugger in the world, and I'd missed being in his arms more than I could ever describe.

He held me tight against his chest, resting his chin on top of my head. "It killed me to know you were out there all on your own. I went looking for you, you know."

"You did?" He wasn't lying. His voice was completely honest and sincere. I felt him nod.

"Of course I did. Couldn't find you, though. I knew Nick had the P.I. on you, but I didn't want to ask him. It felt like too much of an invasion to your privacy."

"You cared about that?" Nick didn't seem to.

He nodded again. "You and the guys mean everything to me. I'd never do something I thought would hurt you."

"But you did."

His chest expanded on a sharp breath, his hand rubbing my back as his grip on me tightened even more. "I know. We didn't think we had a choice. We were wrong, and we were idiots."

I sighed, but snuggled deeper into his chest. He smelled like spice and cinnamon.

Home.

The thought hit me like a freight train to the chest. "You were, but you aren't the only ones to blame."

"Maybe not, but we carry a lot of it." He dropped a kiss on top of my head. "Don't leave us again, okay? Yell at us, hit us; do whatever you need to do, but let us prove to you that you belong here with us."

"I'll try," I promised, but that was the best I could do. Especially considering everything they didn't even know yet. Fear filled my heart and uncertainty made my stomach flip. *What am I doing?*

I needed to get away from him and I needed to do it right now. "Good night, Con. I'll see you in the morning, okay?"

"Okay." He gave me a final squeeze and then let me go, lifting his hand in a wave as he headed toward his own room.

It came as no surprise that sleep wouldn't come to me after all that. I was so exhausted I could hardly keep my eyes open but, once they were closed, so many awful things swirled through my mind that I had to open them again.

Lying in the darkness of my room, I wondered if I was the only one having trouble drifting off tonight. They'd had most of this information for a long time but it hadn't been an easy night for any of us.

My brain refused to shut out any of the events or revelations of the night. It was like I'd marched into a war I'd had no idea was going on and now I was caught in the crossfire. Along with four boys that I wouldn't be able to live without.

Not again. Not now that I knew they weren't the monsters I'd come to think of them as. Maybe *I* was the monster but I still had time to make it right.

One thing I was certain of was that it'd take all of us to figure this out. All of us to win this war, especially since we didn't even know who the enemy was yet.

Another hour passed, and I was no closer to sleep. Rolling to my side, I switched on my lamp and searched my drawer for a book or something to distract me.

Reading had always been a hobby of mine and there had to be a book in here that would distract me enough that my damn thoughts would switch off. It wasn't a book my fingers hit first, though. It was the slim, solid length of the vibrator.

I paused, not even having remembered it was in there. *An orgasm would be pretty distracting, too.*

Plus, it felt like forever since I'd last had one. Considering I had no idea what we were facing, who knew when I'd get another chance?

It took replacing its battery with the one in the TV remote but I got the sleek thing buzzing in my hand and laid back again. I wasn't feeling the least bit sexy but as I ran its tip up and down the length of my thighs, bare in the cotton shorts I'd put on to sleep in, I felt those parts of me coming alive.

Swiping my tongue along my lips, I closed my eyes and let my imagination run wild. The first place it ran to, much to my dismay but not very surprisingly, was the last time I'd been on this bed with Nick.

It'd been only hours before everything changed, but I didn't focus on that part of the day. I thought about what he'd been doing before those phone calls.

I remembered the feel of his tongue as it ran through my slick folds. I thought about how it felt when he'd sucked my swollen clit into his fiery mouth; about what it might have felt like to have more than one set of hands on me.

My hips arched off the bed and a soft moan spilled out of me. Only, my moan wasn't the only one I heard.

Heart hammering as my eyes flew open, I sat bolt upright in bed. Nick stood in my doorway, his black hair tousled and his top half bare. He wore black sweatpants that did nothing to hide the bulge in them.

He watched me with heavy eyes, his chest rising and falling slightly faster than normal. He had his lower lip between his teeth and a slight flush on his cheeks.

While he'd always been well built, I didn't remember every line on his body being so damn well defined. His abdomen was a delicious series of ridges and valleys, but not in the obnoxious way that would've made him look like a bodybuilder.

Blue eyes latching onto mine, he stalked toward the bed. The mattress dipped when he crawled onto it, not stopping until he was straddling me and could both hear and feel the telltale buzzing that I hadn't stopped.

Another low groan rumbled from his chest. It was the same sound he used to make when he was so turned on that he was half-crazed. And hearing it again made me feel the same way.

"Is it the one I got you?" he bit out, his gaze dark with lust.

I nodded. My cheeks heated, but I refused to let him know I was embarrassed about him catching me red-or purple- handed. "It's not like I carry a vibrator around in my purse just in case of an emergency quarantine situation."

"I couldn't sleep." His voice was rough. "I thought I'd come to see if you'd managed to fall asleep. But now I'd rather you come while I watch."

"Nick," I met his heated eyes and decided to toss caution to the wind. Having his strong, hard body above mine might just be the very oblivion I needed to stop thinking, even if it was only just for tonight. "This doesn't mean anything."

"Yes, it does," he said before sliding one of those muscular arms underneath the covers and around my waist, hauling me closer to him as his other hand caught the side of my neck. "But we don't have to talk about it right now,"

When his lips met mine, I knew I'd made the right decision. It might end up destroying me but it sure as hell shut my brain up.

Nick used to be a good kisser, but now he could've taken gold at the

Olympics. It was a near-dizzying experience, one that took my breath away with the soft but insistent touching of lips and tongues. While it had never happened to me before, it was like his kiss suddenly transported me into a bubble of light where nothing else mattered.

I leaned into his touch and dipped my head back to give him better access; he took it without holding back. I felt his muscles flexing as he moved to get under the covers with me, their powerful strength rippling beneath my palms.

We lay back on the bed with Nick hovering above me. He propped himself up on one elbow and took control of the purple toy in my hand. Almost instantly I started feeling that familiar pressure building between my thighs when he held the light vibrations to my clit.

When Nick locked eyes with me, the pure need I saw drove me over the edge. I didn't even try to fight it, letting the waves of bliss sweep me under as exquisite pleasure spread from my fingers and curled my toes.

I heard him moan out loud right along with me and reached up to bring his head down and crush his lips to mine again. Nick kissed me until the world came back into focus, then rested his forehead against mine.

"I'm going to have to see that again. Often," he said, his breathing labored.

There was so much unsaid between us, so much I still had to know about what they'd been up to. What I had. But all of that could wait.

We might only have this one night together and I wasn't letting it go to waste. Running my fingers through his hair where his head was now buried in the crook of my neck, I spread my legs and hooked one around his hip.

"See it again now, then. I want you, Nick. Always have, always will."

He lifted himself up and pulled his head back to look into my eyes again. "Are you sure?"

I kissed him again, deeper than before. "I've always been sure about you."

It was myself I was unsure of but that would also have to wait. For the rest of the night, all I wanted was to give myself to him and, hopefully, have him remember it tomorrow.

Because tomorrow, when I finally gave them the only secret I'd ever kept from them, all hell would break loose.

Maybe, just maybe, after tonight he'd know that not everything had been a lie.

10

NICK

I woke up with a bang. I might've taken a minute to appreciate the irony of having fallen asleep after one, too, but it wasn't the same kind of bang. That one had been a transcendent experience that felt like it'd left an imprint of Archer on my soul.

The bang I woke up to, however, was one that sounded a hell of a lot like a gunshot. My heart instantly started pounding as I sat up, already moving forward to shield Archer's body with mine.

As I twisted around to search her room while shoving my hand underneath the pillow, I simultaneously saw a figure standing in the door and remembered that we'd fallen asleep in Archer's bed. My gun wasn't here.

But the figure who'd run past the door before backing up wasn't an enemy. It was Alex. He gave the scene in front of him one look before shaking his head.

"Get some fucking clothes on. Both of you," he barked. "We've got company."

"I'm assuming he doesn't mean someone's come over for tea?" Archer said as she reached for her shirt. She slid it over her head, giving me what I knew to be her nervous, scared but still trying to lighten the mood smile, "What do we do?"

"You need to hide. We'll take care of this." I'd already jumped out of bed and as I spoke, the waistband of my sweats snapped into place. "At the back of your closet is a panel that's loose. Behind it is an opening big enough to fit you. Stay there until one of us comes to get you."

"Like hell," she said, her expression fierce and every trace of the smile gone. She ended up dressed at the same time as me then jerked her thumb toward the door. "I'm going with you. Either accept it now or find it out later when I walk into the fight all by myself."

"Fine," I grunted. "There's no time to argue but you stay behind me or one of the others at all times, okay?"

"We'll see how it goes." Her gaze met mine one final time before she took off running after Alex. I muttered a string of curses as I raced out of the room, vowing that no matter what happened, she'd be safe.

Alex, Connor, and Jax were all crouched on the second-story landing, their hideout an alcove in the wall where the staircase curved to the bottom. Alex dropped to his haunches beside Connor, who shoved a gun into his hand and then eyed me.

He sighed when he realized I wasn't carrying either, silently shaking his head as he unclipped a spare from his belt. *Trust Connor to have kitted himself out with enough weapons to stage a small country' coup when he'd only had a minute's notice.*

I heard scuffling downstairs but whoever had fired before seemed to have stopped. Taking the firearm from Connor, I checked out everyone else. They were all fine-- or so I thought until I saw Jax wince and press a hand to his side.

"Did you get hit?"

He pressed his lips into a thin line but he finally nodded. "I was going downstairs to get a glass of water for Evan when they came in. We locked the tunnel up behind us earlier but they definitely came in through the study."

"How bad is the wound?" My pulse, which had already been thrumming with the adrenaline coursing through me, kicked up another notch. Dread pooled in my stomach. I couldn't lose him; I couldn't lose any of them.

Also, if whoever was down there had gotten in through the tunnel when it'd been locked, someone with a key must've let them in. That left very few options as to who was behind it. As far as I knew, only the three of us in my family had any of the keys to anything in this house.

Jax held my gaze for long enough to let me know it was more serious than he wanted the others to realize. The icy tentacles of fear wound their way around my insides but I gave him a nod. "Go to Evan. Patch yourself up as best you can. Keep your weapon on you and stay the fuck safe."

"Got it." Although he was doing his best to hide it, I could see how much of a struggle it was for him to move. *Of course it is, you idiot, he just got shot.*

"Is he going to be okay?" Archer asked as she watched him backing up down the hallway without another word.

I looked right into her gray eyes and did something I'd sworn I wouldn't do to her again. I lied. "Sure. Of course. Jackson's the one with the most first aid training of us all. He'll slap a band-aid on it and keep Evan safe."

Doubt flickered in those gorgeous, stormy eyes but she let it go. "Do we know if Evan said anything yet?"

"No," Alex said, his voice quiet but not quiet enough to hide the tremor in it. "Chances are excellent that he'd just woken up and Jax was going to get him water before he could talk."

"I guess that--"

Archer was cut off by a loud, sing-song voice coming from the base of the stairs. "Come now, children. Nobody needs to get hurt tonight. You took something of ours and we need it back."

"Maeve." I glanced at Archer, who nodded her confirmation. "That's just fucking great."

She rolled her eyes at me before she started standing up. I knew she thought her own aunt wouldn't shoot at her but I also knew a lot more about how unhinged the woman was.

As her head breached the wall keeping us safe, another gunshot rang out. I'd acted just at the right time, grabbing her wrist and yanking her back down so hard she toppled onto me.

Her eyes were wide as she looked up. "That bitch just shot at me."

She must've been in shock because she hadn't kept her voice down. Laughter cackled from downstairs. "I'm not the bitch here, honey. You are. None of you have any idea what you've gotten yourselves caught up in."

"We know a lot more than you think," Alex called out. "Who's with you?"

"Stop this foolishness, Alexander Montgomery. You're coming with me tonight, either at will or by force," his father's commanding voice rang out.

Archer and Alex both paled even more than they had before, but then they glanced at each other for only a second. As if they were both supercharged by just that one look, they gritted their teeth and rallied.

"That's never going to happen, Father," Alex responded, after which another volley of fire broke out.

When it died down, his father spoke again. "That was your only warning, you insolent fucking children. Put down your weapons and come downstairs. Let's talk. This is ridiculous."

"Insolent fucking children?" I laughed, the sound coming out bitter and brittle. "You're the one who sounds like a villain in a kids' show. How about you leave my house and we'll all have a talk with the police once quarantine is over?"

Another laugh filled the air. It sounded so similar to the one I'd just let out that my spine turned to ice. "Please, Nicky. The police aren't going to help you. Nobody is."

"Father. This is a surprise. Tell me, are Stone and Cant also down there?" Revulsion traveled through me. *My own fucking father?*

He chuckled again but I heard the sound of a gun being loaded. "No, those two imbeciles don't have the balls to do what needs to be done to change the world."

"Change the world?" Archer murmured. "What the fuck is he talking about?"

I never got to ask my father the very same question. Maeve yelled something incomprehensible and, the next second, all hell broke loose. I didn't know how many people were down there but shots fired into the wall above us, bits of debris falling down. One of the bullets ricocheted and whizzed right past my head.

My first instinct was to keep Archer safe and that's what I did. Alex and Connor must've had the same thought because we formed a tight circle around her.

Connor ducked forward and fired off a round of shots. They rang out so loudly that my ears buzzed but I didn't care. All that mattered was getting out of this alive.

"We're separated," Alex stated, adjusting his position so he could see me. "We need to get to Jax and Evan."

"We can't back down. There's nowhere for us to go, remember? We can't leave the house," I whispered furiously. "They're between us and the tunnels."

Alex licked his lips, his eyes darting between mine until he nodded. "They are, but we know this house even better than they do. I don't think your Dad has slept here one night in the last five years. Do you think he remembers about--"

"The staircase in the back?" I questioned, understanding what he was referring to. "I don't know, but it's a better option than trying to get down there using this one."

"Someone has to distract them," Connor grunted. "Or they'll know we've gone."

He popped off two more shots, grim determination in his eyes when they met mine over the top of Archer's head. "Go. I'll meet you down there."

"We'll barricade the entrance once we've made it into the tunnel. As far as I know, that's the only way into the tunnels from this house. They'll be stuck here long enough to give us a chance to get away. Into one of the other houses for now, at the very least."

"Look for something to use as a barricade once you get to the study," Connor agreed.

Archer tried arguing but Connor gave her a firm shake of his head. "This is the only way. Go get Jax and Evan then get the hell down there."

"I could stay with you," I offered, but he shook his head again.

"You need to stay with them. Alex is useless with a gun, Archer doesn't even have one, Jax is injured and Evan's been tortured. This is the only way."

I gave him a long look, but eventually agreed. "Okay. We'll wait for you before we barricade the entryway."

Connor nodded but he didn't seem convinced he'd be meeting us there. We couldn't argue about it, though. The shots were coming in fast and heavy again, some of them now coming from on top of the actual staircase.

The assholes were closing in on us and I had to get them out of here. If I needed to, I'd come back to get Connor. Fuck him, we weren't leaving him behind.

The bullets kept coming, as did the shouts of glee from Archer's crazy aunt. Given everything we'd learned, I wouldn't be surprised to find out she'd set up her own brother and his wife all those years ago.

We'd get to the truth, though. We were closer than we'd ever been before, but I had a feeling this was only just the beginning. To get to the end, we needed to get out alive first.

A screaming match started up below. The deep voices of our fathers' clashed with Maeve's. All I could make out above the fray was my father yelling, "This is fucking insane. Stop it now."

The gunfire didn't stop, and neither did I.

Archer gave Connor a hug, brushing a kiss to his cheek. She whispered something to him and he nodded at her with a soft smile playing on his lips. My heart did something strange at the sight of them together but I ignored it-- for now.

"Come on," Alex whispered. "We're running out of time."

"I'll bring up the rear." I cradled Archer's hand and put her between me and Alex. "Let's go."

Hugging the wall, we moved away from Connor. Just before we slipped out of sight, I looked back at my friend. A steely expression had crept onto his features and he'd wiped the slate clean of all emotion.

Archer didn't know but we'd all done a ton of training while preparing for whatever was coming. Connor was an excellent marksman if anyone could get out of this alive, it was him.

He dropped to his stomach and crept closer to the top of the staircase. The next moment, his return fire rang out again and I heard at least one thud as one of his bullets hit its mark.

We didn't stop, though, moving as fast as we could to the guest room where Evan and Jax were waiting. Archer took the lead once we'd turned the corner, running at a full sprint to their door.

She didn't even really stop running when she reached it, turning the knob and shoving at it with her shoulder as she barreled inside. Alex and I were right on her heels but she came to an abrupt stop just as she entered the room.

When I flew in after her just a moment later, I realized why. Evan was standing up with Jax's gun in his hand. Our friend kneeled at his feet, his shirt now soaked through with blood and his skin an unhealthy gray. His forehead and cheekbones were shiny and there was a ring of sweat around the collar of his shirt.

Evan looked deranged; his brown eyes were flat, his brunet hair plastered down in places and pointing straight up in others. He smiled but Jax must've gotten in a hit before he went down because Evan had blood staining his teeth and a trickle of it running from his swollen nose.

"You guys are so fucking stupid." He coughed, but the gun in his hands remained stable and aimed right between Jackson's eyes. "I volunteered to be down there." I swore my heart stopped beating. We'd planned for just about every possibility, but this hadn't been one of them. Evan smirked at me, blood pooling at the seam of his lips. "You should've let things be, Kent."

The gun suddenly trained on Archer. "But you just couldn't let this one little bitch go, could you?"

None of us moved. His finger was on the trigger and it didn't take a genius to figure out that, as battered and bruised as he was, he could kill Archer before any of us reached him.

"It was all perfectly planned, assholes," he gloated. "All you had to do was to be good little boys and let her go."

"Archer has nothing to do with this," I said, moving slowly to her side.

Evan's eyes widened and he let out a god-awful laugh. "That's where you're wrong. She had everything to do with this, didn't you, sweetheart?"

Sweetheart? My blood froze in my veins and I felt Alex stiffen beside me.

Archer turned to face me, her eyes dark with regret. But she nodded and walked backward toward the asshole.

"I'm sorry, Nick. I didn't have a choice." There was a storm of emotion building up in her, I could practically see it happening but I had no idea why.

"We trusted you," Jax grunted, pain lacing every syllable.

Archer looked down at him. "Yeah, I trusted you once, too. Look how well that turned out for me."

With that, she turned her gaze on Evan and screwed her eyes shut. "You got what we agreed to. Now let them go."

"Let them go?" Evan lowered his chin and frowned at her. "But sweetheart, the party's just getting started. We have so much more in store for them."

Archer studied him for a minute before she shrugged and pulled out a small silver handgun from God only knew where. Without hesitating for a second, she swung it up and took aim at his chest. Before I could even begin to make sense of what was happening, a single shot rang out.

Both of them dropped to the floor.

I had no idea what was happening but something was off. Archer had been honest with us, I believed it with everything I had. Whatever *this* was, it wasn't what it looked like. There had to be an explanation.

Before I could find out what it was, though, I still needed to get all of us out of here alive.

With no further thought, I rushed to her side and dropped to my knees. "Come on, baby. Live. Breathe. Just stay with me, okay? I'm not losing you again."

Jax let out a cry beside me, collapsing as well. Alex knelt down between the two of them, stone cold terror in his eyes when he lifted them to mine. "It's too late, Nick. We've lost her."

TO BE CONTINUED...

ABOUT CHARLIE JULES

Charlie is a writer of all things romance. She's not fussy. When the characters speak, she listens. A lover of coffee, wine, chocolate and magic. Mother of one with the personality of five and wife of one incredible human being.

Join Charlie's Readers Facebook Group at
www.facebook.com/groups/202990620928884/

facebook.com/charlie.jules.501
instagram.com/charliejulesauthor

YOU MAKE ME SICK

BY J. C. SMOAK

A one-night stand.
Two lies.
Three years apart.

SAOIRSE

In college, we were inseparable. He was my best friend, but I was secretly in love with him.

Our connection was so strong, I thought it would carry us beyond school all the way to our new careers in Europe.

The night before our flight, passion took our relationship to a new level. It was amazing, beautiful, earth shattering.

Then he disappeared.

FINN

In college, we were inseparable. She was my best friend, but I was secretly in love with her.

I never wanted to be away from her and it looked like I'd never have to be. New jobs in a new country but still the same old us.

I thought we'd taken a step that would finally take us out of the friend-zone and bring us together for good. That night was mind-blowing but, the next morning, I made a huge mistake. And the cost? Her.

She never spoke to me again.

Now, I have one shot to fix what I broke.

Because I won't live without her.

I can't.

I'm hers. It's time she knew it.

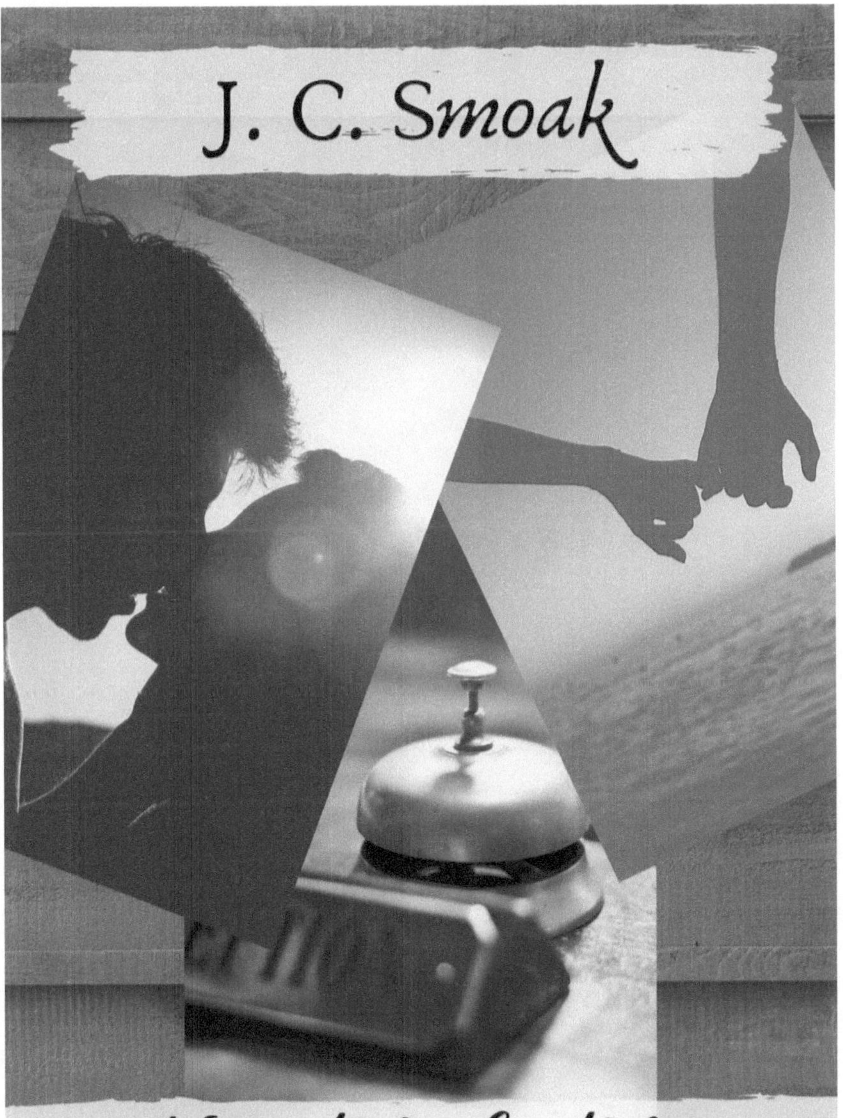

You Make Me Sick

To Jem De La-La and Jean Bicbie, thank you for talking me through this process and offering your help when I needed someone to hold my hand. You made me believe this was worth a shot.

To Charlie Jules, thank you for being an amazing critique partner who gave me so much praise while also being brutally honest. You gave me courage.

To my husband, thank you for laughing when I'm freaking out. In your own weird way, you always let me know that it's ok to be scared. Your unshakable faith in me is probably misplaced but always appreciated. Ich liebe dich.

PROLOGUE

Three years ago...

SAOIRSE

Get on the plane, Saoirse.

As I read the text from my *best friend* again, I struggled to accept what I knew to be the truth. The empty airplane seat beside me was hard to deny and a giant slap in the face. How could I have read the situation so wrong? He was supposed to be on this plane with me, flying off to a new adventure together. Instead, I was alone.

We'd had a beautiful night together, a night I thought would grow our friendship into something more. It was like breathing after years of holding my breath, finally being able to show my true feelings for him after years of pretending he was just my friend. Now, I felt like I couldn't breathe at all.

"Miss? All electronics need to be turned off during the flight."

I glanced up at the flight attendant and watched as her expression changed from professionalism to pity. Obviously, I wasn't hiding my pain as well as I would've hoped.

I tried to draw a breath and responded with a nearly unintelligible, "Sorry, I'll turn it off."

Her eyes quickly glanced from mine to the empty seat beside me and back, and I felt a heavy dose of humiliation join with the heartbreak ripping me apart from the inside out. I opened my mouth to attempt an explanation but there was nothing to say. How could I possibly explain something I didn't even understand?

She placed her hand on mine, made sure I was making eye contact with her and said, "If he's not here with you, you're probably better off."

I tried to swallow past the lump in my throat so I could say... what? What could I say? I'm sure my eyes were pleading with her to make it better, make it hurt less, help me breathe, something. *Give me something that'll make it all stop before I lose my mind.*

All she could give me was a gentle, "It won't hurt forever."

I watched her walk away, trying to accept her words but it just didn't seem possible. This pain tearing through me and leaving nothing in its path was a forever pain. It wasn't even pain, it was devastation. Cataclysmic devastation.

I felt a sob making its way up my throat and I bit my fist to contain it. I managed to mostly silence it but I couldn't stop the tears. I looked out the window of the plane, letting them fall and praying that I'd see him running across the tarmac to stop the plane or something. But this wasn't a fairy tale and, as much as I wanted to push back against it, I had to come to terms with reality.

Best friends for years have a night of passion and the result was an empty seat, an empty promise and an empty heart.

Alone.

1

SAOIRSE

I have never been so humiliated in my life. It was supposed to be a guest spot in a conference to speak about the proper handling techniques for unstable chemical compounds. Twenty minutes tops and I should've been on my way back home where I didn't need to be smart in front of a hundred strangers. Instead, it ended up being over an hour of being attacked by the ghost of bad decisions past.

"Asshole. The nerve of that guy." I muttered while shoving clothes into my suitcase harder than needed. "He thinks he can just show up after three years and completely undermine my intelligence? Why? What the hell did I ever do to deserve this? Is it really so much to ask to just be left alone?" My dog, Moose, looked at me from the bed like I was wasting his time before repositioning himself to face away from me. *Thanks for the support buddy*.

The ringing of my phone interrupted my would-be rant. I had to dig through the clothes covering the bed to find it, before answering with a rather unpleasant, "*What?*" I glanced at the adjoining door in my room, afraid I was being too loud. Adjoining doors in hotel rooms always freaked me out.

"Well, I guess I don't need to ask how the conference went." The sarcastic voice of my best friend was a welcome comfort. We'd been friends since kindergarten.

"Jameson," I said on a relief filled sigh. I took a deep breath, trying to calm down so I wouldn't take my shit out on him. "I don't even know where to start. You would not *believe* what happened." One more deep breath, "Finn's here."

"McAllister? McAllister's there?" Jameson sounded as shocked as I was when Finn first stood up in the crowd. "As in '*holy shit, Jameson, why couldn't I keep my legs closed and not ruin my friendship with him?*' That guy?"

Cringe, his imitation was both impressive and horrible. "Thank you, Jameson! I really needed the reminder of my single act of incredible stupidity." *So damn humiliating.*

"Single act? I thought it was multiple times that night." Annoyed, I growled to get him back on track. "Sorry. I'm guessing this isn't just a random observation, something happened?"

"He was in the audience at the conference and he basically tore apart all my research without even letting me explain it. Every time I tried to, he'd just cut me off and make me look like I didn't know what I was talking about." I was getting more and more upset the more I explained. "First, he asked for my credentials, like they weren't on the damn sign outside of the auditorium, then he asked how old I was and how long I'd been working in my field, as if I'm too young to be good at my job or something. And after that humiliating run-through, he asked questions that were completely random about every single one of my points that I looked like I hadn't done my research." *Deep breaths, don't cry.* "After all this time, why would he show up? Why did it have to be at the moment I'm finally in a position to gain some respect from the scientific community? Explain this to me!"

"Whoa, Saoirse, chill chica. You'll blow a blood vessel." He had a point. "Maybe he just really wanted to understand your research, maybe that's why he asked so many questions. I mean, he graduated second in your class, and we both know who was first."

Now that *did* make me feel better. "You're right. I need to calm down and just forget about that jackass; I have more important things to focus on. Like getting Moose home before he decides we're staying in the hotel forever. He's become quite attached to the staff here always giving him treats." With the thought of home, I felt the last of my tension melt away.

"Born to be a diva, that boy. Let me know when you're on your way and I'll meet you at your place with Chinese food. Drive safe."

"Sounds good, see you soon." The second I ended the call, there was a knock at the door. "Coming."

Upon opening the door, my calm vanished into thin air. Standing in front of me was a six foot five, blond haired, blue eyed Finn McAlister. *Damn, why does he have to be so good looking?*

"I don't have time for this." I swung the door shut, hard, and spun away. The resulting thud and pained groan were satisfying; a little petty, but I wasn't going to apologize. I had no idea which part of him it connected with, but I hoped it hurt. "What do you want? Humiliating me wasn't enough for you?"

"Humiliating you? How do you figure?" He'd followed me into the bedroom, as if he weren't completely invading my space. "Moosey!" *Jesus.* His shout scared the hell out of me as Moose jumped up and barked, excited to see him. *Infuriating.*

"Moose." My whispered correction went unnoticed as Finn dove onto the bed to wrestle with my traitorous Pitbull. The same bed covered in my bras and panties. *Kill me now.* "What do you want?"

He continued playing with Moose as if I hadn't spoken and I was reminded of how adorable they'd been when Finn brought home a puppy as a house-warming gift for me. As much as I didn't want to admit it, their love for each other had always been kind of beautiful. Which is exactly why I needed to get him out of here and away from me, I didn't need Moose and I wanting to keep him around. "Hello? Can you tell me what the fuck you're doing here, or do I need to call security to get rid of you?"

"What would you even tell security? 'Please come save me from the hot guy in my bed playing with my dog?' I'm not sure that's reason enough for them to come running." As Finn made himself comfortable on my bed and Moose made himself comfortable on Finn's chest, he finally seemed to realize what he was laying on. "Now wait a damn minute." Excitement filled his expression as he grabbed a piece of black lace near his head. "What's this? A thong? Are you wearing something like this right now?"

I felt myself blush under his scrutiny and the intrigue in his eyes only made my embarrassment worse. "Oh-ho-ho, she is. Scandalous. Can I see?"

"No, you cannot." I tried to grab the panties from him, but his reflexes were impressively quick for someone with a sixty-pound dog on his chest.

I huffed, exasperated. "You're not that hot." At that point I abandoned my carefully planned out packing in favour of stuffing my clothes in my bag as quickly as possible. "And you still haven't told me what you're doing here."

"Oh..." He was interrupted by what sounded like the room door opening followed by an insistent knock. He raised his eyebrow and sent me an accusatory look, which I didn't appreciate.

"What? I don't know who it is. Everyone I know in this entire hotel is in this room." I shot him a glare on my way to the door and hoped it communicated to him that I was not happy about this detail. When I grabbed the knob to pull open the door, I almost dislocated my shoulder because it didn't move at all. "What the hell?" I tried again and the handle turned but the door still wouldn't move. "I'm sorry, the door won't open," I called out. "Who is it?"

"Hotel Security."

FINN

Did I think she would show me the cock-hardening thong she was wearing? No, but I couldn't stop myself from asking. This girl had the ability to make me stupid. She was gorgeous and brilliant and funny and amazing - it was all I could do to breathe around her, let alone think. As demonstrated by the fact that I'd made a complete ass of myself at the conference because I couldn't stop asking her questions just to hear her talk a little more.

With the knock at the door, I realized I'd probably gone a bit too far. I couldn't regret anything that got me just a little closer to her though, especially when it was the most progress I'd made with her in three whole years. I had to do it.

"Hotel Security? What are they doing here?" I asked, but I knew exactly why they were there. I felt like a tool for lying to her, but a guy had to do what a guy had to do. *Especially one as desperate as me.*

"What am I, a mind reader? How the fuck would I know what they want?" She was so sexy when she was mad... or happy or sad or... yeah, she was just sexy. When emotion lit those beautiful green eyes and added that stubborn tilt to her chin, it took her from the raven-haired beauty she always was to a complete knock out.

"I'm sorry, ma'am, but I'm going to need you and Dr. McAllister to stay in your room until further notice," came the very official sounding voice from the hall.

"What? Is something wrong? Did something happen?"

"I'm sorry but I'm not at liberty to say." Yeah, no way was she going to just let that go. I felt a little ashamed for enjoying this so much.

The look on her face was pure indignation as she planted her hands on her hips, ready for battle. "Well, maybe you should find someone who *is* at liberty to say. *Now*!" Her tone made it clear that the door wouldn't protect the poor security guard on the other side; I wouldn't be surprised if he'd just pissed his pants. I loved her voice, so sultry and powerful, but people tended to focus on the intensity with which she spoke and ended up thinking she was bitchy. So passionate. *Swoon.*

I snorted at my own ridiculousness. "Wow Finn, why don't you just grow a vagina already."

"What?" She didn't even spare me a glance, still staring daggers at the door waiting for a response from someone in charge.

Oops, I needed to keep my obsession inside my head and try to only let intelligent thoughts come out of my mouth. Here it goes... "You are so hot when you're bossy." *Congratulations; still a tool.*

The look on her face when she looked back at me was so telling, she didn't even need to speak her next words. "Are you drunk or something?"

I was saved from responding by the security guard's voice coming through the door. "Dr. Black?"

Saoirse jumped and spun back to face the door. "Yes! Can you please tell me what's going on? I can't stay locked in here with him, I need to get home."

"I'm sorry for the inconvenience, Dr. Black. As I understand it, there may have been some kind of contamination and you need to remain isolated until further notice. They're running tests to find out for sure but, until then, they've asked us to provide a place to help limit his exposure to civilians." *Wow, that was very official sounding.*

Saoirse gave me a suspicious look over her shoulder. *Maybe not official enough.* "What kind of contamination?" She never broke eye contact with me while she waited for an answer.

"I'm sorry, ma'am, but I'm not at liberty to say." *Yikes, she wouldn't like that.*

Still with the heavy eye contact, she narrowed her eyes at me and ground her teeth in frustration. "Again? Where's the person who *can* tell me something?" she snarled through the door.

"Um... I've asked the manager to come speak with you but she's incredibly busy so it could take a while." There was a noticeable tremble in his voice.

Saoirse let out a closed lipped scream and stomped her foot. "You're joking, right?"

"N-no ma'am. She's asked that you be patient and stay in your room. As soon as we have more information, someone will come update you." *Poor guy.*

"Come on, Saoirse, give the guy a break. You know how this works and there's nothing he can do to change it. Stop scaring the hard-working security guard." I laughed at the glare she shot my way for defending the innocent dude on the other side of the door. After all, this whole thing was my fault.

She dropped the glare from her face and raised her eyes to the ceiling as if she were in deep contemplation. "You know what, you're right. I shouldn't be taking my anger out on him, I should be taking it out on you. I should've known that you showing up here would cause trouble."

Guilty. "Look, we're stuck here for a while so we may as well get comfortable." I patted the bed beside me in invitation and, for a second, she looked almost tempted.

She flinched and shook her head, narrowing her eyes at me again. "I may be stuck here but I definitely won't be getting comfortable with *you.*"

Saoirse crossed her arms and spun back to face the door. She tapped her foot in aggravation for a minute before taking a deep breath and nodding her head in acceptance. *Game on.*

2

SAOIRSE

I was wondering what cruel twist of fate put me face to face with him after three years of successful avoidance and it turned out I would have to keep wondering since no one would tell me anything. It seemed like nobody even knew what the hell was going on and I needed answers. Contamination, he'd said. *So vague.*

Finn seemed perfectly fine with being locked up in here for however long it took and I had no idea how to deal with him, so I just stood staring at the door. Praying for a miracle, or a lightning bolt. Anything that would put some distance between Finn and I. *Maybe a tornado to take me away from this nightmare; even with the wicked witch, Oz has got to be better than this.* "If there was an earthquake, they'd have to evacuate us and I could just make a run for it as soon as we got outside."

"Yeah but they'd make you leave all your shit behind," Finn said matter-of-factly.

I jumped and spun to face my doom, hoping the fear of being stuck with him wasn't showing on my face. "Things can be replaced, sanity on the other hand..."

He chuckled knowingly, testing my patience. "Tell me about it; sanity is probably the hardest thing to regain once you've lost it. Three years and I still haven't regained mine." *Ignoring that and moving on.*

"I don't have time for this. I need to go home and get ready for work on

Monday; I can't be stuck in a hotel room. Especially not with *you.*" If my emphasis on that word hadn't gotten the point across, hopefully my overly-dramatic hand gesture had.

"Whoa, what's wrong with me?" He gave me a hurt look before turning his attention to Moose as if my dog knew what my problem with him was.

Deep breaths. I knew I was stuck with him for the foreseeable future because I wasn't about to climb out the window and I obviously couldn't convince the hotel staff to let me out, so there was no point in losing my shit. "Like I said, I don't have time for this."

I grabbed my phone and headed for the only privacy I was going to get: the bathroom. I needed someone to talk me down off the ledge I was on before I did something stupid like crying over the one-night stand that pulled a Houdini the morning after.

The phone barely rang before Jameson picked up. "Miss me already? Always so fucking clingy."

As soon as I heard his voice, I started to freak out. There's something about a trusted person that just brings walls down without permission. "I don't have the patience for you to be a smart-ass right now, Jamie. I'm literally locked in my fucking hotel room with fucking Finn fucking McAllister and I have no fucking clue what the hell I'm supposed to do."

His silence was like a flatline; like I'd killed his internal smart-ass with one statement. He was quiet so long I was actually starting to worry. I'd just opened my mouth to yell at him when he finally said, "What do you mean you're *locked* in your hotel room?"

"Yeah, locked in my fucking hotel room." I hoped my exacerbation made it obvious that I was pissed. I was really trying to hold on to anything that would keep me from crying and I wasn't above holding a grudge.

He laughed like an excited kid at Disneyland, he obviously found my predicament hilarious. "You're actually locked up with him? Man, that's some karma right there." *Asshole. My best friend should be supporting me because he's* MY *best friend.*

The clearing of my throat was loud and aggravated. "Excuse me, can you focus please? You need to call the hotel and tell them there's been an emergency and they need to let me out."

"Why would I do that?"

I flopped down onto the edge of the bathtub in despair. "Because I can't be trapped here with him." I needed him to wake the fuck up and smell the disaster.

"Why can't you be trapped with him?" Jameson asked slowly, as if he really didn't understand. "I know you don't want to be but it sounds like you don't have a choice. Why don't you just try to make the best of the situation?" *Oh, he's not helping at all.*

I couldn't believe I had to explain this to him just because he was being a douche and pretending he didn't remember why I didn't want to be near Finn. "For fuck's sake. I can't be locked up with him because I don't want anything to do with him, Jamie."

"Well that's true. Why is that, again?"

"Jesus, are you trying to make me blow a gasket?" His silence was answer enough. "Fine. I guess I just would've preferred to talk to him in a more controlled way, where I could walk away if I felt I had to. I would've talked to him eventually but not like this."

Jameson snorted so loud I had to pull the phone away from my ear. "You expect me to believe that?" This time it was *my* silence that answered *his* question. "*I've* talked to him more than you have in the last three years and he's not even my friend."

"Wait, you talked to him? When? Why? How could you talk to him after what happened?"

"I didn't really have much of a choice, Saoirse. He's basically the anti-Waldo, he's everywhere! He calls, texts, shows up at my gym, my house. I couldn't avoid him." He begged for understanding.

I facepalmed so hard, it actually hurt but I couldn't believe this was the first time I was hearing about this. "Why didn't you tell me?"

"How? You made it pretty clear that you didn't ever want to hear his name again."

He had a point. As childish as it seemed, I was so in love with him that, after he disappeared on me, it just hurt too much to think about him. I was humiliated and crushed, I couldn't move past it so I shoved it deep into the back of my mind and pretended he didn't exist. Being thousands of miles away helped a bit. "Why was he doing that?" My voice was whisper-quiet; I could barely breathe with this new information.

"What do you mean *was*? He was at my house yesterday." At that, I breathed in so hard that I promptly started choking on my saliva. *Classy*. "Soarsh, you ok?"

When my coughing settled down, I was finally able to speak. "Ok, I really need you to start explaining right now."

"Nope. Sorry, I'm not getting involved. It's time for you guys to figure this shit out; I'm now Switzerland. Call me later. Love you, bye."

"Jameson, no. You can't just leave m..." The click on the other end of the line may as well have been the final nail in my coffin. *Now what?*

FINN

Well, it seemed like Saoirse was all caught up and now knew how much of a psycho I'd been, following Jameson around just to get updates on her. I wasn't entirely sure how to navigate our situation but at least we were face to face for the first time in three years; hopefully we'd figure out the rest together. I just had to wait for her to come out of the damn bathroom and, for the first time in a long time, I was actually really nervous.

She only hid for about five minutes after the end of her phone call but it felt like an eternity and the only thing that kept me on planet earth was playing with Moose. I really had missed him; almost as much as I'd missed Saoirse. "You get everything figured out?" I couldn't help poking the bear; she really was gorgeous when she was mad.

Her glare was like an electric shock that shot through my whole body. "As a matter of fact, I didn't figure anything out. I don't understand any of this and I'm not sure I want to." She ran both her hands through her gorgeous black hair and slowly spun in a circle before coming to a stop facing away from me and staring at the ceiling like she was praying for patience. "Do you want to tell me why you've been stalking Jameson?"

"Ah yes, the very not short Mr. Short."

"Wow, you really do have an issue with the fact that he's an inch taller than you, eh?" I could hear the smirk in her voice.

"Whatever, I'm taller laying down." her face when she turned towards me was half *what the fuck is wrong with you* and half glaring disapproval. "What? You know it's true."

Her blush was instant and sexy. "How exactly would I know that?"

"Do you need a reminder?" I reached for my pants.

She stormed forward to stop me. "No, I don't need a reminder, you pervert. Would you please take this seriously for once?"

"You mean you haven't seen Jameson naked? I thought you guys had some kind of thing going on at some point." If I were being honest, I knew they'd never been together but it's called irrational jealousy for a reason.

She growled at me again, which I was really starting to like. "You're insufferable." I was just about to defend myself when, with surprising force, she shoved me off the bed. My ass hit the floor so hard, the wind was knocked out of me because I wasn't expecting her to be that strong or that aggressive. "So, why have you been stalking him?"

I didn't bother moving from my position on my back on the floor.

"Maybe because, over the last three years, you wouldn't talk to me and if I wanted to find out if you were alive, I had to be pushy." Hopefully my tone made it clear that I was extremely unimpressed with her for that.

"Why would you even care?"

That made me sit straight up like an old-fashioned horror movie. "What the hell is that supposed to mean?" The look of disbelief on my face must've been comical.

She was grabbing armfuls of clothes and lacy underthings and stuffing it all into her bag without a care for organization. "It means that if you cared about me, you wouldn't have disappeared. It means that if you cared how I was doing, you would've been on that plane." Her voice was gaining volume the more she talked. "It means that if you cared about my feelings, you would've been with me for those three years and I wouldn't have been all alone, in a foreign country, at a job you were supposed to be at with me!" With that last statement, she slammed her suitcase shut and threw it on the ground. She was breathing heavily and looking at me like she wanted me to fix it but couldn't stand the idea of hope. Her beautiful green eyes were a horrible combination of lost and crushed, drowning in a quickly rising sea of tears. "*If* you cared, we would've been together."

With that, she stormed back to the bathroom and I had a feeling I wouldn't be seeing her for a while. I could live with that because I'd been rocked to the core by her words and I thought it was going to take some time to recover.

I knew she was mad at me, but what I'd heard in her voice and seen in her eyes was a shock after three years. I loved her, I missed her and it hurt to be without her, but it never occurred to me until that moment how much I could hurt her; *had* hurt her. Her pain was so palpable it lingered in the air like acrid smoke, making it hard for me to breathe or even see. It was destruction, betrayal, disenchantment, abandonment and a slew of other soul-deep emotions that I was struggling to grasp. What I'd just experienced was beyond anything I could've imagined and I felt, in that moment, like the biggest asshole that ever lived.

And there I was, locking her in a room with the person who'd caused all that pain so I could explain... what? What could I explain that would make it better? What could I say that would change anything for her? The more I thought about it, the more the truth became clear; nothing. There was nothing I could do except try to fix what I'd broken and move forward with her.

Hopefully she'd let me.

3

SAOIRSE

What a disaster. I'd completely lost my shit out there and let him see everything. I hadn't meant to; I never wanted him to know how much power he had over me. And now he did.

I started running a bath because I really needed some calm. "When all else fails, take a bath." My mother's words were perfect in that moment because everything felt like it was failing. I felt like there was no way to survive this, like I wouldn't be leaving my hotel room the same person I was when I first stepped into it and I didn't know what to do with that. I was trapped in a situation where I had no control and, if what had happened with Finn was any indication, I didn't have the weapons required for this fight. And this was going to be a fight; for strength, for truth, for healing and hopefully for closure because I needed to be free of this.

I never seemed to have the weapons required for dealing with Finn.

As I tried to calm down in the bath, I practiced a meditation breathing technique I'd learned. It consisted of breathing in for a count of three Mississippi, holding for three Mississippi and exhaling for three Mississippi. The thing I didn't consider when doing this was the release of emotion that usually accompanied the technique and, in no time, I found myself crying. I was a giant mess.

I realized in that moment that I'd had a lot of shit bottled up and, being face to face with Finn again, I couldn't hold it in anymore. The walls were coming down hard and fast and not with any kind of finesse or class at all. "Get your shit together, Saoirse. You need to face this and move forward." *No more hiding.*

After drying off and washing my tear streaked face, I wrapped myself in the hotel robe and left the bathroom with every intention of faking it until I made it. I only made it one step out the door before I completely forgot about my decision to woman up.

Finn was sitting on the couch with a spread of amazing looking food and alcohol in front of him. I had no idea where any of it came from. "Peace offering for a temporary ceasefire?"

He looked at me pleadingly, so I decided to take pity on him. "For now." Not too much pity; this wasn't a charity, after all.

"I'll take it. I wasn't sure what would get me into your good graces better; cheesecake or jalapeno poppers, so I got you both and a bunch of other stuff I remember you liking."

"Yes to all of that and I'll decide on the status of my good graces later." I grabbed a piece of cheesecake and planted my ass in the chair across from him. "So, how are you? What have you been doing with your life for the last three years?" I steered clear of the topic of his disappearance.

"I've actually been working at our university; teaching is my passion now and I still get to do research. It's been really rewarding, helping shape the minds of the future and really being challenged by some of those minds. I'm amazed at how much I learn when I'm supposed to be doing the teaching. Maybe that means I suck at my job or something." He chuckled and averted his eyes, which told me he was genuinely concerned about being a good teacher.

"Are you kidding? I wouldn't have gotten through our third year if it weren't for you; I don't think you could be a bad teacher if you tried. You're so smart and you have a way of explaining things that makes sense even when nothing does."

The look he gave me was grateful and his exhale, one of relief. "Thank you, Saoirse. I don't know how I've survived the last three years without you constantly boosting my ego."

A surprised laugh bubbled out of me and, just like that, we were right back to that easy friendship that got me through university and so much more. "Fair point. There really aren't many people in the world who know that the egomaniac you portray is a mask. You're secretly a scared little girl on the inside."

"Hey!" He threw a jalapeno popper at me and I caught it in my mouth.

I gave him a closed mouth smile before chewing and swallowing the popper. "Ew, jalapeno poppers and cheese cake do not mix. Bad combination."

"I can't believe you can still do that."

I winked at him. "Product of a misspent university education."

He returned my wink. "Oh, believe me, I remember. So many damn parties. You probably still hold the record for the only undefeated beer pong champion of all time. Such a party girl."

"What else was I supposed to do? I don't like beer so I had to make sure I drank as little of it as possible." I knew what he was going to say next; same as every other time we had this conversation.

He smiled so big that I could literally see all of his pearly whites and said, "How about pick a different party game to perfect?"

I rolled my eyes at him. "Yeah, yeah. You know, you better stop calling me a party girl or I'm going to start telling people about the pizza and the cop car." I gave him a pointed look.

"That wasn't me."

I smirked at him. "You might not have stolen the pizza out of the delivery driver's car but it was your idea." He popped a grape in his mouth and gave a nonchalant shrug, but the slight pinking of his cheeks betrayed him. "And I know it was your idea to tip the cop car over while the cops were interviewing everyone who hadn't run away about the missing pizza."

"How do you know that?"

I gave a very unladylike snort. "Oh, come on, Finn. You might have the surfer name and looks with your blond hair and blue eyes, but you're from Alberta. I can actually imagine your voice in my head saying something stupid like '*trust me, guys, pig tipping's probably easier than cow tipping.*'"

He cleared his throat and declined to respond to my assessment, but the mischief in his eyes showed how hilarious he still thought it was. "*Anyway*, it was a wonder we graduated at all with you dragging me to every campus party you could find. I still can't figure out how you kept your grades up when you went to half of our classes barely functioning from lack of sleep and being hungover."

"I already told you; I had a good influence. Pig tipping aside." I gave him an exaggerated wink. "Now, why don't you make me a Caesar." I batted my eyelashes at him like the retarded cartoon princess that I was not. "And don't forget..."

"Lots of vodka, no ice, extra pickled beans and extra salt. Stop treating me like an amateur, I spent years as your personal bartender; I couldn't forget this shit if I tried." His tone made it clear that my need to remind him was misplaced, but the affection in his eyes told me that he had no intention of trying to forget.

FINN

She seemed to be relaxing a bit in my presence and I was grateful. I didn't want her to be uncomfortable; a fact that may have been less than clear since I'd locked her in a room with me against her will. *Semantics.*

After mixing her third drink in quick succession, Saoirse shifted drinking speeds to a slightly more respectable rate and threw her legs over the arm of the chair, making herself comfortable. I'd kept her entertained with stories about students blowing up beakers and graduated cylinders, which explained my new scars; one above my right eyebrow, one centered just above my chin and one on the upper part of my left ear. "In the movies, they never mention the flying broken glass when someone blows something up in chemistry class."

"Probably because they figure it should be obvious." Her shoulders shook with silent laughter and the gleam in her eyes was mocking.

I knew that no matter how much I pleaded with her for understanding, she was never going to let me off the hook for not ducking when something exploded in my classroom. "Come on, you can't tell me that's never happened to you before; where something happens and you just don't react in the way that should be obvious."

She gave me a bewildered look. "*Three times,* Finn?"

Shit, I'm never going to live this down. "Four."

"What?" Her expression changed to one of disbelief, her chin lowering as her eyes widened and searched my face. "I only see three new scars on that handsome face of yours. Where's the fourth and how'd you get it?"

I'd never understand why I thought telling her all this was a good idea. "It's not on my face and that's all I'm saying."

"Oh no, sir. You can't tease me like that, we have rules."

Never thought I'd regret our drunken rule making. "The Rules of Truth and Friendship for True Friends. I can't believe you remember that."

"Of course I do." A hint of sadness entered her eyes. "The rules state that if we start telling each other something, we have to finish." Though she tried to control it, with each word of that sentence her voice got quieter; as if someone was turning her volume down.

The sadness didn't leave her eyes and I could see that it was dragging her down; I knew I had to do something to bring her back so I told the truth. "It's on my left ass cheek."

Her face filled with excitement and she sat back in her chair again as my face flushed with embarrassment. "Oh, I can't wait to hear this. *Please*, do explain, Dr. McAllister."

Mortified. "I was on my way to my classroom to check on some students who were working on a project and there was an explosion that shattered the window in the classroom door as I was about to go in."

"Wait, I'm confused. How did you get a scar on your ass if you were about to walk into the classroom?"

She just couldn't let it go. "I dropped some tests I'd been grading and when I turned to pick them up..." I couldn't get the rest out and, based on the quickly changing shade of her face, I figured I didn't have to.

Just as her face changed from red to purple, a sound escaped her that was somewhere between a rapidly deflating balloon and the sound Moose made the first time he met a porcupine. Her whole body shook in the gray hotel robe that was driving me crazy and she finally burst out laughing. "And a piece of glass ended up in your ass?" She spoke between heaving breaths.

"Cheek! A piece of glass ended up in my ass *cheek*, don't make it sound gross." That didn't stop the laughing at all; it seemed the distinction made no difference to how hilarious she found my pain and humiliation. "Would you stop laughing? It actually really hurt and took forever to heal."

She dragged in a deep breath to temporarily stop her laughter and stared wide-eyed at me. "Did you have to use one of those ass donut things?" With that level of focus, she couldn't miss my face going up in flames and she lost it all over again.

"Thank you for being such a wonderfully understanding friend and not making me feel like a total idiot." I glared at her to let her know that this was becoming a lot less fun for me. "Can we talk about something else now? I don't think my ego can take much more of this."

She seemed to realize she was being insensitive and did her best to take deep breaths and calm down. "I'm sorry. I'm just really enjoying the idea of people hearing an explosion and running to the rescue only to find you bent over with a shard of glass sticking out of your ass." More laughter.

"CHEEK!"

4

SAOIRSE

Watching him storm away to the bathroom was almost as fun as watching his face turn red; I know it may have been a little mean, but I still felt the need to punish him. Even though I wanted to move forward and get closure, it seemed I wasn't quite ready. Maybe it was time to get to the hard stuff, but I wanted to delay the heartache as much as I could. The hard stuff was called hard for a reason and I wasn't in a hurry to get there.

I was dressed when he came back because I felt like I needed the extra defense against what I knew was coming. And I wasn't just talking about him, I had some things of my own that he probably didn't see coming. "How about a game of cards?"

He seemed relieved that I wasn't bringing up his ass donut again. "Yeah, let's play cards." He turned in a circle before facing me again with a sheepish look on his face. "Shit, I don't have any cards in here. You still stash a deck in your purse?"

"Yep, I still prefer actual Solitaire when I'm bored. Keeps my hands moving and off my phone. I truly believe playing games on your phone is the quickest way to get in the habit of wasting time." I nodded toward my purse on the table by the door. "So, what are we playing?"

"Strip Poker?"

I rolled my eyes. "How did I know you were going to say that? You're such a guy sometimes. I'm not playing Strip Poker with you."

"Afraid you'll lose?" His taunt was not even close to subtle but it still managed to poke my competitive side.

"Of course not."

"Well then..." He spread his arms wide, cards in his left hand, challenging me to prove that he had no chance of winning.

After some careful consideration, I had an idea. "How about we play Strip Poker for questions instead of clothes? Like a combination of Strip Poker and truth or dare. If I win a hand, I ask you a question and if you don't want to answer it, you take off a piece of clothing. Deal?"

He thought about it for a few seconds and then seemed to come to the same conclusion I had. It was the whole reason he'd been stalking Jameson - he wanted me to listen and by doing it this way, I got to choose the pace. I would decide what I wanted to know and when, and he would decide the same when he won a hand. "Deal." He sat back on the couch and started shuffling the cards while I moved the food to the side so we had use of the table. "Texas hold 'em?"

"Sure. I don't think you know any other types of Poker, do you?" I couldn't help poking back at him after he'd poked at me; it was a good way to distract from how nervous I was.

Like the grown adult he was, he stuck his tongue out at me and dealt us each two cards. "How's the betting going to work? I don't have any change or chips."

I looked around the room for something to use. "I think there's one of those jumbo bags of Cadbury Mini Eggs in the side pocket of my purse."

"That'll work." He went back over to my purse and opened the side pocket, just as I remembered what else was in there. "Wait a damn second, what the hell is this?" He didn't sound very happy about the book he'd pulled out.

"A book?" I said it like a question so he'd realize how ridiculous his question was.

His disapproving look was sexy as hell and it almost made me forget about my embarrassment over him finding a smut novel in my purse. *Almost.* "I'm aware of the fact that it's a book. Why does it have a naked man on the cover?"

"He's not naked, he's shirtless and I think you'll have to ask the author why." I watched him carefully. To anyone else, the look on his face would've seemed disturbed but I noticed the subtle change; the moment his mind switched from intimidated to intrigued. My embarrassment drained away and I was instantly excited and curious to know what he was thinking. *Bad Saoirse.* "Something wrong, Dr. McAllister?"

He jumped slightly which confirmed my assessment that his mind had wandered but I doubted he'd let me in on where it had wandered to. "No, nothing. Just a little surprised since I barely remember you reading anything other than textbooks. On the rare occasion that you did read something else, it was never something like this."

"I didn't have much time to read anything else back then." *Liar.* "Did you find the eggs?"

"Oh right." He reached into my purse and grabbed them before setting the book down and giving it one last long glance. "Let's do this."

FINN

Fucking fuck. My brain was no longer on point after the discovery of the bodice ripper in Saoirse's purse. How was I supposed to think straight when all I could do was think of all the things I'd heard about these types of books and imagine doing every one of them with her. I needed to focus but I feared I'd need to just pretend that I wasn't drowning in mental images of her in many, *many* compromising positions.

We divided up the Mini Eggs - a stroke of genius on her part because we both loved them and would fight for them – and began to play.

I barely glanced at my cards before saying, "I call."

"Full house, kings and sevens. Beat that." Damn, I loved the way her face lit up when she was showing off. I'd never been a good poker player but that would work in my favour. If she kept winning, she'd keep asking questions and end up hearing the things I needed her to know anyway.

I laid my cards on the table to show that I had two pair and watched her grab the half of my Mini Eggs that I'd used to bet. I really needed to start playing a little smarter and betting more conservatively or I wouldn't get any eggs. "Take your victory lap; what's your question?"

"Are you seeing anyone?" Her eyes widened slightly and her cheeks reddened which told me her question was more telling than she'd intended for the first one out of the gate. I wasn't about to complain when I was being afforded a rare look inside her thoughts, no matter how brief.

"Nope."

Oh, she didn't like the one-word answer. She clenched her jaw and tried to maintain a straight face to hide the fact that she'd been looking for details. "How long's it been?"

"Now, that wasn't the deal. The deal was one question. If you want to ask another one, you'll have to win another hand, Dr. Black." My lips spread into an over-exaggerated smile, earning me a glare but I needed to throw her off a bit so that I got to ask some questions too.

I won the next hand and decided to be a little shady. "What's your address?" I wasn't about to lose her again and I was willing to do whatever it took.

"*What?* You can't ask that, that's not how this works."

I looked around the room as if I was confused. "I don't remember any rules that said we couldn't ask questions like that. Did I miss that part of the conversation?"

She rolled her eyes and rattled off her address so quickly, it was obvious that she hoped I'd miss part of it. *I didn't.* Unfortunately for her, the fact that she'd decided to answer instead of removing a piece of clothing made it obvious that she was less averse to me knowing her address than she'd like me to believe.

"Thank you," I said with a smug smile.

"Just deal the next hand and get ready for payback, McAllister." I wasn't worried, I'd tell her anything she wanted to know.

As luck would have it, I won the next hand too. "Phone number?" The smile I flashed her this time was more than a little self-satisfied and not in the least bit remorseful.

She threw up her hands in annoyance. "Oh hell, what's next? My bra size?"

"Thirty-six double D."

She grabbed both her breasts as if blocking them from my eyes would somehow make me unknow her size. "What the hell, Finn? How do you know that?" I guarantee she would've slapped me in that moment had I been within arm's reach. "Wait, my neon green bra. I couldn't find it after I moved to Paris. You have it? Finn, that's my favorite bra."

"What is it with girls and their bras?" She actually seemed really upset about this one bra going missing.

"Finn! Why did you take my bra?"

I gave her a confused look. "Was that a question? I'm sorry but it's not your turn." I wagged my finger at her. "No breaking the rules. Now, phone number?" I held my phone, waiting for her answer.

She growled at me, aggravated. *Adorable.* "You're playing dirty." Her phone number came flying out of her mouth twice as fast as her address had but I was ready for it. "Is this how this whole game is going to go?" There was an obvious pout in her voice; her lower lip jutted out a little and she crossed her arms, making it clear she was feeling sorry for herself. Her jaw was set with determination, however, which told me she wouldn't be giving up any time soon.

She won the next hand and gave me a smug look over her Caesar. "Did you tip over the cop car?"

"Whoa, low blow. And you say *I'm* playing dirty." I shook my head; impressed, as always, by her brilliant mind. I'd already forgotten that we'd talked about that. "Fine, yes. You happy?" I pointed at her to make sure she listened to my next words. "If you ever tell the cops, I'll lie and tell them you did it."

"Ha! I knew it! And did you say something about tipping cows? Was it your idea to steal the pizza out of the delivery driver's car?" She was enjoying this way too much.

I frowned at her; I wasn't about to reveal all my secrets in one go. "Again, trying to break the rules. How many questions was that?" I raised an eyebrow at her and started counting on my fingers. "Too many."

"Deal faster then; this is taking too long. I need answers."

5

SAOIRSE

I was serious when I said it was taking too long, but I doubted I would feel that way once we got to the heavy stuff. Part of me felt like suggesting we just put the cards away and talk but the other part was still afraid; afraid of telling the truth and afraid of knowing the truth.

My three aces took the next hand. "What did you say to convince the others to help you flip the cop car?"

Finn groaned and rolled his eyes before reluctantly answering, "I think it was something like, 'come on, pig tipping's got to be easier than cow tipping.' Satisfied?"

"Immensely," I responded with a cackle, and proceeded to beat him again with a flush. "And who set up the whole pizza delivery thing?"

He glared at me playfully. "It was my idea. I called the pizza place, made an order for the house next door, called again and made a second order of twenty pizzas for the house party. While the delivery driver was arguing with the neighbours about the pizza they didn't order, I got some people to sneak out to his car and steal the pizzas. When the driver realized what had happened, he called the police. Thus, the cops showing up and ending up with their cruiser on its roof."

As for my favorite green bra, he decided to remove one of his shoes instead of answering for that one. No matter how much I pushed, he wouldn't budge - it was maddening. I had a feeling he was enjoying how crazy it made me. *Jerkface.*

"Would you at least take off your other shoe? You look ridiculous."

He laughed and kicked his other shoe off, lifting his foot and wiggling his sock covered toes at me. "Happy?"

"Ecstatic." I hoped my bored tone conveyed how much of a tool I thought he was being. "Call. I need more answers."

But his four of a kind wasn't going to get me any. "Well well well, seems the student may have finally learned something."

"Uh huh, you're still no Poker shark. What do you want to know?"

No smile this time. "How have you been over the last three years?" His quiet voice was indicative of his fear in asking me. He wanted to know but he was also afraid of the answer.

Well, he had nothing to be afraid of because I wasn't going to answer. I kicked my slippers off and nodded to the deck of cards. "Deal." I knew it was a chickenshit move but I kind of hoped we could deal with *what* happened before we talked about how it felt. I wasn't even sure if *I* was ready to deal with those emotions, let alone spill them to him.

"Fair." He seemed to realize that this was not a joking matter and started shuffling the cards without further comment. I'd never get over how forgiving he was of me; I swore sometimes that I could do absolutely no wrong in his eyes. Well, we'd soon find out how accurate that was.

As he dealt the next hand, I decided that I could maybe make this a little easier on both of us by simply asking for easier questions. I cleared my throat to try to clear the tension and prepared myself for what I was about to reveal - my fear. "It's hard to answer such an all-encompassing question because three years is a huge amount of time to sum up in one answer."

I watched as he seemed to catalogue every part of my facial expression, as I knew he would, then nod his head in acceptance. "Ok, smaller steps."

"Thank you."

I felt exposed; a strange thing to feel around him. I didn't think I'd ever felt less than completely comfortable with him; it was how our friendship was built… and destroyed. My heart constricted at the thought and I did my best to keep it from showing on my face but it was a truth that was part of why it was so hard for me to move past this. I'd trusted him and felt comfortable enough with him to let my guard down that last night and it had cost me. Years of pain and confusion that got me nowhere except stuck in a foreign country feeling alone and betrayed by someone I loved. Not that he knew I loved him but, when we got together the night before we left for Europe, I thought he might've felt the same.

When I woke alone the next morning, I realized I might've been mistaken; when I got on the plane and the seat beside me stayed empty, I knew for sure. He was just gone and, as much as I wanted to know why, I couldn't risk letting him in again - I shut him out and ignored every attempt he made to contact me. It wasn't that I didn't believe in second chances, it was that I didn't want to risk getting hurt again and I couldn't see myself not opening back up to him. Just look at what was happening in that hotel room; a couple hours and we were already getting back into our old stride.

"You ok?"

His voice broke me out of my internal struggle but didn't stop the pain it caused. "Yeah. Sorry, I'll be right back."

I locked myself in the bathroom again, which made me feel weak, but I needed to breathe. I could feel the tears coming; all the pent-up pain and anger flying to the surface with nothing left to stop it. I realized that I'd been able to ignore most of it for the last three years because I'd been ignoring how it used to be with us; how easy and comfortable. I couldn't ignore it anymore. He'd brought my walls down and opened me back up to him; the thing I'd been trying to avoid. Those walls didn't just keep him out, they kept all of this in and I felt like I was going to explode with it.

My eyes frantically searched the bathroom for some kind of relief from the tidal wave of emotions I was about to drown in. I wanted to break something; smash it, crush it, rip it apart, hurt it... the way he'd hurt me. I didn't care anymore about hiding it from him. Why had I even been doing that in the first place? Was I trying to protect him? Did I not want him to feel bad? *Fuck him!* He's the one who'd fucked it all up and yet I was the one suffering because of some subconscious need to not hurt his feelings. It was bullshit and I felt a crazy amount of anger rise up at the injustice of it all. Why did I have to suffer twice for his indifference while he didn't suffer at all? I wanted him to suffer and I could no longer justify my self-imposed silence. *Fuck him.*

I swung the door open so hard, it slammed into the wall, and stormed back to him - finally ready to make him pay for what he'd done. "HOW COULD YOU?" I screamed so loud I could likely be heard for ten blocks and I probably looked crazy but that's how I felt. I'd decided not to hide anymore; so now he'd get to experience what he'd done. *Eat your fucking heart out, McAllister.*

FINN

When she'd gone back to the bathroom, she'd had that devastated look on her face again. *Not anymore.* I'd never before seen the look on her face when she came flying out of the bathroom - honestly, I wasn't even aware that she was capable of that level of anger. Saoirse was anything but soft, but she certainly wasn't aggressive in the way I was seeing now. Usually, she had a kind of strong assertiveness going on that made you think twice before you crossed her. *This* wasn't that.

She stood rigid and tall with her hands fisted at her sides, her chin tilted down and her green eyes burning holes into my soul. The tension in her face, shoulders and arms betrayed how much she was holding herself back from physically lunging at me and I wouldn't have been surprised if she pulled a Jean Grey and everything in the room began to levitate.

I kept my mouth shut and focused on what she had to say; something told me that I needed to hear this. An even stronger part of me told me that I needed to feel it. If I wanted us to move past this then it was time for penance.

Her voice had lowered when she continued, but not by much. "How could you do this to me, to us? How could you just disappear like that? We were best fucking friends for years, Finn. How could you do that? I can't begin to understand how you were even capable of something so cruel. You were nowhere to be found and you didn't answer your phone. I spent the whole morning wondering if you were fucking dead. Do you know what that's like?"

She didn't give me time to respond. "And then you text me, *'get on the plane, Saoirse.'* What the fuck was that? Were you just in that much of a hurry to be rid of me? Couldn't even spare the time it would take to call and talk to me like the friend you were supposed to be? You got what you wanted and you were done with me, is that it?"

"Saoirse, you know that's not true." I basically had to yell to get a word in.

She yelled louder. "Do I? How could I possibly know that? Maybe you were just playing the long game? Maybe you thought I'd be an easy target in the beginning and when I wasn't, you saw me as a challenge. I don't know anymore. I stopped knowing anything about you the moment I woke up alone in your dorm. Because up until that point, I would never have believed that you could do something like that to someone who was supposed to be your friend."

"It wasn't like that," I tried to interject.

"I was in love with you!" With her shouted words, I lost the ability to breathe. "I was in love with you and you ripped my fucking heart out. How am I supposed to know if it was just for sport when I wouldn't think you capable of it for *any* reason? I trusted you with everything, you knew everything about me and I obviously knew nothing about you. I would never do something like that to you, no matter what the reasoning behind it. I would never abandon you without so much as a phone call to explain why I'd bailed. I guess I wasn't worth the effort to you. Did I mean anything to you or was it all just some fucked up act to get into my pants?"

She wouldn't believe how much she meant to me, but I still couldn't breathe enough to say anything. Not that it mattered because I was pretty sure she wouldn't believe a thing I said about my feelings for her right now. She was too angry and the attempts I'd already made showed me that she wasn't ready to listen to my side yet.

I watched in horror as her whole demeanor crumbled before me; where a second ago I would've believed she could slay a dragon, now she looked like the most fragile thing I'd ever seen. I couldn't hold myself back anymore from wrapping my arms around her and trying to give her some of my strength or comfort or anything she wanted from me. She tried to push me away but I wouldn't let her stop me. I couldn't watch her go through this pain alone.

I'd just gotten my arms around her when the sobs started and I felt myself being ripped apart by every agonizing sound that came from her. It occurred to me that I had gotten this very wrong; thinking that all I had to do was come back, explain what happened and we could move forward. I felt like a chump for thinking it would be that easy, that she would so easily forgive me because she always had. Maybe she always had but I didn't think I'd ever hurt her like this before and that knowledge tore me up inside.

I wrapped her up tighter, trying to hold us both together while we fell apart but I knew that I might not be what she needed. I wanted to be, more than anything, because she was everything I needed.

"I'm sorry," I whispered but it wasn't enough. The tears in my eyes were a direct result of my shame and how helpless I felt to fix what I'd broken. She was right, I hadn't treated her like a friend. In fact, the helplessness I was feeling was very similar to how helpless I'd felt back then. It was a shitty situation that I'd handled in the only way I could think of that would cause the least amount of damage - though that no longer seemed to be the case. It seemed like I'd unwittingly chosen to handle it in the most damaging way imaginable and I would never forgive myself for that. How could I expect her to forgive me?

"Let go of me." With those broken words, she started struggling in my arms to get free, but I wasn't sure I could let her go. If I let her go, I didn't think I could look her in the eyes and I felt like holding on was the only thing stopping me from losing her forever.

"Let go," she said again. Her voice was stronger but I held on, even when her struggling turned to fists beating against my chest.

"Let me go!" Her scream startled me as her palm connected with the side of my face. Saoirse was not a violent person, so I knew I needed to listen and stepped back from her. I felt myself becoming exceptionally angry at all of my *many* fuck ups as she shoved me further away.

"See? This is a perfect example of how fucking selfish you are. You don't care what I want at all, even when I'm screaming it at you."

"DID IT EVER FUCKING OCCUR TO YOU THAT I DON'T KNOW WHAT THE FUCK YOU WANT, SAOIRSE?" I didn't mean to yell but I was so overwhelmed with emotion that I couldn't stop myself.

6

SAOIRSE

I finally understood what 'stunned silence' meant. Being someone who never lacked in the words department, I could honestly say I'd never come across a situation where I had nothing to say but there I was; stunned silent. I couldn't say if it was that I had nothing to say or if I was just so shocked by his outburst that I was curious to know what he'd say next. Finn had never raised his voice to me before; even when we argued, his voice would fill with passion but would never actually gain volume. I would've sworn, in that moment, that even my tears stopped dead on my cheeks from the shock of Finn losing his shit on me.

I stood still as a statue, not even sure I was breathing, trying to remember what I'd been saying ten seconds before but nothing would come to me. It was like he'd knocked my brain loose, opened some valve and let all my steam out, and I had absolutely no idea where to go from there. Luckily, I didn't need to know because Finn McAllister wasn't anywhere near finished.

"Did you ever think about why I followed you around like a lost fucking puppy for all those years? Sure, I guess it could be considered playing the long game but it would be the longest game known to fucking man and the dumbest because you never looked at me as anything more than a friend." His jaw was clenched, chest heaving with deep breaths and I could swear I saw tears beginning to well in his eyes. "Don't get me wrong, I loved being your friend and I still consider you my best friend but it's a poor man's substitute. What do you do when the person you're in love with never shows any interest in you after years of mooning after them?"

"Love?" I got stuck on that word for a second before I heard the rest of what he'd said. "Wait a minute, it's not like you showed any interest in me either."

He threw his hands in the air like I was the most difficult person in the world. "Saoirse, I spent every minute of every day with you. Do you know anyone who spends that much time with someone they're not in love with? You're a great person; you're smart, funny and gorgeous but don't you think I'd have my own life outside of you sometimes? To me, it seems pretty obvious that I was basically obsessed with you." His face turned sad and he walked to the window, staring out in quiet contemplation.

"I didn't think it was that obvious."

He spun back around to face me with a baffled expression. "Oh, real nice. Rip my heart out. Why don't I just jump out this window and save myself from you killing me slowly with your words?"

"Go ahead, we're on the first floor."

For once, he was the one to roll his eyes. "This isn't getting us anywhere. So, we were both in love with each other and didn't know it. Doesn't it seem stupid to let a misunderstanding that happened three years ago get in the way of us being together?"

That pissed me off all over again. "Oh, a misunderstanding? That's all it was? Just a misunderstanding that caused me all this pain? That put me in a foreign country alone. That lost me my best friend and the man I loved. That was a misunderstanding?"

"Yes," he responded in an insistent tone.

"Please explain to me how you abandoning me could possibly be a misunderstanding."

He took a deep breath and ran his hand through his hair, making a mess of it. "I honestly thought I was making it easier for you. I went to grab us breakfast that morning and my phone rang. It was Dr. Bissette."

"My boss?"

"Exactly. He told me they'd decided to only hire one of us and that they wanted to do one more round of interviews. I couldn't go without you and I couldn't stand the idea of us competing against each other for that job."

His eyes were begging me to understand but all I could feel was dread at what I knew was coming. "Don't say it. Please."

"You would've turned down the job, Saoirse, or tried to convince me to take it. There's no way you would've gotten on that plane and I didn't want you to miss out on the opportunity to work for one of the best labs in the world. It wasn't until after you were gone that I realized I wouldn't be able to see you until you got back. The only reason I'd been allowed to travel out of the country was for that job and, without it, I was still on lockdown. I'm still on probation from the cop car incident." He shook his head. "And then you wouldn't answer any of my calls."

I was so angry at him for making that decision for me. He was right; I would've turned down the job, I would've stayed. And that was my choice, damn it. Instead, he made the choice for both of us and, as much as I understood it, I didn't understand it. "So, you're telling me that making the decision to separate us was somehow a good idea in your mind? How can I believe that you loved me when you made a decision like that? That's something we should've discussed and decided together. Even if we didn't love each other, we were best friends and we should've been making that decision together. How could you do that?"

"I didn't know that it would hurt you that much - hell, I didn't know that it would hurt me that much either. It seemed like it would just be a few years apart where we would keep in touch and try to see each other as often as possible. I knew that I didn't want to be away from you but I figured the light at the end of the tunnel would make it bearable."

I scoffed at that. "But I didn't deserve a light at the end of my tunnel?"

"I didn't know you'd completely ghost me and I couldn't exactly drop by when my stupid criminal record made it impossible to leave the country." His insistent tone gave me pause but I was still too angry with him to let it go. I wasn't about to take the heat for this.

"Still, to put me through all of that without even talking to me about it, without giving me a say in a decision that affected both our lives. You had no right to do that, I don't give a shit how altruistic you thought it was. You have no idea what you put me through, things you couldn't possibly understand."

"Then help me understand!" He stomped back over to me and grabbed my shoulders in a firm hold. "I'm sorry, I don't mean to sound insensitive, but you keep talking about all this pain you went through and you still haven't explained it to me. You know I'll do everything I can to understand you, if you'll just help me out a little. Trust me enough to at least tell me what happened. I know us being apart was hard, but this seems like more than that."

"It is." *This is going to hurt.* I took a deep breath and spoke the words I'd been dreading, "I was pregnant."

FINN

My hands dropped from her shoulders and the air rushed out of my lungs at such an insane speed I would've sworn I'd been hit by an invisible truck. *Pregnant? I have a kid?* I felt like I was going to be sick. *Good job, Finn. Not only did you abandon the woman you love but your kid too. And the award for the biggest piece of shit in the history of the world goes to...*

"You were pregnant?"

She looked so ashamed and I couldn't understand it. It was me who should be ashamed, not her. "Yes."

"I have a kid?" I'd always wanted kids with Saoirse but I thought it would be something we decided together and planned for. I wasn't about to look a gift horse in the mouth though - if this was how we started our family, I wasn't going to complain. I could feel my shock turning to excitement until I noticed the look on her face.

The shame in her eyes was growing. "No."

Oh no. I was almost too scared to ask but I had to know. "What happened?"

I expected her to break eye contact with me but she didn't. "I didn't know. I was starting work in two weeks, so I guess I'd been there for about a month, when I started to realize something was off. I mean, I was basically walking around in a fog when I wasn't crying my eyes out over you and I definitely wasn't paying attention to anything other than that." Still with that eye contact.

She seemed like she was not only punishing me, but herself too. I wasn't sure why. "I was barely keeping anything down and that was only when I could convince myself to eat in the first place. With how all over the place I was, my stomach was always upset and I was struggling with severe migraines. I don't know that I would've noticed anyway because I had no frame of reference. I don't know the first thing about pregnancy and what it entails other than the fact that you have a baby at the end."

She chuckled and shook her head at herself, but she wasn't fooling me. I could feel her tension and see the tears she was trying to keep at bay. I rubbed her upper arms, trying to sooth us both but I didn't think anything would. "It's ok, just take your time."

"I feel so stupid. How could I let that happen?" Her voice was thick with despair, so much so that it broke my heart.

"It's not your fault."

She pushed my hands away as the tears finally started falling. "Of course, it's my fault. You don't know."

"How can you say that? It's a miscarriage, Saoirse, it's not something you can control."

"It was a miscarriage due to excessive stress. It was because I was such a mess." She shook her head sadly. "I should've been able to keep from crumbling like a child. I should've been able to bounce back; instead I was so fucked up that I was making myself sick every day and I couldn't drag myself out of the darkness long enough to see what I was doing."

"You were going through hard shit, Saoirse." She could try to convince me all day but I knew it wasn't her fault - it was mine. Eventually, she'd realize it too and then it'd be up to me to convince her to forgive me. If she ever spoke to me again.

"Everyone goes through hard shit, Finn. But I let it destroy me and, because of that, I destroyed what could've been a beautiful thing. Don't you see?" What I saw was a tsunami's worth of emotions rising to the surface in her and I didn't know how to stop it. "I killed our baby, Finn. Me. I let the heartbreak get to me so much that I killed an innocent baby. I'll never forgive myself for that."

She was hyperventilating and I rushed to grab her to offer comfort just as her knees gave out and she began to collapse. I lifted her up and carried her over to the bed where Moose had been silently watching from this whole time. I laid us both down and hugged her tightly; trying to be her thunder blanket and bring her breathing back to normal. "Just breathe, it'll be ok, just breathe."

"It will *never* be ok; I killed our baby."

"No." I did my best to speak in a soothing voice. "It was an accident. You didn't do anything wrong, Saoirse. Just breathe."

"How can you say that? You know it's true. I'm a horrible person who did a horrible thing and you lying to me won't change that." Her breathing hadn't calmed and I could barely understand what she was saying. "How can I ever forgive myself? How can I even look at myself in the mirror?"

"Enough!" I yelled, I couldn't listen to this anymore. "You are not to blame here. If anyone is to blame, it's me. I did this to us - I made a stupid decision that caused us so much pain and put you in a terrible situation that you had to go through alone. I should've been there. I shouldn't have left you the way that I did. I'm so sorry, Saoirse."

"Yeah, but if I'd just answered one of your calls then maybe this wouldn't have happened."

I had no idea how to pull her out of this spiral. "You don't know that, Saoirse. You don't know what would've happened and you can't say for sure that it would've changed anything. It just wasn't the right time and that's ok. These things happen."

"But if I'd just..."

"No." I had to make her see. "Remember that book you told me about?"

She pulled her head out from under my chin and gave me a confused look. "Can you be a little more specific? I've read more than one book in my life."

"I don't remember anything about it other than that someone in it had a miscarriage. Do you remember?"

She thought for a second and then nodded her head slowly. "Yeah, I think so."

"Remember you told me that the hero said something to the heroine after her miscarriage that you thought was the most beautiful idea." I hoped she'd see where I was leading her.

Her tears didn't stop as she squeezed her eyes shut and told me again what this fictional character had said that moved her so much. "He said that a miscarriage wasn't losing anything - that baby is yours, that soul is yours, it just wasn't ready to be brought into the world yet. That someday, when the time is right, that baby will be mine because it's meant to be mine. Someday." She wrapped her fists in my shirt and cried herself to sleep.

7

SAOIRSE

Finn was right. Although we'd both played a part in what happened, it wasn't anyone's fault and there was nothing we could do to change it. As hard as that was to accept, we needed to accept it and try to move on from here. I didn't have the slightest clue where that left us but I hoped we'd figure it out.

When I woke up, Finn was still wrapped around me and sleeping soundly while Moose, who'd obviously felt the bed was too crowded for his liking, was sprawled on the couch.

I took a long look at Finn and, for the first time, noticed the signs of stress on his face. He wasn't the carefree Finn I remembered anymore; he looked older and tired. Even in sleep, he didn't look as relaxed as he used to be. I realized then that it was time for me to accept the fact that I wasn't the only one who'd suffered during our three-year separation; he may not have suffered as badly as I did but he hadn't come out of it completely unscathed either. However, he was the one who'd unilaterally made the decision to separate us; something that still pissed me off and made me sad the more I thought about it.

But I had a choice - punish him forever and keep suffering with this separation or let it go as the mistake it was and try to fix what could be fixed. Part of me was very against letting him off the hook so easily and it was probably the part that was still hurting over what he'd put us through. The other part was just tired - tired of living without my best friend, tired of hurting and tired of being angry. I just wanted the merry-go-round to stop spinning. There was only one problem: where would it stop?

We'd finally confessed our love for each other but was he just talking about the past? I knew I wasn't. Loving Finn was like breathing - it felt like I couldn't stop even if I tried and I wasn't going to try. I wanted to be with him but I had no idea where he stood on it. Three years is a long time to be away from someone and it was entirely possible that his love for me was borne from spending so much time together - something that certainly could've changed now that we'd spent all this time apart. *God, why does this have to be so confusing and terrifying at the same time?*

Moving as little as possible, I leaned forward and gently pressed my lips to his because I might not get another opportunity. I was more than a little surprised when he rolled on top of me and kissed me back. It felt so good to be this close to him again; though it'd only happened once in the past, it was a memory not easily forgotten.

His hands found mine and pinned them above my head, holding me in place while he kissed the hell out of me, our tongues warring for dominance. His possessive hold on me reawakened senses I'd forgotten I had. Wrapping my legs around his hips, I pulled him in tight against me and moaned when he bit my lower lip. I rubbed against him as much as I could, trying to create some kind of friction to help relieve the tingles running all over my body. I loved the rough play and the power struggle, it made me lose the ability to think, a fact he obviously remembered from our one amazing night together. He also knew I liked to role-play but I didn't think we were at that point yet.

"Tell me I'm not dreaming." He spoke between kisses on my lips, chin and neck, and I noticed that he didn't open his eyes, like he was genuinely afraid that he was dreaming. "Saoirse, tell me I'm not dreaming, please. Tell me I'm not going to open my eyes and find that I'm making out with a damn pillow again."

I couldn't stop my burst of laughter and his eyes popped open to glare at me. "Sorry."

"It's not funny. You can't imagine how horrible it is to wake up from a dream so real that you're sure it's really happening, only to find that it was all in your head."

The look in his eyes said that he was dead serious and, though I'd had many dreams of him over the years, I didn't ever remember them being that real. “I’m sorry. I didn’t mean to laugh. No, this isn’t a dream and I’m not a pillow.”

“Well, some parts of you are rather pillow-ish.”

I smacked him on the back of the head. “How about you try not to be a bottom-dweller while you’re on top of me? Otherwise, I might just have to keep my pillows to myself.”

“That would be a damn shame.” He focused on my tits with an appreciative smirk and I almost smacked him again. “Oh, I did have one question.”

“Ask away.”

He seemed less sure of himself. “Why didn’t Jameson tell me? I saw him all the time. Did you ask him not to?”

Oh. “He doesn’t know. I never told anyone; it didn’t seem right.”

He looked at me sadly. “So, you really were alone in all of this.” Not a question. “I really am so sorry, Saoirse. I hope you know that I would’ve moved mountains to be there, if I’d known.”

“I know but it all happened so fast. By the time I realized that there was something wrong, I went to the hospital and it was already basically over.” The memory was still hard. “I think the worst part about it was finding out I was pregnant at the same time as I found out I’d miscarried. It’s like it was too much for my brain to process all at once. To lose something so amazing before you knew you had it - the universe is cruel sometimes.”

There was so much understanding in his eyes in that moment that I was reminded, once again, why he was one of my most trusted friends.

The phone beside us rang and Finn rolled off the bed and handed it to me before heading into the bathroom. “Hello?”

“Dr. Black? This is the hotel manager,” said the female voice on the other end of the line.

Oh yeah, I’d completely forgotten about my current situation. “Yes, are we ever going to be let out of this room?”

“Are you sure you want out?” The giggle that accompanied her question told me exactly who I was speaking to.

“T? What the hell?” I sat up, trying to process the fact that Finn’s sister, Tessa, was the hotel manager and keeping my voice down so he didn’t hear me. “What the fuck is going on?”

“Ok, please don’t hate me.” *Oh shit.* “He begged me, Saoirse.”

No way. “He begged you to lock me in here with him? And you said *yes*?”

“You kept shutting him out, you refused to talk to him. Hell, you basically stopped talking to me too just to avoid him.” *And the worst friend in the world award goes to me.* "Look Saoirse, he's been in love with you since he met you. You guys belong together, you're soulmates and he knows it. It's time for you to catch up."

I was stunned silent for the second time and slowly laid back down as she whispered, "Please don't let mistakes of the past get in the way of your future."

Tessa's parting words rang in my ears. Finn came out of the bathroom and crawled back on top of me. "I have a question," I said, still working to understand. "What's Tessa doing here?"

He froze and examined my face. He could obviously see that there was no point lying to me anymore and admitted, "This is one of the family hotels. Tessa runs it."

This was sounding a little too convenient for my presence here to be a coincidence. "So, you're telling me that your sister runs the hotel that your family owns, which just happens to be where the conference that I was asked to be a guest speaker at, was being held?"

His eyebrows dropped with his quizzical look while he mimed 'following the bouncing ball' with his right index finger. "Yes." His cocky smile was back. "Weird, right?" Cue the blush. *Not sneaky enough, Dr. McAllister.*

"You set this whole thing up, didn't you?" I crossed my arms over my chest; not an easy feat while laying on my back with boobs the size of mine. "I mean, not just the locking me up against my will thing but the whole conference. You set it up, didn't you?"

I glanced at the adjoining door in my room. "Oh my God, Finn! You're in the room next door, aren't you, you fucking perv?"

FINN

Busted.

"Hey, there's no need for name calling." But her expression told me that she wasn't seeing the extremely romantic gesture that this was supposed to be.

"Ok, fine. I just wanted to be close to you and I wasn't sure you would let me anywhere near you since you seemed so hell-bent on never speaking to me again. I figured if I was in the adjoining room and you decided not to speak to me, maybe I could just talk through the door and then you could pretend you weren't giving me a second chance while still hearing me out."

She scoffed at me. "I wasn't in my right mind, Saoirse. I've been without you for three years and I had to do something to get you back - I would've done anything."

Her expression turned sad. "So, the whole conference was a sham?"

I could see the confidence slowly leaking out of her eyes and I had to stop it. "No. I'm on the board that holds this conference every year and I merely offered this hotel as host and suggested you as one of the guest speakers. The board then did the research and voted on the featured speakers they wanted to attend. To be fair though, I knew there wasn't a chance in hell they wouldn't want you on the docket; your reputation precedes you and your work speaks for itself. You've already made a name for yourself in just three short years... you're amazing."

I managed to get that all out in one breath and her wide eyes told me she'd noticed. "Ok."

"Ok? That's all you have to say after all of that?" That was a level of trust I didn't feel I'd earned yet, but leave it to Saoirse to keep surprising me.

"Well, yeah. There's nothing I can do about it now and I can't say I wouldn't have attended anyway even if I'd known you'd set the whole thing up. So... ok." She gave a curt nod like that was the end of it.

"Ok." I thought about it for a minute. "You know, I'll never understand how you can be so much work and so damn easy all at the same time."

She narrowed her eyes on a cute playful glare. "I am not that much work. Wait, did you just call me easy?"

"That's not what I meant." I placed my elbow on the bed beside her shoulder and dropped my face into my palm, releasing a groan. "See? Work."

She chuckled before sobering. "So, where does this leave us?"

"Well, that's really up to you." I took a deep breath in preparation for the vulnerable position I was about to place myself in. "I never stopped loving you, Saoirse - never stopped wanting to be with you. But it's like I said: I would rather have you in my life as a friend than not at all. It'll be hard for a while but I have no doubt that it'll be worth it. I couldn't imagine my life without you."

She gave a small nod and broke eye contact. "There's a lot of stuff that can't just be undone, a lot of hurt and there's probably going to be some trust issues. It's going to be a lot of work to deal with."

"We can deal with it together." I rubbed my nose against hers the way I used to when I wanted her to smile. "I'm not naïve, I know that it's going to take time and work but I'd rather do that work with you than without you.

We'll get back there again. The important thing is that we love each other and we want to do that work together."

She stared into my eyes for a long moment before seeming to find what she was looking for and exhaling a breath I hadn't realized she was holding. "Ok."

I kissed her nose. "Ok."

We talked for hours and, although I could sense that we both wanted to go further, we kept our physical affection PG for the time being - it seemed important to reconnect without getting too physical. We were rebuilding our relationship and neither of us was in any hurry. But we would get there soon enough, and I couldn't wait.

I lay there staring into the eyes I'd longed to see for the last three years and felt awe at finally being with her again. She was perfect, every time I looked at her, I felt this strange combination of home and unworthiness. She just had a way of settling me and part of that was the devotion I could always see shining in her eyes - I'm sure mine were saying the same thing right back and I hoped I made her feel even half of what I felt. Just knowing she cared for me that much was enough to bring me to my knees, I didn't think I could ever express how much I loved her or how sorry I was for what happened but I hoped she'd let me spend the rest of my life trying.

Tessa had come by to pick up Moose a few hours ago and he would be staying with her for the night while we took this time to reacquaint ourselves. It was around midnight when Saoirse started struggling to keep her eyes open and I felt bad for everything that'd happened today to cause the exhaustion I could see in her eyes.

"Let's get some sleep."

"Nuh uh." She shook her head even as she yawned into the back of her hand. "I'm afraid that if I fall asleep, you won't be here when I wake up."

The vulnerability in her whispered words broke my heart and I felt my eyes well with tears of shame again for what I'd done. I'd never get those years back and I'd never get over the pain I'd caused us both. I would do everything in my power to fix what I'd broken, to take that sadness out of her voice.

I kissed her forehead and wrapped my arms around her. "I'm not going anywhere ever again. I swear I'm going to be around so much that you'll get sick of me and beg me to leave."

Her very unladylike snort was adorable. "Not possible."

"Either way, we're meant to be, baby. Therefore, we will be."

She hummed contentedly and tucked her face into the side of my neck. "*We will be*. I like that."

"Good because I love you."

"I love you too." The snore that followed those words made me love her just a little more.

And that was the thing about Saoirse; every time I thought I couldn't love her more, she did something that made me fall just a little deeper. I couldn't wait to see what that love looked like in fifty years.

EPILOGUE

Four years later...

SAOIRSE

The quiet was unusual in our house with three boys under the age of five running around constantly, so I was taking advantage of their visit with Aunty Tessa and Uncle Jamie. I stood at the kitchen island working on an article for Science Magazine while also preparing dinner and trying to decide if three kids was enough, if I should just give up on having a girl.

Finn and I had gotten married a millisecond after reconnecting - it hadn't taken us long to realize that we didn't want to be apart ever again and we'd welcomed our first son into our lives barely a minute later. To be honest, I felt like I'd been pregnant non-stop since we got married and, after three pregnancies that resulted in three sons, it was doubtful that any other result was even possible. I loved my boys but having a daughter was something I'd always wanted and I was having a hard time shaking the thought.

Suddenly I was pinned to the counter from behind and a large hand covered my mouth to muffle my shock. "Shhh... wouldn't want to wake up your precious children when we have so little time before your husband gets home."

His other hand made its way into the neckline of my dress and dipped down to my breast. His palm dragged across my nipple, making it tighten, and he massaged my breast roughly. I bit back a moan as he sank his teeth into the side of my neck where it connects to my shoulder. An unavoidable shiver ran through my body that didn't go unnoticed. "Mmm, such a dirty girl, standing here in front of all these windows wearing a dress so thin that your braless tits are obvious to anyone looking."

He dragged his tongue up my neck, nibbled my earlobe and pinched my nipple hard while pressing his large erection against my ass. "Is that what you want? You want people to look? You want people to see you and know that they could pull this dress up, bend you over and go to town on you with nothing to stop them. I bet you're not even wearing panties, are you?"

His whispered words turned me on so much that I could barely breathe. He was right, I wasn't wearing panties, but I hadn't wanted to attract attention from anyone other than him. I could feel him, out in his car watching me through the windows and I'd dressed to drive him crazy, to draw him to me, to have exactly this happen. I turned my head to dislodge his hand and look at him. "So, what's stopping you?"

A feral growl ripped out of him and faster than I could've expected, my right cheek was against the counter and my dress was around my waist. "No panties, bad girl." His hand connected with my left ass cheek in a hard slap, making me moan at the sting as delicious tingles ran up my spine. "And look how wet you are, you're just begging for it, aren't you?"

Two fingers slid into me hard and fast, causing me to lose my breath and turning me on more than I thought possible. We were in clear view of the windows and just the idea that someone could be watching this was so hot; I wanted more. "So, what are you waiting for?" I taunted.

The answer was apparently nothing because, in the next second, he'd dropped his pants and shoved his cock so deep inside me it hurt in the best way. The suddenness of it sent me into a mind-blowing orgasm and I screamed as the world exploded around me. He slammed his hand over my mouth again to keep me quiet. "Always sassing me when I'm already on edge, no wonder you're always pregnant. Is that what you want? You want me to knock you up again?"

I moaned into his hand and felt myself climbing toward another orgasm simply from imagining him getting me pregnant. "Fuck yes, do it." My moaned words were barely above a whisper with how quickly I was spiraling toward that incredible peak.

His thrusts sped up to the point that I could barely catch my breath and I felt like a pulsing current of electricity was travelling all over my body. "You want that little girl your husband can't seem to give you? Need me to get the job done for you?"

He held my right hip tightly and threaded the fingers of his left hand with mine on the counter in front of my face, his wedding ring glinting in the light of the kitchen.

"Yes." I couldn't believe he knew that - I'd been doing my best to keep it to myself.

He ran his nose up the side of my face while whispering, "Beg me for it."

"Please." The humiliation of begging for something like that was intoxicating and I felt my body reacting to the intensity.

"Not good enough." He stopped thrusting and a pitiful whine escaped me. "Do it properly, Saoirse, you know what I want to hear."

He fisted my hair, pulling me upright so my back was against his chest and wrapped his left arm around my waist while still holding my hand tightly. His right hand wrapped around my throat and squeezed, driving me wild - I loved his possessive hold.

I knew what he wanted to hear but I was so far gone that I wasn't even sure I could string words together at that point. "Please... fill me with... your cum... get me pregnant... let me make you a daddy again, Finn. Please."

When he groaned and started thrusting again, I knew that he didn't mind my broken words and he'd gotten the message loud and clear. "Fuck, I could feel you gripping my cock while you spoke. You love when I make you say dirty shit like that, don't you?"

"Yes... yes." I wasn't sure if there were actually words coming out of my mouth at that point, I was already drowning in my second orgasm. My head tipped back onto his right shoulder, my mouth open in a silent scream and barely able to breathe, I lost it completely.

"Good girl. Come on my cock, let me feel how much you want my cum." His upward thrusts were so hard my feet were lifting off the ground. I was grinding myself onto his cock with mindless abandon, completely unable to focus on anything other than my pleasure and him getting me pregnant.

He growled and slammed into me one last time, holding me tight to his lap as I basked in the feeling of his cock pulsing deep inside me. "God, I love that feeling," I moaned.

"You should. That's your daughter I just gave you," he responded through panting breaths and I smiled at the certainty in his voice, secretly hoping he was right but not willing to get my hopes up. "So, what's for dinner?"

I elbowed him in the stomach. "Are you kidding me right now? You're still inside me, Finn."

"And?"

I rolled my eyes and pushed my hips back, hard, to shove him away, my dress falling back into place. Watching him stumble back and land on his ass on the kitchen floor was satisfying.

"You make me sick. How about you finish making dinner while I go have a nice hot shower," I said as I made my way to your bedroom.

He had no problem making dinner and often helped with everything around the house. However, he knew I preferred baths if I wanted to be left alone; saying I was going for a shower was basically me inviting him for round two.

"You mean lovesick, right? I make you lovesick?" I didn't answer and continued down the hall. "Wait, did you say shower?" he called after me.

At our bedroom door, I glanced back at him with a wink and laughed as he scrambled to his feet, trying to come after me with his pants still around his ankles.

I'd never get tired of his obsession with me.

Nine months after that...

FINN

"FINN MCALLISTER, I'M GOING TO FUCKING KILL YOU!" I cringed and gave the security guard at the door an apologetic look for the shouted words from inside the car.

"Wheelchair?" I asked sheepishly. He met my expression with a shake of his head and an amused smirk.

I heard laughter coming from behind me and glanced in that direction to see the very not short Mr. Short getting out of his car and striding toward us. "Well, I'm really glad I didn't miss this."

"Hey Jameson..." The sweet voice of my wife pissed me off for a second. Why was she being nice to him and not me? Then I saw her face.

"Yeah, Soarsh?" He smiled smugly, but it didn't last long.

"This is *not* a *fucking sideshow*! If you're just going to be a fucktard then I will *revoke your fucking godfather title from all of my children*! And I'll tell your wife what you said when she was in labour with your daughter." She wasn't really yelling but the force in her voice made it very clear that she wasn't above doing physical damage to him just because she was in labour.

Jameson blanched and swung his gaze behind him to make sure Tessa hadn't gotten out of the car yet. "Yeesh, ok, sorry. I'll shut up." He ran to help

Tessa out and kissed her sweetly - the picture of innocence and devotion. I still wasn't over him marrying my sister.

I chuckled and looked down at my badass wife with pride, only to be met with a look that told me I was still in the line of fire. "Are you planning on helping your pregnant wife out of the car before she gives birth or do you want to watch me do this in the passenger seat?"

She might have stopped yelling, for now, but that was of little consequence when she had murder in her eyes. "Sorry."

I grabbed the wheelchair from the guard, helped her into it and wheeled her into the hospital, heading for the familiar walls of the maternity ward. "Hey babe?"

I loved when she called me that in her sweet voice. For Saoirse, it was a term of endearment reserved for those she loved most because it was what her mom used to call her.

"What's up, honey?" I responded.

"Did you hit your fucking head or something? You passed the hall that goes to maternity and you're moving so slowly that I have no fucking idea how you could *possibly* miss it." So much for her sweet voice, that was like a whiplash. *Jesus, I don't know if I'm going to live through this.*

After more glares than you could fit in an ocean and language that would make a sailor blush, she was finally situated in her room and hooked up to the fetal monitor. My mom was holding her hand, Tessa was sitting against the wall with Jameson beside her reading... was that a Cosmo?

"Why do I keep letting you do this to me?" Her words were accompanied by a pained groan as another contraction hit.

"Probably because you can't stay off my dick long enough for me to put on a condom once the doctor clears us for sex." It was out of my mouth before I thought about it and I was met with a variety of reactions.

Jameson looked like he was going to explode as he tried to hold in his laughter, Tessa looked at me like I was drunk, my mom's face was a study in shock and disapproval, the way only a mother could look at her child and I was too afraid to check Saoirse's reaction.

"Get out!" Her shouted words made it so I didn't need to see her face to know how she felt about what I'd just said.

I left the room just as my dad was about to walk in. "Trouble in paradise?" he asked.

I shook my head and smiled my dopey love sick smile. "Nope, perfect as always. She's just working through her process."

The comment that got me kicked out wasn't completely unfounded. Four babies in five years, all Irish twins. That meant we wasted no time getting her pregnant again after every baby.

He gave me a skeptical look and was about to comment when Saoirse yelled, "Finn!"

I gave him a triumphant smile and made my way back to my wife.

"Ok, everyone out please. We'll see you in a while." My eyes met the panicked eyes of my wife and held while everyone made their way out. I took her hand and pressed my forehead to hers, ignoring the nurses around us. "Ok Saoirse, let's have it."

"I'm scared," she whispered as if she was worried the baby would hear her and her eyes welled with tears.

Fuck, she was always so beautiful. "You're always scared, Saoirse, and you always rock it. I don't think you could fail at anything even if you tried. You're the best person, wife and mom I've ever met, and you're going to be the best at this just like you were the last three times. You've got this and I'm right here with you."

"Always?" she asked in a watery voice.

"Fucking right, always. Aren't you sick of me yet?" I smiled at her and kissed her nose.

She returned my smile and took a deep breath to calm herself. "Yeah, but you just won't fucking leave me alone." She gave me an annoyed look.

"Sassy, sexy Saoirse, love of my life, I love you so damn much."

She leaned forward and kissed me softly. "Love you too."

"Ready to meet your daughter?"

She glared at me. "The doctor said it was another boy."

"I don't give a shit what the doctor said. I know you and I'm telling you, this one's your girl. Who are you going to trust? Me or some know-nothing doctor? I'm a doctor too, you know?"

She laughed at the same argument we'd been having for months since we were told the gender and gave a short nod. "Let's meet our girl," she said.

I climbed into the bed behind her, with her between my legs and her back to my chest as the doctor entered the room. *It's go time*. "You've got this." I kissed her temple and prepared to watch her be the superhero I knew she was.

We met our perfect little girl 6 hours later.

Want to know what happened between Finn and Saoirse three years ago? Join my reader group "JC's Vixens" on Facebook and receive the prequel for free.

ABOUT J. C. SMOAK

J. C. Smoak is a born and bred Canadian with a passion for romance of all kinds. Living in Alberta on an acreage with her family, eight dogs, four cats and one chicken, she's surrounded by cows who thankfully aren't easily offended by her frequent use of cuss words (luckily, no one's started a swear jar yet).

J. C. loves to laugh and usually thinks she's way funnier than she actually is. With a lifelong love of writing, she is a gold-medalist grammar freak and, thanks to Disney, she's a Happily-Ever-After addict. She believes that books and movies should be an escape from real life, like a mini vacation. As a true hermit, J. C.'s an expert at quoting movie lines, and when she's not writing, reading or singing, she can usually be found watching her favorite movies for the millionth time with her tail-wagging best friends.

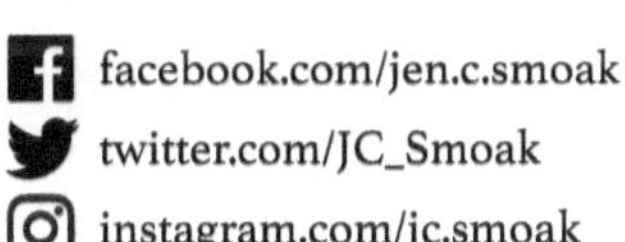

BEAUTY AND THE LYCAN

BY KAYLA MAYA

In a disease ravaged world ruled by a new breed of vampire, Clementine has been caught and encaged in a never ending game of cat and mouse.

Bound by her captors and thrown into a deadly prison home to a vicious Werewolf. Clementine has two options; befriend the wolf or get killed by the vampires.

But, when her heart makes the decision for her, can she escape her fate?

1

Clementine kept her head down as she poured a pitcher of scarlet blood into a cup. The cup was held by a gnarled, pitch-white hand with long, sharp, almost talon-like fingernails. The vampire's complexion was more ashen than usual today, Clem noticed. Usually, there was more color to them - not much, but enough to notice that something was wrong. She hoped that it had nothing to do with her, yet hope was all she held. The vampire swatted her away with his other hand, nail scratching her upper arm and drawing a thin line of blood that began to seep out from the wound. She hissed in pain, drawing back as the vampire gripped her wrist, drawing her closer.

Clementine shuddered, eyes wide in horror as the vampire, known as Father McGuire, dug his fangs into her wound. She bit back her cry for help as the pitcher fell from her fingers, shattering on impact with the ground and blood splattering out to coat the floor. Clem had been drunk from several times before; each time they almost left her dry. She had recently heard stories from the other servants about how the pretty ones become concubines - and then bloody banks to drain after other primal urges were satisfied. She shuddered once again. Sleeping with a vampire was by far the last thing on her list of things to do today. Father McGuire reached out, grabbing Clem's waist and bringing her to his lap.

"You taste very lovely." His voice was gravely, almost unused, as he pushed her upper arm away. Her blood coated his lips as his fangs protruded from the corners of his mouth. "Would you like to pleasure me in other ways?"

It was more of a command than a question, but Clementine had been compelled more often than she could even recall and it didn't affect her anymore. She played along regardless. Life was too precious here lately; the last girl that disobeyed his command ended up being his five-star course for a solid week, giving the other servants a few days off to recover. Clem included. But now, sitting on his lap, feeling his desire mixed in with his carnal ways, she wanted nothing more than to stake him in the heart and watch him explode into glittering dust. She noticed the way he almost purred, his beady, hungry eyes watching her body movements.

"Atta girl," he soothed. He reached out, combing her dark, midnight hair with his talons, his hand straying towards the nether region.

"Get. Off. Me."

"What did you say?"

The vampire grabbed her wrist, swinging her from his lap to right in front of him, red eyes blazing with fury. His teeth were elongated, the blood he drank from her coating his fangs a dark crimson. Clem's knees locked and shoulders hunched as she began to shudder, her teeth starting to chatter at seeing the vampire so angry. She had seen them angry before, but never like this. Had she really upset him this much by denying him her forbidden fruit? Clem hissed in pain as his claw-like nails dug into her wrist, drawing more blood for him to suckle on.

"I asked you a question."

Clem remained silent.

"I said, I asked you a question. You had better answer before you really start to anger me."

She bit her lower lip, trying her best to remain calm as her blood rushed to her ears, her heart hammering against her ribcage. She was beyond frightened. The threat from earlier was abysmal; this was something far worse. Clem mustered up as much courage as she could, not looking the vampire directly in the eye.

"I—I didn't mean what I said," she swallowed, "I did not mean it."

The vampire pulled her closer, his breath stirring her hair. She knew that they didn't need to breathe anymore, but sometimes, no matter how old they seemed, it was harder to get rid of old habits. Especially when one was this angry. "How did you manage my compulsion?"

Clem blinked. "I'm sorry?"

"How," he yanked her closer, teeth nipping her ear to draw more blood, "did you manage my compulsion?"

"I—I don't know," she lied, "I don't have a clue."

"Hmm..." he licked the blood that dripped from her ear, his tongue grazing his lips and almost savoring her taste. He smacked his lips together. "You are human. Mortal. There should be no reason for you to endure my compulsion."

"Maybe I'm special."

"Hardly," He snorted. "Regardless, you disobeyed and now I have to figure out what to do with you. Shall I have you as a snack or a meal? You decide, my dear."

Clementine began to hyperventilate, her body being convulsing by fear. Was death really worth disobeying her vampire captor? She tried to speak, but her voice was lodged in her throat, her fear taking over her as she fell to her knees. She scraped her right knee on the broken glass of the pitcher and fresh blood welled from the wound, mixing with that of the other servants. Was this really how she was going to die? Becoming lunch - or rather, a meager snack to a hungry vampire?

"I am waiting," he told her.

Her eyes went wide as they locked onto a large shard of glass. She grabbed it, her movements lucid and slow. With shaking hands, she held onto the glass, once again cutting herself along the palm. She felt her blood trickle down her wrist before the vampire reached out and grabbed her throat, lifting her in the air. Clem struggled, her feet kicking at nothing as the vampire's fangs slowly formed into large points. His tongue lolled out the side as he brought her neck to his lips. Clementine screamed, raising her shardt in the air and striking him in the chest, right in the heart. The vampire growled, throwing her away and against the drawer at the far end of the room. She hit her head with a bang, immediately feeling a large bruise forming along her cheek. Her right temple was badly cut, blood seeping out onto her face.

"How dare you!" he screamed. He grabbed the shard and ripped it out of his chest. He threw it on the ground and covered his injury with his hand, fangs still bared. His eyes were bright with red hot fury. "You dare kill me? A vampire? Your captor!"

"I—I," Clem stammered.

"I am over two-thousand-years-old, little mortal." He grabbed her throat, almost crushing her windpipe as he brought her closer. "Tell me, why should I spare your pathetic life? Other than that pretty face you have."

"My blood," she said.

"Oh?" He seemed to ponder this for a moment, "I don't think so."

Clementine closed her eyes, a single tear rolling down her cheek. *I am going to die,* she told herself. With a growl, the vampire threw her back into the wall, teeth bared and gleaming as he licked his lips. "You know," he mused, "I think I have a better idea."

2

The vampire dragged Clementine down the endless, cold hallway. Clem kept slipping and sliding from the fresh blood cascading from her open wounds. Her hair was crusted with dried blood – her own mixed with that of the vampire's. While she knew that she'd lost a lot of blood, it still wasn't enough for her to lose consciousness. It felt like her soul was draining from those open wounds. He kept a firm handle on her wrist as he led her down to the depths of the castle. They eventually stopped in front of a cell, the cold seeping into her very core as a deep growl emanated from within; dark, blood-red eyes glowed from the darkness. Clem gulped as the vampire forced the cell's door open and tossed her in. She flopped to the floor, knees and elbows skidding. Clem sat up, throwing herself against the wall as the vampire laughed and walked away.

She cursed inwardly as she noticed that the glass wound to his chest hadn't slowed him down at all. Not even a little bit. No limp to his step, no arm covering his chest. Clem huffed and stamped her foot in frustration at her lack of knowledge about killing the vampires.

Clem examined the darkness. She could distantly hear the sound of breathing and the scraping of chains along the ground. Those blazing eyes peered at Clem as she stood on shaky legs, trying to push her hair away from her face to catch a glimpse of who would kill her instead of the immortal bloodsucker. A mangy, grey wolf stalked through the darkness, its fur standing on end as it marched closer. Its ears were large, with a slit on the right ear, and the wolf had a massive maw filled with dozens of sterling white fangs. Saliva dripped down from the side of its mouth, its long tail thumping from behind. A massive chain was wrapped around its neck, dragging the links behind to make that loud scraping noise. Clem noticed that the wolf favored its back-right leg, almost dragging it across the floor behind it.

"Who are you?" The wolf's voice was husky, almost hoarse, as it smacked its maw a few times.

"I—I'm sorry?" Clementine asked.

"Who. Are. You?"

"My name is Clementine. I—I tried to kill Father McGuire."

"Obviously unsuccessful," the wolf remarked. It sat on its haunches, wincing as the leg flopped to the side.

"Your leg..." she gestured at the limp appendage. "It's broken."

The wolf's head jerked in her direction. "It is not broken."

"Yes, it is," she frowned, her worry all but forgotten. In fact, this wolf was almost formal with her. "Here, I used to be a nurse. Let me help you."

"No." The wolf drew its tail over the injured leg, eyes narrowed in suspicion.

"You're rather nice. I assume you're a werewolf."

"I do not enjoy killing, but you are correct. I am what you call a lycan."

"What's your name?"

"It does not concern you."

"Fine. At least let me help set that leg before you lose it completely."

The lycan's eyes narrowed, a low growl coming from his throat. "Fine." He moved his tail to the side to reveal the broken leg. "I will let you do this."

As Clem crawled to the lycan's side, she caught wind of the god-awful smell that came with his leg. It was swollen, the edges crusted with a dark film and dried blood. Puss oozed out of the wound, and his leg shook slightly whenever the yellow-white puss came flowing out. It looked rather painful. Her suspicions were confirmed when the lycan growled in his throat, a small and feeble cry escaping his maw. As Clem dressed the wound, she tried desperately to not notice the breath that stirred her hair or feel the soft fur beneath her fingers.

"Why are you down here?" She gained the courage to ask.

"The same reason you are down here," the lycan responded, "the immortals."

Clem nodded and continued her best attempts to work out the wound and keep it clean. Her fears were replaced with keen interest. If the lycan had wanted to kill her, he could easily do so with a single bite to her windpipe. However, he had chosen the more civil route, sitting down and talking to her. For that, she began to realize that he could be the key to helping her help *him* escape this captive prison. Maybe, just maybe. If she could convince him. Right now, she didn't dare utter a syllable - not when his massive canines were far too close to her face for comfort.

"How long have you been down here?" she tried again.

He glanced up to the single cell window, barred with rusted silver pillars. Lethal to lycans, yet harmless to humans like Clem. "Almost fifty-two full moons."

"You've been in here for almost *four* years?!" Clem exclaimed shrilly.

"Keep your voice down!" he nearly shouted. "I do not wish to speak about how long I have been away from my kin."

"Why are you being so cordial with me?"

He paused. "I do not know."

"You don't know? Or you won't tell me?"

"For some reason, I do not wish to harm you. Who can say why?"

"Right." She sucked air in through her teeth. "Well, seeing as how we're stuck here for a bit, why don't we get to know each other?"

The lycan regarded her with bloodshot eyes, tongue lolling out over the massive, gleaming canines. He opened his maw but thought better of it, opting to just turn around and sit on his haunches. He stared up at the bright, almost baby blue moon. Clem's eyes traveled the length of the lycan's magnificent body, observing the taut muscles, almost like he was about to pounce at any given moment. His ears flicked from side to side every now and again, watching for danger. Once, she saw his tail thump the floor, skittering dust into her face and making her cough. After a while, she noticed that he took refuge over by the window, body curled in a tight ball. His eyes were like two burning coals, never moving from her face as he regarded her.

"Why do you stare at me like that?" she questioned.

"Like what?"

"Like what you're doing now."

"I am not staring," he huffed, "merely, watching you."

"Why?"

"I do not know."

She huffed herself, going over to her own corner to watch him like he had done to her. The lycan regarded her, tail slapping the ground as his right ear twitched. He lifted his head as a large, heavy metal door slammed shut. A few moments later, footsteps could be heard coming closer down their way. A forked nose came first, followed by gnarled fingers and then wispy red hair.

Father McGuire.

The lycan stood, a low growl emanating from his throat as his eyes blazed. He kept a close eye on the vampire as the immortal came closer, wrapped gnarled fingers around the bars, and leaned in, lips raised in a small smile of victory. The vampire gazed into the lycan's eyes, mouth moving in a silent voice. The werewolf's eyes went from the immortal to Clem, eyes narrowed and muscles pulled taut before he opened his massive maw.

The lycan sprang.

Clementine skidded back on her heels, her butt sliding over the cold floor and palms scraping against the concrete. Fresh blood welled up along the injured hand, the blood dripping down her fingers to the floor. The vampire licked his lips, fangs looking just as lethal as the lycan's massive canines and claws.

I am going to die here

No

I will survive

I will not allow him to win

The lycan's hot breath stirred Clem's hair, almost salivating on her lap. Was Father McGuire using his compulsion on the werewolf? If so, why wasn't he affected by it like she had been earlier? She shook my head and bolted to the side as the lycan rushed her again, head going straight into the wall and sending cracks out through the stone. After several long minutes of cat and mouse, the vampire had finally had enough. He dropped his compulsion and the wolf collapsed in front of the girl, groaning as the injured leg flopped to the side.

"I will see you later, my sweet snack." The vampire smiled and turned to walk away from the duo. "And maybe next time you will not avoid my attacks."

3

For several weeks, the routine was the same. Clementine and the lycan spent several long hours together talking. After several brutal days of earning his trust, Clem was finally able to relax whenever the vampire came down to sic the lycan on her. While she had still not learned the origins of his namesake, she took comfort in the fact that her healing had done him some good. His leg was almost at a hundred percent – but that also meant it would be ten times harder for her to avoid him whenever McGuire compelled the wolf to try and mutilate her. Luckily, she was fast enough to dodge the lycan's attacks. Mostly, that is.

With several scraps and scratches, she had come out relatively unscathed. In fact, the worst of her injures was to her heart. She had grown to love the lycan - not just his body, but his soul. He had informed her that his wolf form was not the usual form he would have taken, but that of his human form. At first, she hadn't trusted the were. Over time, however, she began to realize that he had more humanity in him than Clem herself, even though he was a magical beast. That's what originally drew her to him; his humanity.

"When can I see your human side?" Clem asked one morning.

"I do not know," he confessed.

Clem held the cup around the handle, discreetly trying not to show her desperation. "We need to find a way out of here."

"That we do," he confirmed. "However, that does not seem possible - not with these chains around my neck."

"I'll help you with them."

"Foolish," he told her. "You are not strong."

"Yes I am!"

"Are not."

"I am!"

"Are not."

"Are you always this infuriating?"

He tilted his head to the side. "No," he confessed. "But you bring out the best in me, as they say."

Clem relented, opting to rest in her corner, eyes warily checking the perimeter. It had been almost a week since the vampire's last visit. A week free of torture. The lycan, who still refused to grace her with his name, held a kinship towards her. They needed each other to survive, but she wouldn't push his boundaries. Despite being two separate species, they had formed a tight bond and a deep friendship. While she watched him resting in the corner, tail curled around his body and ears flicking back and forth every so often, she often confused him for a dog rather than a large beast that could potentially kill her. She settled into her corner, mulling over events. All humans had been enslaved by the vampires almost a hundred years ago. Since then, anyone spotted was captured - Clem's entire family included.

"My name is Desmond."

Clem jolted out of her thoughts at the sound of the lycan's voice. He lifted his head, ears pricked forward and glowing eyes assessing her. Had she heard him correctly? "I'm sorry?"

"My name is Desmond," he repeated.

"I'm Clementine."

"I know who you are." He glanced up. "My ears pick up everything. Right now, as we speak, that vampire is on his way."

"What do you mean?"

"He is coming."

"Father McGuire?"

"Correct. And he is not alone. Prepare yourself."

Clem bounded to her feet, glancing back and forth as she heard the huge, heavy, metal doors clang open and then shut once more. She heard scuffling followed by an inhuman scream as the vampire appeared, clutching a young girl around the throat. Veronica. The same girl with whom Clem had a deep connection. Clem remembered when she first arrived and Veronica, a short blonde-haired girl with bright ocean eyes, was there to lend a hand. Through the years of their enslavement, they had become close friends. Her only friend. Why did he have her in his clutches?

"I see you two have become acquainted with one another." The immortal smiled. "However, if you do not give up your secrets soon, I will kill this other girl."

"I told you before, I don't know what I did," Clem defended herself.

"A pity." The vampire shifted his weight and then sank his teeth into Veronica's throat. Clem screamed as the immortal drank her friend dry before discarding the body to the side, blood dripping from his mouth and red eyes blazing with fury - and a fresh kill. "I will bring down as many humans as possible until you talk."

He left, leaving Clem to fall to her knees and hug herself as fresh tears streamed down her face. Because of her, an innocent girl had perished... and many more would follow if Clem couldn't figure out why not being compelled was such a bad thing. She desperately tried not to glance down at her dead friend - at those lifeless blank eyes and pasty white skin.

"He sees you as a threat," Desmond sat up. "Why?"

"Because I can't be compelled."

"Oh? What sort of trickery is that?"

"I don't know," she confessed.

"Is that what brought you down here?"

She nodded. "He...wanted to do more than drink my blood. Vampires have other primal urges that humans used to have. I did not want to share a bed with him, so I staked him in the heart with a piece of glass." She paused. "Needless to say, it did not end well for me. He found out that I had faked being compelled and nearly killed me. Then, he sent me down here in this prison. Isolated, trapped, and alone."

Desmond regarded her. "I was brought here because I killed a vampire."

Clementine's eyes bulged out of her sockets. "You killed one? How?"

He glanced away. "My mate was killed by a group of them. I went after them. Lycans' bites are very deadly to vampires. With a single bite, I took them each of them down, one by one. This vampire you call 'Father McGuire' was the one who caught me and sentenced me to a life in this prison. I kill those who defy him because, if I do not, I will be killed myself."

"Why didn't you kill me?"

"I do not know. You are special. I cannot seem to want to harm you."

"I don't understand."

"Neither do I."

She sat back on her heels. "Well, that's weird. I can't be compelled and you can't kill me for whatever reason."

"I must transform," Desmond sat up straighter. "It is nearing time for my shift."

Clem opened her mouth to say something, but just then a blinding bright light exploded in front of her. Where the Lycan once was, now sat a tall, dark, tanned man with an eight pack. His hair was just as unruly as his coat in wolf form and he had dark, hooded eyes. He wore nothing from the neck to his waist, only a pair of shorts hunging low over his hips. Clem found herself drooling over his muscled human form. If anything, she imagined herself running her fingers over those toned muscles and feeling him on top of her in a way she had never felt before. The attraction was instant and her heart was beating wildly in her chest. She wanted this man.

"This is my human form," he told her.

"Why did you transform?"

He furrowed his brows. "Because I did not trust you."

"And you do now?"

"Partially. I saw the way you looked at the immortal."

"Like what?"

"With hatred."

"They took everything from me," she told him. Her eyes roved across his body, eager to run her hands over him. "They'll suffer if I have anything to do about it"

Desmond cocked his head to the side, eyes narrowed. "They took everything from me as well. What happened to you?"

Clementine sucked in air through her teeth. "My family. We... we lived on the outskirts of the forest, hidden beneath the ruins of the Old World. My sister, Mandarin, went with me. We were out in the apple orchard, collecting as many of those succulent fruits as we could before the sun went down. We were too late. Father McGuire found us, killed my sister, and took me to his home where I was beaten, almost sucked dry, and many other unthinkable things that I will never repeat again.

"I blame myself for my sister's death. If I hadn't forced her to come along with me, if I hadn't told her to help me grab a few more apples... she would still be here. If I had fought back - no, if I had offered myself to be killed first, then she would be alive." Clem brought her knees up to her chin, resting there. "I often wonder if my parents blame me. I keep wondering if they went out to find us and found Mandarin's corpse instead. Maybe I can find them again and tell them what happened. Oh, who am I kidding? That won't ever happen. I'll never get out of here."

"Clementine... Mandarin... those names are of fruits long-forgotten. Long deceased. Why do you have names of old fruits?" he asked.

Clem tilted her head to the side. "My parents decided that they wanted us to be remembered. They wanted us to have hope, since the world went to complete shit. Ever since that disease wiped out half of humanity and the vampires rose to power, we were the only beacon of hope that blossomed from my parents. I had a friend back in the place we had stayed before I was captured. Her name was Creek, a symbol of what used to flow through the mountains. That's what we are. Hope. A symbol of hope and love."

"Interesting."

"And you?"

"What about me?"

"Why are you down here?"

"I have already explained it to you - my mate was killed."

"I feel like there's more to it than that. I told you my life story—"

"Through your own choice," he huffed.

"But," she continued, as if he had not spoken. "It would be nice to hear your own story since I told you mine."

"Fine," he sighed. "My species is just like you mere humans. We are a limited breed, meaning three to four males can have a female mate. Females are limited now but, before this 'disease' you mentioned before, there were numerous she-wolves. Back then, males and females could only mate and marry another wolf if they were seen as destined mates."

"I don't understand."

"A destined mate is when a male and female share half a soul. Once they are reunited, that half-soul morphs into a full soul that is shared by each wolf. My mate, Aya, was killed before our souls could connect and become one. Her death literally took a part of my soul. She-wolves could only mate with their destined mate, but since we are so few in numbers now, destined mates no longer matter. We mate because we have to, not to find our true loves. Not anymore, at least."

"I'm sorry."

"There is nothing for you to be sorry about. But first, I must ask - what is this disease you mentioned before?"

"Oh. That's the disease that wiped out almost all of humanity. It was once known as the zombie plague, but then morphed into the new name: Humanity Killer. It was a small virus that wormed its ways into the human flesh, where it would lay dormant for a few weeks until it manifested. It ate the humans from inside out, sometimes killing almost instantly. Others, their skin rotted from their bones, making them look almost like a zombie. Soon, they discovered animals could carry it, even if they didn't always die from it.

"Many people died, but many rose up from their graves with unnatural healing abilities. They grew fangs, talons, and eventually became immortal.

And that's how we know them today: vampires. Once a thing of myth and legend, now made a reality. When the vampires took over, humans became a thing of the past. The virus is now long gone, but the age of humanity lost its reign on the world. Most say it was Mother Nature returning the favor - there we were too many people. I'm curious, did the Humanity Killer affect your kind like it did humans?"

"It did," Desmond acknowledged. "But not like it did to you mere humans."

"How so?"

"It started with the morphing. First, they started getting larger, more sinister. They did not die to begin with, they simply changed. Their fur fell off, leaving them mangy. Welts filled with blood and burst, coating our coats in diseased blood. Then, we grew more appendages, such as an extra arm or leg. It continued until they morphed into the Dark Wolves. I am sure you are aware of them."

"Barely. We lived underground, we didn't really hear about the monsters in the world above. When we did, we were mostly told to watch out for the vampires, not the Dark Wolves that crept in the shadows. Although, they were mentioned several times. Unlike vamps, the wolves could come out during the day time, but only where the shadows were. Sunlight doesn't hurt them like it does vampires, but it does make them uncomfortable enough to not venture out beyond the Dark Wood."

"I am impressed," Desmond smiled. "You know a good chunk of lore."

"Hardly," Clem snorted. "I just grew accustomed to listening to tales and then re-telling them to the other kids."

Clementine couldn't help the small smile that crept along her lips. Her heart grew for the werewolf. Being isolated in this prison for weeks with him made her realize that she was falling dangerously in love. Not just for his body, but his soul. Her cheeks flushed bright scarlet when she noticed that Desmond had his head tilted to the side, nose twitching as he assessed her.

"What is the matter?" He asked.

"Uh... nothing. I was just... thinking!"

Desmond huffed. He glanced out the single window, where the moon had already risen to its full height. She began to wonder what her life would have been like if she had not been reckless and gotten herself captured and her sister killed. Would Clem have met Desmond if he, too, hadn't been captured? Rather unlikely, seeing as how he would have been more than happy to be with his destined mate. Sadness crept inside her bosom. While she knew being in love with a werewolf was completely insane, she still couldn't help but feel her heart ache for him, for his arms wrapped around her torso. What would a life be like with Desmond? Would it be full of love and devotion, or just plain out terrible? Either way, the only way out of that prison was through death. Whether by Desmond's own hands or the vampires, it still remained uncertain.

"Do you think we'll be able to escape this place?" Clem asked.

"I do not want to alarm you, but I fear we cannot. Not without the cost of our lives. Vampires only exist to extoll torment; keeping us locked up together is that for him."

Clem sighed. "I feared you would say that."

"I am sorry."

She shrugged. "I figured as much. I would die being happy."

"Happy? How so?"

Clem bit her bottom lip. "No reason. I just enjoy your company."

"You are hiding something from me."

"Am not."

"Spill."

"It doesn't concern you."

"We have limited time together," he reminded her. "If I want to talk with a beautiful human in my last hours, then so be it."

Clementine's face flamed. "You...you think I'm beautiful?"

"I am not blind. I appreciate beauty."

"But your destined mate—"

"What about her? Do you think that just because she is gone, I am suddenly in love with you, Clementine?"

Her face turned even redder. "I didn't mean—"

"I know what you meant," he snapped. "I like you, that much is true. That is probably why I cannot harm a single hair on your head. But I cannot love you like I did Aya. I am sorry."

Clementine's face fell, a single tear falling from the corner of her eye. "I... I understand why you can't. I can't help how I feel, though. I love you, Desmond. I know we have been isolated in this prison for so long now that I can't tell if it's been weeks or months anymore, but I can't help it. I am in love with you, Desmond."

He sighed. "My intention was never to harm you. I didn't want you to fall in love with me because... I could not bear the thought of losing you like I did Aya. But, despite everything, Clementine... I did fall in love with you. I could not help myself."

"But you just said—"

"I know what I just said," he told her. "But I couldn't tell you the truth. I have no heart to tell you that I am in love with you and then lose you." He sighed. "I didn't want to tell you earlier, but I overheard Father McGuire talking. He is done playing with us and he will kill us tomorrow."

Clementine shuddered. "Will you stay up with me? In our final moments?"

Desmond smiled, standing and walking over to her. He caressed her cheek, sending shivers and tingles all over her body. Clem kept her hands at her sides, trying her darndest to keep her hormones under control as his fingers trailed down her face and to her collarbone. Before she knew it, she was laying on her back, Desmond on top of her. He was kissing her. Clementine wrapped her arms around him, crushing his body to hers as her mouth explored his. A moment later she was naked and he was making his way inside her. She gasped at the pleasure as his mouth closed over hers once more. Clementine wished she could live in this moment for her entire life.

4

Clementine awoke wrapped in Desmond's arms. They were both fully clothed, with wide smiles on their faces. The Werewolf nuzzled her neck, licking her earlobe. She giggled as she pushed against his chest, laughing as he tickled her. Seconds later, a horrible racket sounded farther down the hall. Desmond sprang up, morphing into a wolf, fur standing on end as he stalked the length of the cell block. Clementine stood up, straightening her shirt as best she could before Father McGuire rounded the corner.

"I see you've been... well-acquainted." McGuire smiled, pointed fangs dripping with fresh blood. Three other vampires fell into step beside Father McGuire, then two more. Six vampires in total and only one human and werewolf to fight. "Since I cannot compel you, I might as well do the next best thing."

"You will not touch her," Desmond roared.

Father McGuire smiled and raised a finger at Clementine. "Get her."

Within moments the cell door was broken and the five vampires swarmed in, McGuire hanging back and laughing. Desmond rose into action. He bounded in front of Clementine, using his body to push her closer to the wall to keep her protected from all sides. The dark-haired vampire lunged at Clem, earning a large bite in the thigh by the werewolf. The vampire dissolved into ashes, the remains bubbling from the bite of the wolf. Father McGuire jumped into the fray, helping the other four vampires grab hold of Desmond and holding him down as Clementine screamed.

"Such beauty," McGuire cackled. "Too bad it is going to waste."

Clem screamed and thrashed as he dug his fangs into the soft point in her neck. She continued to kick and try to get herself loose, but the vampires' hold on her wouldn't relent. She quickly began to weaken, her heart pumping as the loss of blood went to her head. Desmond roared and howled as he tried to get free.

"Desmond..." Clementine's weak voice floated over to his ears. "I love you."

"Clementine!" Desmond broke free as Father McGuire drank the last drop, flinging her body to the wall. "No!"

Desmond's vision turned red as he went into a frenzy. He ripped apart the closest vampires, their ashes flying into the air and clinging to his coat. Ashes coated the ground and filled the air as Desmond tore apart another vampire, holding onto the last one with his eyes locked on Father McGuire. The elder vampire smiled, running a hand over his mouth where fresh blood dripped down from the corners of his mouth. Without another word, Desmond roared and attacked the elder vampire, his teeth sinking into the vamp's arm. The fangs dug in deep and Father McGuire smiled has he crumpled into dust, a long laugh floating into the air. The werewolf whirled around as more vampires rushed in, surrounding him.

"I will see you again, Aya," Desmond's eyes trailed over to Clementine's dead body. "And I will get to see you again, Clem."

Desmond howled before the vampires attacked. Soon, all that could be heard was the last, soul-wrenching howl before Desmond lost his life.

ABOUT THE AUTHOR

Kayla started writing at the age of four and has not stopped since then! She enjoys all things fantasy with sparks of romance sprinkled in. To this day she spends countless hours on her laptop and with pieces of paper where ever she can find!

Website:
https://kaylabuenrostro16.wixsite.com/kaylamaya

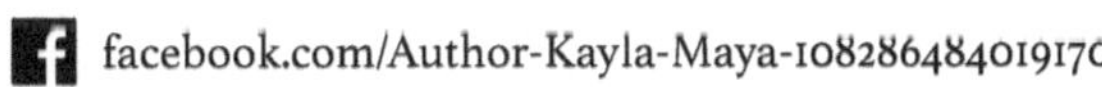

RAIN DELAY

BY TINA GALLAGHER

Rusty Russell thought Ivy Sherman was flaky and shallow. She thought he was an arrogant ass. When a hurricane confines them to a house they'd both expected to be empty, their opinions change and things heat up inside as the storm rages outside.

1

RUSTY

I glanced out the car window as the Uber pulled into the circular driveway.

"You sure this is it?" I asked.

"This is the address," the driver said.

"Ok then. Thanks." I grabbed my duffle and stepped out of the car. After slamming the door behind me, I turned and looked at the two-story house. "It's pink," I muttered to myself then followed the sidewalk to the double-door entryway.

After typing the six-digit code into the keypad, I heard the deadbolt shift and opened the door. It seems kind of strange to secure a house worth millions of dollars with six random numbers, but to each his own, I guess.

My phone rang just as I stepped into the foyer, and there's no doubt in my mind who's calling.

"I just got here. Literally just walked in the door," I said without checking the Caller ID. "And not for nothing Mom, this place is what Sam refers to as his bungalow in the Keys? Holy hell. The foyer is as big as my condo."

"I'm glad you're safe," my mom said with a sigh.

Since my dad died six years ago, she's been really nervous that something is going to happen to me anytime I'm not within her sights. Which is quite a lot since I'm on the road playing baseball half the year.

I walked into the open-concept dining room, living room, kitchen area and then over to the wall of windows overlooking the water.

"I'm fine. Tell Sam I said thanks again for letting me use this place. It looks like the perfect spot to decompress for the week."

"He's happy you took him up on his offer," she said. "I think he feels like you're finally accepting him."

My mother started dating Sam Sherman a little over a year ago. He comes from old timber money and made a small fortune himself with his own gaming company. This "bungalow" in Marathon, Florida is well over three thousand square feet, sits right on the Gulf, and from what I understand, is the smallest of his five properties.

The fact that my mom has a boyfriend is still a little strange for me, but Sam seems to make her happy and treats her well, so I can't complain.

"What are you guys up to tonight?" I asked.

Since Sam is retired and my mom doesn't work, it's not unusual for them to just jet off to somewhere. This week they're in Tuscany.

"We're going to a pizza and gelato cooking class, which I think is going to be a lot of fun. After that, we're supposed to be meeting Ivy's mom Kelly for a drink. Sam is hoping they can figure out where Ivy is. He's really worried about her."

From what I've been told, Sam's ex-wife is an artist and a bit flaky, and his daughter seems to follow suit. I've only met Ivy a couple times, but she didn't leave a very good impression.

I slid the patio door open and stepped out onto the balcony. Looking left to right and then toward the water, I was happy to see the closest property was far, far away. This place definitely has the privacy I'm looking for right now. Hopefully I'll be able to get my head on straight and my pitching back in line this week. I don't want to go back after the All-Star break and suck like I did the past month.

Settling into a lounge chair, I asked, "Why, did something happen to her?"

"She was fired from her job and left the house in Aspen a week ago. Sam hasn't heard from her at all and her cell phone must be off because he can't track it. He's worried."

"I'm sure she'll turn up. Hasn't she done this before?"

"Not like this, according to Sam. She usually lets him know where she's going, or at least lets someone know. This time she just disappeared without a word."

"Are you nervous about meeting Sam's ex?"

"A little, but I'm sure it will be good. They haven't been together for a really long time," she said. "But enough about that, how are you?"

"I'll be fine. I just need to figure out what I'm doing wrong and I think having time to focus will help with that."

"Oh Christopher, you put too much pressure on yourself. You're an amazing pitcher. Just go out there and play catch like your dad used to tell you to do."

Only my mother uses my full name, which is better than Christy, which is what she used to call me when I was younger. To everyone else, including my father, I've been Rusty since a coach gave me the nickname back in middle school. Between my hair color and having the last name Russell, it fits.

"I try to remember that every time I pitch, but some days it's harder than others."

"Relax and enjoy your time in Marathon. I know you'll be back to your old self when you start after the break," she said. "I have to go get ready for our cooking lesson now, but I'll talk to you tomorrow. I love you, honey."

"Love you too, Mom."

I ended the call and placed my phone on the table next to me. My father's advice has always worked in the past, and hopefully it will help me now. I'm not the fastest pitcher, but I've always earned my position by being accurate and hitting any spot I want at any time. For some reason, my pinpoint control is evading me and for the past month, I've been throwing meatballs and getting crushed.

Settling further into the lounge chair, I closed my eyes, took in a deep breath of salt air, and slowly let it out. I'm not going to think about that today. I'm just going to relax and enjoy the Gulf breeze and maybe take a swim. Tomorrow will be soon enough to figure out how to save my career.

IVY

"I'll be right back baby, I just need to open the door," I said to Finn who was sleeping in the back seat.

I stepped out of the car and walked over to the keypad mounted next to the garage door. It would have been easier to use the app on my phone to open it, but it's turned off and stashed in my purse. I'm sure my dad is trying to track me at this point and right now, I just want to be alone.

Thankfully the six-digit code hadn't been changed and the door opened immediately. Running back to the car, I got behind the wheel and pulled into the garage. I sat forward and rested my head on the steering wheel, exhausted. I've been driving for the better part of three days to make my way from Aspen to Marathon as fast as possible.

Finn whimpered behind me and I looked over my shoulder and spotted his head between the seats, ears raised, waiting to follow my lead. Traveling across a good part of the country with a one hundred thirty pound Irish Setter could have been challenging, but he's such a sweetheart, we didn't have any problems at all.

I stepped out of the car and stretched then walked over to close the garage door. Once it was all the way down, I opened the car door and let Finn out. He jumped out and sniffed his way around the three-car garage. While he did that, I retrieved my suitcase and the bag of Finn's supplies from the trunk then slammed it closed.

"Let's go inside, then I'll let you out to explore the yard. I'm sure you want to stretch your legs too."

He wagged his tail and followed me up the stairs and into the kitchen. I dropped my suitcase then placed the grocery bag on the counter, pulled out Finn's bowl, and filled it with water.

"Come on, buddy. Let's go outside."

I led him out the patio doors and down to the yard so he could do his business. Of course, he was more interested in sniffing and checking out the new space, so I put his water down and got comfortable in a lounge chair. This could take a while. I doubt he'd wander off, but I don't want to leave him alone just yet.

Closing my eyes, I tried to relax and enjoy the atmosphere. The house in Marathon has always been my favorite place in the world and I'm hoping that being here helps me figure out my life. I mean, I'm thirty years old. When am I gonna get my shit together?

I'm what you might call a Jill of all trades, master of none. I went to college for seven years and after trying out that many majors, quit to figure out whated I want to do. In the past five years, I've had more jobs than I want to think about, trying to find one that I love...but they all end in disaster.

Before I could do a mental play-by-play of all my failures, I felt water drip on my cheek a second before Finn licked me. I opened my eyes and smiled up at him.

Cupping his face in my hands, I kissed him on the top of the head.

"You are the best boy in the world, you know that?" He wagged his tail and rubbed his face against my chest. "Let's go inside and get comfy." I stood and grabbed his water bowl, and he followed me back up the stairs and into the house. "I know you slept most of the way but I didn't and I'm exhausted." Closing the door behind us, I clicked the lock and walked over to the kitchen. "But you're probably hungry. I know I am." I pulled his other bowl out of the grocery bag, filled it with food, and set it on the floor then rinsed and refilled the water bowl and placed it next to its twin.

Once Finn was taken care of, I looked in the freezer to see if there's anything for me.

"Score." I pulled the frozen pizza out and closed the door. "And since you were such a good boy all during our trip, I think you deserve some crust." Finn picked up his head and swallowed a mouthful of food then licked his mouth and wagged his tail. I think he approves.

After setting the pizza on a stone and putting it in the oven, I pulled a pitcher from the cupboard and placed it in the sink so I could make some lemonade. I turned the handle all the way to the left, but the pressure was low, as though water was running somewhere in the house.

"That's weird." I turned off the water. "I'm gonna go check to see what's going on."

I looked in the half bath near the front entrance before making my way to the other side of the house. A light shone under the door of the bedroom at the end of the hall and I walked that way. I know, I know. I'm being that girl in every horror movie that you scream at who goes to the basement or the barn or wherever and gets herself killed.

Finn came up behind me and let out a soft burp. He'll have to go out again shortly, but for now, I need to find out why there's a light on and water running in a house that's supposed to be empty.

Grabbing the vase off the hall table, I crept toward the door, slowly opened it, and peeked my head inside. The light on the nightstand cast a soft glow through the room and I spotted a duffle bag on the edge of the bed. I stepped inside and Finn followed. The bathroom door was half-closed and I heard the shower running. Tightening my grip on the vase, I crept across the room and pushed the door open. Finn bumped into the back of my legs as I came to an abrupt halt.

The shower was occupied by a man. My eyes locked the part of his anatomy that identified him as such and I licked my lips. I'm not a woman who finds that particular body part attractive to look at, but I gotta say, his is pretty nice. And there's a lot to look at if you know what I mean. Before I could examine it further, he turned around giving me a good look at an amazing ass. Shampoo streamed over the perfect globes and down his long legs.

My eyes took a lazy tour up his muscled back and broad shoulders. He turned again, giving me a nice view of his profile. Something about his chiseled jaw and straight nose looked familiar, but I couldn't quite place him. I know I should do something other than stand in the doorway watching the man shower, but I'm frozen in place.

Finn sat next to me and nudged my hand with his nose. I patted his head but didn't take my eyes off the man in front of me. He hung his head and rolled it from side to side as the water sprayed against his shoulders. I heard a low groan and took a step forward. He must have sensed my movement because next thing I knew, I was staring into silver-blue eyes.

"What the fuck?"

I took in a sharp breath and dropped the vase. Finn went into full attack mode and started barking. I grabbed his collar and held him back so he didn't get cut on the shards littering the floor.

At that moment, I recognized the man in front of me. Christopher Russell, the son of my father's girlfriend.

"Shit," I said as I also realized that I was still standing there staring at him in all his naked glory. Keeping a death grip on Finn's collar, I backed out of the bathroom and slammed the door behind me then ran out of the bedroom and down the stairs.

2

RUSTY

I turned off the water and stepped out of the shower. Grabbing a towel off the rack, I dried myself, tied it around my waist, and walked into the bedroom. Still a little shaken from the *Psycho* moment in the bathroom, I sat on the edge of the bed and dragged my fingers through my wet hair.

The only reason I took Sam up on his offer to come here is because he swore it was secluded and empty. It seems his missing-in-action daughter decided to take advantage of those things too.

Even through the fogged up glass of the shower stall, I recognized Ivy Sherman. Her mass of curly, honey-blonde hair is hard to miss.

I haven't unpacked yet, so leaving wouldn't take too much effort. But instead of storming out, I'll get dressed, go downstairs, and have a polite conversation before figuring out my exit plan.

After pulling on boxer briefs, shorts, and a T-shirt, I opened my bedroom door and headed downstairs to face my little peeping Ivy. As I walked down the hallway, her slightly off-tune voice floated up the stairs as she sang a song I recognized from childhood. Or at least her rendition of it.

"There was a pup named Michael Finnegan, he had whiskers on his chin-ne-gan, the wind blew them off and blew them on again, poor old Michael Finnegan, begin again."

Ivy sang the verse again as I walked down the stairs and stepped into the living room. The dog watched her adoringly as she tickled his chin while she sang between bites of pizza. Her back was to me as she sat cross-legged on the couch, but he noticed me immediately and stood, then growled, baring his teeth.

I stopped just behind the couch and Ivy looked at me over her shoulder. Squatting down, I rested my forearms on my thighs, letting my hands hang loose.

"Finn doesn't really like men," Ivy said as she shifted to grab his collar.

"Let him go. He'll be okay."

Her dark brown eyes met mine as she slowly settled back onto the couch. Finn looked from her to me, seeming to wonder why he was being left to his own devices. When Ivy didn't reach for him again, he stood and tentatively made his way toward me. I didn't move, but talked to him in a soft, soothing tone.

"Hey buddy. What are you doing? Huh? You having pizza?"

His tail wasn't wagging, but didn't look like he wanted to attack me either. I took that as a good sign.

"Who's a good boy?"

Finn moved within sniffing distance and, seeming to like what he smelled, moved closer still. When his nose touched the back of my hand, I flipped it over to pet the side of his face. That did it. His tail started a slow wag and soon I found myself on my ass as he butted up against me to get closer.

Ivy ran over, but I stopped her from pulling Finn off just as he licked me from jaw to temple. Her eyes widened and I laughed and rubbed his sides as he snuggled against me.

Finn slowly slid down until half his body rested on my legs.

"We're good here," I told Ivy. "You can go finish your pizza."

She blinked and opened her mouth to speak, then closed it and silently walked back to the couch. Her back to me, she picked up another slice and took a big bite. I continued to pet Finn and he rested his head against my thigh and closed his eyes.

We sat like that until my legs started to fall asleep.

"Hey buddy, let's go get some pizza." I slowly shifted my legs to the side, giving him a chance to sit. Once he did, I stood and pointed. "I think there are a few crusts waiting over there for you."

He looked over his shoulder then ran the short distance toward Ivy. I went into the kitchen and pulled a Sam Adams out of the refrigerator.

"You know, your dad is freaking out since you've gone off the grid," I said and walked back to the living room, grabbed a slice of pizza, and settled into the love seat adjacent to the couch.

She watched me take a bite, then said, "Help yourself."

I took another bite and chewed. "I'm serious. My mom and your dad are in Tuscany as we speak. They were meeting your mom to see if they can figure out where you are."

Sitting back, she patted the spot next to her and Finn jumped up, resting his head on her thigh.

"Please don't tell them I'm here," she said looking up at me, her brown eyes shining with tears. "I just need a minute to figure some things out before I talk to my father."

I totally understand needing time to yourself, but instead of answering, I leaned forward and grabbed another slice of pizza.

"This is pretty good for a frozen pie," I said and took a big bite.

She watched me eat then narrowed her eyes. "Wait. What are you doing here, Christopher? Shouldn't you be off playing baseball or whatever?"

"Please call me Rusty." I finished my slice, saving the crust for Finn, and took a long drink of beer. There's no reason for her to know the whole truth so I decided to go with the shortened version. "It's All-Star break and since I'm not on the team, I have some time off. I told my mom I was going to take a vacation and your dad offered this place since he didn't think anyone would be here."

"I figured it would be empty because my dad never comes here in the summer. He doesn't like the heat." She looked down and focused on her fingers as they ran through Finn's fur. "Are you going to tell them I'm here?"

I finished my beer and placed the empty bottle on the coffee table. Finn lifted his head when I whistled and grabbed the crust I tossed to him out of the air.

I'm not normally the type of guy who invites women to dump their problems on me. Not unless I have something to gain from it, if you know what I mean. But right now, I really want to hear what's going on with Ivy. Maybe her issues will help me take my mind off of my own.

Shifting to lean against the armrest, I crossed my ankles, and put my hands behind my head.

"Why don't you tell me your story and then I'll decide?"

IVY

Rusty looks like such a smug prick sitting there and part of me wants to tell him to kiss my ass. What's the worst thing that can happen —he'll tell my father where I am?

But Finn's reaction to him holds me back. He's an excellent judge of character and I wasn't lying when I said he usually doesn't like men.

And obviously Rusty likes dogs, so that's one big check mark in the positive column for him as far as I'm concerned. I looked down and watched Finn chew the crust Rusty had thrown in a perfect arc into his mouth. That's when I realized something.

"Did you notice that you and Finn have the same color hair?"

He glanced at Finn and the corner of his mouth kicked up into a small smile. Instead of answering my question or making some snide comment, he said, "Stop trying to stall. Spill."

I took in a deep breath and let it out on a sigh.

"I was let go from my job. Which might not seem like a huge deal in the grand scheme of things, but it's just the latest in a long line of failures. I went to college for seven years and ended up quitting without a degree and I've either been fired or quit every job I've had since." Rusty's image blurred as I met his silver-blue gaze. "I turned thirty last month. Not having my life together is getting embarrassing."

Surprisingly Rusty looked at me without judgment. The last time I'd seen him, it had radiated off him in waves. But now, he seems different. Nicer. I mentally shrugged. Or maybe I'm just letting Finn's reaction to him sway my opinion.

"Why do you think you've had such an issue?"

I shifted and waited for Finn to settle back into place before I answered.

"Well in college, everything interested me. I initially went in undeclared and then ended up changing majors every time something different caught my attention. The problem was that each of those changes added time to my schooling and I just wanted to get out, so I quit after I got a summer job I wanted to continue doing. And I probably would have, but I got fired." His raised brow prompted me to explain. "I was a submissions coordinator for a publisher and opened a phishing email. The company's entire system got infected and that was it for me."

I stroked Finn's neck, making sure to scratch under his collar the way he likes. He let out a soft snore and I smiled.

"And stupid stuff like that has happened at every job I've held since. This most recent one lasted the longest, just short of two years. I was a line chef at a pretty upscale restaurant in Aspen. I mostly did prep work, but I also made sides and sauces. All that mixing, chopping, and stirring was so soothing and I really enjoyed it. I'd hoped I finally found my calling."

"So what happened?"

"I started a fire in the kitchen."

"Literally?"

I nodded. "Not on purpose, obviously. I heated oil in a pan to sauté onions and took my eyes off it long enough for it to start on fire. By the time I threw my towel on top to smother it, the flames were too high so it caught on fire too and burned the whole stove up. Before I knew it, the grease traps and ventilation system got involved, then the sprinklers went off. They had to evacuate the restaurant. The kitchen was a total mess and when I offered to help clean up, I was asked to leave and not return."

"Shit. That's brutal."

"Yeah. Finn and I had a pity party for a couple days in Aspen and then I decided to come here to hopefully figure things out. I haven't called my dad because I really don't want to hear the disappointment that will be in his voice. I've always loved this place and I hoped it might inspire me."

"According to my mom, he's kind of freaking out. Not that it's any of my business, but you might want to at least let him know you're here and that you're okay."

"Does your mother always know where you're at?"

"Yeah. I mean, obviously not every second of every day, but she at least knows what city I'm in. And I usually talk to her at least once a day. Especially since my dad died." He shrugged. "If a simple phone call stops her from worrying, it's the least I can do."

I rested my head against the back of the couch and looked up at the ceiling, letting out a sarcastic laugh.

"For the past week, I thought I was acting like an adult taking care of myself and now I feel like a rebellious teenager who ran away from home."

His low chuckle echoed through the room and seemed to vibrate through my body, making my stomach feel like I'd just gone down the first hill of a rollercoaster. I placed my hand over the affected organ in an attempt to settle it down.

"Just let him know where you're at and tell him you'd like to be alone. I'm sure he'll understand."

Rusty swung his legs to the floor and stood. I didn't have to shift my gaze too far down from the ceiling to look at his face. How tall is he anyway? I didn't realize I'd said that out loud until he smiled and answered.

"I'm 6'5". Why?"

Geez, no wonder he looks like a giant to me. At 5'3" I'm a bit height challenged. And for some reason, my curves make me seem even shorter. The man in front of me is the total opposite. He's well-muscled but his long arms and legs give him a lanky look.

I shook my head before my mind could focus on the fact that *everything* about the man is big.

"Just curious."

"I'm gonna head up to bed. It's been a long day." Finn lifted his head and Rusty walked over to scratch him under the chin. "I'll see you tomorrow, buddy." Shifting his gaze to me, he added, "I'll be out of your hair by noon."

It took me a couple seconds to process his words and once I did, my eyes rounded. "What? Why?"

"It is your father's place," he said. "You came here to be alone so it's only right that I leave."

"My dad offered the house to you and I barged in. I'll go." I looked down at Finn then back up to Rusty. "But if you wouldn't mind, I'd like to hang out tomorrow to give him a break from the car." His eyes narrowed and I continued before he could turn me down. "It's a big house. I'm sure we'll be able to stay out of each other's way for twenty-four hours."

He nodded once. "Okay. We'll give it a try and see how it goes."

That said, he scratched Finn's head one last time and I watched him walk through the living room toward the hallway to the bedrooms. Finn rested his head against my lap and looked up at me with his cognac-colored eyes. Leaning down, I kissed his forehead.

"One day here then we hit the road again. If you have any suggestions where we should go, I'm all ears."

3

RUSTY

I paddled up to the dock and grabbed onto the ladder. After climbing up, I reached down and pulled the kayak out of the water then hefted it up onto my shoulder. Walking toward the house, I looked around taking in the sandy beach to the right and the blue sky above. This place is really beautiful. The pink house is even growing on me.

I'm glad I got up and out on the water early. It's barely eight and the heat and humidity are off the charts. The ocean breeze kept me from getting too overheated, but it also made the water super choppy and my workout was that much harder.

After storing the kayak in the rack under the porch, I stepped under the outdoor shower to wash off the salt and sand. I'll get a real shower after breakfast but right now I just want to eat. I'm starving.

Finn greeted me as I walked into the living room. I looked around and spotted Ivy curled up on the sofa. I'm guessing the big guy woke her up to go out early.

"Come on, let's get you some breakfast."

The dog followed me into the kitchen and watched my every move as I put a scoop of food into his bowl. He dug right in and I double-checked that he had water before moving on to my own breakfast.

I'd gotten some basics at a small corner store yesterday, but want to find a supermarket today to better stock the refrigerator. But I have eggs, milk, and bread so I'll make French toast. I grabbed everything I'd need and also a box of frozen breakfast sausage I'd spotted in the freezer yesterday.

Finn had eaten all his food and now made loud lapping sounds as he moved to his water bowl. I laughed when he paused and let out a loud burp.

After beating a few eggs in a large bowl, I added milk, vanilla, and cinnamon then tossed in eight slices of bread, pushing them down so both sides could absorb the mixture. Once that was settled, I pulled a griddle out of the cupboard and set it on the stove to preheat. Grabbing a frying pan from the overhead rack, I dropped in the sausage and put it on the back burner.

I tested the griddle and decided to give it a couple more minutes. Finn sat at the edge of the island watching me.

"Do you need more water?" I walked over and checked the bowl. Yep, it was empty. I reached down and picked it up then gave him a refill. "It's hot down here. You need to stay hydrated." He watched me as though he understood every word I said. "Let's see if the griddle is ready." I pulled the fork out of the bowl of soon-to-be French toast and let the egg mixture drip onto the griddle and smiled as it popped and splattered. "Looks like we're good."

I pushed the bread down again, giving it another good dunk before lifting a dripping slice and placing it on the griddle. I repeated that three more times, then checked on the sausage.

"I hope your mom likes French toast." Finn watched my every move, probably hoping I'd drop something. "Don't worry, I'm sure you'll get a taste."

I flipped the slices in quick succession then used the spatula to roll the sausage before setting it on the edge of the griddle. Pulling a coffee pod off the rack, I dropped it in the machine, and pushed the start button, remembering to place a mug underneath at the last minute.

"That was close," I said to Finn.

I placed the first batch of French toast on a platter and added the remaining four slices to the griddle. While that cooked, I washed the bowl and cleaned the countertop before setting the table.

Finn had settled right next to the island so I had to step over him as I walked back and forth. It's been a long time since I've had a dog and I've forgotten how great it is having one around. I was telling him exactly that when Ivy peeked up from the couch, her honey-blonde curls wild around her head.

"You're just in time. Breakfast is just about ready."

"You made breakfast?" she asked as she sat and dragged her fingers through her hair. I watched as she wrangled it into a ponytail then did some sort of magic trick that tied it into a loose knot on the top of her head.

"French toast and sausage," I said and added everything to the platter and turned off the stove. "Finn said you like both."

As soon as he heard Ivy's voice, Finn had stood and walked over to her. He had a huge smile on his face as she rubbed his sides. Can't say I blame him.

"He did, did he?" She kissed his head and scratched his neck.

"Did you want coffee?"

She stood and Finn followed her to the island.

"I'll get it. You don't have to wait on me." Looking around she asked, "Is there anything I can do?"

"Just make your coffee. There's no juice or creamer. But there is milk if you don't take it black."

I inched by her and carried the platter of food to the table then sat and filled my plate. Ivy joined me as I poured syrup over everything.

"Sorry about conking out on the couch. Finn was up early and we hung outside for a while. I planned on sitting down for a minute when we came back in, but obviously fell asleep." She added two slices of French toast to her plate along with a couple pieces of sausage. "I hope he didn't bother you too much."

"No, he's great."

I placed the syrup on the table and pushed it in her direction. She picked it up and tipped it over her plate.

"I'm still amazed he took to you so fast. It usually takes him a long time to warm up to new people, especially men."

"Gingers stick together. Right buddy?"

Finn turned his head in my direction, probably hoping food was coming his way. But I'll follow Ivy's lead on offering him something from the table.

"This is so good," Ivy said around a low groan, taking my attention from Finn. She licked her lips and took another quick bite.

"Thanks." I took a long drink of coffee, hoping it would clear the husky tone from my voice and shift my focus off her mouth. "So how old is Finn?" Thankfully it worked.

"Two," she said. "I adopted him last year. A friend of mine volunteers at the rescue he was brought to and ended up fostering him. I've never had a dog and wasn't looking for one, but I applied to adopt him right after I met him. It was love at first sight. Right baby?" Finn wagged his tail. "He was in horrible condition—malnourished with matted fur and cracked pads; he was definitely abused. He had lash marks on his back and a wound on his right paw that was infected."

She took a few more bites before continuing.

"They think a man abused him because he freaked out anytime a male volunteer went near him. He still growls at men until he gets used to them." She smiled. "Present company excluded. For whatever reason, he took to you right away."

"I told you, it's a ginger thing."

"Are you forgetting that he's color blind and can't see red?"

"He can sense it."

She rolled her eyes and chuckled. "What about you? Do you have a dog? Or any kind of pet?"

"I had dogs as a kid, but not since I'm on my own. It'd be really hard with my lifestyle. I'm on the road half the year and have long hours when I am home. I live alone so it really wouldn't be fair to the dog."

Ivy ate everything on her plate then reached over and grabbed a sausage off the platter and handed it to Finn.

"And that's it for the table food," she told him. "I don't need you having stomach issues while we're on the road."

Which reminded me that she'd be leaving in the morning. It's funny, the last time I saw Ivy she seemed shallow and flighty and I couldn't wait to get away from her, but now I'm really enjoying her company. I'll definitely be sad when she and Finn leave. I'd ask her to stay, but I don't know if that's smart.

I'm not blind and Ivy is definitely attractive. I'll admit, I've found myself checking out things on her that I have no business looking at. I'd feel guilty but I've caught her doing a pants check or two on me. Of course, I have to use my imagination when looking at her curves. I haven't had the privilege of seeing her naked in the shower.

Before I could start imagining that scene, I decided to change the subject.

"I'm running to the supermarket. Do you need me to pick up anything for you or Finn?"

"A case of water would be great. It would save me from stopping with him in the car tomorrow. Thank you."

Ivy stood and picked up her plate. "Are you finished?"

"I got it."

"You cooked, I'll wash the dishes. It's only fair."

Considering how Ivy grew up, I'm surprised she knows how to wash a dish. Then again, I've been surprised by her quite a bit in the past twelve hours.

IVY

Rusty had showered and left as I finished washing the dishes and cleaning up. I still can't believe he made me breakfast. Not to mention he fed Finn while I was sleeping.

I really like his mom Marian but until seeing him here, I thought Rusty was a pompous prick. I've only been in his company on two occasions prior to this and avoided him as much as possible each time.

It's actually a good thing that I'm leaving tomorrow because he's really hot and the only thing that kept me from being even somewhat attracted to him before was his shitty personality. And now it turns out he's actually a nice guy. Plus Finn likes him which gives him tons of bonus points.

My last boyfriend had been around for two months and Finn still growled and bared his teeth at him, even after being in his company for hours at a time. That guy seemed to think I should lock Finn up when he was around. He even mentioned getting rid of him. Like that was going to happen.

I broke up with that guy and haven't felt the need to date since.

"Come on Finn, let's go for a walk on the beach."

I grabbed a ball from his tote and he followed me out the door. We made our way to the sandy beach and I tossed the ball for him to chase. Running at full speed, he grabbed the ball and brought it straight back to me and I threw it again.

My hair blew against my face and I wished I'd thought to secure it with an elastic. A loose knot won't do in this wind.

Finn and I played fetch until he got tired then I sat in the sand and he walked around exploring. I laughed out loud when he got too close to the water and a wave crashed into the shore soaking his legs, chest, and face. He ran over and plopped down next to me. The beach probably wasn't the best idea the day before a car ride, but at least I'll be able to rinse him off in the outdoor shower.

Resting back on my elbows, I looked out at the horizon. It had been sunny earlier, but it's overcast now and the wind helps the heat and humidity from being too overwhelming. Lying down, I tucked my hair beneath me. I'll have to shower sand out of my mass of curls too, but at least this keeps them from whipping against my cheeks. I took in a deep breath and let it out slowly enjoying the moment. Finn rested his head against my hand and I looked over at him and rubbed his ear.

For ten months, one week, and two days, Finn has been the only man in my life and I've honestly been okay with that. That is until I saw Christopher "Rusty" Russell in that shower last night. Now I can't help but wonder what it would feel like to be with a man so tall and muscular and confident.

"Yep, it's a good thing we're leaving tomorrow," I said to Finn.

4

RUSTY

When I had to circle the supermarket parking lot three times before snagging a spot, I should have known something was up. But I'd parked the Mercedes coupe Sam had said I could borrow and grabbed a cart that had escaped the corral on my way toward the store blissfully ignorant of the chaos I'd find inside.

As the doors swished open, I walked into a store full of people and found the shelves not so full.

"What's going on?" I asked the guy who was attempting to stock the bread display just inside the doors. Every time he added a loaf to the shelf, someone grabbed it.

He gave me a sarcastic side glance and continued doing his work.

"Didn't you hear there's a hurricane coming?"

"A hurricane?" He nodded. "It's July."

I'm guessing he took pity on me since I'm an uneducated non-local because he explained, "Hurricane season is technically June 1st through November 30th. Just because we normally get them between August and October, doesn't mean it can't happen now."

"How bad is it supposed to be?"

"Bad enough to be a pain in the ass but not bad enough that we have to evacuate." The guy looked at me and tossed a loaf of bread into my cart. "Do I know you?"

"I doubt it. I'm not from here."

"You look really familiar." His eyes narrowed then widened when he figured it out. "You're Rusty Russell. Holy shit."

He looked around, as if trying to decide if he should shout what he'd just discovered to the whole store or keep it to himself. I was so relieved when he chose the latter.

"You a baseball fan?"

"A huge fan and the Waves are my second-favorite team."

I held out my hand to shake his. "Well, it's always nice to meet a fan. Mr. —" I paused so he could supply his name.

"Walters." He pumped my hand up and down, more vigorously than was necessary. "Tom Walters."

"It's nice to meet you, Tom Walters," I said, then directed my cart toward the produce. "I better get shopping before everything is gone."

"What are you looking for? I'm the only one stocking shelves right now and as you can see, what I'm putting out isn't lasting long." I pulled my list from my pocket and showed it to him. "There's no plain water over there right now, it's all in the back. See those double doors over there?" I looked across the entire store to the back corner and nodded. "You go back there and ring the bell when you're ready and the guy working the warehouse will get you the water and anything else you need." He pulled a walkie-talkie out of his back pocket. "I'll let him know you're coming."

"Thanks Tom. I really appreciate it." He held out my list, but instead of taking it I said, "Do me a favor and write your address on that paper. I'll send you a couple T-shirts so you can represent your second-favorite team every once in a while."

He smiled and pulled a pen from his pocket and scribbled on the paper before handing it back to me.

"Thanks again for your help. It was really nice meeting you."

I hustled through the store filling the cart with enough food for two people for a few days. Although I'm sure there are flashlights and candles at the house in preparation for this sort of thing, I picked up some just in case, along with a lighter.

With a hurricane coming, there's no way Ivy and Finn can leave. That reminded me. My cart was just about full when I turned down the pet food aisle. Thankfully I'd fed Finn earlier so I recognized his brand of food as soon as I saw the bag. He had a decent amount left at the house, but I don't want to take a chance he'll run out during the storm. I also grabbed a box of treats and a bone for him.

That done, I headed toward those double doors and rang the bell. Sometimes being a minor celebrity has its privileges.

IVY

I heard the garage door open and close a minute before Rusty appeared at the top of the stairs carrying at least four bags in each hand. I met him in the kitchen as he set them down on the counter.

"Are there more bags?" I asked.

"I'll get them. You can start putting that stuff away."

Finn followed him to the steps but came back into the kitchen.

He'd bought so much stuff. Steaks, hamburg, chicken, cheese, and a bunch of fresh fruits and veggies. But I guess being a professional athlete burns a lot of calories so he must eat a lot. I'd just finished placing the last of the perishables into the refrigerator when he plunked another load of bags onto the counter.

"One more trip should do it," he said before heading back to the garage.

After stuffing the freezer with a few pizzas, a couple pans of lasagna, and two trays of macaroni and cheese, I moved onto the non-perishables.

Finn let out a playful bark when Rusty came back up the stairs. I looked up and realized it was because he'd spotted the dog food on Rusty's shoulder.

"I left the case of water down next to your car."

"Thanks, I appreciate it."

"But there's no way you can leave tomorrow."

"Why?"

"Apparently there's a hurricane coming. The store was crazy." He pointed to the bag of food he'd placed next to the island. "I grabbed another bag of food for Finn just in case we're stuck here for a while. I didn't want him to run out." He bent down and picked up a bag, holding it open so I could see its contents. "I got him some treats and a bone, too." Glancing at Finn, he added "I didn't want to take them out before making sure he can have them."

Where did this guy come from?

It's bad enough he cooked breakfast and went grocery shopping, but then he remembered the kind of food Finn eats and got him treats and a bone. There's no way I can stay here with him, no matter how big the house is. He's just too tempting.

"Those treats are good and he's okay with rawhide bones. I know some dogs have issues with them, but he never has. And he loves both of those things, so thank you for thinking of him."

"He's a good boy," he said, reaching down to pet Finn whose tail thumped against the wall.

I walked past them into the living room and picked up the remote. Turning on the TV, I flicked through the channels to find the weather. The local channel had broken into regularly scheduled programming with hurricane coverage and it wasn't looking good.

"The guy at the supermarket said it's not bad enough to evacuate but will probably still be a pain in the ass," Rusty said from behind me. "I wasn't sure what's here so I picked up a lantern, a couple flashlights, and a bunch of candles. The shelves were pretty picked over, but we should be okay."

My stomach fluttered at the word *we*.

Walking toward the wall of windows, I watched as the waves crashed to the shore, choppier than they had been just a couple hours earlier. The sky looked heavier too.

"Maybe if I leave now I'll be okay."

The words had just left my mouth when a commercial ended and a video of bumper-to-bumper traffic appeared on the screen. Even though evacuation isn't mandatory, enough people were trying to leave, making the highway look like a parking lot.

Rusty had settled onto the couch so I took a seat in the chair across from him.

"Have you ever been here during a hurricane before?" he asked.

"No, but so far, the property hasn't sustained any significant damage even during the worst storms." I pulled my phone out of my pocket and searched through the apps, making sure the one I want is still active. "We can close the remote control shutters once it starts getting bad. There's also a standby generator but it won't power everything all at once. It'll keep the appliances working but we won't be able to sit here binge-watching Netflix with all the lights on and the AC cranked."

"I wasn't expecting a generator at all, so that's good to know," he said. "I'm glad you're here because I wouldn't have known about the shutters either or how to close them if I did."

"I imagine my dad would have let you know once he heard about the storm."

"They're enjoying themselves in Tuscany. I'm sure Marathon weather isn't high on their priority list."

"By the way, I spoke to him today so you don't have to keep the fact that I'm here a secret anymore."

"My mom called me while I was at the store, but I couldn't talk to her too long anyway. But she did mention that you'd spoken to your dad."

The corner of his mouth kicked up.

"What?"

Those silver-blue eyes met mine and my stomach did that crazy flip-flop thing again. Why the hell can't they pick one color or the other? As if the man isn't attractive enough, he has to have mesmerizing eyes and eyelashes I couldn't achieve with the best mascara. It's really not fair.

"She told me to be nice."

"Nice?" He nodded. "What does that mean?"

He shrugged then rubbed his chin with long, blunt-tipped fingers. "I'm thinking she means that I should be nice to you. I didn't read more into it than that. Why? What do you think it means?"

"Just that, I guess." I cleared my throat. "I'm gonna take Finn out to run around for a while since he'll be cooped up inside once the storm starts."

Thankfully there's enough of a grassy area for him to explore so I don't have to take him in the sand again. All I can say is thank God for the outside shower because the two of us would have made a hell of a mess if we had to get cleaned up inside earlier.

"Why don't you relax and I'll take him out?" Rusty stood. "You had a long trip here and it's been a long time since I played fetch with a dog." He placed his left hand on his right shoulder and rotated his arm. "Plus it will be good for me to throw."

He's killing me. But at least if he goes outside I won't have to look at his long, lean yumminess.

Deciding to keep things light—*needing* to keep things light—I said, "Please don't hurt my baby with your million-dollar arm."

He grabbed Finn's ball from the tote and whistled. "Come on, buddy." They walked toward the patio door and wind gusted in as he pulled it open. Finn walked out onto the deck but Rusty glanced back at me and said. "That's multi-million-dollar arm, and don't worry, I won't." Then he winked and closed the door behind him.

That should have sounded cocky, but instead it came out playful, like he was making fun of himself and dare I say, flirting with me. I'd rather be stranded here with the arrogant asshole I'd met before instead of this hot man with a sense of humor who is good to my dog.

The storm brewing outside has nothing on the one raging within me.

5

RUSTY

A loud rattle woke me from a sound sleep. I sat up in bed and placed the book I'd been reading before I conked out on the pillow next to me. The noise sounded again and I looked toward the window in a futile attempt to see what's happening out there.

Ivy had closed all the shutters when the wind kicked up earlier. If it weren't for the lamp on the nightstand, the room would be completely black. At least the power hasn't gone out. Yet.

I got out of bed and pulled on a shirt then headed downstairs. Finn lifted his head from Ivy's lap as I approached.

"Sounds nasty out there," I said to Ivy.

She took a sip of wine and nodded. "He kept pacing in the bedroom so I decided to come down here. These shutters don't seem to make as much noise. Which is funny because the windows in the bedroom are smaller than these."

I nodded to acknowledge her words.

"Have you seen the weather report lately?"

"About an hour ago they said this is the first of two storms that are hitting. This is basically just a thunderstorm. The one coming tomorrow is the actual hurricane."

Looking around at the elegant beach house, I said, "Well, I guess there are worse places to be stuck during a storm."

"True."

"Are you hungry? I was gonna have a snack."

I don't know what it is about being on lockdown that makes me want to eat more than usual. And after skipping lunch, we'd had an early dinner and both went to our rooms. So it feels late but it's just past eight.

She glanced at the clock. "I should be full from that huge steak I ate for dinner, but a snack sounds good." Standing, she added. "I'm gonna take Finn out before it gets worse out there."

"I could take him."

"Thanks but you took him before. I got him." She stood. "Come on baby." He jumped down from the couch. "I'll take him through the garage. So he can go on the patch of grass out front."

Finn followed her down the stairs and I went into the kitchen to whip us up something to eat. I opened the refrigerator and grabbed a beer, twisting it open while I figured out what to make. Spotting the leftover steak and Mexican blend cheese, I decided on nachos.

Placing the bottle of Blue Moon on the counter, I dug through the shelves, grabbing everything I'd need. I set the ingredients on the counter and pulled a pan from the rack and placed it on the cooktop, setting the flame to low heat. Grabbing a cutting board and knife, I diced the steak into bite-sized pieces and tossed it into the pan then sprinkled it with chili powder, paprika, and cumin I'd found in the cupboard. While that heated, I removed the seeds from a jalapeno and minced it as small as I could then scraped it into the pan, giving everything a quick stir. After scrubbing the cutting board and wiping it dry, I chopped two tomatoes then found a platter and loaded it with a layer of tortilla chips.

Now comes the fun part.

Turning off the burner, I stirred the contents of the pan one more time then used the wooden spoon to scoop some of the steak and jalapeno onto the tortillas. I topped that with a healthy dose of cheese then added another layer of chips and toppings. I put the platter into the oven.

I glanced at the clock and realized fifteen minutes had gone by. I'm thinking Ivy should have been back by now. I was just about to go check on them when I heard her voice followed by the sound of Finn running up the stairs.

"Well look at you." I chuckled.

Finn ran over to my side, skidding as he stopped in front of me. I patted his wet fur. Ivy must have at least towel dried him because he's not dripping. That thought had just left my head when the woman in question appeared in the living room.

The dog's soaked appearance had amused me. Ivy's not so much. My eyes skimmed her from head to toe, lingering on the see-through T-shirt and the plump breasts it's clinging to. She's wearing a bra, but it must be a light color because it's pretty much transparent too and I swear I can tell the color of her erect nipples.

Realizing I was just standing there staring at her with my mouth hanging open, I blinked and shifted my eyes up to meet hers.

"The uh—" I cleared my throat. "The nachos will be ready in a couple minutes."

She nodded and licked her lips, her eyes glancing down at the semi-erection I'm sure my athletic shorts aren't doing a thing to hide before meeting my gaze again.

"I'll go change and be right back." She looked at Finn. "You behave and stay off the furniture."

I watched her walk down the hall toward her bedroom, noting the perfect globes of her ass visible through her white shorts. Ivy is tiny but she's curvy in all the right places.

Finn nudged at my hand. If he could read my thoughts, he probably would have bitten it instead.

"You deserve a treat after going out to do your business in this mess."

I reached into the box of treats and pulled one out. As soon as he'd heard me digging in the box, he sat and watched me. He's really trained well and as I held out the treat, he leaned forward and gently took it from my hand.

The oven timer sounded and I opened the door and glanced inside.

"Perfect," I said to Finn who was watching my every move, probably hoping I'd give him another treat.

Sliding on oven mitts, I pulled the platter out of the oven and placed it on the cutting board. I figured it could serve as a trivet and it's large enough so I won't need the oven mitts to carry it.

I sprinkled the tomatoes over the top of the bubbly cheese then added some sour cream, spreading it around as much as I could.

Sliding my hands under the cutting board, I lifted my masterpiece and walked toward the dining area. I started to set it on the table, then stopped.

"We might as well make use of the coffee table, don't you think? That way you can cuddle up to your mom while she eats."

He seemed to like that idea and followed me while I leaned over and set the platter down. Ivy walked into the room just as I straightened, looking adorable in a pair of sweatshorts and an oversized T-shirt. She'd pulled her hair back into a braid that rested between her shoulder blades.

I went back into the kitchen and pulled two plates out of the cupboard and grabbed a couple napkins.

"Do you need a drink?"

"No, thank you. I still have wine."

I picked up my beer and walked into the living room, setting everything down before sitting cross-legged next to the coffee table. My hips protested and I made a mental note to stretch them out before bed.

"These look amazing. Like something you'd get in a restaurant," she said, surprising me when she sat in the space between the couch and table adjacent to me.

I handed her a plate and napkin.

"I added a jalapeno to the leftover steak, but I took out all the seeds and cooked them a little so it shouldn't be too spicy."

She reached out and dragged a bunch of nachos onto her plate then looked at Finn and stood.

"I think I'm going to give him the bone you got him."

Her leg brushed my shoulder as she walked by. I filled my plate with chips and shoved a couple into my mouth. As I heard her approach, I braced myself for contact again and was disappointed when there wasn't any.

"Here you go," she said, handing the bone to Finn who had settled on the other side of her. "'Rusty got this for you today. Wasn't that nice of him?"

His eyes shifted to me before he took the bone from her and placed it between his paws and went to town on it.

"How was it out there?" I asked.

"It's a mess." She shoved a nacho into her mouth and chewed. "Mmm, these are amazing. The perfect amount of spice." Meeting my gaze, she said, "You're a really good cook."

"Thanks. I have a few go-to things I can make, otherwise, I'd have to either go out or order in all the time. And I do that enough when I'm on the road. It's nice to stay in and cook for myself when I'm home." I took a drink and directed the subject back to her venture out into the storm. "I'm guessing Finn didn't want to go out alone."

She rolled her eyes. "Back home, he has a fenced yard so he's able to wander to his heart's content and take his time. But he doesn't like going in new places or when I have him on a leash so it takes forever and a lot of cheerleading on my part. He's very peculiar about doing his business."

"I guess it's like someone who doesn't like using public restrooms."

"I've never thought of it that way, but I suppose it is." She finished her wine and grabbed the bottle she'd stashed next to the couch and refilled the glass. "Do you want to watch something while the power is still on?"

"Sure," I said. The homerun derby is on but I'm not even going to suggest watching it. It'll make me feel too shitty about not being there and I don't want to ruin my good mood. "You pick something."

She glanced at me out of the corner of her eye. "What if I pick some sappy chick flick?"

"Finn and I will deal with it."

I stood and walked to the kitchen to get another beer while she flipped through the channels.

"Oh, I love this movie." I looked up and saw the opening credits to *Trouble with the Curve*. "Is this okay?"

Setting back into my spot at the coffee table, I nodded. "It has baseball and Clint Eastwood. What's not to love?"

After she put the remote down next to her, she picked up a chip.

"Don't forget Justin Timberlake."

"And Amy Adams." I waggled my eyebrows.

She looked up at the ceiling and shook her head. "Such a guy."

"Hey you started it."

"Just watch the movie."

We'd put a good dent in the nachos before either of us slowed down. I really needed to stretch my legs and I turned sideways and straightened them out in front of me.

"I was just gonna move," she said. "My butt is numb."

I watched her shift back onto the couch, careful not to focus too much on her ass, but her toned legs are just as distracting.

Finn continued to chew his bone contentedly so he didn't try to join her. I looked at the empty space next to her and decided I would. After wiping my hands, I shifted onto my knees then pulled myself onto the couch, careful to stay close to the armrest so I don't crowd her.

We both got more comfortable as the movie played on. I slouched down against the armrest and spread my legs out in front of me. Ivy pulled a pillow to her side and rested her feet on the coffee table, ankles crossed.

I eventually stopped noticing the sound of Finn chewing his bone and the wind howling outside and became engrossed in the movie. Justin and Amy had just jumped into the lake in their underwear when a loud boom of thunder shook the house.

Ivy lunged toward me, digging her fingers into my chest. Finn barked and hopped onto the couch snuggling against Ivy's legs. She shifted even closer to me to make room for him. Her wide eyes met mine before dropping to her hands. She loosened her fingers one by one and started to pull away. I placed my hand over hers, holding them in place. Her gaze slowly rose to meet mine again.

I should let her pull away, but that's the last thing I want. And if I'm reading the look in her eyes right, she doesn't want to either.

After spending just twenty-four hours together, my previous opinion of her has totally changed. She's not the ditzy, aimless scatterbrain I thought her to be. Just the way she takes care of Finn tells me that. And now that I know what a smart, caring, and thoughtful person she is, her physical attributes have become amplified.

She's sexy and adorable and so unassuming, it's a nice change from the women I usually meet. Kissing her probably isn't a good idea, but it's the only one I have at the moment.

Dragging my hand up along her arm, I squeezed her shoulder before sliding my fingers under the thick braid at the nape of her neck. She didn't flinch or move away. Instead she bit her bottom lip as her gaze dropped to my mouth before meeting mine again, her eyes wide.

I leaned forward slowly, giving her a chance to push me away, pull back, or turn her head but she did neither of those things. Instead her dark eyes continued to stare into mine as I moved closer then fluttered closed as my lips met hers.

IVY

The moment Rusty's mouth met mine, everything else ceased to exist. The feel of his lips on mine, his stubble against my skin, and his heart pounding under my hand became my whole world. And I wanted more.

I moved my hand up to dig my fingers into his hair, the motion smashing my breasts against his chest. His answering groan vibrated through me, making my nipples tingle. He wrapped his arm around my waist, pulling me closer, engulfing me in his embrace. His big hand cupped the back of my head holding me still as he teased me with hot, open-mouthed kisses.

Pulling back slightly, he nibbled at my bottom lip then slipped his tongue inside. The man is absolutely delicious and I eagerly met him stroke for stoke as our tongues tangled, tasting and sharing.

His hand slipped around to cup my breast and I let out a low moan when his thumb flicked back and forth across my distended nipple sending a zing down to my clit. My core clenched and I squeezed my thighs together to ease the ache.

I was torn between moving closer and staying in place, allowing Rusty to continue his sweet torture of my breast. He took the decision from me when he removed his hand from the back of my head and used it to cup my ass, pulling me closer until I was basically lying on top of him. His erection poked into my thigh and I shifted my hips, trying to get it closer to where I needed it.

Rusty reached down and cupped the back of my leg, pulling it over his until I straddled him. I let out a long groan as his thick erection poked against my clit, the layers of fabric between us doing nothing to hinder its effect. Our mouths remained fused together as I rubbed myself against him, mimicking the rhythm of our tangling tongues.

My core clenched on every downstroke and I moved faster. Rusty's hands down cupped my ass, pulling me harder against him, his counter-thrusts pushing me closer to the edge. I'm not sure I've ever had an orgasm from just dry humping. It's usually an achievement when I have one at all.

I widened my legs and his hard length slid between my folds, and I lost it. My movements became faster, more frantic, and Rusty squeezed my ass, holding me down against him as his mouth continued to devour mine.

My nipples tingled just as my inner walls fluttered then clenched as I continued to thrust against him. I couldn't move fast enough and lost my rhythm, but Rusty took control and helped me find a new one that was just as pleasurable. My orgasm seemed to go on and on and I needed to breathe.

Pulling my mouth from his, I sat back, dragging much-needed air into my lungs. His silver-blue gaze never left my face as I came down from the best release I've had in a long time.

"Wow." The word came out on a gust of breath as I struggled to get my breathing under control. Once I did, I wasn't sure if I should thank him or apologize. After all, I've had mine and I can still feel his erection pulsing between my thighs, solid proof that he hadn't had his.

He leaned forward and placed a soft kiss on my lips then sat back, his hands still gripping my ass, holding me flush against him.

"That was the most beautiful thing I've ever seen." I felt a blush spread from my chest, up my neck, to my cheeks. "But I have one question."

"What's that?"

"Is Finn gonna bite my dick off if I take you to the bedroom and get naked?"

That's definitely not what I expected him to ask and I looked at Finn passed out on the

other end of the couch and laughed.

"I hope not, but I can't promise anything." I met Rusty's gaze again and added, "But I'll take it as a good sign that you've gotten this close to me. Plus he seems to really like you."

He shifted forward, holding me against him as he stood. My arms circled his neck as I wrapped my legs around his waist. I glanced at Finn as Rusty walked toward his bedroom, but my dog didn't even open his eyes. Pretty amazing since he never left my side whenever my ex-boyfriend was around.

Rusty set me down next to his bed and went back to close the door. His gaze never left mine as he walked toward me. As he got closer, I had to tip my head back to maintain eye contact.

He reached for my hands and wove our fingers together, lifting them between us to kiss my knuckles.

"Are you sure about this?"

I don't think I've ever had a man ask me that at this point in the game. Usually my participation is enough consent for them. But I understand that taking this next step could complicate things. Hell, the steps we've already taken could. But despite that, I want this. I want him and told him so.

"Thank fuck."

6

RUSTY

Whipping Ivy's shirt over her head, I tossed it to the floor, releasing the latch of her bra with one hand, impressing myself that I still have that particular skill. At the first sight of her breasts, I swear I audibly gulped. They're perfect...plump and perky, tipped with rosy nipples. I cupped one then the other, testing their weight before leaning down to have a taste.

I teased her nipple with my tongue, before drawing it further into my mouth to suck.

"Mmmm." I groaned against her then swirled my tongue around her stiff nipple before pulling her deeper into my mouth to feast.

I pulled back, releasing and looking down to admire my handiwork.

"Gorgeous," I said as I dipped my head to her other breast, giving it the same treatment.

Ivy's fingers dug into my scalp holding me to her as her moans and sighs cheered me on. I backed her toward the bed. She's a lot shorter than me and I want to stretch her out horizontally so I have full reign of her body without stooping down.

She sat on the bed and I pushed her back just enough so her legs dangled down the side. Kneeling down, I tucked my thumbs into the waistband of her shorts and panties and tugged. Ivy lifted her hips helping me to get her beautifully, gloriously naked.

My gaze took in her perfectly-painted toes before following her shapely legs to their juncture. Neatly-trimmed honey-blonde curls glistened and would have brought me to my knees if I wasn't already on them.

"Lie back."

She followed my gravel-voiced command and rested back on her elbows, her dark gaze watching my every move.

I rested her legs against my shoulders and spread them wider so I could fit. Placing my hands on her hips, I pulled her forward until her pretty pussy rested right in front of my face. I placed an open-mouthed kiss right at her core before licking her from bottom to top, circling her clit, before doing it again and again.

When her hips thrust up, I placed a restraining hand on her belly as I slipped a finger into her wet heat. Her answering groan echoed through the room. I added another finger and plunged deep before curling them to stroke her from inside and teased her clit with the tip of my tongue.

"Rusty." She twisted her fingers into my hair. "Oh God."

Her walls squeezed against my fingers so I pulled out and added a third. She's so tight, it's a snug fit and I groaned as I imagined how she'd feel wrapped around my cock.

I pumped faster, then faster still as my tongue kept pace on that tiny bundle of nerves, before I opened my mouth and sucked on it. That's all it took to throw her over the edge. She screamed my name then chanted nonsense words as her inner walls squeezed my finger and her clit throbbed against my mouth.

I stayed with her, pumping slower and slower through the last flutter then slowly removed my fingers.

Standing, I pulled off my T-shirt and tossed it to the floor. As I went to remove my shorts, I remembered protection.

"Shit."

I glanced at the nightstand. If we were at my house, it would be fully stocked, but I doubt Sam Sherman keeps condoms in his guest rooms.

"What's wrong?"

The sight of post-orgasm Ivy cleared every word except one from my brain. *Mine.*

"Rusty?"

I blinked, pulling myself out of my Ivy-induced trance.

"Sorry, I lost my train of thought for a minute." Her shy smile made my heart pound. "But I'm not sure if I have a condom."

"Oh." She didn't look any happier about that than I was. "I could—"

Instead of finishing her sentence, she gestured toward my very visible erection.

The thought of her lush lips around me made my dick twitch. Her eyes widened, making me chuckle. Something I didn't think possible at the moment.

Her mouth curled into a sexy smirk. "Does he do any other tricks?"

"If I can find a damn condom, I'll show you."

I walked toward the bathroom and frantically searched through my toiletry bag before finally dumping it out onto the counter.

"Thank you," I said to whoever the patron saint of condoms is and grabbed the strip of four foil packets and ran back into the bedroom.

Pulling off my shorts and underwear, I stood still and let them fall to the floor before jumping into bed next to Ivy.

I pulled her against me, covering her mouth with mine. The feel of our naked bodies against each other is almost enough to push me over the edge.

Ending the kiss, I reached behind her and removed the elastic from her hair and worked my fingers up her braid, loosening it as I went along. Her long curls fanned around her on the pillow, making her look like an angel.

"I want to apologize in advance because this is not going to take very long."

I leaned onto my side and opened one of the foil packets. Ivy nibbled at her lower lip and watched me roll the condom down my throbbing length. Closing my eyes, I took in a deep breath and let it out slowly, trying to drum up some measure of self-control. She was still watching me when I opened them again and saw the want I feel mirrored on her face.

She shifted to her back as I moved toward her until I rested between her legs. Placing her feet next to my hips, she opened herself further and I took her invitation. I pushed forward and filled her with one powerful thrust. She screamed my name and I held still.

"Shit, are you okay?"

"I'm fine," she panted. "It just feels so full."

When she wiggled her ass and readjusted herself beneath me, it was the sweetest torture I've ever felt. Her inner walls gripped and released me as she adjusted to the intrusion.

"Okay. I'm good now."

"You sure?"

She nodded.

I moved slowly in and out, in and out, in and out. Her inner walls gripped me each time I retreated and welcomed me back on every thrust. I moved faster, then faster still when she wrapped her legs around my waist and I slipped further inside.

Exhaling through gritted teeth, I fought off my release as the feel of her tightening around me bombarded my senses. I leaned down and licked her nipple before pulling it into my mouth and sucking in rhythm with my hips. I wanted to sing my thanks to every deity known to man when I felt the start of her orgasm.

"Ivy," I groaned against the curve of her breast as my own orgasm pulsed through me and seemed to go on forever.

Resting my forehead against her shoulder, I took in deep gulps of air as I tried to get my breathing under control. Ivy's legs slid down and rested beside mine on the bed. I shifted to move back, but she held me in place.

"Don't move." She tucked her arms under mine and wrapped them around my back, pulling me closer. "You feel good against me."

"I can't argue with that, but I don't want to crush you."

She let out a contented sigh. "No, you're good."

I don't know how long we stayed like that, just enjoying the feel of the other when I heard a sound. Lifting my head, I listened and realized what it was when I heard it again.

"It sounds like we have company."

IVY

I felt cold when Rusty moved off me so I pulled the cover over me. He walked into the bathroom, then came back and pulled on his boxer briefs and went to the door. Finn came bounding in and jumped onto the bed, settling right next to me.

"How did you know he was out there?" I rubbed Finn's ears and he rewarded me with a smile.

"He knocked at the door." Rusty climbed into the other side of the bed. "I'm guessing he has to go out. It's been a while." Leaning forward he kissed me, then stood and put on his shorts. "I'll take him. You relax."

"Are you sure?"

"Positive."

That said, he whistled and Finn jumped off the bed and followed him out of the room. I'm still amazed at how my dog has taken to Rusty. The only other person he's ever been that comfortable with so fast is me. It's the main reason I adopted him. We fell in love at first sight.

I settled against the pillows and closed my eyes, mentally replaying the last couple hours. One minute we were watching a movie and the next I was dry humping Rusty until a mind-blowing orgasm tore through me. Then he'd given me two more right in this bed.

I've heard about multiple orgasms but had never experienced them for myself. I may petition for this date to be made a national holiday.

Finn's paws sounded in the hallway seconds before he came bounding into the room. Thankfully he didn't jump on the bed this time because I'm sure he's wet. Rusty walked in shortly after and did get into bed. Shifting closer, he put his arm around my shoulders and pulled me against his chest.

"How'd it go out there?"

"He stepped just outside of the garage and peed on the driveway so he didn't get too wet."

"Thank you for taking him out. It sounds like he was better for you than he would have been for me."

"I think he just really had to go." Kissing the top of my head, he settled further down on the pillow and pulled me closer. "Plus it was just number one. Number two takes a little more strategy."

I turned my head and kissed his chest then looked up at him through my lashes.

"Thank you."

"What for?"

"Not making me feel like a freak because I talk to my dog and for understanding his eccentricities."

"Don't forget the singing."

His full smile made my heart skip a beat. It is truly a beautiful thing.

"The dog's name is Finnegan and he actually has whiskers on his chin. How could I not sing *Michael Finnegan* to him?"

"You do have a point."

Finn had sniffed his way around the room and now stood at the side of the bed, watching as I snuggled with another male. I was about to tell him to go relax and we'd head to our room soon when Rusty reached out and patted the bed. Finn jumped up and spun in a circle three times before settling at our feet.

"Are you sure you want him up here?"

Rusty nodded and closed his eyes. "I definitely want you in my bed and I understand that you guys are a package deal."

His image blurred and I blinked back the tears. I sniffed and he peeked one eye open, offering a small smile.

"Get some rest. We'll have plenty of time to talk about everything that's running through your beautiful head tomorrow."

I rested my cheek against his chest, closed my eyes, and immediately fell into a contented sleep.

I'm not sure what woke me, the sounds of the storm outside or the man who was now spooning me from behind. It wasn't so much the fact that we had changed positions as it was what his roaming hand was doing to me.

His hand kneaded and squeezed one breast, twisting the nipple between his thumb and forefinger before moving on and offering the other breast the same treatment.

Rusty kissed his way across my shoulder and licked his way up my neck, before licking at a spot behind my ear. How does he know that drives me wild?

Groaning, I squeezed my thighs together and rubbed my ass back against his erection.

"Shhh, you'll wake Finn." His warm breath tickled my ear a second before he nibbled at my lobe and pulled it with his teeth.

His hand slid down my body and between my thighs. I shifted my legs further apart to give him better access and was rewarded when he slid his long middle finger through my wet folds and slipped it inside.

"Mmmm, you're so wet."

He pumped his finger in and out, his palm pushing against my clit. I wanted to move, to touch him, but his forearm against my hip held me in place.

"Just relax and enjoy."

My heart threatened to pound out of my chest and my breath came out in shallow pants as I fought the urge to alternately groan and scream his name.

His arm barely moved as he pumped his finger in and out of me, pushing me toward my fourth—FOURTH!!!—orgasm of the night.

It didn't take long before my inner walls fluttered then clenched down on his finger. He stayed in place through the aftershocks, then slowly pulled out.

"Don't move."

He shifted away and then I felt him at my back again, his condom-clad penis resting against my ass. His fingers wrapped around my knee and he pulled my leg back over his hip and shifted me up enough so he could slip inside.

This time was unhurried and more deliberate. Each measured thrust dragged his dick against my swollen walls, building me up slowly. His hand roamed up and down my body, his thumb alternately grazing my nipples and circling my clit.

When my orgasm came, it washed over my entire body like a wave, leaving me shaking. Rusty groaned into the back of my neck as he reached his own release.

7

RUSTY

I felt someone watching me and opened my eyes. Finn stood on the other side of the bed, dancing in place. Ivy rested against my chest, her breathing deep and even. I shimmied out from under her and shoved a pillow in my place.

Slipping into my shorts, I gestured for Finn to follow me out of the room. He ran into the hallway and I slowly closed the door behind me. Already knowing the routine, Finn ran down the hallway and to the stairs that led to the garage. I followed, pressing the garage door opener as I walked through.

He looked back at me as the door opened, revealing the storm to us. With the shutters down, we've been pretty isolated from it beyond some howling wind and the sounds of the rain against the house. And the thunder. I smiled at that last thought, remembering my first feel of Ivy's warm curves resting against me.

"It's gonna get worse before it gets better buddy, so you might as well go now."

He slowly stepped outside, looking around for shelter. He'd stayed under the slight overhang above the garage doors last night, but the rain is blowing too hard for that to be effective now. We'll have to figure out somewhere else for him to go after he eats, when he'll inevitably have to poop.

Finn did his business with the least amount of exposure to the elements possible and stepped back into the garage. I closed the door then looked around, checking out the shelves lining the walls and finally spotted something we could use. On the bottom shelf, there was a low, long plastic container we could line with something to turn it into a Finn-sized litter box.

I pulled it off the shelf and Finn looked over my shoulder as I removed its contents and set them on the shelf.

"Hopefully your mom can talk you into using this."

"Using what?" Ivy's voice sounded behind me.

Removing the last item from the container, I placed it next to the others and stood.

"It's a mess out there. I was thinking we could turn this into a sort of litter box for him."

She looked between Finn, the container, and me.

"What even made you think of that?"

"I was just looking around for ideas, spotted the bin, and it came to mind. It's really nasty out there now and it's supposed to get worse. He can't be going out in a hurricane to do his business and you definitely can't go out with him. It's not safe."

As if to punctuate my words, the wind howled and rain pelted against the garage doors.

"There should be some old beach blankets in that container up there." She pointed to the top rack. "We can line it with those and just throw them away."

I reached up and pulled down the bin she'd pointed to and placed it on the floor. She watched me, her eyes fascinated.

"What?"

"It must be amazing being that tall."

I shrugged. "It comes in handy sometimes. But squeezing into the middle seat of a flight isn't very fun."

"I'm sure a multi-million-dollar pitcher like you can afford first class."

"I was this height junior year in high school. I didn't become a multi-million-dollar pitcher until a few years ago."

Leaning down, I gave her a playful kiss then opened the bin and pulled out a beach towel. She watched as I folded then tucked it into the low container.

"What?" I asked her again for the second time in five minutes.

"You're very domestic for a jock."

"Why do you say that?"

"You cook, you have no problem taking care of Finn, and you folded that blanket like a pro. I'm half tempted to run upstairs and grab a fitted sheet to see what you can do with it."

That last comment made me laugh. "I'm not that good, but I can do the basics. My mom was determined to raise me so I could do all the things my dad couldn't."

"Like?"

"The things their generation thought of as women's work." I used air quotes with those last two words. "Cooking, ironing, washing and folding clothes, and cleaning the bathroom properly because men can't aim straight."

"Go Marian," she said, pumping her fist in the air.

"Speaking of cooking, let's go upstairs and I'll make you breakfast."

As if he understood my words, Finn ran past us and bounded up the stairs.

"I'll do it. I owe you a couple meals," she said. "What are you feeling? Pancakes, eggs and bacon, omelet?"

"Eggs and bacon sounds perfect. I take mine over easy so of course I'll need extra toast to dunk into the yolk."

"A man after my own heart."

Ivy preceded me up the stairs, giving me a chance to ogle her ass.

"How do you take your coffee?" she asked. "I didn't notice yesterday."

"Just a little cream. No sugar."

She walked into the kitchen and instructed me to sit and relax. Finn jumped up beside me as I settled onto the couch and rested his head on my thigh. I turned on the TV and decided mindless comedy was a better choice than the weather and found *The Office* on Netflix.

Just after the opening credits, she brought me a mug of coffee, just the way I like it.

"Thank you."

She smiled and offered a mock curtsy. "You are more than welcome, sir."

That said, she returned to the kitchen and soon the smell of bacon filled the air.

The past couple days have felt so domestic, which would normally freak me out. I once dated a woman for nine months and almost freaked out when she asked to leave some things at my place. We broke up shortly after that when she realized we had two totally different ideas about our relationship.

It was just two days ago I turned around in the shower and found Ivy Sherman staring at me. My opinion of her has done a complete one-eighty since then and I know it's ridiculous, but I can't stop thinking about where we can go from here.

I'm not sure how my mom and Sam will feel about us dating, but if we can handle them being together, they should give us the same courtesy.

"What do you think buddy?" Finn lifted his eyes at the sound of my voice. "Do you think your mom would be willing to give us a try?" His tail thumped against the couch, which I took as a good sign, even though he's most likely just reacting to my tone of voice rather than my actual words. "I guess I'll just have to ask her then, huh?"

IVY

It had taken some convincing, but thankfully Finn had finally used the litter box Rusty created for him. The storm had intensified, so as predicted, going outside is not an option. We walked upstairs after he peed and I sprinkled baking soda over it. That seems to be working to both keep the smell down and absorb the moisture so I don't have to change the blanket every time he goes.

Rusty and I spent the day binge watching *The Office* and snacking, while Finn happily chomped on his bone. But the power had gone out a little while ago, so no more TV for us. We could have left some of the lights on, but Rusty had turned them all off and placed lit candles throughout the room.

When I reached the top of the stairs, Rusty met me with a glass of wine.

"Thank you."

He followed me into the living room and sat, pulling me down onto his lap. He shifted beneath me until my butt rested on the couch with my back against the armrest, my legs over his. I felt his gaze on me as I took a sip of wine.

He's been watching me intently all day, as though he has something important to say. Or maybe I'm just projecting my feelings onto him. There's a lot I want to say, but I'm not really sure where to begin.

The thoughts running through my head are crazy. We've only known each other, really known each other, for two days. And no matter what's happening here in our little isolated world, it's nuts to think it would last when we get back to our real lives.

"I want to talk to you about something," he said, looking so nervous, my heart began to pound.

"Okay." I leaned forward and placed my glass on the coffee table.

"This thing..." He trailed off and I watched his Adam's apple bob up and down as he swallowed. Weaving our fingers together, he rested our joined hands against my legs and met my gaze again. "This thing between us is crazy. Three days ago, if someone mentioned the name Ivy Sherman, my mother's boyfriend's flighty daughter is the only thing that would come to mind."

I'm really not sure what to say to that, so I remained silent and urged him to continue with my eyes. I must have done a good job because he started speaking again.

"But now, I'd think of the amazing, smart, funny, sexy woman who sings to her dog and gets soaked in a thunderstorm so he doesn't have to go to the bathroom alone."

His image blurred as I listened to his words. No one has ever thought of me like that, not even my father.

"I've never felt this way about anyone. Emotionally, mentally, physically, you just do it for me and it feels right. More right than anything I've ever felt. And I know we're here under extreme circumstances, but I doubt that if I'd found another woman ogling me in the shower the other night, I'd feel the same way. It's you."

I smiled and sniffed. Rusty reached up and wiped his thumb across my cheek to clear away a tear that had escaped.

"I don't know where this will go, but I want to explore it beyond this house, beyond this city. I know you and Finn live in Aspen but we can see each other when I'm out that way playing or when I have a couple days off in a row. We can video chat in between, then get together again once the season ends."

"You'd do that for me?"

He cupped my cheeks and slowly stroked with his thumbs.

"I'm pretty sure I'd do anything for you."

He leaned forward and kissed me, just a soft kiss that seemed to seal his words.

"This is insane," I said when he pulled back.

"I'm aware, but for some reason it seems to make sense."

"What about our parents?"

"If we've dealt with them dating, they can do the same for us, right?"

"I guess so."

A million things ran through my head...reasons why I should just let whatever this is between us end when the storm does, but I don't listen to any of them. Instead, I nodded.

"Yes?" he asked flashing one of his mega-watt smiles.

"Yes."

"Yes, yes?"

"Is there another kind?"

His mouth crushed against mine and as our breath mingled and our tongues tangled, I knew I'd made the right decision.

EPILOGUE

RUSTY

The umpire shouted "play ball" and the batter stepped into the box. I stood on the mound, and looked to my catcher, Leo Marakis, as he flashed the sign for a fastball, waist high, inside corner. I nodded, then placed my foot against the rubber and stared down the batter confident I can place the ball exactly where Leo wants it.

Ever since I got back from Marathon, my pitching has been back to normal, if not better. My mom thinks it's because of Ivy and I don't totally disagree. We've been together for two months now and I've never felt happier or more settled in my life. Both of our parents were thrilled when we told them about our relationship, so that was one worry out of the way.

Going into my wind up, I reached my arm back then brought it over the top and followed through, my feet ending at the edge of the grass. I watched the ball sail right into Leo's waiting mitt. He didn't have to move an inch.

Strike one.

Next was a curveball inside that the batter nearly screwed himself into the ground trying to hit.

Strike two.

Leo called for a fastball, low on the outside corner. It will be a strike but will look outside to the batter since the first two pitches were inside.

Called strike three.

The crowd jumped to its feet at that first out and did the same for the next two—a ground ball to first base and a broken-bat line drive right back to me.

She caught my eye as I jogged off the field. I stopped in front of the dugout and smiled up at her. The half of the stadium that can see me probably thinks I'm insane, but I don't care. Ivy is here and not only that, she's wearing a Waves jersey with my number.

The little minx told me she couldn't get away this weekend. She's been staying at the house in Marathon and finishing her degree in graphic arts. It seems Ivy has gotten both of her parents' talents and she can create some amazing art on the computer. She's been designing logos and website graphics pro bono for nonprofits for years and really enjoys it. I have no idea why she never considered it as a career before.

Despite my crazy schedule, we've managed to see each other pretty often since she's on the East Coast. She and Finn even stayed at my place for a week during a home stretch. But when I asked her about coming up this weekend for the start of the playoffs, she said she had too much school work to do. I was disappointed, but totally understood.

But Ivy must have plotted with Hannah Reagan, who works for the Waves PR Department, in order to surprise me, since they're sitting next to each other in the wife and family section. Hannah's husband, Jack stepped out of the dugout and followed my gaze into the stands, mirroring my sappy smile when he spotted his wife.

The bottom of the inning was about to start and he slapped me on the shoulder before heading to the on-deck circle.

"Don't fight it," he said as he walked away.

"I don't intend to."

I glanced up at Ivy and flashed her another smile before heading into the dugout.

The End

ALSO BY TINA GALLAGHER

Check out the rest of the books in the Carolina Waves Series!

On the Mend

Waste of Handsome

Once Removed

ABOUT TINA GALLAGHER

As a tween, Tina Gallagher and her best friend would create happily ever afters for their favorite soap opera couples. Eventually, the soap operas lost their appeal, but the writing never did.

Before living her dream as a full-time author, she worked a spectrum of jobs ranging from baking and cake decorating to marketing and project management.

In between creating memorable characters, traveling, and taking pole dance lessons, Tina enjoys spending time with her handyman husband and two grown children.

Visit Tina's website at www.tinagallagherbooks.com

Sign up for Tina's newsletter and receive a FREE book!

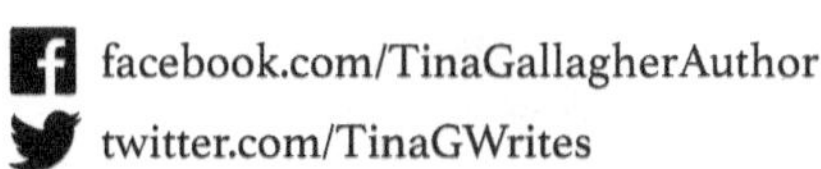

ROCKS, BUT NO ROLL

BY DENISE WELLS

1

MAGS

"Tell me you're bringing at least one cute outfit?" My roommate, Tricia, sits on my bed watching me pack for a company trip. When I say company, I mean smallish startup ISP (internet service provider) on the West Coast that has just merged with a larger small startup ISP from the East Coast. And when I say trip, I mean some stupid glamping type thing in the middle of the Olympic National Forest meant to bring us all together like one big happy family.

"Why would I? One, I don't have anyone I need to impress. Two, they said we could, and I quote, '*kick back, connect, and let the creative juices flow,*' so I ask you, what do I need cute for when I have leggings?"

"Mags," she scolds. "Have I taught you nothing in the years we've known one another?"

"You've taught me plenty and I appreciate it all. But, you're a makeup artist, you have to look good all the time. I write ad copy, no one cares how I look. They just care how I make their shit sound."

Still, when she's not looking, I throw in a nicer pair of jeans and a cute boho top, in addition to what I've already got in my bag, which is a lot. It's not that I'm overpacking, it's just that I won't know what I'll be in the mood to wear. What if I wake up and feel fat and leggings are an automatic no because I'm self-conscious about my ass? Leaving me with jeans as the only other choice. Then I have to decide if I want skinny jeans or boyfriend jeans? Cuffed bottom or straight leg?

I really hate traveling for this very reason. I believe in comfort where my clothes are concerned, but only if I'm staying home. If other people are going to see me then it must be comfort with a small modicum of style. I bitch all day long about comfort over fashion, but I'm living a lie. I *want* to be the girl who can effortlessly throw on any old thing and exude enough confidence that I still look hot. But in reality, it takes a lot of forethought to look this carefree casual.

"What about the promotion?" Tricia asks.

"What about it?"

"You want to make a good impression because you want the promotion," Tricia says.

"No way is my promotion going to be based on what I wear," I say, even knowing as I do it might not be true.

"Uh, absolutely it might be."

"Why?" I whine.

She hands me a basic black dress, one that's made from some crazy non-wrinkle material, and a pair of ballet flats. "Here, bring these, just in case."

"Fine."

"What else do you have in there?" she asks.

"An extra pair of underwear for each day, because what if I fall in a river and my pair for that day doesn't dry in time and I'm left a pair short by the end of the trip."

"Yeah, cause *that's* likely," Tricia says drily.

I roll my eyes at her. "Socks, in case my feet get cold. Hair ties, baseball hat, sun hat." I put it on my head. "What do you think, sun hat, no sun hat?" I pull it back off my head.

"Ditch the sun hat."

I toss it in the direction of my closet. "Okay, I think that's it."

"How many pairs of leggings do you have?" Tricia asks.

"Four."

"How many days are you gone?"

"Three."

"Lose two leggings." She rummages through my bad until she finds them. "And how many pairs of jeans?"

"Three." I leave out the extra pair I threw in.

She pulls one pair out. "Why the maxi skirt?" she asks, pulling that out as well.

I shrug.

"So, four bottoms for three days? And we haven't even gotten to the tops yet. You know if you'd just let me mix and match a few things, you could have, like, seven cute outfits from four pieces of clothing."

"No need, I've got this covered," I say zipping up my bag. It barely closes. I chose a duffel bag because I thought it looked more casual, not so high maintenance. But every so often, at times like this, I have to wonder if I really *am* high maintenance? I start to ask Tricia, then decide against it. Does it really matter? I mean, how much will I really change at twenty-six years old?

"Do you have a jacket?" she asks.

"Yep."

"Toiletries?"

"Yes."

"Okay, want me to drop you at the train station?"

"Please."

Halfway through the depot I begin to realize the folly in packing a duffel bag that I have to *carry* as opposed to just going with a small suitcase I could have wheeled. By the time I reach the train, I'm winded, sweaty, and my shoulders are aching. I find an empty seat, stow my bag, pull out my earbuds, and my e-reader.

I know a few other people are taking this train too, but I don't know what car they will get on, so I don't keep an eye out for them. Besides, I've been dying to finish this book, it's the first in a trilogy by an author that I love. And I waited until the other two were released to start reading it. So, I have all three and I can binge through the entire long weekend away in my down time.

I lose myself in the first chapter and am starting the second as the conductor calls, "All aboard." I hear, rather than see, someone jump on the train at the last second, breathing heavily and stumbling through the aisle. The seats facing me are open, but I'm really hoping no one sits there. I'm a big believer in personal space, so if this person keeps walking on by that would be—

"Hey, Mags, I thought that was you." Chaz, one of my co-workers, flops into the seat facing mine. I guess if someone had to sit in my space, I'm glad its him. I have a small crush on him. He's cute and funny and we don't work in the same department.

He works in the IT department. Which I found funny at first. That an internet company would have IT too, like wouldn't that just be something they would all know how to do for themselves? The answer to that, in case you're wondering, is no.

If I were someone who would allow myself to date someone I worked with, it would have to be someone in another department, because otherwise: *awkward*. And, if I were to allow myself to date someone in another department, it would be someone like Chaz. But I'm not that kind of someone, so nothing will ever come of my crush. Because dating someone you work with is just messy, all the way around. I don't know from personal experience, I've never done it, I just imagine it would be.

"Hey, Chaz. Wow you just barely made it," I say, pulling my earbuds out.

"Yeah, I thought it would be quicker to take a Zippycar instead of a LYFT. Boy was I wrong."

"Did you get lost?" I ask.

"No, I couldn't find a place to leave it."

"Oh yeah, I can see where that would suck." Zippycars are cool, especially in a downtown space like Seattle, you can use an app to pick up a car pretty much anywhere, drive it to where you need to, and then leave it there. Just paying for the time you used it.

Unlike renting a car where you take it for an entire day plus go through all the paperwork and insurance crap, with Zippycar you just get in and drive. "I've never actually gotten one before," I admit.

"I use them for dates all the time." He smiles and looks down slightly when he says it, like he's bashful or something. The dimple in his left cheek calling out to me, like a beacon in the night. I want to stick my finger in it. Or my tongue.

Wow, where did that thought come from?

"Cool," I say.

"Yeah," he agrees. "So, what do you usually do on train rides like this?"

"Read." I hold up my e-reader. "Listen to music." I show him my earbuds.

"Makes sense," he says. "I didn't bring anything with me.

I nod and smile sympathetically. I would never be caught on a train or plane or any mode of public transportation without an e-reader or a book and my earbuds. I'd go insane if I had to sit there with nothing to do. Case in point, Chaz starts drumming his fingers on his thigh, his foot bouncing in time.

"What are you drumming?" I ask.

"Oh, it's just some new piece my band and I are working on," he says.

"You're in a band, I didn't know that, that's so cool! Do you play an instrument? Or sing? Or?"

"Drums," he shrugs sheepishly.

"Oh, yeah, duh. I should have guessed that based on the finger work." I gesture toward his wiggling fingers

"Yeah." He glances down at his hands and smiles, like they are something to be admired. "So, what are you listening to?"

"Me? Henry Files. Loved him in One Movement and I love him even more as a solo artist."

"Really, you like that shit? No offense but that's not music."

"Of course, it's music, it's on the radio, they've won awards, their last hit is in a car commercial for god's sake."

"Yet it still sucks." He crosses his arms over his chest, and I can't help but notice how puny his biceps are. Shouldn't he be more muscular as a drummer?

"It's better than that other crap people love so much," I argue.

"Like?"

I shrug. "Take your pick: Weigh Station, Slitherbox, or even worse, Faux Fisted."

"My band does covers of Faux Fisted songs all the time. It's our best material."

"Oh. Shit. Sorry."

"Yeah." He looks out the window, hurt blanketed across his face.

I'm not sure this conversation could get any more lame or awkward.

"So, Chaz, what are you most looking forward to learning on this trip?" I ask.

I take that back, since I just brought us to next level lame.

"I really want to see what kind of hotties the East Coast has to offer."

"Hotties? Like from the other company?"

"Yep."

"You can't date co-workers."

"Who said anything about dating?" He smirks.

"You can't do *that* either."

"Why not? Is there a rule?"

"I don't know. It doesn't matter. Even if there isn't, office romances never work out."

"Says you."

"Says everyone. It's a well-known fact that workplace relationships don't work. Either someone gets divorced or someone else gets fired."

He waves me off. As though nothing I'm saying makes sense.

I make a show of putting my ear buds back in and searching for music on my phone screen.

He rubs at non-existent facial hair on his chin, then motions towards my head. "Hey, can I borrow your ear buds?"

"They're ear buds." I pull one out to show him.

"Yeah, I know, can I borrow them?"

"They go inside your ears."

"And?"

What does he mean by *and*? I feel like he's not getting it. I don't want something that was in his ear to then go back in mine.

"Ear. Buds." He says it like I'm the stupid one, holding his hand out for them.

"No!"

"Why?"

"I . . . uh, have an ear infection. I wouldn't want you to get it. Especially not when you're a musician. It might throw off your balance or something."

"Good point." He nods in agreement. "Thanks."

"No problem."

We settle into an uncomfortable silence, so I return my attention to my book. What should be a two-hour train ride lasts six years with Chaz interrupting me every third paragraph or so to engage in disjointed small talk.

Still, we decide to share a ride to the cabin and continue the self-induced hellish torture of one another's company. Remember like two hours ago when I thought I had a crush on this guy? Yep, that's gone. Long gone.

Chaz and the driver spend the entire forty-minute drive to the cabin discussing the merits of *hunter class* versus *warlock class* on some X-Box game called *Destiny*. In case you are wondering, most people prefer to be in the hunter class, because X-Box clearly caters to them. But the warlock class is obviously superior if you pay attention to anything at all.

As we pull up at the cabin, all I can do is hope that the karma gods see fit to bless me with the good stuff.

And by good stuff, I mean no annoyances (read: Chaz) and no surprises.

I hate surprises.

2

DEVLIN

"How does it feel to be the big boss?" Brittni slinks up to me as she asks the question. She hasn't stopped following me around since I got this promotion. You're looking at the National Vice President of Subscriber Enrollment and Retention. A title so long and convoluted, it doesn't even fit on one line beneath my name on my new business cards. Nor does it fit with my new duties, but it's one that I'm excited about, nonetheless.

"I gotta be honest, it feels good, Brittni. I think this retreat is a great idea and I'm excited to create some real synergy and cooperation. You know, open the lines of communication and really nail down where we are looking to go as a company."

I wince at how corporate I sound. Five years ago, I would have hated myself for it. But somehow, I've melded into this person that spews the company idioms with ease. And, surprisingly, I don't hate it.

"I knew you were going to get the promotion," she says, smiling. "I read it in the cards before they announced it. Plus, it was written all over your aura; so commanding." She rubs her hands along my biceps. A move from a girl I normally like since I work hard for them. But when she does it, I feel dirty.

"Just like I knew we were going to absorb the Seattle company. I could have told you about it. And I would have except you've been so busy lately; I hardly ever see you."

"We see each other every day at work," I return. I know where she's heading with this conversation and I don't like it. She's asked me out countless times and I've said no each time. But still she persists. At one point telling me we are soul mates who are meant to be together.

"This takeover—"

"Merger," I interrupt.

"Is taking all your time."

Our company has absorbed a smaller one headquartered on the West Coast—Seattle to be exact. I'm responsible for bringing the separate sales and marketing teams together into one cohesive unit. This retreat is meant to help that process along so that when we return to our respective locations we can still be doing so, just separately.

"Anyway," Brittni shakes her hair and fluffs the sides. "I'm so excited about everything we are going to learn. How many new people will we meet? What are you going to have us do first? Will you save me a seat next to you?" She prattles off questions she doesn't even wait for answers on. I'm not sure if she wants to talk to me or just hear herself speak. Either way, I'm growing weary of it.

She tried to maneuver a seat next to me every step of the way here. We've just arrived at the cabin after an early flight from JFK to Olympia, and then a long, winding van ride here. Somewhere in the Olympic National Forest, where we are going to spend three days *team building* and brainstorming how to grow the company brand.

In addition to believing we are soul mates, Brittni also wants my old job. And she wants me to recommend her for it. But I'm not going to. That honor is going to my buddy, Sam.

Because he deserves it. He works his ass off, he doesn't rely on low cut shirts with big tits to get attention (read: Brittni) and he'll make a good manager. Technically, I'm supposed to include candidates from the Seattle office too, but I already know Sam can do the job, so he's my pick. To save the morale on this trip I'm going to refrain from announcing it until after we go back to NYC.

I look at the surroundings before heading into the cabin. Thousands of mature evergreens and firs in every direction. And dozens of other tree varietals that I don't recognize on sight.

There are parts of Central Park that are like this, beautiful and green, at least in the late spring and summer, but nothing that smells like this. It smells clean, like nothing but air. No smog, no diesel fumes, no trash, no restaurant grease. Just air.

Being here reminds of my ex from college—the one who got away. Well, not so much got away as left me and never looked back. I can't blame her entirely. I changed the plan. She didn't.

We met our junior year in college, one of those lust at first sight situations in a bar. I took her home with me that night, then didn't let her leave.

I couldn't.

After that first night, I was smitten.

And she was too, even if she wasn't as open about it as I was. For the next two years we were inseparable. Since we were graduating at the same time, we devised a plan for how to spend the summer after. Driving across the US stopping at every cheesy tourist spot we could find: Carhenge, Enchanted Highway, Cadillac Ranch, Flintstone's Bedrock City, World's Biggest Ball of Paint, Dinosaur World, Roswell—we had a list and it was long. Then end up in Seattle, WA, where her family is from, and get amazing tech jobs with a big software company or online retailer.

Then the unexpected happened. I got a job offer I couldn't refuse. I hadn't even applied for it. One of my professors had sent in my resume along with a letter of recommendation. The job was for a media and marketing specialist at a tech start up, an ISP. My dream has always been to be a part of something from the ground up, and this was that chance.

I took the job without a second thought. I didn't even discuss it with my girl first. I just assumed she would stay with me. She didn't see it that way. I haven't seen her since. I tried to contact her a few times that first year, not as hard as I should have. That was my mistake.

That was five years ago, and I've yet to meet a girl who excites me as much as she does. But I blew it, and I know it. So, on the days that I'm feeling emotionally charitable I admit to myself I hope she made it to Washington, and that she got an amazing job with some fabulous company, and that she's happy.

Other days, not so much.

"Dude," Sam interrupts my reminiscing. "I grabbed us a room with two twin beds. Not all the rooms have more than one bed."

"Shit, I didn't even think about that. Thanks, man."

"No problem, boss." He winks exaggeratedly, making me laugh.

"I think I'm going to unpack and grab a quick shower, try to wake up before the West Coast team gets here."

"I'll distract Brittni, so she doesn't try to crawl in there with you."

"Ha, thanks." I laugh, but I also wouldn't put it past her. Brittni is one of those people who looks together on the outside, then she opens her mouth and you wonder how the same company hired her as you?

Not that she's dumb, quite the contrary. But her head is in the clouds, literally. She prefers to live, as she puts it, in the spiritual realm. Where everything happens for a reason and at the same time, she can predict the future. Tarot cards, energy healing, aura reading, palm reading—she does it all. And what's worse is she really believes in what she's saying.

I head inside the cabin. And to call it a cabin is silly given the size. While the decor is exactly like what you would expect in a log cabin with lots of wood and windows, raised ceilings and a great room. The livability is more like a communal hotel. Ten bedrooms, six full and three half bathrooms, game room, home theater, dining for thirty people family-style.

The entire downstairs is one great fifteen-hundred square foot room of living and dining areas plus the largest residential kitchen I've ever seen. I know from the brochure that the basement houses a large game room and home theater, and that all ten bedrooms are upstairs, five and five on opposite sides of a loft area.

I head up the grand staircase in the middle of the great room leading to the loft then turn to my left, second bedroom on the right, like Sam told me. I can see everyone unpacking and settling in and hear the murmurings of the West Coast team arriving. I'm going to need to introduce myself at some point, but for now I just want a moment of quiet. My assistant, Nancy, is here to organize everything and I'm happy to let her do just that.

I'm going to need to stay on point this entire stay, it's kind of my show. It was my idea to bring the two coasts together, and to make it a working vacation for everyone. And, since we are the larger company absorbing the smaller, we chose their home turf of Washington for the retreat. Even though the office is in Seattle and we're in Olympia. Nancy said this was the closest she could get.

The goal being to inconvenience them as little as possible since this trip is also to help us evaluate who we will keep and who we'll let go. As such, there are going to be a lot of team building and trust exercises. I have Nancy, Sam, and a couple other guys helping me with the initial selection process and then I will narrow it down from there. We automatically elected to keep their tech support on staff, so of the twelve remaining employees here, we'll be keeping five.

My least favorite thing about this new position is exactly what we I'm here to do.

Fire people.

3

MAGS

A small, peppy woman welcomes me the moment I step into the cabin.

"Hello! I'm Nancy. Assistant to the National Vice President of Subscriber Enrollment and Retention. What's your name and we'll get you all checked in?"

"Magdalena Stratton." I hold out my hand to shake hers. "But everyone calls me Mags."

"That's so pretty," she says, staring at me for a moment longer than is polite, before shaking her head as though to clear it. "Well, here you go, one name tag, one swag bag. You should only need the name tag for a day or so, by then we should all know one another. But until then this will definitely help. The bedrooms are all upstairs and first come first served, and if you pick a queen or king size bed you may be sleeping with someone else, so just keep that in mind. But there should be plenty to choose from."

I nod my head and gather my things, attaching my name tag as I climb the massive stairwell in the middle of the room to the loft above. I head to the right and make my way down the hall, passing the two bedrooms and a bathroom on the right, and the two bedrooms and a bathroom on the left, only to end up at one large bedroom on the end. Each bed already has a suitcase or duffel on it, so I make my way over to the left-hand side. The first room on the right has an open bed, so I grab it without even looking at the rest of the rooms.

I just want to get settled in before this whole thing starts. Now that I'm here, I wish I'd listened to Tricia more about my clothes. From what I've seen of the other girls, they are wearing cute skirts and shorts. Suddenly the idea of spending the weekend in leggings feels regrettable. I pull my reusable water bottle from my purse and squirt a long drink into my mouth.

Sharing a room with a stranger, as an adult, whether as a team-building exercise or not, is not my idea of a good time. I don't even know if it's a girl or a guy. Would they even let a girl and a guy share a room? Surely that goes against some sort of sexual harassment policy somewhere.

I sit on my bed and take it all in. The entire place is decorated like a log cabin, with wood and windows and leather furnishings. As far as I could tell, all the beds have quilts on them and big cushy pillows. The only difference being my room.

The decor in here is . . . interesting. Scarves have been draped everywhere. Over the windows and lamps, wound around the raw iron headboards—oh god, what if my roommate is some kind of bondage freak who ties him or herself to the headboard at night? Or worse yet, me? I unwind the scarf from around my headboard as fast as I can and try to drape it decoratively back over the other bed.

My headboard is now conspicuously bare, so I throw a jacket over it hoping she or he, doesn't notice. Though I seriously doubt a guy would have this many candles. At least I'm assuming they are my roommate's candles since none of the other rooms had them. And it's a lot of candles, like on every flat surface, none of which are burning.

Except. . .

A decidedly not good smell drifts from the walk-in closet. I peek my head inside. A tall blonde girl is standing in the middle holding what looks like a plant that is on fire.

"Ohmigod! Fire!" I aim my squirt bottle at her and fire. Water dousing both the plant as well as parts of the girl.

"Oh my stars!" she shrieks. "What are you doing?"

"Putting out the fire."

"That wasn't a fire! It was a purifier."

My eyes bug.

She rolls hers. "This entire room is absolutely stifling in its lack of creative energy and reduced metaphysical awareness. I can't handle it. Look around, we need to let go of what no longer serves us: mentally, physically, and especially spiritually." Water travels down her cheeks to her chin, dripping to her chest and rolling into her cleavage.

"Let go of *what*?" It bothers me that she hasn't wiped the water from her face.

She tilts her head. "Wow, you're really clogged, aren't you?"

"Clogged?"

"And so celestially simple."

"Excuse me?"

"It's not your fault." She walks past me, patting me on the shoulder as she goes. "You were born this way. But I can help."

She rummages through her suitcase until she finds what she was looking for. "Here, this will get rid of all that negative energy in a jiffy." And proceeds to spray me with the most foul-smelling stench I've ever inhaled. If you mixed dead skunk with rotten eggs and a bag of fresh dog poo, it wouldn't smell this bad. My stomach rolls.

"I'm going to throw up."

"That means it's working," she beams.

I gag. "I mean it, where's the bathroom, psycho?"

"Right through that door." She points to my left. "And I'll ignore the psycho comment since sometimes the negativity has to peak before it begins to disintegrate. Also, not your fault," she calls after me.

I race to the door and fling it open. My eyes film over.

Oh god, she's blinded me!

I stumble into the toilet, flinging the lid up seconds before draping myself over the seat and dry heaving. Again, and again before angling to rest my cheek on the cool porcelain.

"My god, what is that smell?" The shower curtain slides open and a blurry figure materializes. I turn my head back into the bowl to wretch some more.

"Is that you, that smells?" the voice asks.

"I'm being cleansed," I groan, lifting my head only to realize, with little relief, I'm not blind. The film over my eyes is the steam from the shower.

"Oh god, that's awful." The voice is muffled by a second towel over his face in what I imagine is an attempt to staunch the stench.

I can barely make out a deliciously defined male chest and abs peeking from above the towel wrapped around the voice's waist.

"At least I'm not going blind," I mumble, to myself.

"Were you sprayed by a skunk?"

"No, I'm being cleansed by my psycho roommate."

His laugh filters through the towel over his face. "Oh, you must mean Brittni. She's harmless. Mostly."

I stand and move to the sink to wash my face. "What she's done to me is not harmless. I'm going to need that shower if you're through." I splash water on my face trying to rid myself of the smell in any way possible.

"No problem." He steps out over the ledge of the built-in tub, brushing against my backside as he tries to pass in the small space. "Sorry, it's a little cramped in here." He lowers the towel from his face, as I turn to move out of his way, our eyes meet.

His face whitens as my stomach plummets anew.

"Mags?" he asks.

"Dev," I breathe, then lower my head and vomit for real in the sink below.

4

DEVLIN

Mags is here.

My Mags.

The girl I've thought about every day since she left after graduation and I moved to NYC.

How the hell is she here?

She must work for the Seattle company.

I hold her hair back as she throws up into the sink. It still just as silky as I remember.

I run my fingers through her soft strands as her body convulses and another stream of vomit spews from her mouth.

Not exactly the romantic reunion I might have imagined over the years.

The smell of her vomit mixed with whatever Brittni has doused her with, makes me want to join her. I close my nose and breath through my mouth, trying to lessen the effect.

"What are you doing here?" I can't help but ask.

"Puking apparently," she moans. "Will you turn on the shower, please. As hot as it will go."

She didn't need to tell me that. I remember it about her. One thing Mags and I had in common, well one of the many things, was a love for long hot showers. I turn it on, adjusting it to just past the setting I'd had it on for mine.

She turns from the sink to step into the shower, clothes and all, tugging the curtain closed with a jerk.

"Um, I'll just, uh," I stammer.

"You know I hate you, right?" she says. Her words emphasized by the sounds of wet clothing dropping to the shower floor.

The memory of her naked body sneaks into my mind. "Yeah. Okay. But, hey, it's good to see you. Let's catch up. Soon." Face palm. Could I get any lamer?

"Catch up?" She peeks her head out holding the curtain closed under her chin, squinting slightly. "Really, Dev?" Her eye makeup has run down her face, whether from the dry heaves and vomiting or the shower, I'm not sure. Wet hair plastered to the sides of her head.

I'd almost forgotten how beautiful she is. And for a moment, all I can do is stare.

She blinks at me, repeatedly. "Get out of here! Go!"

"Yep."

I go back to my room, flinging myself on my bed, feeling dumber than dumb.

"Dude, you take the longest showers in the world," Sam says, barely looking up from his phone.

"You aren't supposed to have your phone turned on. This is a technology free week."

"Says the guy who hasn't unplugged the router yet." He looks up and cocks his head. "I think you left the water on."

"No," I sigh. "That's Mags."

"Ha." He chuckles, then meets my eyes. "Mags?"

I nod.

"As in *Mags*? *The* Mags?"

I nod again. Standing to pull on boxers, a pair of jeans, and a t-shirt.

"What the fuck is she doing here?"

"I would imagine she works for the Seattle office," I say drily, adding Converse and a light hoodie to my ensemble.

"How did we not know that?" he asks.

I shrug in response, finger combing my hair into place. It doesn't matter how I style it; longer front pieces just fall back into my face anyway.

"*Mags* Mags?"

"Yes, Sam."

He rubs the back of his head. "Well, I guess it makes sense. I mean we've never really interacted with this new West Coast division before now. How would we know, right?"

"She said she hates me."

"To your face?"

I nod. "And then I said, *hey we should catch up.*"

Sam winces. "Not your finest comeback."

"No."

"What're you gonna do?"

A knock on the door interrupts our musings. Nancy pokes her head in. "You said to get you once everyone has checked in?"

"Yeah, thanks Nance. Can you let everyone know I'd like to meet in the main room in fifteen minutes?"

"Sure thing." She glances at Sam briefly before stepping back into the hall and closing the door behind her.

I look to him, brows raised.

"I know, I know," he says raising his hands in a surrender pose. "But right now, we're talking about you."

"I'd rather talk about you."

"Don't you have a meeting to lead or some sort of big boss like thing to do?"

I glance at my wrist even though I'm not wearing a watch per my own instructions for the weekend. "We've got time."

"It was one night. It ended awkwardly. And I don't know how to recover. Let alone approach her again. Okay? Happy?" Sam sighs.

"No," I say. "I'm not happy. What happened wasn't a big deal. Just get back on that horse, bud. Ride it all the way into the stables."

"Are you comparing the love of my life to a horse?"

"She's the love of your life?"

"She could be if I hadn't embarrassed myself."

"It happens. There's nothing to be ashamed of."

"Only guys it's never happened to say that," he grumbles.

"Sam, it's a natural part of life—"

"Did it ever happen to you with Mags?"

"Sure."

"On your first date?"

"Well, no, but later in our relationship—"

"Exactly. Once she already accepted you as a person with faults."

"Sam," I start.

"We gotta go," he says. "You've got a meeting to lead, a router to unplug, and a comeback to think up so you don't look like such an idiot around Mags."

"Did I sound like an idiot?" I ask. The sort of question you can only ask your best friend who you've known forever and ever.

"Totally."

"Are you just saying that because I made you talk about Nancy?"

"Probably." He opens the door and steps into the hall, just as Mags is doing the same. "The back of that head can only belong to one person. I should know, I stared at it through four years of business and marketing classes."

She pauses and turns her head slowly. "Sammy?"

"The one and only, baby doll." He opens his arms. "Give me some sugar!"

Mags runs into his embrace. A twinge hits me right in the heart. Partly because I wished she'd greeted me that way, instead of with the cool indifference she'd adopted instead. Well, cool indifference interspersed with actual vomiting.

The three of us had met at first-year student orientation in college and became inseparable. Mags and I in more ways than one. And when she chose to leave me, she left Sam too. Losing his friendship as well. For him she holds no grudge, not like she does for me.

The two link arms and stroll down the hall to the large winding staircase. The faint smell of skunk still lingering in the air.

5

MAGS

Sam and I do the elevator pitch version of catching up as we make our way to the great room, then stand there looking for seats. There aren't two together. Anywhere.

Nancy, the girl from earlier, glares at me. Specifically, the arm that I have wrapped around his.

"I'm going to grab a seat over there." I motion vaguely. "Looks like there's a seat next to Nancy."

Sam's face lights up, making me wonder if they have something going on between the two of them. I watch as he heads over, whispering something in her ear. Her eyes widen, then narrow, as she stares at me.

Great. Just what I need. The assistant to the guy in charge hating me.

Thanks a lot, Sam.

I look around for an empty seat. Most people have already congregated in small groups or pairs and are talking quietly amongst themselves. I don't have a lot of friends at the company. That's not true, I don't have any.

Chalk it up to not doing a lot of socializing outside of work. Happy hours aren't really my thing, and it seems to be the only way that co-workers get to know one another anymore. That and hanging out in the break room. Another thing that's not really, well, my thing. Besides, if I spend all my time in the break room, I'll never get this promotion.

Chaz is sitting on a small couch with an empty seat on either side of him. I take the one on the left and squeeze as far into the side of the couch and away from Chaz as possible. Which I try to reverse as soon as I see Brittni enter the room. I can't have her sitting here. I haven't talked to her since she sprayed me with that obnoxious tonic. And I don't intend to change that now.

I spread my knees as nonchalantly as possible to take up more space on the couch as she approaches. Willing Chaz to scoot to the right with my mind and my thighs.

It doesn't work.

"Hey, roomie," she says as she wiggles her ass into the inch of space between me and Chaz, creating a space for herself.

Surprisingly, she doesn't smell like the tonic. More like a spice or an herb.

Patchouli?

Sage?

"What'd I miss?" she asks.

"Nothing, we haven't started yet," I tell her.

"Oh, good. Any chance I get to see my man in action, I take it."

"Mmmm." I keep to non-committal responses in the hopes that she stops talking.

It doesn't work.

"He's running this entire show. And with any luck at all, I'll be taking his old job." She continues talking, her voice not a whisper, but not at full volume either. "I mean, we can't be too obvious about it or everyone would think I only got the promotion because of our feelings for one another."

"Promotion?" I ask, despite myself.

"Yes, to Marketing and Acquisitions Manager."

"Oh, for the East Coast?" I ask.

It must be since that's the promotion I'm going for in our office.

"No, for the whole thing. That's why we're here, you know. To officially announce the merger, lay a bunch of people off, and become one big happy family."

"What?" My voice is louder than I intend it to be.

Heads turn in my direction and I shrink back into the couch cushions. I don't like attention on myself. And I especially don't like it when I cause it.

"You didn't know?" Brittni asks, her voice at a normal octave.

"No," I whisper.

"They really keep you West Coasters in the dark about everything, don't they?"

I nod in response.

"I'm lucky, my guy tells me everything," she gushes.

"Very cool." I envision some senior exec, divorced, with kids, who's happy for the attention she and her double-D breasts give him. Dishing out the dirt on the company right before it's announced publicly. Making her feel special and still not breaking any major rules.

Despite myself, I look around the room for Dev. It's only natural that as she prattles on about her guy, I look for the one that used to be mine. Not that I still have feelings for him. I don't even *want* to be looking for him. It's just something to do. A way to pass the time until this meeting gets started; at five minutes past schedule according to my calculations. I hate when there's an agenda and it's not followed.

I check and double check my pencils. I have three, each sharpened to precision, because I hate writing with a dull lead. I don't like how wide and sloppy the letters start to look after a while. Plus, a brand-new pad of paper, making me ready to take notes on everything we learn on this retreat. I know, I could use an automatic pencil and have a constant sharp lead, but I don't like the way they feel in my hand. I don't like that I must click somewhere to get new lead, whether on the eraser or the little clip thing. And don't even get me started on the clip thing. A pencil should not have a clip thing. It should be yellow, made of wood, and have six even sides. Clip things are for ball point pens only. Pencils are to be stuck behind your ears, or in your—

"There he is now." Brittni bounces in her seat, causing me to bump into her each time her ass returns to the cushion.

I look up to check out her mystery man. But all I see is Devlin. I laugh to myself. Because no way would he ever be interested in someone like her. She's too annoying. Too flighty. Bubbly. And booby. And—

"I want to thank everyone for making the trip out here today," Devlin begins. "For taking the time out of your lives and away from your friends and family to devote to the company. We are appreciative."

"Isn't he great?" Brittni squeals into my ear.

"*Dev* is your guy?" I hiss.

"His friends call him Devlin," she says, leaning into me.

My jaw clenches, my teeth grinding together near the back. Something my dentist has warned me about, or I'll need to start sleeping with a mouth guard every night. Because I need one more thing to inhibit my dating scene.

Dev?

And Brittni?

Fuck it.

I keep grinding.

6

DEVLIN

I make it a point to look around the room as I'm welcoming everyone here, meeting each persons' eyes as I go. As much as I don't want to admit it to myself, I'm looking for Mags. I'm still amazed that she's here, that we work for the same company. How did I not know that?

I find her in the crowd, sitting next to Brittni, her jaw clenched and eyes hard. I move on quickly, not wanting to dwell too much on why she looks like a powder keg about to blow. I remind everyone that this is a technology free retreat as Nancy walks around the room collecting cell phones. Not that we had much reception up here anyway.

Then, make a production of unplugging the router and giving it to Nancy to tuck away somewhere. She has a list of teambuilding and trust exercises that we'll be doing starting tomorrow. But for tonight, we've just got a small ice breaker, then a pizza making party for dinner with beer and wine.

"Before we get to the pizza making and the beer, we're going to do introductions."

A collective groan sounds through the room. I know that people hate introducing themselves, so I'm hoping this twist will help.

"You won't be introducing yourself, however. You'll be introducing the person next to you. Nancy is coming around now to make sure that everyone is paired off, and you've got five minutes to learn three things about one another you will then share with the group."

Mags gets paired with Brittni, something I'm sure she's not happy about.

I'm paired with a guy named Chaz who'd been sitting next to Mags on the couch.

"So, you're the new head amigo, huh?" he asks first thing.

"Devlin McGuire, nice to meet you." I hold out my hand, he's reluctant to take it.

"Are we allowed to just, like, shake hands?"

I wait to see if he's kidding. Making some kind of manager/employee joke. But, no, he's serious. "Yes," I tell him. "In fact, it's encouraged."

He shakes my hand, letting me know he's in the IT department and is ready to take care of any technology issues we may have.

"It's a technology free weekend," I remind him.

"I know," he says. "Weird right?"

"Tell me a little bit about you, Chaz."

"Well, first," he leans in close. "I need to know, how are the betties on the East Coast anyway? You know, man to man. Anyone lookin' for a little afternoon delight?"

My head rears. I'm surprised at both his candor and idiocy. "I'm not sure that's appropriate. While we don't specifically prohibit employee fraternization, it's not encouraged either. I'm not going to help you single out someone on my staff for you to sleep with."

"Well, when you put it like that, it sounds kinda bad, you know. Hey, did I mention I'm in a band?"

"Oh, what do you do? Or play?"

"Drummer." His chest puffs out. "Sometimes I sing too."

"What kind of music?"

"Rock mostly. We do some covers of Faux Fisted that'll blow your mind, man."

Not being a Faux Fisted fan, I decide to change the subject. "So, what led you to the company?"

"I was working for a major electronics store chain, can't mention any names, you know how it is, seeing as they went out of business and all. I'm sure if you think about it though you can figure out who it was. I was tech support in the store. You know, people could bring in their computers and stuff and we'd help them fix it. That gig ended, with the whole out-of-business thing, and now I'm here."

I open my mouth to reply, but he keeps talking.

"I got a girl I'm interested in. She's in marketing. I'm gonna plant the seeds while we're here, you know, for a little one-on-one consummation."

I nod, as though I understand. Which I don't.

He continues, "We sat together on the train ride up. I let her know that

I'd be cruising for chicks here. But if I do, that's just to sow my oats, you know? Get it all out of my system before I settle down for good."

I respond despite my better judgement. "You thought telling her you're pursuing other girls would be a solid plan for courtship?"

"Court *what*? No man, I'm making her jealous. Chicks only love what other chicks love. That's what makes the world go 'round."

I hate to admit he has a bit of a point.

"I let her know I'm in demand, then suddenly she wants it." He elbows me in camaraderie. "We shared ear buds."

"Is that a thing now?"

"Well, we would have if she didn't have an ear infection."

"I see." I wonder who it is that has an ear infection and how the altitude is going to affect that. Making a mental note to have Nancy ask around if anyone is sick. At the same time wondering what woman here would share ear buds with him. "How do you know she wasn't just saying that?"

"What do you mean?"

"Maybe she didn't want to share her earbuds, so she lied about having an ear infection."

"Oh, man, that's cold. Supremely smart, but also cold. As ice." He licks his finger and makes a sizzle sound.

I really hope for his sake that Chaz is amazing at his job.

"So, you're in a band. Ready to settle down in a relationship. And in IT? Do I have it right?" I ask.

He nods. "Yup. What about you?"

Nancy rings the bell that time is up.

Chaz smacks his forehead. "Dude, we didn't have time to do you."

"Not a problem. You can just say that I'm enjoying the Pacific Northwest and I hope to see a lot more of it."

"I got you, man."

Nancy starts the group on the other side of the room, so we have some time before getting to Chaz and me. So far it seems everyone is enjoying the exercise and getting to know on another. And then it's Brittni and Mags' turn.

Brittni stands, and steps to the center of the room, even though it's not needed. "Hello everyone, I'm Brittni and this is Mags." She motions like a game show host to a prize. "Mags is a Pisces—"

"Aries," Mags interrupts. "And that wasn't one of my three things."

"She loves long walks on the beach—"

"No, I don't," Mags protests.

"I'm intuiting. It's a process," Brittni says.

"It sounds more like a personals ad." Random voices start shouting out questions and comments. "What's intuiting?"

"Well, I'm very spiritual, by nature. And having been blessed with the gift of the sense, the sixth sense," Brittni explains.

"Do you see dead people?" More random comments filter through the air.

"Yes, I do. Live people too. I'm clairvoyant."

"Ohmigod. Can you tell my future?" someone asks.

Mags throws a hand up in the air and flops back against her seat on the couch as people start to surround Brittni and ask her various questions. Most of us from the East Coast have experienced this with Brittni already. She rarely foregoes a chance to show off her *skills*.

With only Chaz and I left after Brittni and Mags, I don't make a big deal out of Brittni's disruption and let her steal the show, so to speak. Instead, moving over to sit next to Mags.

She stiffens the moment I'm seated. "You could have told me you were the boss," she hisses.

"In between you throwing up? Or as you were kicking me out of the bathroom?"

"You know what I mean."

Actually, I don't. But I don't mention that.

"You must be M. Stratton from marketing?" I confirm.

"You knew I was going to be here!?" she shrieks.

"No. I just got a list of the employees names. That's it. I purposely did not look at any background info on anyone ahead of time so I wouldn't have any preconceived notions when I met them."

"Why would that matter?"

"For deciding—" I stop myself before I say too much. But she sees it on my face anyway.

"You *are* firing a bunch of us, aren't you?"

"No. I don't know. Nothing has been decided."

"Your little girlfriend was right."

"Who's my little girlfriend?"

"And I'm sure I'm at the top of your list because of our history. I can't believe you. Can't even man up enough to work with your ex. We wouldn't even be on the same coast. Ohmigod, are you deciding on the promotion for Marketing and Acquisitions Manager? Of course, you're going to give that to her—"

"To who?"

"That's so like you, taking the easy way out. Hiring your girlfriend instead of someone with actual qualifications. Someone who has worked their ass off to prove their worth. But do you know anything about that? No, because you didn't want *preconceived notions.* You have no idea about our accomplishments or work ethics. You don't know how hard I've worked for this. You're just making a decision blindly based on emotion. Or worse yet." She gestures toward my lap. "You disgust me. And I don't even care that I said that to the new boss because I didn't stand a chance here anyway. Not with you making the decisions. I hated you five years ago for breaking my heart and I hate you still for ruining my dreams."

She gets up and stomps across the room, not stopping until she's up the stairs and turning down the hall to where her room is.

"What was that all about?" Nancy asks coming to sit beside me.

"That was Mags."

"Mags? Like from college? That Mags?" Nancy knows my history. We've worked closely together for five years and she's an amazing assistant and friend. I brought her with me up the ranks as I was promoted. She went from a temp, to receptionist, to department administrative assistant, to my assistant.

I adore her as a person and she's invaluable to me at work. Not to mention that my best friend is half in love with her. If he could just pull his head out of his ass and get over his *first date faux pas.*

"Wow," Nancy continues. "She looked really pissed off."

"You think?" I run my hand through my hair, the front falling right back down into my face. "I may need you to do me a favor. I'm just not sure what it is yet or if it will work."

"My favorite kind." She smiles.

I head outside for a moment to myself so I can get my thoughts together and develop a plan to make Mags talk to me.

7

MAGS

My intention was to stay in my room all night. But the smell of pizza and the sounds of laughter is too much. So, when my stomach growls for the third time in as many minutes, I leave the sanctity of my room and make my way downstairs.

I keep an eye out for Dev, if for no other reason than so I can avoid him, while I grab a beer and a piece of pizza. I'm not proud of the way that I reacted before. I should have been more professional. But the idea of him holding my future in his hands drives me crazy.

I've worked hard for this promotion and to watch it get handed to my psycho roommate just because they are sleeping together—well, that sucks to say the least. And don't even get me started on the thought of them together.

Brittni is holding court with much of the West Coast office, blathering on about seeing things in their lives. She sees me watching her and calls me over. "Mags, Mags, come here."

I ignore her at first, but it's hard when everyone else has heard her call me, I'm within earshot, and they are all looking my way. I make my way over to the group.

"Mags, let me read your palm." Brittni takes my beer from me and places it on the counter, then holding my one hand in both of hers, turns it over and begins tracing various lines with her fingertip. "I see that you and your brother are very close."

"I don't have a brother," I tell her.

"Well, I mean, someone you are close to. Like a brother."

"I don't really have anyone like that."

"Well, you went to school with a boy, right?"

"I went to school with a lot of boys."

"That must be it. One of them looks at you like a sister. I see it very clearly here." Brittni closes her eyes as she says that. I fight to control my laughter.

"I see the number sixty-eight in your life. Does that number mean anything to you, Mags?"

"Umm, no. I don't think so."

"Are you sure? Is your father sixty-eight?"

"No."

"Your mother?"

"No."

"Hmm." Brittni takes a deep breath and lets it out slowly. Her breasts pushing at her blouse, straining the button closure as she does. Chaz's eyes nearly pop from his head. She opens her eyes again. "It must be your address."

"Nope."

"Your favorite number?"

I shake my head.

"Okay, well, just think about the number sixty-eight, okay?!"

"Will do." I pull my hand from hers and grab my beer from the counter, snickering as I hear Chaz say to her,

"My favorite number is sixty-nine."

Brittni giggles in return.

I throw up a little in my mouth. A common reaction I seem to have toward Brittni.

What can Dev possibly see in her?

Brittni continues with Chaz. "Oh, I see that your grandmother had a dog."

"No, no dog," he says. "But she did have a cat."

"Yes, definitely a pet. I see that now. It was you who had a dog."

"No, I'm allergic to them," Chaz says.

"Oh. . . I mean. . . someone in your family had a dog."

"No." Chaz sounds sad as he answers her.

"How about someone you hung out with growing up."

"Oh, yeah, I knew a girl who had a dog."

"THAT MUST BE IT!"

You got a real winner there, Dev.

I head outside to the fire pit where a few people are sitting around it toasting marshmallows and making s'mores. Sam is there with a seat next to him that I quickly grab.

"I'm saving—" he starts, then looks at me. "Oh, hey Mags. I didn't realize that was you."

"You saving Dev a seat? I'll go." I stand to leave.

Sam reaches out and grabs my wrist. "No, I was saving it for someone else."

"Someone else, huh?" I wiggle my eyebrows at him, and he laughs.

"Yeah."

"Tell me about her."

He looks around before scooting his chair closer to me. "Have you met Nancy?"

"Dev's secretary?"

"Assistant, yes."

"You like her?" I ask.

"Like her? I'm fairly sure I love her."

"Oh, that's awesome, Sammy. Does she know? How does she feel?"

"I think she likes me."

"Well, all right then. What's the problem?"

"It's complicated," he sighs.

"She's married?" I ask.

"No."

"On the rebound?"

"No."

"Celibate?"

He laughs. "No. Nothing like that. It's something I did. I can't talk about it."

"You're married." I deadpan.

"Shut up, dork." He laughs, backhanding me in the bicep. "Something happened on our first date. Something terrible. And I don't think I can get past it."

"What did she do?" I lean in closer, eager to hear whatever dirt he's dishing out. Maybe next I can get him to tell me about Brittni.

"It's not something she did. It's something I did. Rather, something that happened to me."

"Oh no. What happened?" I put my hand on his shoulder in what I hope is a reassuring gesture.

He looks down at his lap, shaking his head. "This is so embarrassing. I can't believe I'm telling you this."

It dawns on me, what must have happened. "It's okay, we don't have to talk about it."

"I need to tell someone. Especially a girl. I need to know how bad it is from a female perspective."

"I get it," I tell him. "And it's not that bad. It happens to all guys, totally normal."

"Yeah. Dev said it happened to him when you guys were together, but not until further into your relationship."

I think back to Dev and I and can't recall a single time he was, *ahem*, unable to perform. "Really? I don't remember that happening. But if he says it did, then it must have."

Sam nods. "He said a few times."

"A few times? Jeez, my memory must just be glossing over the bad times. Er, not bad. I don't mean it's bad. I just mean regrettable. No. Like . . . um . . . fuck. Sorry. I don't remember it happening ever. But, hey, see how insignificant it is? I don't even remember. Besides, I'm sure he made up for it after." I cringe at my words but continue anyway. "And, so can you." I end on an upnote, hoping I sound encouraging.

"How do I make up for it, exactly?" Sam asks.

"Well, I don't know. Maybe try not to think about it, so it doesn't happen again," I suggest.

He looks at me, head cocked, brow furrowed.

"You know, and don't drink beforehand. Or just have one beer. There's a reason it's called *whiskey dick*."

Sam takes a pull from his beer, promptly spraying it into the fire in front of us. "What does *that* have to do with anything?" he yells.

"Everyone knows that if you drink too much, you go from"—I hold my index finger straight out—"to." Then let it bend down.

He starts to laugh. And laugh. Soon having to push his chair back from the fire so he can bend over, head between his knees, because he's laughing so hard.

I look around the fire pit. People are looking, but not really staring.

"Oh my god, Mags. Holy shit. Oh, shit."

"What's so funny?" I hiss.

He sobers after another moment of glee. "I didn't have a problem getting it up. We didn't even get to that point."

"Well, then what happened?"

"I had the shits. Clogged up her toilet and it overflowed. I had to call out a plumber to fix it." He laughs some more. "Suddenly that doesn't seem so bad considering what you had me doing."

I perch my feet on the cement surround of the fire ring and lean back in my chair, taking a long draw on my almost warm beer. "Oh, *that.* Yep, that totally happened to Dev. More than once even."

I look over at Sam and hold his gaze for a second before we both dissolve in laughter.

And for just a moment, I remember what it's like to live and feel happy. Much like how I was five years ago before Dev tore my life apart. Before I shut myself off from the world, any new personal connections or friendships, social interactions, and of course, dating.

8

DEVLIN

Today is a full day of team building exercises, and the day I put my plan into place. Much like I worried she would, Mags has avoided me every possible second. And since we go home tomorrow, this is my only chance.

While most of our other activities have centered around groups of five or six, today we are pairing off. Nancy is making it appear as though names are drawn at random, but she is making sure to partner Mags and me. Because I asked her to. She's also going to make it appear as though we randomly select an all-day activity. Because I asked her to.

So, whether she likes it or not, Mags and I are spending the day together and she's going to listen to me about why I didn't go with her five years ago.

Clearly, thinking that just because Mags was a captive audience, she would listen to me was futile.

"The map says we need to go another five hundred yards west." Mags points to her left and heads in that direction.

"I don't think that's west," I tell her.

"Well, you aren't the map and you don't have this." She holds up the compass, which she has refused to relinquish the entire time we've been hiking so far. Our activity is a mini-survival hike/scavenger hunt, simulating what thrill-seekers on a reality show might encounter, but shrunk to a day with no real danger, and no audience or cameras.

I follow behind her, trying not to stare at the sway of her ass. She's wearing leggings that are so sheer I can practically see the outline of her thong. Black leggings, a white tank top, and bright pink converse, with a baby-blue hoodie tied around her waist. Not exactly hiking gear, but fine for what should be an easy day of roaming the mountainside. Her fashion choices haven't changed much in the last five years. Then again, neither have mine.

"Do you see it yet?" she asks, referring to the giant Douglas Fir we are supposed to find. Rumored to be over three hundred feet tall with a trunk girth of over thirty-eight feet. Once we take a picture in front of it, we can move on to the next item: finding black bear scat. Which is similar in shape to human feces, only much larger.

"Nope. But it shouldn't be too hard to miss, right?" I swing my backpack around and pull a bottled water from it, taking a long swig as we go. I packed a light blanket, some small snacks, and a few bottled waters. Romanticizing the idea of a hike and a picnic.

"Well, if we don't find it soon, we're never going to get through everything on the list. Then we lose. And I hate to lose," Mags grumbles.

I already know this about her, the competitive streak. But this isn't a win or lose activity and I remind her of such.

"Of course it is. Everything is win or lose, Dev, you know that. God, where is it? It should be right here." She stomps her foot.

I grab her arm and twist her around to face me. "This isn't a competition. It's just an activity meant for us to work together on. As much as I enjoy watching your ass, I think we should collaborate a bit more instead of me just following you."

"Shut up about my ass. You get zero say about me."

"I wasn't saying—never mind. Look, can I just see the map for a minute?"

"You know I can read a map," she huffs.

"Yes, I do. And so can I." I hold out my hand for the map. She hands it to me reluctantly. "Okay, so the fir should be here"—I point to the spot on the map—"and it looks like we're here." I move my finger to the left.

She stands next to me, bending her head to see better. "That's not where we are. We're over here." She points to a spot much further to the right, which is most definitely not where we are.

"Mags, listen—" I start.

"No, you listen," she interrupts. "You aren't the boss of me. Well, I mean you are, but not for everything. And I don't have to do what you say just because you say it. We aren't at work."

"Technically, we are on a work a retreat, but that's not what I meant. I meant for you to actually listen, you'll hear a stream."

She cocks her head, then nods slowly. "Okay." But she says it more like a question than an agreement.

"So, that puts us here." I point to my spot on the map again. "There's no stream near where you say we are."

She studies the map again. "Oh." Her face falls.

"Look, can we just work together on this? It's meant to be team building not individual competing. We can read the map together. Make decisions on where to go together."

"Pfft. Says the guy who can't be bothered to make a decision *together* when it really counts."

"Good point," I concede. "Can we talk about that?" I know she's referring to when I took the job in NYC, after college, and didn't talk to her about it first.

"No need. That was five years ago. Water under the bridge. You made your choice, I made mine." Her words are nonchalant, but she's still bothered by it, I can tell.

"I thought you'd stay," I tell her.

"On the East Coast? And what? Move to New York? Why would you think that? The plan was never to stay. It was always to leave."

"Plans change."

"We had those plans for over a year."

"I know. It was an amazing opportunity. I didn't seek it out. It just fell into my lap."

"Then you shouldn't have been so prepared to say yes."

"I didn't . . . I thought . . . You're right. I should have talked to you first. But, shit, Mags. It truly never occurred to me that you would still leave."

"You never even asked me to stay."

"Yes, I did!"

Her voice lowers as she looks down to her feet. "No, Dev, you didn't."

I think back to the day she left. And the days leading up to that day. Not that it was a long span of time. It wasn't even a week between the time I said yes and when Mags left. And though I can't remember those specific words leaving my mouth, I also can't imagine that I wouldn't say them.

"I . . ." I start, not knowing what I want to say until the words leave my mouth. "I'm sorry."

"Yeah, well." Her voice wavers and I see a tear fall through the air and land on the tip of her shoe, making a dent in the dust left there by the path.

"Mags." I tilt her face up so I can see her. "I never, ever wanted to hurt you. Or us."

She turns her head to the side, not meeting my eyes. But the tears are still there in hers, threatening to spill over at any moment. I take a chance and pull her into my arms for a hug. Her slight body stiffens at first before melting into me as she slides her arms around my waist and buries her face in my chest.

I use the opportunity to sniff the top of her head, something I've not been able to do for the last five years. I've missed it every day. She still smells the same. Like fruit and vanilla, and all Mags.

My cock starts to harden as I take in her scent and she presses her body against mine.

She pushes away suddenly. "Oh no," she says, circling her index finger at me. "There will be none of that."

"None of what?"

"That. You. Your body. Your dick. Those feelings. Nope. Not happening, Devlin." She spins to head down the path. Which is when she disappears.

9

MAGS

One minute I'm back in Dev's arms, feeling safe and secure, getting a little turned on at the feel of his hardening dick. The next I'm careening down a hill.

Hill is putting it nicely, what this is, is more like a cliff.

Ohmigod, I'm falling down a cliff.

The back of my tank scrunches up as I go, rocks and twigs scratching at my back and pulling at my hair. My hoodie falls from around my waist as my body continues to propel itself down the side of this . . . let's face it, it's a fucking mountain.

I'm falling down the side of a mountain. Heading for god knows where. My final resting place, I'm sure.

What's that noise?

Oh fuck.

Here's the stream.

My body stops its tumble. Finally. But not until I've completed an entire rotation at the edge of the stream, effectively drenching my entire body. You might think you know what cold is, but you don't. Not until you've submersed yourself in a stream that originates from the thaw of the snow atop Mount Olympus.

My scream hurts my own ears it's so shrill.

I look up to see Dev in the water, and he's pulling me out. Then pulling me against him, touching me everywhere at once.

"Are you okay? Mags? Talk to me? What happened? Are you hurt?"

"Cold." My teeth already chattering.

He half carries, half drags me up the shore, grabs my lost hoodie from the atop his backpack and wraps it around me. "Let's get you into the sun." He tosses his backpack over his shoulder, then scoops me into his arms and begins walking up the shoreline toward a patch of sun.

I don't even care if I'm heavy. I'm simply happy to be alive.

"I fell down a mountain," I stutter into his chest.

"It was more like a small hill," he says.

"It felt like a mountain."

"I'm sure it did." He kisses the top of my head. I'm not even sure if he realizes he did. Regardless it makes me feel good. I snuggle closer to his body heat.

He doesn't stop at the small patch of sun like I thought he would. Instead finding a less steep section of the mountain and effortlessly climbing to the top.

Devlin does cardio, apparently.

He sets me down gently, then pulls out a blanket from his backpack and spreads it out. "I know you're tempted to curl up, but if you can, lie flat in the sun, your clothes should dry faster that way."

I nod and follow his instructions. He surprises me by wrapping his own hoodie around my shoulders after laying mine out to dry, then lying down beside me and pulling me into him. "The body heat should help," he says after I look at him questioningly.

I settle back in, and it's like no time has passed. Like we are back in college slowly waking up after spending the night together or picnicking in the quad on a warm day. My body fits into his like a missing puzzle piece and I don't even care that I hate him. Or that I've missed him. Or how cold I am.

All I care about is how good he feels after my near-death experience.

His arm tightens around me in a brief squeeze, as though he could read my thoughts. There was a time when I would have sworn to you that he could.

"We should probably head back instead of continuing this hike," he says. "We need to get you out of those wet clothes, and it's best that we do that before the sun starts to set."

"What time is it?"

"I'm guessing maybe four o'clock based how long I think we've been gone and where the sun is at," he says squinting at the sky.

"Okay," I sigh, sitting up. His eyes drop to my chest and widen. I look down, realizing my white tank top is completely see through. The little lavender flowers on my bra, that were so subtle, are now screaming for attention. I cross my arms over my chest and glare at him.

He holds his hands up in a surrender pose. "I'm sorry. You can't blame a guy for looking."

"Isn't that sexual harassment, Mr. McGuire?" I smirk.

His expression goes flat and he stands quickly. I immediately regret my comment and want the warm look back on his face. The teasing eyes and the knowing smile. "I'm sorry. I didn't mean it like that," I tell him.

"No, you're right," he says. "That is no way for a manager to treat his employee. I'm not setting a good example and I'm sorry for that." He grabs the blanket and shakes it loosely before stuffing it back in his backpack.

"Plus, what would your girlfriend say," I taunt.

"What girlfriend?" he asks.

I hand him his hoodie, but he waves me off and starts walking down the path. I shrug and put it back on. Grateful for the warmth it provides and the scent that is all Dev I'm enveloped in, then scramble after him.

"Brittni."

"Brittni's not my girlfriend," he scoffs.

"Your fuck buddy then."

He stops and turns to face me. "She's not my fuck buddy either. She's my employee. I don't appreciate the implication there is anything more than that. Where would you even get such an idea?"

"From Brittni, she told me."

"Well, she lied." He spins and begins walking again. "She's not my anything. We've never even dated or seen each other socially. She's tried, but I haven't done anything. You want to know why?"

Relief floods through me.

Followed by fear.

The idea of Dev with Brittni sickens me. Not just because I think she's off the deep end, but also because she is the opposite of me in every single way —looks, personality, drive. And, I can't stand that she packs a suitcase better than I do. I mean, how did she get all those candles and shit in that tiny suitcase, plus clothes?

Dev pauses on the trail but doesn't continue talking or move to face me.

"Why?" I don't say it loud enough for him to hear. Because I'm not sure if I want to know. I do, but only if it's something I want to hear. The problem is,

I don't know what I want to hear. Dev destroyed me when he didn't go with me after graduation. Once the novelty of traveling cross country by myself wore off, it was all I could do to keep going. Keep waking up each day. Keep breathing each moment.

He has the power to do that again. To reduce me to mere nothingness. I'm not sure that's a chance I want to take.

Ha, not that he's offered.

He continues up the trail, shaking his head and muttering to himself.

I debate whether I should say anything about what he said or just continue like I heard nothing. "Shouldn't we at least look at the map to make sure we're going the right way?" I ask, deciding.

"Sure." He stops and begins digging through his pack. "Where is it?" He narrows his eyes at me.

"How should I know?"

"You had it last."

"You mean before I plummeted to my near death? You think I'd hang on to the map during such an ordeal? Besides, you had it. Remember? You were pointing out how I was wrong about where we were?"

He crouches down, pulling everything out of his backpack: Two unopened bottled waters, and one opened one, a few granola bars, the blanket, the list of items we are looking for, and the digital camera with which to prove we found them. "I don't have it," he says gesturing to the small pile.

"Is it in your pocket?"

He pats down his pockets. "No."

I check, the pockets in his hoodie are empty as well. "Where did it go?"

He shrugs his shoulders. "I don't know. We can walk back toward the way we came to see if we can find it."

I shudder visibly at the thought of returning to the place that will surely haunt me forever.

"Still cold?"

"No," I shake my head. "I mean, yes. But that's not why I was shivering."

He looks at me, brow raised.

"I don't want to go back to the place where I nearly died."

"You didn't nearly die."

"Says you. You didn't fall down the side of the mountain."

"No, I walked down it. Because it was a hill."

I wave him off. "Let me see the compass."

"I don't have the compass," he says. "You do."

"Oh, not this again, come on, Dev. Give me the compass." I stomp my foot slightly and squint my eyes at him as he shoves everything back in the pack once again.

"I. Don't. Have. It."

"Well, I don't have it." I unzip his hoodie and motion to my still damp clothing, which clearly conceals nothing from view.

His eyes heat as they travel down my body and up to my face again. Another shiver runs through me, this time one of expectation and satisfaction. Because as much as I love knowing that Dev still wants me, I'm quite sure I love the possibility of what that might mean more.

10

DEVLIN

Her clothes leave nothing to the imagination. Not that I've forgotten what she looks like naked. I haven't. It's still my number one go-to in my spank bank. But she wasn't wrong earlier which what she said about sexual harassment. There is still the issue of me as her boss. And while the company doesn't prohibit employees dating, they certainly don't encourage it. And that's if we ignore that we live on opposite coasts from one another.

"Let's go," I say. My voice coming out harsher than I'd intended. "We have a general idea of where we are in relation to the stream and where the cabin might be. We should be able to wing it."

"Wing it? You want to wing it in the middle of the wilderness?"

"We're in a national park. It's hardly unchartered territory."

"One of the items on our list was to identify black bear scat. A bear, Dev!"

"Black bears don't hurt people, Mags. You're thinking of grizzly bears."

"Oh, 'cause you've asked them personally?"

"Come on." I wave her forward. "You'll get warmer faster if you move."

"Lead the way." She waves her arm at me and begins to follow.

"Are you sure you know where we're going?" Mags asks for the five-millionth time.

"No, Mags. I don't know where we're going. I'm just guessing. Like anyone would who doesn't have a map or a compass!" My voice rises, causing her to shrink back just a bit. But I see it, the moment when the fire kicks in and she rears back at me.

"You think I'm responsible for the map and the compass? Are you crazy?"

"You'd be the one to recognize it. Like is as like does." Once again, not my finest comeback, but I'm tired and hungry, embarrassed, and a little worried.

Her eyes tear up.

"I'm sorry, Mags," I sigh.

She brushes me off. "I'm not upset about you. God. I'm getting my period soon and I'm over emotional."

"I thought women didn't like to use that excuse?"

"We can use it all we want. It's when *you* use it that pisses us off."

I nod even though I don't it. "Why don't we take a little break. Split the other granola bar and see if we can recognize anything around us. Like a landmark or something."

She nods tearfully, not arguing for once, and joins me on the blanket for our third such picnic of the day. This will be the last of the water and granola bar. The sun will be going down soon, and we are no closer to finding our way back than we were three and a half hours ago. The only upside being its summer, so the temperatures won't fall below mid-50s if we're forced to spend the night out here.

Which means at least we won't freeze to death.

We finish the other granola bar and last bit of water in comfortable silence, until Mags speaks again. "We may as well admit it. We're going to have to spend the night out here."

I open my mouth to argue before thinking better of it and choosing to nod instead. The sun sets late this time of year, but it's still setting much faster than I'd expected. Even though I'm not from around here, I can tell it will be dark soon.

"So, maybe we should focus on building a shelter instead of walking more. Besides, I have a blister the size of a quarter on my left heel and it's killing me."

I want to argue again, mostly out of habit from the day we've had. But instead stand and start to gather fallen pine branches to make a bed of sorts for us to rest on. There isn't much. I can't believe I didn't think to bring a pocketknife or anything remotely utilitarian.

My thoughts return to those final days after graduation, before Mags headed west and I stayed east, and how we got to that point. The point where she was leaving, and I wasn't going with her. Or where I remained, and she wasn't staying with me.

I thought our future together was a given, from day one, we just clicked. Our friends described ours as the relationship to aspire to. Sure, we fought, but we made up. I genuinely liked her and enjoyed being around her. And the sex was mind-blowing. Had you asked me, I would have said that nothing could bring us down.

Until it did.

I bring back what I can and pile it beneath a tree. Mags stands off to the side, head cocked, obviously thinking.

"Whatcha thinking about?" I ask.

"The best way to share the warmth of the blanket if it gets too cold."

"I have an idea," I tell her.

"Okay."

"You may not like it."

"Okaaaay." She draws the word out this time, like she's hesitant to hear my idea.

"We need to swaddle ourselves in the blanket and our clothes."

"What do you mean?"

"I'm going to take back my hoodie," I start.

Her eyes widen, resignation falling over her face at the same time as she begins to unzip it.

"You're going to put yours on, then I'm going to zip mine around both of us," I continue.

"How?"

"Okay, we're going to sit on the blanket under the tree here." I point out my makeshift resting place. "I'll have my back against the tree, with the blanket pulled halfway up my back." I take the blanket from her to demonstrate. "You sit between my legs, like so." I pull her down so she's sitting in my lap, her back to my chest. "I'll zip my hoodie around us, and we pull the blanket to our chins." I mimic the motions since she has yet to take mine off.

"You think that'll work?" She spins to face me, our mouths mere inches from one another.

"I do." My gaze darts back and forth between her eyes and her lips. She clears her throat and backs away smoothing the blanket down as she goes.

"Mags, can we talk?" I ask.

She looks up at me from across the blanket. "Sure, but not when we're all cuddly like that." She wiggles her index finger between us.

"I'm kinda cold," I lie. Looking pointedly at my hoodie.

"Here, take it." She unzips mine and tosses it at me. Leaving her in just her own over her tank. She shivers at once.

"Don't be silly. Come here," I beckon.

Mags hesitates, but I can tell by the look on her face that she wants to.

"Please?" I use the smile that used to make her melt. Pleased to find, once she settles in between my legs, that it still works. I zip my hoodie around us, then wrap the blanket burrito style around our legs and chests. It's instantly too warm for me, but when Mags sighs with satisfaction, it's all worth it.

I wait a moment before asking her the question I'm dying to know the answer to. "So, Mags, I need to know. Why did you go after graduation? Why did you leave instead of coming with me to New York City?" Then I brace myself for her answer.

11

MAGS

My heart pounds as I settle in between Dev's legs, mentally preparing myself for the close contact I'm not yet ready for. This is different from the hug earlier, or even the cuddles on the blanket. I'm not ready for him to have an impact on me like this again. But, I'm not surprised by his question. He'd hinted at it earlier in the day and I'm sure in his mind that's exactly how it seemed. That I just chose not to go with him. But he's misremembering the facts.

I take a breath before answering. "Like I said earlier, you didn't ask me to."

"But I did," he protests.

"You didn't." I tilt my head back against his chest and look up, trying to catch his gaze. All I can see if the bottom of his jaw and a small patch of whiskers he missed when he shaved this morning.

"In what universe do you think I would leave and not ask you to come with me?"

"In the one we live in, Dev. Because that's what happened."

"It's not." His arms tighten around me as though to emphasize his point. "I've been thinking about this all day, since you said that earlier. And I distinctly remember the conversation. I said *when you get to New York, we can do a bunch of cheesy touristy stuff* and you completely ignored me."

"You think *that* was you asking me to go with you?"

"I do, because it was." He takes a deep breath, then lets it out slowly, the force brushing my hair against my cheek. "I get where you think I didn't ask—"

"Because you didn't."

"—but at the same time, it never occurred to me I had to," he finishes.

My brow furrows as I try to decipher what he means by that. Finally, I just ask him. "Why not?"

"Because our future together was the one thing I never doubted."

"So, you just assumed I would follow you wherever, without even discussing it with me first, and give up all my plans, and for what?" My face heats, it's getting warmer under the blanket, but I don't want to open it for fear of being cold again.

"For us, so we could be together." He leans in a nuzzles the side of my face gently. I don't even think he realizes he did it. Much like the kiss to the top of my head earlier, it's like muscle memory when I'm near.

I've missed that.

"But I had plans too, Dev."

"You didn't have a job offer."

He's right.

"Well, no. But we had a plan."

"Plans change, Mags. They are flexible by nature. An intention by definition. And if that road trip meant so much to you, why didn't you just tell me? I could have tried to postpone my start date and we could have still done it."

"That wasn't the point." I pound my fist on my thigh, tears pooling in my eyes once again. I squeeze them shut until I feel more in control. I hate my emotions.

"What was the point?" He takes my hand in his, unfurling my fingers and laying them out flat, covering mine with his. As always, his touch has a calming effect on me.

"The point was that you didn't even tell me about the job before you accepted it. We had all these plans and you changed them singlehandedly, without even thinking about or consulting me."

His chin drops to my shoulder and I expect him to argue with me.

"I'm sorry."

His apology deflates me and I'm not ready for that. I'm ready for a fight. A knockdown, drag out where I hurt him as much as he hurt me.

"You're right. I didn't consult you. I just expected you'd be as excited as I was, and we'd adjust. Then when you left, I didn't know how to take it. It killed me."

"You never even called. Or texted. Or emailed."

"Yeah, I did. Every day for over a year."

"I never got anything."

"I never sent them."

"Why not?"

He shrugs. "Part of me figured you left because you wanted to. You were done with me. I didn't know how to combat that, at least not then."

His words give me hope. "What do you mean *not then*?" I ask, despite myself.

"Well, now I would just come after you. Ask you to stay, if that's what you needed. Admit how much I want you in my life, make sure there were no misunderstandings or miscommunications. Make my intentions clear: to have you by my side."

My breath catches.

Does he mean he's doing that now? Or that he *would have* done that if then was now?

"Do you ever wonder how life would be if we'd stayed together?" He hasn't taken his chin from my shoulder. The faint scent of his aftershave floats between us.

"Sure, I guess." I don't want to give him too much. I'm feeling vulnerable and scared, but the rush of adrenaline pumping through my veins makes me feel like I can do anything at the same time. My body tenses as I wait for him to continue.

"I think about it all the time. No one has ever measured up to you, Mags. And I've looked, believe me—"

"I don't want to hear about you all your girlfriends, Dev."

"That's just it, there weren't any."

"None?"

"Nobody serious, no. What about you?"

I consider lying, telling him I've had many boyfriends, that I have one now even. But it's the truth that comes out instead when I open my mouth. "I've dated, but nothing major."

He makes a non-committal noise but says nothing more. I want to continue this conversation. I want to hear more about how much he missed me and how no one else compared. Well, not more about other girls, unless we focus on all the ways they were lacking. I want him to say he still loves me. That he wants me back. That we belong together.

He stays silent.

I force myself to relax against his chest, he rewards me with a soft sigh in my ear.

"I like having you here," he says.

"In the middle of the wilderness, facing untimely deaths?"

He chuckles. "In my arms, facing a night together, in a national park."

"People still die in parks, Dev. It happens all the time. Selfies near waterfalls: poof, they fall in and drown. Hiking off path, someone breaks a leg and is eaten by bear. Hypothermia."

"It's not cold enough to get hypothermia and we aren't taking any selfies."

"So, you admit we could break a leg and be eaten by a bear?" I ask.

"Only twenty-three people have been killed by a black bear."

"That's still a lot."

"Since 1900."

"Oh."

"Exactly."

The sun has mostly gone down and the moon hasn't risen all the way, but it's still not as dark as I imagined it would be. Surprisingly, I'm not scared. I'm sure due to Dev and being here in his arms. But it feels more like an adventure than an emergency. Like we are here by choice as opposed to stranded or lost.

Which makes me want to be brave. As in tell Dev what I'm thinking, even what I'm feeling.

"I'm sorry for leaving after graduation," I blurt out before I can stop myself.

Dev sighs. His chest filling behind me, his cheek brushing against mine as he lets the air out. "What if I said I thought we should try again?"

"Try . . . us?"

"Yeah. What would you say?"

I summons as much bravery as I can, pulling from every individual source I can imagine, just so I can give him this:

"I'd say, no."

12

DEVLIN

"No?" I confirm. "Did you say, no?"

"Yes, I said no."

"But why?"

Mags takes a deep breath before letting it out slowly. Weighing her words before speaking.

I guess I should have done the same. I feel like I'm just flailing in the wind right now, waiting for her to either anchor me or set me free.

If I'm honest, I don't see why we can't just pick right up where we left off. At the same time, I don't want to make assumptions again. I did that when I moved to NYC and look where it got me. Plus, long distance relationships never work; I live in New York and Mags lives in Seattle. Not to mention that I'm technically her boss.

Unless I fire her.

If I did, would she ever forgive me?

"First," she starts. "Is the obvious: you're my new boss."

"Unless I fire you." I test the waters to see what she'll say.

"In which case I would hate you forever and never, ever forgive you."

Good to know.

"So, of course, I would never do that," I reassure her.

"Second, we live on opposite sides of the nation."

"We could change that," I interject.

She ignores me. "Third, we don't even know if we are still compatible. Fourth—"

"Turn around," I interrupt.

"What do you mean?"

"I mean what I said. Turn around. On my lap. Straddle me." I list the instructions for her as clearly as possible.

"Dev, I can't just strad—"

I stand up, forgetting we are still zipped in the same hoodie, my hoodie. She slides out the bottom and stays on her ass.

"Wow. You really—" she starts again, so I grab her upper arm and pull her up so she's standing in front of me. Then, before she has a chance to say anything else, I back her up against the tree behind us and capture her lips with mine.

She protests at first, if you could even call it that, but within seconds her body melts into mine. Her arms crawl up my chest to around my neck, her breasts smashed between us, my dick throbs against her hip bone. I push my tongue into her mouth, trying to sample everywhere at once. Mags tastes new yet completely the same and I can't get enough.

I kiss her until I can hardly breathe and still, I don't want to stop. My hands move up her sides to grab at her breasts, fingers pinching her nipples as she writhes against me. I never want this moment to end. I want to rip our clothes away and bury my cock deep inside her, lose myself in a way only Mags has been able to provide.

"Devlin," she pants into my mouth, her leg snaking around my thigh pulling me closer. I grab her hips and lift her up, her legs wrapping around my waist, just where I want them.

It's been too long since I've had her like this. In my arms. On my lips. Wrapped around my waist.

"God, I've missed you," I mumble against her lips. No longer caring about my pride, what she thinks, or how it looks. All I know is we have this moment, together, and I need to make it clear that I want her.

"I've missed you," she returns.

I need to make this work. I don't even care how. All I know is I can't lose her again. I can't let her go. I won't be that guy. My lips leave hers only to travel down the delicate skin of her neck, biting softly as I go.

"Dev," she moans. "We need to stop."

"Why?" I lose myself in her scent, nuzzling my nose behind her ear.

"I don't know." Her legs release from around me and she slides her feet to the ground.

I raise my head to meet her eyes, her features softened by the dimming light in the sky. "You're so beautiful."

She blushes and looks down, making a noise of disbelief, her forehead stopping when it meets my chest.

I rest my chin on the top of her head and wrap my arms tighter around her. "I don't want to lose you again, Magdalena," I admit.

"I don't see how we can avoid it." She sounds as miserable as I suddenly feel. I lower us back to the ground and pull her into my lap, then wrap the blanket around us in case she's cold. Mags burrows inside my hoodie and curls into my chest, I can feel her breath through my t-shirt.

I lie my head back against the tree and look up into the waning light of the sky, feeling oddly at peace for the first time in five years. Sitting here in the middle of the forest, not knowing what the future holds. My shoulders relaxing as the stress leaves my body and I enjoy this moment with my girl back in my arms.

And just like that, I'm not worried about being stuck under a tree for the next six hours or so. We'll make it back to the cabin in the morning, I'm sure. I'm also not concerned about the job; or the bi-coastal living situation.

"We're going to make this work, Mags." I place a lingering kiss on the top of her head.

"Promise?" She looks up at me and I lower my lips to hers.

"I promise," I say against her mouth. And I have every intention of keeping that promise. We're adults with choices and if we are open and honest with our communication, we can make anything work.

Mags sighs, but it's a happy sound. I wait for her breathing to even out before closing my own eyes and succumbing to sleep. I may not know everything that will happen after we wake in the morning, but I know that I have this woman back in my life and this time around nothing is going to change that.

THE END

ABOUT THE AUTHOR

Denise Wells has been reading since before she could talk. And to this day, escaping into a book is her go-to activity before anything else.

She likes to write about sassy women and semi-flawed alpha-esque men. Denise's female characters always have strong friendships, potty mouths, and like to drink—a lot.

Denise is loyal to a fault, a bit too sarcastic, blindingly optimistic, and pretty freakin' happy with life overall. As a diehard fan of the band The Replacements, Denise would be a rock star in the band if she couldn't be a writer. She's even kissed the lead singer, Paul Westerberg, ask her about it sometime.

Home is in the Pacific Northwest where she lives with four special needs dogs, one senile cat, and a husband (BW) who has the patience and tolerance of a saint. And, lest she forget, Denise also lives with too many to count characters inside her head, who will eventually have their stories told.

For more about Denise visit her website at: www.DeniseWells.com

facebook.com/denisewellsauthor

twitter.com/denisewells

instagram.com/denisewellsauthor

amazon.com/author/denisewells

bookbub.com/authors/denisewellsauthor

goodreads.com/denisewells

pinterest.com/denisewellsauthor

ON THE LAKE IN THE DESERT

BY ANGIE JONES

Jen and Nick have been treading water in their marriage for years. In a last-ditch effort to salvage the relationship, they plan a camping getaway to scenic Lake Powell hoping the sheer cliffs, deep water, and seclusion will bring them back to each other. Leaving their busy lives and cell phone reception at the marina, they embark on their adventure with the best of intentions. When the wild elements begin to highlight the cracks in their relationship, they finally agree to cut their trip, and their marriage short. Before they can give up on each other their situation turns from volatile to deadly. They have felt alone in their marriage before, but they have never known isolation or desperation like this. With only each other to rely on, Jen and Nick must put aside their differences just to survive.

DAY 1

We had only just arrived, and the implausible Lake Powell in the middle of the sweltering Utah desert felt surreal to me. It was like I'd been dropped on Mars. Adrenaline and perhaps a bit of fear pumped through me as I took a moment and soaked up the view. The slate grey lake was striking against the burnt orange sandstone cliffs. Dark streaks seemed to drip down the slick rock. It reminded me of tears carrying mascara down a face.

This trip was supposed to be a hard reset for our marriage. We were on the brink of giving in when Nick suggested we get away to get some clarity first. In fact, it may have been our therapist that originally suggested a trip away, but Nick had really championed the idea. Away from cellphones, Nick's career in international trade, my volunteer work on every committee under the sun, and all other obligations, we hoped to rekindle some of the sparks between us. We'd already given up a lot for this relationship. One more week and we'd know, with certainty, the right decision for the future.

Maybe we had been too busy and lost sight of each other in the bustle. The truth was, even though I'd already started looking for a decent divorce lawyer, I wasn't certain I was done being married. We hadn't made our marriage a priority in years, but I wasn't ready to give up yet and neither was Nick.

The dreamlike setting did little to distract me from the work of getting the boat onto the water. Launching the boat from the ramp had always formed a knot in my stomach. The anxiety was something I built up on my own. I'd always been high strung, but I especially hated backing the trailer down a launch or even backing the boat off the trailer onto the lake. Boating had never been relaxing for me. There was too much to worry about on a lake.

I tried to stay positive. There wasn't a huge line waiting to drop into the lake, as I'd feared. Some of the negative reviews online indicated that it took hours to launch. There was no line at all, which was a relief as the sun was already causing sweat to collect on my face and my clothing to cling to my body.

This time we launched without a hitch. I'd gone through the mental list; boat straps removed, battery switched on, propeller up, plug in, and blower on. The completed checklist soothed me, but I had no way of knowing what would happen next.

The boat slipped off the trailer and with just enough confidence, I steered it away from the ramp. I tied it off to a clamp on the hot metal floating dock.

"Be right back, Jen!" Nick, my husband, cupped his hands around his mouth and hollered.

He pulled the truck and empty boat trailer out of the water and drove up the long boat ramp, disappearing at the top. I felt a pang of jealousy because he hadn't felt any anxiety at all. Of course, I had enough for both of us.

I sat in the open bow of the twenty-one-foot powerboat and stretched my lo ng, tanned legs across the seats. I applied sunscreen all over my exposed and sweating skin. It wasn't even noon and the sun's glare already forced me to fish one of Nick's hats out from under the seat.

I looked down into the water and saw movement just under the surface. I squinted and identified several large carp investigating and nibbling around the boat. I pinched a dinner roll from a bag and tossed tiny pieces in the lake for the fish. They enjoyed the free meal. Once I ran out of the roll, I spent a few minutes taking in the grandeur of the lake.

The lake was at a lower level, exposing a band of rock that looked like sun-bleached bones. I'd read this band was commonly called the 'bathtub ring' and that seemed like an accurate description.

Perhaps beautiful wasn't the right word to describe the scene. It was remarkable, too wild, and too unearthly to be pretty. The velvety water was unsettling and breathtaking at once as it lapped against the roughness of the sandstone. The dry air was still and hot as I waited for Nick to park the truck and the trailer. I worried he would forget to put the trailer lock on, and the trailer would be stolen while we were merrily camping.

I watched as a lady effortlessly backed a trailer into the water and a man guided the boat onto it. I saw the panic on his face and realized he had forgotten to raise the motor and propeller. He scrambled to fix it, yelling at the woman to stop the truck. Of course, the woman couldn't hear him over the truck. The metal screeched against the concrete boat ramp until he was able to adjust the switch and raise the drive. I grimaced on his behalf, knowing he might have to replace the skeg, the shining fin under the propeller. I could hear him cursing to himself as the truck finally pulled to the side of the ramp. The man raised the propeller, while his wife stood crestfallen, examining the damage. The man joined her and put his arm around her shoulders. He tilted his head back and laughed, I couldn't hear the couple, but I could see them comforting each other.

I felt a pang of jealousy at their easy intimacy. There was a time when a scenario like that would have drawn Nick and me together. But now? Now it would have caused a heated argument, blame analysis, weeks of giving one another the coldshoulder, and the grand finale of pretending it had never happened at all. The couple finally got back in the truck and disappeared at the top of the long ramp. It was quite an end to their vacation.

I couldn't help but wonder how our vacation would end.

I peered over the side of the boat to watch the carp busily scouring below. I dipped my hand in to see if they would bite but they didn't. Even the water felt hot today.

Nick finally reappeared at the top of the ramp. He was happily jogging toward me, a wide grin on his face, despite the oppressive heat. From this distance, I could admire him freely. Nick's tall, athletic frame hardly bounced as he ran. His tan skin and long blonde hair looked too dazzling under the glaring sun. As he got closer, I felt slightly peeved that he wasn't even sweating. I was sweating from just sitting, meanwhile, he was jogging in a desert looking like he was relaxing under an AC unit.

When he stepped onto the boat, he was still cheerful but breathless from the exertion of jogging down the long ramp. I pointed out the carp and he appreciated the view. He switched the blower on, and the fish swam away.

Nick situated himself behind the steering wheel and the boat glided away from the dock. He gunned it after we passed the buoys that marked a wake-less speed. I couldn't help but cringe. He knew he was supposed to let the engine warmup before speeding off like that. I held the nag inside, desperate to get the trip off to a good start and keep up his cheery mood.

As the boat rushed over the water, I felt a sense of hope for us. Besides, all the sweat on my skin started to dry in the wind and it cooled me down considerably as we traveled. I felt like we were flying across the lake and leaving our problems behind us. I looked over at Nick steering the boat, a man at perfect ease with the world around him. Maybe this was exactly what we needed.

He looked up at me and smiled, perhaps thinking the same thing. Were we finally on the same page? Maybe Nick was right, we just needed to get away from the daily grind and we'd be ourselves again.

I allowed some of my nervous tension to dissolve and tried to focus on soaking up the scenery. The roaring boat engine was soothing, and I forced myself to take some yoga breaths, demanding relaxation. I started looking forward to eating dinner. I'd always been a bit of a food snob and I found a lot of the joy came from the process of planning and preparing a meal for Nick to enjoy. Cooking while camping presented some challenges, but I felt up to it.

Despite my efforts, with so much to look forward to, and the outlandish scenery, I still felt uneasy. There was an odd sense of foreboding hanging over me as we sped across the lake. Perhaps it was just a lack of a definite plan.

We would explore by boat until lunch and then find a campground. We didn't have a campsite reservation or any idea where the best spots were. The camping was mostly primitive at Lake Powell, and it was a little too casual for my taste. There were some easily accessible spots, but the sites were crowded together without any barriers between them. Light and sound from other campers wouldn't set the romantic tone that Nick and I were looking for.

The growing heat made us more uncomfortable, and I already felt dehydrated. I knew Nick hadn't put on sunscreen, so I'd casually placed the bottle in his cupholder. I wasn't his mother but the idea of enduring Nick whining about a completely preventable sunburn all week exhausted me. He ignored the sunscreen.

There was no shade when Nick stopped the boat and announced it was lunchtime.

"Let's put the Bimini Top up for shade, the sun is brutal," I suggested.

"Nah, let's just hurry and eat so we can find a good spot and set up camp," Nick countered.

I hated to rush and when I looked at his shoulders, I wondered if he was already sunburnt.

"We're going to want some shade while we eat," I reasoned.

"Fine," he set the cooler down and fished out the unwieldy Bimini frame. Impatient to eat, he thrust two bolts into my hand.

"I can't get it to reach," I complained to him as I struggled with two metal pieces that were supposed to be attached to the side of the boat. The frame would then unfold, and a piece of canvas would provide excellent shade cover. But not until it was appropriately fastened by the bolts.

"Try pushing it forward instead of pulling forward," he suggested as he struggled as well.

"Is it backwards?" I asked.

"Ah, the short ends do go in the back," he agreed. Without any warning, Nick wrenched his end of the Bimini frame around, knocking one of the screws from my hand into the water.

He looked up when he heard the ominous plop. We'd both heard it before, and we both recognized it immediately. He looked at me panic-stricken.

"Hand me the toolbox, it's still under the captain's chair. There's an extra," I said.

Nick didn't move.

"Nick?" I urged, impatient to put something in-between me and the sun.

"Last time I went fishing the guys we lost one while we were putting it up. I used the spare and then we couldn't find either when we put the Bimini away," he confessed. Without apologizing.

"And you didn't replace it? Or say anything to me?" I whipped my blonde ponytail so I could glare at him. I was honestly astonished.

"It's okay, Jen. Calm down, we will just unload the gear at camp and pick up an extra at that marina shop later. You know, they make nicer ones that attach to the side so they can't fall in," Nick informed me.

I huffed, indignant at how blasé he was playing it.

After giving up on the Bimini we ate lunch in silence, under the blazing sun.

I privately hoped Nick did get a sunburn. It would serve him right.

We boated miles and miles, heading away from civilization. I kept prompting him to just choose a campsite because we were getting too far away from the marina. We kept stopping to check out potential campgrounds but there was always something wrong.

Nick scoffed at one of the sites I thought was perfect. "It's not flat, where would we put the tent?" He was right, but I was eager to settle somewhere sooner than later.

The next site was too rocky.

The further we got from the marina the fewer boats we saw. A romantic getaway didn't need overly friendly neighbors or their noisy generators. I'd reasoned that the closer to the marina we camped, the easier the trip would be to get gas or supplies.

"If we can get away from the light pollution, you'll be able to see your stars so much better," Nick said. Stargazing sounded romantic.

So, we kept going down narrow canyons, one after the other, and no two were alike. It was easy to get carried away exploring canyons and racing past the buoys that marked each canyon. There were rocks looming just under the surface in some places, so close I could see marks where propellers had cut into the top of the sandstone. The ugly scars in the rock must have spelled disaster for past boaters. At the very least their propellers would have been ravaged when they hit the rocks. I shuttered to think the worst-case scenario would have been.

"Watch out for those chunks of wood there," I pointed ahead.

Nick slowed down for the floating wood and we noticed several submerged dead trees. We'd never seen anything like it, but the changing lake levels had left small clusters of entire trees.

"One more thing to watch for," Nick slowly navigated through the narrow canyon without incident and our search continued.

Oddly, I found myself worrying less. I wasn't even that concerned over the Bimini Cover anymore. We had hats and sunscreen. We were in the full shade of the towering cliffs occasionally, so we'd just have to choose a shady spot to pitch the tent. We would also need to venture back to civilization to replace ice and dispose of our trash within the next couple of days. All the ice in the cooler would surely melt quickly in this heat and we'd want to restock the groceries as well. I was sure we were getting too far away from the marina. Now it would be a pain to go to the Boat N' Go shop to pick up the bolt. On the other hand, even though the lake wasn't crowded noise tends to carry over the water so I could hardly blame Nick for wanting to ensure that we had our privacy.

The ride was incredibly scenic, and we wouldn't mind spending hours making it more than once.

We found a very secluded long canyon; the first branch we took led to a dead-end but about halfway up the forty-foot cliff, there was a small cave that was filled with rocks, trees, driftwood, and who knows what kinds of critters. Above the small cave, the sheer cliff was ominously straight and smooth, without a single imperfection.

The second, longer arm in the canyon had high vertical walls that would have made beach camping impossible except one small patch of sand tucked in the very back. There were a few rocky bits, but it was mostly flat. We would be able to have a fire, pitch our tent, and our small, screened shade tent as well. Despite the water at the back of the canyon looking a little stagnant with some debris, the spot looked ideal.

We tied the boat off and waded to shore carrying loads of gear and coolers, then we began setting up our campsite.

In the depths of the canyon walls, we were finally in full shade. As the light changed, I barely recognized the canyon. The top of the wall was still in the sun and looked almost blood red, but the base of the same cliff was pale. The evening cooled off alarmingly fast, so I got our heavier jackets out.

We worked quietly and as a team to pitch the tent and unrolled the sleeping bags. There wasn't a lot of space on the small sandy beach, but there were so many bugs in the canyon that we were forced to set up the little screened-in camp kitchen.

Nick started a fire and I began preparing dinner.

I cubed cheddar cheese and potatoes, butterflied chicken breasts, sliced mushrooms, and chopped a small yellow onion.

"Do you need help, Jen?" Nick settled into the camping chair across from me.

"No, thank you though. How is the fire? Do we have coals yet?" I asked.

"Not yet, but we will manage," Nick assured me.

I placed a small pile of baby carrots on two sheets of aluminum foil. Next, I topped them with generous chunks of cold butter and sprinkled some brown sugar and curry on top. I stuffed the chicken breasts with cheese, onions, and mushrooms. I then added the potatoes, with some chopped rosemary. For good measure, I split a can of green beans between them. I salt and peppered the whole meal, especially the potatoes. Nothing tastes as good as salty potatoes while camping.

I folded the aluminum foil around each dinner into a pouch and added a second layer of foil.

We moved the camping chairs from the impromptu kitchen and Nick placed the tinfoil dinners in the fire.

I took out my phone to set a makeshift kitchen timer. Nick made a sucking noise against his teeth, and he raised his eyebrows pointedly.

"It's just for a timer," I explained. We had agreed to no phones, but of course, he couldn't use words like an adult.

"Oh," he relented.

"I don't have a watch," I reasoned. But my fingers were itching to open my e-Reader app or any mindless game. Watching the fire was peaceful but we weren't connecting or engaging with each other. At home, we would turn on the tv and waste time on our phones to fill this type of uneasy silence. I wondered if we really had said everything we needed to say to each other.

We sat in dead quiet for ten full minutes until my phone timer startled both of us. Nick flipped the meals over with long grilling tongs and I reset the timer.

I was just about to open a puzzle game when he moved his chair closer to mine and asked out of nowhere, "Would you like one?"

"One what?" I questioned as I slipped my phone into my jacket pocket.

"A watch, would you like a watch? I mean, would you wear one if you had one?" Nick clarified, and I couldn't help but notice that he sounded nervous.

I smiled, "Maybe. I had a good one in high school. The face was shattered at a high school baseball game. I wasn't paying attention and a foul ball ticked it."

"You're lucky you didn't get hit in the head. I suppose the baseball pants distracted you?" Nick laughed.

I giggled, "I was not there for the riveting athletic ability if you must know. Wearing a nice watch just seems a little risky, you know? I wasn't completely lucky that day though. The watch really was ruined, and not to brag but it was a Swatch. They were a really big deal back then, remember?" I reflected.

"I remember. I didn't have one, but most kids did," he said.

"I don't think I would wear something expensive on my wrist now though. Maybe something understated and inexpensive," I answered his original question. "You stopped wearing your watch," I had noticed months ago but I hadn't bothered asking him about it. We had skipped a lot of simple conversations lately.

"Yeah it turns out my watch was only water-resistant and not waterproof. It got so foggy I couldn't even read it anymore."

I forced a smile, knowing he'd been spending a lot of time swimming laps the Rec Center near our house.

At first, I had wondered if he was preparing for an adulterous affair. You always hear about men getting in shape to cheat, right? But I didn't think he had the time or energy to chase women. On the other hand, who can ever be completely certain? Maybe he wasn't even swimming at all. Maybe he was just meeting some woman. My imagination had run wild at the time.

I smiled in earnest now, remembering the time I'd finally confronted him, asking point-blank about who he was seeing.

"I'm not seeing anyone. I barely have time to see you. My dad's first heart attack happened when he was my age, remember?" he had said. Of course, I remembered.

We'd just started our sophomore year of college and Nick had to fly home because his dad's situation was quite serious. We hadn't been an official couple, but I booked his flight and packed a bag for him with everything I could think of to make a hard trip more comfortable. He always said that made him realize I was the one for him.

"We should get smartwatches that track our lives and remind us to drink water," Nick's voice brought me back to the present.

"Hmm?" I asked.

"We should get smart-watches. They're the new Swatch. It would be nice to not rely on phones so much. You know they don't even teach kids how to read face clocks anymore?" Nick asked.

"You're joking," I said.

"No, I'm serious. Next time you see a kid, ask them if they can tell analog time, they really can't," Nick said somberly.

"I mean, does that matter? Is that a skill they need? Everything is digital now," I sighed.

"Schools don't teach cursive either," he added.

"Yikes," I was surprised how easily we were chatting now. "I think kids do need cursive. How will they write love letters or sign checks?" I asked.

"Or read America's founding documents. Letters? You mean text messages, right?" Nick snorted.

"Yeah, I think they need to teach kids how to write in cursive," I agreed.

"My wrist still hurts from those drills in third grade," he mused.

"Between cursive worksheets and times table drills it's a wonder we don't have carpal tunnel," I said.

We both stretched our hands and shook them out, recalling the agony that was grade school and #2 Ticonderoga pencils.

The timer for dinner went off again. The packets sizzled as Nick scooped them from the coals. We unwrapped the foil and savory steam hissed as it escaped.

The dinner was lovely. We didn't talk too much as we ate, but we enjoyed our time by the campfire in the comfortable silence.

Once the fire was extinguished, the stars were incredible. I don't know what Nick was thinking about, but I was questioning whether the trip was working to repair our previous missteps. Everything seemed to be going well. Maybe it was a little overly ambitious to think we could undo damage and distance that took years to create in a single week. But for tonight, I saw a lot of potential. If Nick was really committed to putting the time and work in, I was in as well.

We picked up dinner and extinguished the fire.

Afterwards, we'd tucked into our sleeping bags early without a goodnight kiss, and I started second-guessing everything all over again.

DAY 2

The following morning, I woke up alone and disoriented in the stuffy little tent. Sleeping on a foam mattress left me feeling a bit stiff. The optimism from the day before was gone, but I've never been a morning person. I pulled my hair into a ponytail and tucked it into a hat. I hadn't bothered running a brush through it before I stumbled out of the tent. The wildness of Lake Powell felt surreal and jarring. The rock looked vibrant in the morning light, and I was fascinated all over again. We had full sun in the mornings, I realized.

Nick, ever the early bird, had already built a fire and was warming up the breakfast burritos I'd made before we'd left home. The smoke from the campfire must have woken me because my body really feel ready to be awake.

Nick very charmingly —or perhaps it was just a practical matter of self-preservation— handed me a cup of instant coffee with a splash of milk. His fingers grazed across mine and for the first time in a long while I felt butterflies in the pit of my stomach. We locked eyes and he smiled down at me.

I didn't always like my husband, but he was classically super-hot. He was also a classic workaholic who had put me on the back burner on a regular basis. His work was all-consuming. After long hours at his office, he'd come home exhausted and spend most of his time on the phone saving deals or talking strategy with his partners. The money was excellent, but the hours were brutal.

Somewhere throughout the years, I'd stopped waiting at home for him. I'd made friends with some of the neighborhood stay-at-home moms. We got together two or three times a week. We'd do yoga by the pool, which left my skin tan and my body firm. Some evenings we'd get together, everyone would bring a different appetizer, and we'd drink too much wine and not eat enough food. If this made me less available to Nick, he didn't say a word about it.

The little group of women from our neighborhood had helped me survive suburban life, but Nick couldn't be bothered to learn their names. On the other hand, he had generously thought to make me some coffee when I surely would have perished without it.

It was entirely too hot to sit by the fire, so I sat in the screen tent sipping my coffee, away from the smoke and the bugs. Instant coffee is another food that tastes so much better while camping.

The burritos were left on the fire too long and were a bit charred around the edges. We still got enough to eat and started preparing for a long day trip to Rainbow Bridge.

We took a break from boating and ate lunch in a small cave under a towering cliff. I served croissants stuffed with hand-carved turkey and butter leaf lettuce. To make them pop, I slathered them with cream cheese and cranberry sauce. The result was a savory, sweet and tangy masterpiece; if I did say so myself. The sandwiches paired nicely with plain potato chips and carrot sticks.

I wanted a glass of red wine but had to settle for water since I was constantly feeling dehydrated in the heat. Once lunch was over, we continued boating. After a short but hot hike, we reached the beautiful natural bridge.

"The sign said it's almost 300 feet high, and it's sacred to Native Americans," Nick said.

"It does feel kind of magical, doesn't it?" I asked.

"Yeah, it does," Nick smiled. He rested his arm against my shoulder despite the heat.

The boat ride back to camp felt longer than the trip to Rainbow Bridge. We barely talked over the motor, but sometimes we held hands.

We got back so late there wasn't time to make a big, fussy dinner before dark. We cracked open cans of ice-cold white wine, laughing at how surprisingly good it tasted.

"The coals aren't ready yet," I sighed.

"We are too hungry to wait for decent coals," Nick insisted, and I agreed for once.

Our hot dogs were cold in the middle and burnt on the outside.

"It's harder to keep track of wine by the can, honestly. When you empty a bottle of wine it's an excellent stopping point," Nick mused

"More of a yield point, but yes; I see what you mean," I said as he handed me a new can.

"We are on vacation, after all," he smiled as I popped the top and took an appreciative sip.

If we finished two bottles at home, we knew there might be headaches the following day. But the cans seemed to flow freely, and we took turns walking to the cooler for more.

By the time we were finished with the hotdogs the fire was huge, and blazing coals were ready to toast the marshmallows for s'mores and of course, we had even more wine. We sat by the fire talking about the rock formations we'd seen on the trip and eating leftover chocolate. We finally had the conversations we'd been putting off.

"I think we need to make an effort to spend more time together. And not just going to movies or whatever. Like, actively sharing quality experiences like the hike today," Nick said. I was taken aback but appreciated that he'd been putting some thought into coming up with a plan.

Nick walked over to the cooler to grab more wine but returned instead with a chilled bottle of cinnamon-infused whiskey.

"We had all the wines," he shrugged, sitting down heavily. This surprised me as it seemed like there had been quite a lot of cans when I'd loaded them onto the cooler.

"Do you remember that business trip?" he asked.

"And which one do you mean?"

"I mean the one to Time Square where you drank all those Cosmos at the hotel happy hour and puked in the bathtub," Nick reminded me.

"Yes. Vaguely, I do remember. That bartender was very polite, wasn't he?" I ribbed him a bit.

"Ha, I remember your bill being non-existent because he was quite taken with you," Nick reminisced.

"Nah, he just felt bad that you were so late because your meeting ran over. You should have been pleased you didn't have to pay for all of them. Manhattan cocktail prices are ludicrous" I pointed out.

"I'm sorry," he apologized.

I wasn't sure how far back the apology was supposed to stretch but I let out a little laugh to bring some levity back to the night.

"You were really nice about cleaning me up and keeping an eye on me that night, even though I was ridiculous," I reminded him.

We drank the whiskey right from the bottle. The cold liquid tasted hot because of the spicy cinnamon flavor. When Nick leaned over in his camping chair and kissed me, I could taste the warmth on his mouth. At first, I was nearly too surprised to kiss him back, but I quickly warmed to the idea as we made out like teenagers.

I felt my stomach flutter, after all these years and all our problems, Nick could still make me feel so good. I told myself to remember this feeling in the morning, Nick wasn't that bad. It was easy to lose track of time, watching the fire burn as we passed the bottle back and forth between us late into the night.

DAY 3

Our promising trip turned on a dime that night. We were exhausted from our adventure and the wine and whiskey only added to the lethargy. Once we were in our sleeping bags, I heard an odd noise right outside the tent. It sounded like a distressed cow to me, but I knew it was impossible. It wasn't coming from the cliffs above us, it was on our level. At first, Nick couldn't hear them. And then when he did hear, he didn't care what it was. I crawled to the tent opening and thrust my feet back into my shoes. I realized I'd had too much to drink as I stumbled around camp, trying to find the origin of the annoying noise. I finally found two bullfrogs sitting in a puddled bowl-shaped depression in the rock.

There was nothing to be done about the noise, but with the mystery solved, I was able to go back to sleep.

I was rudely awakened by Nick tossing everything in the tent around.

"What?" I cried out.

"There's a mouse in here," Nick said gruffly.

"What!" I screeched.

"You left the zipper open while you went out."

I couldn't overlook the note of condemnation in his tone.

"Yeah, I guess I did," I admitted.

Nick upended everything in the tent. I begrudgingly slipped out of my sleeping bag and started moving things outside.

Finally, the entire tent was empty. I shook the foam mattresses and sleeping bags vigorously before returning them to the tent. I started checking bags before putting them back inside. I had to hold a flashlight with one hand, so it was slow work. It was nearly dawn but there wasn't enough light without the flashlight. When I checked Nick's backpack, I found a nibbled Ziploc bag of protein powder, granola bars, and even a few granola bar wrappers.

"It's stupid to keep food inside the tent," I muttered, tossing the bag to him.

"It's stupid to leave the tent zipper open," he retorted.

"Fine," I conceded. I just wanted to go to sleep. My stomach gurgled ominously, and I deeply regretted the wine, whiskey, and the junk food dinner we'd had that night. Who among us can eat hot dogs and whiskey without impunity after thirty? I was eager to try and fall back asleep.

"Do you think the mouse is gone?" Nick put the last bag back inside the tent.

"Yeah, I heard him scurrying around the tent, but I never actually saw him," I said.

"I heard him before I saw him. I thought you were trying to find something. But you were snoring and then I caught sight of him and knew he couldn't stay. They can destroy things overnight. He was a little brown thing, really fast though," Nick said. I could tell he was still a little drunk and I smiled as we crawled back to our sleeping bags. The wind had picked up and it howled around the canyon, making for a very restless sleep.

DAY 4

I woke up disgruntled and well before Nick. That was atypical as I've always loved to sleep late, and he is usually unable to sleep past seven. As quietly as possible, I exited the tent and made my own coffee. I was hungover. My mouth was so dry, my stomach was still roiling, and the worst part was a throbbing headache. After Nick crawled out of the tent, I offered him a coffee. He shook his head. He was obviously hungover, but still good-looking in a tousled sort of way. He lumbered over to the camping chairs near our makeshift fire pit.

I used the leftover croissants to make egg sandwiches. I fried bacon and scrambled eggs on the camp stove. The croissants were a little dry, but they'd do. I felt like a zombie with a roiling tummy as I shuffled over to the fire pit.

I proudly carried Nick's plate to him only to watch him pouring milk over cold cereal.

"Oh, I've made breakfast. Egg sandwich?" I offered.

"I can't stomach anything but this right now, Jen," he turned away from the paper plate holding the sandwich.

I huffed a breath through my nose and sat down hard in my camping chair.

"I wish you would have said," I grumbled before taking a bite of my delicious sandwich.

"You didn't ask," he said around a mouthful of cereal.

"A good meal is the best way to treat a hangover," I urged.

"I am not hungover, I just don't feel good," Nick grimaced.

"Okay, okay," I laughed. "But I am never, ever drinking again."

I powered up my eReader and relaxed under the sun, hoping my punishing headache would soon vanish.

Less than two hours later, Nick asked what was for lunch. I was not hungry at all.

"You can make yourself a sandwich," I suggested, carefully not gritting my teeth.

"They always taste better when you make them," Nick grinned, trying to coax me into caving into making a second sandwich for him.

"I did make you one! You just didn't want it. And now that I'm relaxing you want me to pop up and make you one. No thank you. I am on vacation," I said without getting up.

"Fine," Nick laboriously stood and trudged over to the kitchen tent.

"What sandwich meat do we have?" he asked, without even looking in a cooler.

"There's a little turkey left," I informed him and turned my focus back to my book.

"What cooler are they in?" he hollered.

"Blue," I said, beginning to feel exasperated.

"Do we have lettuce?" he asked.

"Yes, it's in the blue cooler, too," I said snappily.

"Have you seen the mayonnaise?" he asked.

"There are two coolers and one box with food in it. If you can't find what you need, you're not looking. I'm reading, Nick. Cut it out," I seethed.

"It would be easier if you just made it," Nick suggested.

"It would be easier for you if I just made it. I'd like to relax and read," I explained, still heated.

"It's not a big deal. Our eating schedules are just a bit off, that's all," he said.

"They're off because you wouldn't eat a decent breakfast," I said.

"Look I'm sorry, you're just mad I didn't want egg sandwiches," Nick laughed.

"Well, why didn't you tell me, so I didn't make one for you?" I demanded.

"I didn't even know you were going to! I don't think I could have handled a heavy breakfast after we got so carried away with that wine last night," he explained.

"I think it was the whiskey," I reasoned.

"What?" Nick's face and tone indicated he had no memory of the fiery whiskey.

"Yeah, you kept peer pressuring me into binge drinking," I joked. But it landed poorly because we'd been arguing.

"Oh, so your hangover is also my fault. Got it," he chided.

"It was meant to be a joke. I didn't really mean it like that," I said.

"Right," he clipped.

"Okay," I snapped back.

"It was those stupid bullfrogs and that stupid mouse. I didn't get enough rest. I really wish you'd remembered to close up the tent when you went out last night," he said.

My mouth dropped.

"And I wish you wouldn't have left the food in our tent to attract rodents," I volleyed after a beat.

"Is anything ever your fault, Jen?" he spat my name.

"This is what our doctor tried to warn us about," I reminded him.

"She's not a doctor," he sputtered. "She has a master's degree in psychology. That's definitely not a doctor," Nick snorted derisively.

I didn't count to ten as the Not a Doctor Just a Therapist had advised before I continued with, "Thank you, that's such a helpful and super-critical distinction. It completely changes the entire point I was conveying. This is exactly what our *therapist* told you about communication, you're shit at it. Why are you acting like this? Jesus Christ," I hissed.

He narrowed his eyes at that, just as I knew he would. He kept telling everyone he was raised religious but was now more spiritual than religious. As if he owed anyone an explanation. And he wasn't even spiritual at all. He just liked saying it.

I didn't care either way about his spiritual inclinations at that point, but that little dig, not just the lord's name in vain but also the unladylike vulgarity was always a direct hit with Nick. It was the only thing I knew that would really set him off. As satisfying as it felt to say it, I was immediately sorry I had.

He took a deep breath and I waited for him to unload a nice long lecture. He didn't though. He stood up and marched off to the boat. I expected him to relax down there, away from me, and I was shocked when I heard the boat engine roar to life. He backed the boat out and navigated it neatly out of the canyon without even looking back.

At least I could read in peace and quiet, I lamented.

I heard the boat return before I saw it. The evening had turned chilly and I'd been worried about Nick all day. My worry vanished and left anger in its place. Nick tied it off and jumped from the bow, sunburnt but smugly handsome.

"Where have you been?" I snapped.

"I went for a nice long boat ride. And I got hungry, so I ate at the restaurant. The hostess said a big storm is coming through."

"You went all the way to the marina?" I gasped.

"Yes," he nodded without further explanation.

"Did you at least get the replacement bolt for the Bimini?"

"Oh, no," he said, smacking his forehead. One look at his burnt nose, cheeks, and shoulders told me as much. "I completely forgot about that." He admitted, at least doing me the courtesy of looking contrite.

"Well, I didn't like being left alone all day." I stared into the fire I'd built to keep warm in the wind and cold.

"I know," he said.

"I don't like being alone most days at home, and I really think it was awful of you to drag me to the middle of nowhere and then leave me stranded all day in a strange place with no way out. What if something had happened to either one of us?" I demanded.

"Nothing happened," he countered

"It could have, and you don't just abandon someone like that." I said.

"I'm sorry you felt that way, Jen." His tone clearly expressed that he wasn't actually sorry for anything.

"It isn't just a feeling, it's a fact. I hate your stupid non-apologies, Nick. I was trapped here all alone. Anything could have happened. This trip was supposed to help us work things out you cut and run. What a big surprise," I was losing my temper and didn't try to reign it in. I was happily boiling over.

"I just needed to cool off. I didn't want to say anything I'd regret later," he looked at me pointedly. Bold of him to assume I regretted a single thing I'd said.

"Nick, the only time I can be really honest is when you've exhausted my will to be polite anymore. And then the truth just tumbles out," I confessed.

"You are literally the worst at apologies," he said.

"That wasn't an apology because I'm not apologizing. Why would I be the one to apologize?" I demanded.

He didn't respond, and he seemed to check out of the argument. This was one of his irritating tactics. Going into screensaver mode mid-discussion was one of his old plays and it's one I was through with. I was tired of caring more than he did, trying harder than he ever had.

"I wish we could just leave. I'm done," I finally said.

"Done with the vacation or done with us?" he asked.

"Both," I said quietly. I realized how sincerely done I was at just that moment. I wouldn't have been brave enough to say it then, but he'd obviously been thinking it over while he was out on the lake.

"Same," Nick agreed simply.

I sighed with relief, but my eyes were stinging with tears. I didn't dare blink, or they'd roll down my cheeks. I held my breath to keep a sob in. He was done arguing and he was ready to move on as well. That would make it easier going forward. But for now, it left us both stuck in the middle of nowhere for the night with this nearly solved problem weighing on each of us.

We both stared into the fire in complete silence. The wind felt cold on my back even though my face felt too warm. I suddenly resented him for giving in and not fighting a little harder himself. Years of putting me on the back burner and the only change he'd made for me was a stupid camping trip? This was the only sacrifice he was willing to make after all I'd given up for our marriage.

I didn't point any of this out because I knew he'd only point out how hard he'd worked, how many hours he'd spent slaving away. He didn't value my time in the same way he valued his. He didn't weigh the fact that I'd given up a lot to move every time he said we needed to move, or that his long hours made it impossible to chase my own ambitions. Resentment simmered under my skin.

The fire twisted and leaned with the wind, which was really stirring now, even in the protected canyon. It whipped around us, and thunder cracked in the darkening sky.

I didn't look up from the mesmerizing fire when I asked, "Can't we just leave now? It's not quite dark. Could we break down camp and leave right now?"

"It's way too choppy out there, really. When I was boating back there were whitecaps. That wind would make it tricky to get the boat back on the trailer as well. By the time I left the restaurant there every spot in the dock was full and other boats were circling the breakwater. The whole ramp was lined with trucks and empty trailers waiting to pick up and leave. I didn't see many boats on my way back at all. I think the boaters are leaving because they were worried about the weather. The hostess in the restaurant said it could get rough tonight. Plus, even if we started packing up now, it would be dark by the time we left. Wouldn't want to risk hitting anything under the water."

I rolled my eyes at this. Now he was going to be conservative. Even when it meant staying the night on this godforsaken patch of sand in the middle of a lake.

"Just great," I relented. I couldn't stand him for another minute and there was literally nothing I could do to get away from him.

I rose, placing a few things in the tent in case it started to rain. I rage-cleaned up dinner and started packing gear so we could leave first thing in the morning. I felt resentment simmering as he lounged in his camping chair. The wind seemed to be getting riled up right along with me and sand stuck to my lip balm. I could feel the grit inside my mouth and nose. I hated this place with every fiber of my being. I'd come with so much hope for us and it was absolutely gone now. Despite my movement from slamming the camping gear into the boat, I was getting cold, so I returned to the fire.

"Jen. Your hair," he gasped.

"What about it," I growled.

"It's all standing up," he said.

I reached to pat it down, but there was nothing to be done for it as it popped back up. It was like there was a static charge.

Before either of us could realize what was going on, lightning flashed and then thunder crashed immediately. It was so close it hurt my ears and shook my chest. Nick had ducked and covered. He straightened himself and smiled sheepishly, embarrassed at his reaction.

"There's nowhere to go," he muttered grimly, "we're just out in the open."

He was right. I wasn't sure if the canyon walls would protect us or put us at more risk. We were stuck in the back of a canyon, for better or worse. I had to imagine the wind and chances of getting struck by lightning were worse out in the open. I looked longingly at the tent, but I wondered if the tent poles would attract lightning or act as a ground. The shade tent was taller than our sleeping tent, perhaps it would strike there instead.

When the rain started to pour, we scuttled over the uneven ground to the tent.

We sat just inside the sleeping tent, watching the fire extinguish under the sudden downpour.

"Ooh, look!" a gorgeous waterfall had appeared, cascading gracefully down one side of a cliff behind the boat.

"There's another," he pointed to the other side.

It was beautiful and unexpected. Both waterfalls were causing the water in the canyon to churn into a rust color. It was picturesque enough to be magical, but I looked into my husband's eyes and they were full of fear.

The water wasn't trickling but pouring with great force and crashing into the lake. The little beach in front of our campsite was slowly vanishing.

The roaring of the water grew impossibly loud as more water and debris fell from above, crashing from the cliff and roiling in the water before us. A curtain of water came rushing down across from the boat, slamming the boat into the opposite canyon wall. Rocks started being pulled down with the water and I watched two large logs crash into the churning lake.

"Nick," I pointed at the cliffs even though he was staring at them. He already knew the volume of water doubled on both sides and it reached the boat, filling the open bow with water. The force of the water pushed it from one side of the canyon to the next, rocking and lobbing like it was rudderless on the sea in a storm. We sat frozen as the line that tethered the boat to shore snapped and the boat started to spin.

My husband sprung out of the tent and raced toward the boat, but it was too late. It had twisted in the water and capsized in an instant. There was nothing we could do about it. The debris, rocks, and roiling water made it impossible to dare to try anything. He stood on the shore, powerless.

We stared into the water until the waterfalls died down, gone as quickly as they'd appeared.

"I guess you can stop bitching about the Bimini Cover now," he smiled wryly.

We both laughed dryly, and he pulled me to him. I knew we were both terrified, but we needed a moment of lightness. Of course, he would crack a joke just to make me feel better. I could see the panic in his face, but I knew he wanted me to feel better.

DAY 5

We woke up folded into each other, zipped in one sleeping bag that was still damp from the rain. I was once again surprised to feel the tent filling with the dreaded morning heat and an uncomfortable stuffiness. The storm was over.

I tried to fall back asleep, terrified to go assess the damage in the light of day, but my stirring had awakened Nick and he jerked upright inside his sleeping bag, dragging me with him.

"Sorry," he mumbled. "Ready to go take a look?" he asked.

I could never be prepared, but I nodded solemnly.

We both walked to the shore. There weren't any signs of the boat. There was some floating garbage in the water but that had always been the case for the end of this canyon. Last night had been so momentous, how could there be no difference beside some missing sand?

I remembered the shocking amount of debris that fell after the boat capsized. I knew retrieving it would be impossible without real machinery and a lot of help we didn't have access to. Our beloved boat was gone. Real fear nearly closed my throat as I began to fully realize how much danger we were still in.

Our phones had been on the boat and would have been worthless without service anyway. We had limited supplies and no way to get more. We were locked in place, standing on the shore. Nick reached for my hand and I let out a sobbing breath I didn't realize I'd been holding. I began to cry in earnest and Nick tucked me into his chest and arms.

I waited for some words of comfort from him, but none came. That scared me more than anything. Nick always downplayed everything we'd ever faced, told me to not worry so much, and he'd forced things to work out for us. But his silence warned me he wasn't hopeful. He didn't know how we'd get out of this mess and his natural optimism was at the bottom of the lake in the middle of a desert with our boat. Our only means of transportation was destroyed.

"Let's take stock of what's left," Nick sighed.

While some food had been stored on the boat, most of it was still safe in the kitchen tent. The box of dry goods had collected water and was mostly spoiled. The flimsy shade tent had collapsed on itself and one bar was bent.

"The instant coffee tipped over in the collapse and some most of it spilled into the sand," I told him.

"Both coolers are still closed and intact," he added.

The dwindling ice coupled with hot days spelled disaster for perishable items, but neither of us needed to say it.

The firewood was all rain drenched and I kicked myself for not covering it. How long would it take to dry?

"I suppose we should feel lucky we didn't get washed away. If water had come from behind us and gone through the campsite we would have died. We're lucky it's higher right there so the water was forced to go out and in front of us," I sighed. It would be hard to hang on to that positive perspective.

Nick spread the firewood stack out flat to help it dry. I was skeptical that would speed up the process because the sand was still so wet from the rain. It did serve to highlight that there wasn't very much firewood left. I immediately thought of the second branch of the canyon with the little cave up on the side of the cliff. It had wood.

"We haven't seen a single boat in this canyon. A lot of boaters left before the storm, so the chance of a rescue is slim as fuck," I pointed out.

"No need to curse," Nick said in a quiet voice.

I rolled my eyes.

"Yes, let us watch our language. It will be the death of us. There are like a hundred canyons here. I don't like our odds, is all I'm saying," I said.

"We can't even do a signal fire. We barely have any wood," Nick said.

"What about that cave with the wood?" I suggested.

"It's pretty high up and quite a swim. Keeping it dry on the way back would be an issue. But it might be our only option if we are here too long. What if I climb this wall?" he asked, pointing to the wall the first waterfall had come from.

It was at least forty feet tall.

"There's no way. It's not a climbing gym, Nick," I said.

"I see a lot of holds," he assured me.

"Nick, we lost the map. Even if we could climb up safely, we don't know what's up there. If you get to the top, we're still on the wrong side of the bay. You can't get to Bullfrog and you can't walk to Arizona. Especially without water," I reasoned aloud.

"What if I saw another boat from up there?" he asked.

"How would you get to them?" I countered.

"I would yell, and they could radio for help or go get help," he reasoned.

"Last time you were out you said there was a huge line to get out and no one was dropping in," I reminded him.

"I'm going to try it," he said.

"What if you fall? You could get hurt or die," I felt fear creeping up again.

"That's a real concern. But I would fall in the water, Jen," he said.

"Into the water and maybe the rocks," I barely recognized my voice because it was so thick with panic.

"Yeah, do you have a better plan?" he demanded.

"Maybe we focus on surviving and not taking any new risks. I can't imagine what would happen if you really got hurt, Nick. There's no way to get help. Don't do it," I pleaded.

"We don't have very much food and water," he said.

"I mean, plan a route and then we'll talk. I'm worried about the weather, too. What if it turns again?" I asked, hoping to change the subject away from his climbing scheme.

"We don't have anything else to lose, we can weather another storm." He replied.

I thought of the tent and our coolers. Our little stretch of sand. That's how much was between us and death. We had simply lost control.

"What else are you worried about?" he asked.

"I don't know. A lot of things. This place is dangerous, Nick," I said.

"It's a national park, there can't be that much danger, or they'd close it up," Nick tried to sound convincing, but it rang false given what we'd already lived through.

"People die in national parks all the time. They get robbed. They get raped. They drown. There are snakes and heat stroke to worry about. This place is in the middle of nowhere. This lake is well over a hundred miles long and this canyon isn't close to any of the marinas. No one will hear us, Nick. No one can help us. The boat is gone. Bad things happen all the time here. They happen to all sorts of people. We obviously aren't immune. I don't know why you think the rules of probability don't apply to you when your boat just got wrecked by mother nature. You think national parks are safe because you pay a fee at the gate? This is one of the deadliest parks of them all, Nick. This is a wild place, and no one is looking for us yet. You've brought us here to die and you acted like it would be a grand adventure that would solve our marital problems." I spat, really angry then.

"So, the storm and flash flood are all my fault? And I put a gun to your head to come here, didn't I?" he met my energy.

"I didn't feel like I had a choice," I explained.

"You did, Jen. You have always had a choice. Stop with the martyr act. I am not saying nothing bad ever happens to us. It already has, but we always land on our feet," he reminded me.

"We always land on our feet when you take risks because I have always been there to mitigate your fucking risks. Do you know how much pressure it is to always be on my guard, always trying to prepare for anything, for every eventuality? I'm almost always anxious. The stress has taken years off my life, Nick," I said.

"Jen, what good has all your preparing done for us? All your emergency food storage, your emergency savings, your emergency preparedness? We still ended up here," he said.

"And who's fault is that?" I accused.

"Mine?" he raised his eyebrows in surprise.

"Yes, I never would have camped here, trapped like a rat in a canyon. If our boat hadn't been tied back here it wouldn't be at the bottom of the lake. If we were in the bay, we could signal for help or we could just fucking walk to the truck, Nick. But no, you took us to the middle of nowhere," I said.

"I don't control the weather. You're blaming all this on me?" Nick was infuriatingly incredulous.

"Of course, I blame you. I wouldn't be stuck here if it weren't for you; you reckless, arrogant asshole," I screamed.

"No wonder you treat me so bad. You've resented me this whole time," Nick said.

"I treat you bad? Ugh, I do not resent you for being reckless, I resent you for dragging me into your messes. The messes aren't just your problem because I end up cleaning them up," I'd thought this hundreds of times but never expressed it to Nick.

"Well, I am sorry for being such a burden," Nick said, exasperated and sarcastic.

"Thank you so much for apologizing. You will pardon me for not forgiving you straight away. Maybe I will be able to let it go on my deathbed. What do you think, can you wait three days?" I yelled.

"That's a little dramatic. We might find a way out. And if you think I'm such a risk-taker, why do you always come with me? Don't you share some of the blame? We've made every single choice together," Nick reminded me.

"You just talk louder than I do. You talk right over me. You don't listen to my warnings," I shrugged, finally quieting down.

"What are the odds...we couldn't have seen this coming," Nick reasoned.

"You can't ever see anything coming, but I said we should stay closer to the marina, on the bay, and you just pretended like you couldn't hear me," I said.

"I'm sorry you feel that way," Nick countered, but he didn't sound sorry at all.

"How else could I feel. You are so shitty at apologizing. You are sorry for how I feel but you aren't saying sorry for getting us both killed. How about you take some responsibility for this instead of just acting like it's not a big deal? We might die and you still will not apologize. I don't know why I stayed with you. If I would have left you before-" I said.

"—Before what? Before our last hoorah?" Nick cut me off. His voice was harsh with anger.

"You know I didn't think of it like that. I thought of it as a final try," I reasoned, defensive again since Nick was getting heated.

"A final test for me to fail so you could blame a divorce on me too. Why not, everything else is my fault?" he seethed.

"Ugh, I'm tired. Can we talk about blame later?" I was too exhausted to continue.

"You said this is a deadly park, how do people die here?" Nick asked.

"Death, that might be easier to discuss," I laughed. "Drowning is a big one. And boating accidents. Electrocution if you swim near the docks, but that doesn't seem like it will be a problem for us. There are bees and rattlesnakes. It is lucky neither of us are allergic to bees, Nick. Cliff jumping accidents are a big one. I read that if you jump from too high your body keeps going down in the water and your organs separate because they want to go up. Sometimes jumpers get spinal compressions or concussions. Sometimes they never find the bodies, Nick. Visibility is awful and it's a dangerous place, even for professional rescue divers. Pft, just driving into the park on those narrow roads that are easily washed out can be deadly. Then there's heatstroke, of course. I don't even know where the nearest hospital is, let alone how people would contact and get help. It's not an easy vacation. It's not really a vacation at all, more like perilous journey," I recited.

"Why would anyone even come here?" he laughed.

"It is beautiful even though it's so dangerous," I admitted.

"We aren't built to always be safe, Jen. You can't just stay inside," he said.

"No, but you can manage risks and avoid them if it's not worth it. I don't know if this is worth it," I reasoned.

"This was worth it to me, I wanted us to try," Nick said, completely in earnest.

"Next time let's try Cabo like everyone else," I suggested.

"You saying there's going to be a next time?" he asked.

"If I don't kill you and this place doesn't kill us then we'll see. Do you want a next time?" I asked.

"Yes," he said without thinking.

"Why did you give up so quickly when I said I was done. Before the storm?" I wondered aloud.

"I would keep trying through anything, but if you don't love me, if you don't want me, then I need to let you move on. When I said I was done I didn't say it because that's how I felt. I said it to make what you were feeling easier for you. I was trying to let you see that I'm not being selfish and that I respect your wishes. But you said you didn't want to talk about us. Let's talk exit strategies." He said.

"Oh. Okay, we can circle back to us later. As far as getting out of here goes, we can try to swim the canyon and out into the main channel. Maybe we can flag someone down. If that doesn't work, you want to climb. If that doesn't work, we can try to see if we can't dive down to the boat. If that fails, we wait for rescue," I said. I left out the fourth option which was giving up. My mind was still whirling from his confession, but an escape plan was easier to process.

In preparation for our swim, we ate cheese and sliced turkey from the cooler for breakfast, knowing they would spoil first. The food was still cool but not cold.

We sat by the empty fire pit, allowing our food to digest, and dreading the impending swim.

"Ready?" Nick asked.

"Yeah, let's take your CamelBak just in case," I said. I hoped we didn't need to drink lake water to survive but since we were headed to cleaner water anyway, I thought it might not hurt.

The water felt warm around our ankles but when I got to my shoulders it felt much cooler.

The canyon took only a couple of minutes to navigate by boat, but it took much longer swimming. There were more turns than I remembered. When we reached the mouth of the canyon, I was gasping for breath.

"You're lucky you've been training for this," I gulped.

"Yeah, that is fortunate. There aren't any caps like last night but it's way choppier than the canyon," he said.

It felt like a calm sea rather than a lake. There wasn't a boat within sight, and we couldn't hear any engines either. There was nowhere to rest and wait for a passerby. We tried to hang on to the sheer cliff but ended up floating on our backs because it was less work than letting our bodies slide up and down the sandpaper walls. We felt hopeless but neither of us wanted to call it.

When the sun set behind the canyon and our teeth started chattering, we filled the CamelBak with lake water and headed back to shore.

We stopped by a little offshoot on the way to camp and Nick climbed up to the cave. He brought me a few sticks and hiked back up for more. He grabbed some larger pieces of firewood for himself. We were already tired, so holding the wood above water was extremely taxing, and there wasn't even very much of it. He didn't say anything, but I knew he was exhausted by the time we reached our campsite. Unfortunately, we had very little to show for our effort.

We were too cold not to build a fire. I sluggishly gathered everything that needed to be cooked so we could take full advantage of the limited firewood we'd brought back to camp. We lined the fire with the remaining damp wood from the thunderstorm, hoping it would speed up the drying process.

"I think this will be ready by tomorrow night. That's one more day we will be okay, Jen," he assured me.

"Sadly, there wasn't as much food as I hoped. Even fruits and vegetables will rot at this temperature," I answered, feeling less sunny than he was.

There were some hotdogs left but we decided they would keep until the following evening. The ice was completely gone but the melted water was still cool to the touch.

I used the fire to cook some hamburger meat and four chicken breasts in foil. I wasn't sure how long we would dare eat the cooked ground beef but knew our chances would be better if I cooked it sooner than later. The chicken wasn't long for this world. I put lemon slices and pepper on the chicken breasts, and I mourned our lack of potatoes, but we did have some hard rolls that weren't soggy, so we made chicken sandwiches with lettuce and half of the remaining cheese. We each ate the two chicken breasts on rolls and drank the last of the orange juice and the bottled water.

"That was great babe," Nick said after we'd eaten our sandwiches.

"Anything would have tasted great after such a trying day," I offered a tired smile.

"That chicken really was good though. The cold and the swimming really took it out of us, but we did it. We know we can get firewood and there's plenty of water out there," he said in his dry tone.

"The marshmallows melted into one chunk in their bag," I informed him, "but the whiskey is still good."

"Hello, Mrs. I'm Never Drinking Again," he smiled indulgently.

"Oh, we knew that was a lie," I laughed. I'd meant to hand him the whiskey that had been forgotten, but he pulled me down on his lap. His skin felt warm from the fire, and he kissed me with purpose. The smell of smoke in his hair was somehow comforting.

I giggled and looked around as if there was anyone to see us.

"It's fine, we are still married after all," he assured me as he carried me to the tent.

I zipped the tent behind us, and we finally got around to reminding ourselves why our marriage made so much sense.

DAY 6

The next morning, I boiled the water from the CamelBak while the pan was hot. I fried eggs and reheated the ground beef. Such luxury.

The salt and pepper had been out in the rain, but they still worked well enough. The vegetables were not smelling very fresh and the strawberries were covered in mold. I salvaged some but I regretted not eating them sooner. It was difficult to ration without knowing how long things would last in these conditions or how long we'd be stuck.

I apologized when I handed him his plate.

He hungrily ate every bite.

"No complaints?" I asked.

"Never," Nick winked at me like a teenager.

Nick explained today he was going to try and scale the wall. I pushed back, naturally, but he had his mind set on it.

"If I can get up there, I can look over into the other canyons and walk around until I find help. Okay, here we go," Nick started studying the wall of the cliff, mapping a path in his own mind.

My heart started jumping and I wiped the sweat from the back of my neck.

"I'm worried you'll fall," I said.

"Here's what I know. You're the only other person that can help me. All the bottled water we had was locked in the boat Boiling all our water will deplete the butane. There won't be much left to cook the little food we have left. And that food will go rotten fast in this heat and make us sick. Food doesn't really matter if we can't get water to drink. The water at the back of this canyon is too dirty to drink and swimming out to the channel and dragging it back in here is dangerous. And how long can we keep going through that? It was brutal, babe. I've been training for it and it was still brutal. Plus, we still have to boil it before it's suitable to drink. The last thing we need on top of the threat of dehydration is E. coli. We're in this together. Once we get out of here, we can go our separate ways if you still want to, but until then we have to be on the exact same page." Nick reasoned.

"At least you know I'm not going anywhere." I caved. "Okay, try it. Just be careful."

"That looks good over there," he said pointing to the cliff where the boat used to be. "I can't really see each step along the way, but I think once I get up there I'll be able to figure it out," Nick sounded hopeful.

He kissed me soundly on the mouth and walked away.

He waded into the water and stretched his arm as high as he could. I watched him slowly make his way up the wall, keeping his body against the sandstone like a spider. He was deliberate and confident. He was at least twenty feet up when he seemed frozen in place.

"Nick?" I called.

"It's fine, it's just a dead-end," he said, as he began to move laterally to find an upward path.

That's when the rock beneath his foot crumbled. He dangled by one arm before he slid off the cliff and plummeted down into the water.

"Nick!" I gasped and ran into the lake. I started swimming toward the point where he'd disappeared.

He finally surfaced and cried triumphantly, "My organs are fine!"

I laughed in relief.

We swam back to camp and I felt sick from the dissipating adrenaline. We ate the last of the turkey and rolls and I generously loaded on the condiments because they were already room temperature.

"We're really lucky you didn't hit anything on your way down," I said.

"Yes, we're very lucky indeed," Nick scoffed.

"We're still alive, aren't we?" I reminded him.

"Yes. Finally, you're the hopeful one," he smiled.

"It must have something to do with me not jumping off a cliff," I smiled back

"I didn't jump, I just couldn't hang on with that one hand grip. Sandstone is horrible," Nick waved his scraped hand at me. He'd literally sandpapered layers of skin from his fingers trying to hold his body weight and slipping down.

"You won't try again will you?" I asked hopefully.

"Jen, I have to try again," he said.

Nick spent the rest of the day trying to climb different routes. He tried all the surrounding cliffs.

He fell feet-first most of the time but once, he crashed into the water on his side. He never made it above the halfway point, and I was secretly relieved. I didn't know if he could survive a drop from forty feet.

He only stopped for an early dinner, which was the rest of the hotdogs and cheese with some wilted fruits and vegetables. I would have killed for a bag of chips but no such luck.

"I'm going to grab more water from the channel," I told him.

"I'll come with you," Nick said.

"No, I'm sure you're tired from climbing, just stay and relax a minute. Let your food digest," I suggested.

"What if you don't come back? I would never know what happened," he said.

"Yeah, it sucks being left alone at camp," I scoffed, remembering when he'd gone joyriding and left me by myself.

We took some empty water bottles as well as the CamelBak. They were like weights on the swim back, but it was much better than our first trip out to the channel as we didn't waste time treading water, waiting on a rescue boat that never came.

I was ready to call it a day, but Nick tried climbing the canyon walls two more times.

After he gave up climbing, he said, "My hands are worthless, my grip is gone. I think I'm going to try to find the boat down there."

"Oh, please don't. You're tired. That's when people make mistakes. Let's wait for tomorrow morning," I pleaded.

But I couldn't persuade him. There were supplies on the boat we could use so it was hard to argue.

"I guess you better go before it gets dark."

I admired his form as he swam out. He took a deep breath and disappeared below the water.

I held my breath while he was under and saw stars as he came up.

"There are dead trees down there! I think I can use them to pull myself to the very bottom. It's so deep here, Jen!" He called out.

"It's almost six hundred feet deep in some places, love. Ready to come in?" I begged.

"No, I'm gonna try one more time," he said.

"Okay," I sighed.

He inhaled deeply and slipped beneath the surface again.

He came up coughing and I could tell something was wrong.

"I couldn't find the boat and I got cut," he shouted across the water, floating on his back.

"Cut?" I shrieked.

"It's not too bad. I think it was corrugated metal or something like that. But I didn't make a mistake, it just happened. It would have happened no matter when I went, I was pulling myself on the tree and it scraped down my leg. You wouldn't believe how tall those trees are. And I didn't even get to the bottom," he explained.

He slowly swam to shore and hobbled to his camp chair. His leg was dripping with blood and lake water. The gash didn't look that bad until we'd dried it off and it didn't stop bleeding.

I used a beach towel to apply some pressure and that did the trick.

"I couldn't get to the bottom. I didn't even know there were trees right there. We boated over them every day and didn't even know," he said in amazement.

"That's why cliff diving is a bad idea, you can't see what's down there. You could have hit one of those trees yesterday and that would have been much worse," I said.

"They're more in the middle, but you're right. This place is a death trap," he tried to laugh but it rang false as his face was so pale.

"I'm just glad you're okay," I assured him.

"You are?" he seemed surprised to dodge a lecture.

"Of course, I'm glad. You think I want to die alone? Here? Without ever eating creme brûlée again?" I asked.

"We won't die," he said. But I had my private reservations.

"Right. So how does this not get infected?" I asked, knowing it was going to be impossible to keep it clean. The gash wasn't long, but it was deep.

He breathed in through his nose.

"Whiskey is all I can think," I said.

I thought of the first aid kit bolted to the boat, infuriated.

"What a horrible waste," he lamented.

"I wish we hadn't had so much last night," I bemoaned.

"I'm not sorry about anything from last night," he managed a smirk.

"Whiskey is not even that great at disinfecting but it's better than nothing. You won't be able to go back in the water. It's filthy," I said in my most serious tone.

"How can I not go back in the water? I can't just lounge around." He said petulantly.

"Shhh, one step at a time," I tutted as I grabbed the whiskey.

"Take a really deep breath in and out," I waited for the exhale and dumped some whiskey on the gash.

His face contorted in agony, but he kept a howl inside.

I scrambled the remaining eggs for dinner and boiled the lake water we'd collected earlier in the. We drank all of it before it was done cooling off. I had an excruciating headache and wasn't sure if I was dehydrated or if it was simply from stress. We didn't have the spirits to make a fire and fell asleep tucked against one another before the sun set behind us.

DAY 7

We'd slept restlessly and I woke up in an impatient panic. I tried to check Nick's gash without waking him. It was red and puffy; the signs of infection I'd dreaded. I woke him and dowsed it with whiskey again, he didn't cry but I nearly did. I felt powerless and more scared than ever.

I tried not to show how scared I was. I couldn't have him worrying about his leg and me, but I knew in my heart I couldn't do this without him. I couldn't survive without him.

I gave him the water I'd salvaged from the ice bags.

"You stay here and rest," I demanded and then I set my mind on saving his life.

Nick groaned in frustration but accepted his role as patient.

The coolers were officially empty. We had some small backpack snacks and protein shake powder left but we'd eaten everything else.

I took in our little beach area. I kicked the worthless cooler. Empty of ice. Empty...a spark of an idea took hold and I went to work. I set the cooler in the water, and it floated. I smiled. That, at least, was a major victory.

I placed the cooler back on shore while I rooted through the garbage bag and fished out an empty gallon jug that once held water, and I put it in the cooler. I dragged the cooler deeper into the lake. Once I couldn't reach the sand, I floated on my back and slowly swam away from our campsite and Nick.

It took a long while, but I reached the other branch of the canyon.

I looked up the cliff to the small flat area that had caught a messy stack of wood and debris in a long-forgotten flash flood when the lake was much higher. It looked impossibly daunting. I tied the empty milk carton to my swimsuit and started up the wall.

Climbing up the face of the cliff was more like a really steep hill with little ledges here and there, but it was tricky because my body was already tired from the restless night, lack of drinking water, and any semblance of proper nutrition.

I forced myself to keep my body close to the wall. I was able to slowly make my way up the cliff and I dragged the cooler up behind me, wrenching the handle up into the crook of my arm.

Once I got to the little cave filled with wood, I made as much ruckus as I could and listened for a telltale rattle of snakes. I didn't hear or see anything dangerous, so I sat down to catch my breath.

After the luxurious rest, I started collecting wood and filling up the cooler. I couldn't get as much as I wanted because I needed the lid to latch closed lest the wood get wet or the cooler sink like our poor boat.

The cooler was much heavier on the way down. I finally felt confident I could provide both firewood and drinking water.

About halfway down the cliff, I lost my footing. I flailed my arms and I managed to barely keep my balance, but I lost control of the cooler. The lid opened and the weight shifted, and every single stick of wood escaped.

They bounced once off the sandstone and then splashed into the lake water.

I nearly cried then, but I didn't want to waste the moisture.

I took three deep breaths and made my way back up to the cave. This time I skipped the break and went straight to gathering wood. I was worried I wouldn't have the heart to get back up again if I sat down to rest now.

I made my way carefully down to the water and tested the cooler again. It still floated and a wave of relief washed over me. I untied the milk carton, my impromptu floatation device, and made my way painstakingly and delicately to the campsite. I did use the carton as a floatation device, but I made it without dragging the cooler under the surface.

I quickly unloaded the dry kindling and the few large pieces of wood.

I checked on Nick and was pleased to see he was sleeping peacefully. I checked his forehead and it did feel warm, but perhaps it was due to the day heating up. It couldn't be a fever.

I turned back to the water again.

I made the trip to the cave four more times. We had plenty of firewood now. Once more, I took my milk carton and CamelBak out as far as I dared and filled it with fresher water. While the empty gallon container had been a crutch, the container filled with water turned into deadweight and dragging it back was the most difficult thing I'd ever done in my life. I had no idea how much butane was left. I didn't know how many more times I would have to get wood and water. I feared getting to the point where the stove would click, and no flame would appear.

The copper bottom pan would mostly likely get destroyed by the fire. The plastic handle would melt, and the copper would probably separate from the rest of the pan if it stayed hot for too long.

I'd nearly brought a cast iron pan, but it had been so heavy.

"What should I do if we run out of butane?" I asked my sleeping husband.

His voice scared me a little as I hadn't expected him to answer, "Just dig out the green beans can from the trash. You can boil water on the fire in it. Use the tongs to move it around," he said.

"Of course. That's a good idea. We won't run out of water. We can do that as long as we need to," I thought aloud.

"We," he scoffed. He felt helpless but so did I. There wasn't anything to be done for his leg. All I could do was make sure he had water.

"Well, you'd do it all if you could. I know that, Nick," I assured him.

"Thanks, Jen," he sighed.

"While you're up have some of this," I gave him a cup of water and the protein powder. I wished there were more to offer.

He drank it in three gulps. When he fell back asleep, I sat in a camp chair and made a list in my mind.

Every day I had to get kindling, firewood, water, and then boil the water. I cursed the fact that we didn't have any fishing gear, that would have been a source of food. Catching a little darting sunfish by hand seemed out of the question.

The lethargy was making my mind function slower. I was cognizant enough to know that is how people get hurt; they make poor decisions when they're exhausted. But what could be done about it?

I hadn't eaten anything today, but I was too scared to drink the protein powder or the granola bars. Nick needed the nutrition to get well.

I began to cry a little. I thought of all the beautiful dinners I'd made, sometimes the only accomplishment of my day, set on a made table and wasted because Nick's meetings had run late again. My resentment had grown hot as the food grew cold. How I'd put whole meals in the trash and fallen asleep filled with disappointment.

DAY 8

The heat radiating from Nick's feverish body woke me up. The wound was no longer puffy; it was honest-to-god swollen but there were no red streaks to indicate blood poisoning, so I was counting my blessings.

I went through my daily checklist and got kindling, firewood, and water. I boiled the water.

Nick stayed quiet most of the day, nursing a protein shake and looking sullen about not being more helpful. I read aloud from my eReader and Nick listened, even though romance novels have never been his thing. I hoped my battery would outlast our camping trip.

At dinner time, I had a scoop of protein powder with my water. I built a nice big fire to cheer us up a bit.

Nick sipped his protein shake and laughed.

"What?" I asked, perplexed.

"My kingdom for a Black Cherry Propel to drink," he explained.

"My kingdom for a propeller," I laughed.

DAY 9

I took care of the water, the wood, and the fire.

We ran out of granola bars.

Nick slept most of the day but drank plenty of water while he was awake. I found myself sleeping through the hottest part of the day as well, resting my hand on Nick's chest to make sure he was still breathing.

His fever didn't seem any better or worse, but without a thermometer I was just going by touch. I read to him to distract us both.

That night, I fell asleep remembering how he talked me into buying the nicer car model last time we went car shopping. He wanted me to have heated seats so I wouldn't be uncomfortable driving in the winter. There was nothing I could do to make him more comfortable now.

DAY 10

I woke up with a terrible backache. I wondered if my kidneys were giving in. I was trying to drink enough water, but I knew I would have to step it up a little bit.

I dreaded making another trip to get wood. I wasn't sure I could muster the energy today. I stretched my arms over my head and winced.

Nick's eyes were open, but he hadn't moved or said anything since I'd started stirring.

"You okay, Nick?" I asked.

"I'm the same. How are you holding up?"

I was so relieved he was still alive.

"I feel tired is all," I assured him.

"You should have two protein shakes today. You're burning a lot of calories doing all the work," he insisted.

"Maybe," I said, noncommittal. I could not take food from his mouth. I didn't think he was well enough to notice I'd been skimping a little but of course he had.

"You should. If you get sick, then we're not going to make it. You need to make it even if I don't," his tone was somber.

"You're going to be fine. It's just a scratch. We both need to make it, Nick."

"And I hope we do. But you need to try to take care of yourself. I was thinking you could try spearfishing with a hot dog stick and then we wouldn't have anything to worry about," he smiled.

"I'll try that," I laughed, but it sounded hollow.

"Good," he said.

"Nick, if we do make it, let's spend more time together, okay?" I asked.

"What, you've been getting spoiled out here, having all this attention?" he was trying to joke, but I was serious. His face looked pale and this was as weak as I'd ever seen my strong husband.

"I mean it, Nick," I assured him.

"I know. I've been thinking a lot about us. Back home I was trying to show you how much you mean to me in all the wrong ways. And being trapped here made me realize that it doesn't matter how comfortable we make our lives if we are living separate lives. What's important to you should be important to me. I want to spend time with you. But right now, I want you to double up on protein shakes," he said sternly.

"Right, but I don't know how long it needs to last, Nick. How do you plan for—" a noise cut the thought short.

A boat engine. And the speakers were blasting the Beach Boys, the joyous music echoed off the canyon walls. I ran for the edge of the water and started waving my arms frantically and jumping up and down.

The boat rounded the last turn in the canyon and finally came into view.

I cupped my hands around my mouth and called out and waved my arms in the distress signal above my head, but the boat had already started to turn around as the campsite was occupied.

I caught one woman's attention and they circled back to us.

Nick stumbled out of the tent and we sagged against each other with relief, holding each other up, even now.

He held my hand as I desperately explained that we needed help. He held my hand as the boat raced through the canyon and back to the marina. And I held his hand as the doctor debrided and flushed the gash on his leg.

DAY 11

We both had to spend time in the hospital to recover from heat exhaustion and dehydration.

"Who gets dehydrated on a huge lake?" I scoffed at the unexpected twist.

"It's easy when it's a million degrees and you never hold still," Nick said.

Nick was on heavy antibiotics for his leg. Our beds were next to each other and Nick was staring at his phone.

"Whatcha looking at?" I asked.

"Flights to Cabo, Darling. We could use an all-inclusive vacation," Nick laughed.

"You're still hooked to an IV," I scoffed, reaching to hold his hand.

"You said you'd come with me if we made it," Nick said.

"Fine, but no cinnamon whiskey," I smiled.

"No, darling. We will have all the cinnamon whiskey," he assured me.

I had never felt so assured of anything in my entire life.

ABOUT ANGIE JONES

Angie Jones has been writing since she was a toddler and relied on her older sister to serve as scribe. She went on to study journalism in college, where she was the News Editor. On the Lake in the Desert is her first published non-fiction piece. Angie is currently writing in order to procrastinate studying capital market theory as she works toward earning her MBA.

THE TIES OF GRIEF

BY ANNA-MARIE LOPEZ

Death tore them apart. A birthday party might just bring them back together. Savannah and Logan left things on nasty terms, and now, it's the two of them, all alone, in a vacation home for three days.

Savannah was broken after Devon passed. Logan fled town, cutting all ties in her wake. When they get back together for Devon's sake, it takes no time at all for all the tension and unsaid words to rise to the surface.

Is this finally the time for healing? Or, will the weekend end with Savannah and Logan leaving the other's life for good?

A BIRTHDAY PARTY FOR A DEAD PERSON.

It's a birthday party for a frickin' dead person that brings me back to Hilton Head. Logan's idea, and one I want so desperately to turn down the moment she texts me, but one that, goddammit, I just can't ignore.

Devon loved Hilton Head. Hell, Devon loved fucking birthdays.

So, here I am. Staring up at the white, marbled monstrosity of a timeshare Devon's parents were "nice" enough to give Logan the keys to for the weekend. It's just as gawdy as I remember, and the sight fully makes me want to vomit. Logan's absence doesn't help, either. Without her to be annoying and chat me up about every single thing under the goddamned sun, the tableau splayed out before my car acts as the ugliest, most gut-twisting reminder of the end of high school.

Namely, Devon's death.

"The fuck were you expecting, though?" I scoff as I lean my arm against the driver's seat window. "The universe hates you. Obviously, it's going to be an asshole today."

No one answers, of course. For once in her life, Logan is properly late, and despite my slight annoyance over this, I feel way more relieved than anything else. Watching the numbers on my clock switch from 4:15 to 4:16 is like a gift from some magic timeliness god. Maybe I got lucky. Maybe Lo can't come after all. Maybe there's something fancy going on in New York, so fancy she can't possibly pick up her phone and call, and maybe, just maybe I'll be able to get out of this wretched weekend like I fucking hoped for from the beginning.

Believe me: I know how that sounds. I'm the biggest bitch in the world for caring more about myself than Devon. It's his fucking birthday. His twenty-first, for that matter, the one birthday he wanted to have a huge celebration for. He, Logan, and I started planning for it in high school. It'd be this massive thing, the party to end all parties. The only thing I should be right now is selfless.

Only, this whole deal is my worst nightmare wrapped up in a beach-themed bow.

If there's any way I can get out of it, I'm taking that chance, and I'm fucking running.

"Just twelve more minutes, Sav." I tap my fingers against the steering wheel, watching the numbers flip to 4:18. A half hour is pretty generous as far as waiting goes, right? I mean, it was already torture enough agreeing to come in the first place. What does she expect, for me to turn into a total masochist?

On second thought, maybe the description already fits. I'm here, aren't I?

Please don't come, please don't come, please do—

"Oh, my *gosh*! Savannah! Look at you!"

A high-pitched, way too enthusiastic voice screeches out from behind me, quickly shattering all hopes of being able to just go home. I'd recognize it as Logan's even if we weren't supposed to meet up today, and with complete and utter regret lining the bottom of my stomach like rocks in a creek, I swivel my head to find her old, beat-up Sedan pulling in behind my rented SUV. The car looks no different than it did in high school. Still that weird, almost puke-green color. Still covered in dirt. Just the same as always, a notion that only makes me even more anxious.

Great. Apparently, reminders of high school will be following me around all day.

"You're so adorable!" Logan squeals as she throws open her door, jumping from her seat like a goddamned Whack-a-Mole. She beams so widely you'd think she was the sun, personified. Meanwhile, I take a moment to soak her in, feeling both a lump rise in my throat and an awful fluttering start in the pit of my stomach.

Well. She's different, no question about it. Her hair's been dyed pink, a drastic change from her dark brown locks back in high school. In place of those large hipster glasses she always wore, she's traded them out for colored green contacts, and she's clearly gotten way better at makeup, too, since her eyeliner job isn't nearly as clunky as it once was, and her eyeshadow's actually blended.

Shitting fucking fuck. She looks good. It's clear she's come into her own, and butterflies start going haywire in my stomach the longer I stare. Memories of how I fell in love with her in junior year are bombarding me now. All the love notes I wrote, only to crumple up so she'd never see them. All the times I thought about getting up the nerve to tell her about my crush, only to stop myself at the last second. All the moments I wanted nothing more than to kiss her, only to be scared to fucking death she wouldn't even want to be my friend anymore.

Those memories hurt like hell. But the one where I finally did tell her about the crush, where we got together, where everything felt fucking right for the first time since the stupid car accident that took both my parents and both my older siblings?

That one cuts me like a knife.

"Logan. Hey." I force a grin as I reach her, sighing deeply and trying my best not to let a scowl overtake the smile. That's something I've gotten "quite good at", according to Aunt Claire, and despite the fact Logan probably deserves all the bitch faces and more, given just how horribly she left things off with us, I don't want to start out on the wrong foot. It's only the two of us this entire fucking weekend. The last thing I need is for it to be awkward and tense—I deal with enough of that shit in my regular life.

"Sav, my God." She wraps me in a tight hug, squeezing harder than she ever has. "You're a stunner. Like, I seriously can't believe how good you look. And you've gotten so toned! You went out for that running thing after all, huh?"

Instinctively, I pull my sweatshirt tighter around my body, wishing to God she wouldn't have gone to that place right away. It's not that I don't appreciate the compliment, or that I wasn't hoping she'd notice at some point—it's just that being toned at all is a reminder of what brought us here. Devon. More specifically, how I spiraled after he died. Aunt Claire told me about the car accident, and that was it. I was gone. I don't remember anything about the remainder of senior year. Not my SATs, not my prom, not the birthday party Lo threw me, not even us breaking up even though I know it was one of the nastiest fights either of us had ever had. I have the texts still. I don't remember being so volatile with her, and I don't remember being so angry I legitimately wrote out the words *I hate you,* but the timestamps and those dreaded green and blue bubbles don't lie.

I told her I hated her. I fell apart after Devon.

And running—the pastime I always wanted to pick up, but was too chickenshit to actually go through with in high school—is the only reason I'm alive and here today, clinging onto my last thread of sanity on a string so thin it's barely visible to the naked eye.

These days, it's seeming more and more like even that's not enough.

I reach my hand around, starting to rub the back of my neck. "Yeah. Yeah, I do run now. But, uh..." I blow out an exhale. "Can we skip the catching-up stuff for a little while? I'm, uh... cold. And tired. And I could use something to eat. I left this morning without any breakfast."

Mainly because the thought of actually coming to this place was enough to make me want to vomit up everything I've even looked at these past three years.

Logan, thankfully, doesn't comment on my poor eating habits. If we were seventeen-year-old Sav and Lo, she might look at me with that concerned best friend look and ask if I was taking care of myself. Today, though, three years later, it's clearly understood there's a divide between us.

We head inside the house in near silence, me trailing behind her at a pretty sizeable distance. Lo, because she's Lo, moves first to go upstairs and unpack in the room we dubbed as ours every spring and summer from freshman all the way throughout senior year. Meanwhile, I make a direct beeline for the kitchen, already well aware there's a whole stockpile of junk food waiting on both the island counter and in the fridge.

A sudden hitch sounds in my breath as I reach the six-pack of soda near the table. All at once, a profound longing for Mr. and Mrs. Harrington hits me, and it stings a little harder than I'd have thought it would. I haven't seen them since the funeral. Didn't even give proper condolences back then, either. As soon as everyone was leaving and saying their goodbyes and telling the Harrington's how much they'd miss Devon, I got myself right the hell out of there.

I fucking regret that. I hate myself for being so selfish.

I'd give anything to let them know just how damn much their son meant to me.

Of course, though, it seems I've blown my one and only chance. If they won't even come out here to celebrate his birthday like Lo originally wanted them to, I doubt they'll want to see his friends in any other capacity. And that's the thing that's getting to me about this weekend, I think: it was supposed to be this huge, family reunion type deal. Logan and I would come here and celebrate like we are right now, but for the first night or so, Mr. and Mrs. Harrington join us. That way, we could all honor Devon the way he would've wanted.

The Harrington's instantly tapped out after Lo sent her message. It'd hurt too much. They couldn't deal with the reminders of him. And me?

Fucking goddammit. Like a coward, I let my stupid morals get the best of me. When I heard the Harrington's wouldn't be making an appearance, I readily and happily typed out an, "oops, sorry, can't make it" message of my own, prepared to not even think about Lo afterwards. I mean, it's not like his death doesn't hurt me, too. If anything, my hurt is just as strong as the Harrington's.

But it's because of Devon I couldn't do it. He'd have called me a bitch for a move like that. He'd have been so disappointed, so angry, so embarrassed to be my friend.

I couldn't dishonor him like that. So, here I am, regret embedding itself into every fucking fiber of my being because I'm here with my ex and only my ex.

"Next time, just let yourself be a fucking bitch." I scoff, hanging on the door of the fridge. Inside, there's a vanilla cake calling my name, and I have no intention of ignoring the beckon. Emotional eating for the win, right? I mean, it is in my book. Aunt Claire, she'd have a conniption fit over this, tell me that I'm "wearing my body down irreparably", but on my end, I don't give a shit. Life sucks. This weekend sucks. Devon not being here sucks, and holy fucking shit, being stuck with Logan sucks. If I've got any avenue of numbing the pain, I'll numb the fucking pain until the cows come home.

In case it wasn't obvious? This weekend is so not my cup of tea.

"Thank God for Mrs. Harrington, right?"

Logan gives me a raised eyebrow as she comes back downstairs, a small grin dangling on her lips and hair now pulled up into this pretty impressive half-up-half-down 'do. She slides into the chair beside me at the table, grabbing a chocolate bar from the center of it.

Breaking off a piece, she continues, "I'm surprised we didn't both become beach balls in high school. Or, like, that one character from *Willy Wonka.* You know, the one who totally blows up? God." She chuckles, shaking her head. "That scene is hilarious. The whole movie is. I miss watching it. The last time I did was with..."

She cuts herself off abruptly, and as her eyes shift downward, a rush of cold hits the back of my neck. I don't need to ask why she stopped talking. I don't need to ask about the look on her face. I know exactly what she was going to say. *With Devon.* That was how that sentence was supposed to end, and I think we both know it's way too early to bring him up. It was my one and only stipulation for this weekend. I'd come to celebrate him, but neither of us were to bring his name or any memories of him up until I made it clear I was ready. It couldn't be an ambush conversation. It couldn't be something organic. If we were going to talk about Devon, it had to be on my terms.

I clear my throat. Loudly. A little too loudly, actually. My gaze also drops to the wood of the table, and I rub the back of my neck, speaking so quietly I can barely hear myself. "It was kind of a crap plot, anyways..."

The remark dangles in the air. Logan doesn't want to push any further, I'm sure, and I definitely don't fucking want to, either, and so, we're left at an impasse, just staring at one another.

I bite back the urge to let out a scream.

Here's the fucking thing with Devon: losing him absolutely broke me. I wasn't expecting his death. I never even entertained the thought of having to start adulthood without him. My best friend since the very beginning of high school, he was always there those days, and that was how I thought it'd always be. When I lost Mom, Dad, Jules, and Micah? I could at least somewhat handle it, because they'd all been in critical condition for over a week, and the doctor didn't sugarcoat the fact it'd take a goddamned miracle for them to pull through.

Devon? He was gone in the blink of an eye. I went to bed texting him to be safe, and I woke up to the news that my warning wouldn't have mattered. The driver was plowing into him right as I was pressing 'send.' He died on impact.

To make matters worse, he died on Mom's birthday.

So. Yeah. If I'm going to talk about him, if I'm going to be forced to shift from my little fits and spurts of memories to full conversations, I need a warning, and it needs to be on my terms.

"Uh..." Logan lets out a cough, cheeks reddening the way they always did in high school when she'd put her foot in her mouth. "Sav, I didn't... I'm sor—"

"You know what?" I cut her off, waving a hand dismissively. "Let's just skip the awkward small-talk. We both suck at that. This is awkward enough as is. So... I dunno. How's school? New York treating you okay?"

Lo's features ease, like it was the small-talk she was dreading most. I'm not surprised—my ex/former best friend's always been a talkative little shit, but she'll only bore you to death for hours if she really knows you. When we met in the fourth grade, she was so shy she literally didn't say a single word to me for that first week. Meanwhile, I refused to stop pestering her.

The silence between us was so deafening she might as well not have been there at all.

She breaks off a piece of her chocolate. "New York is... weird," she says, shaking her head. "I'm not used to super-cold winters. Like, I'm still not. I've been there two years now, and I still got shocked back in January when I'd go outside and my breath was instantly frozen. I mean, you know how it is back here. We get maybe two snowfalls, and that's it. But up there, it can snow for five days straight, and nothing stops. Nothing shuts down, either—it's all business as usual. Other than that, though, things are going pretty good. I finally don't feel like such an alien when talking about graphic design stuff. Everyone knows exactly what I'm trying to say. And my roommate is literally a dream. She does my laundry sometimes, and I don't even have to ask. Can you believe that? It's like I found a frickin' unicorn."

Like before, I force a grin onto my lips. If I'm being honest, this is shit I really, really don't want to hear about. I'm fully aware I asked, but it was just to be nice. And Lo should know that. Lo should know it was a gesture, but nothing more, and that, in actuality, I couldn't give any less of a shit about this. I don't want to hear about her and her roommate. I don't want to know about all the friends she has. I don't want to think about how happy she is, how happy I could never be.

But because I'm now apparently a self-proclaimed masochist, I still make another gesture.

"And, uh..." I take a long sip of my drink. "Guys? Girls? You, um... is there a lucky Mr. or Mrs. Logan yet?"

A sparkle comes to her eyes—the exact sparkle I saw all the time in high school and could never seem to get enough of. She lets out a laugh, quiet and soft. "Um... no Mr. or Mrs. yet. There are a couple people around campus I've gone out on lunch dates and stuff with. I don't know. I'm just focusing on my studies, you know? Honestly, I'm trying to fast track my degree. The sooner I can get out in the workforce, the better. I'm poor. You should see my apartment—my wall holes have wall holes of their own."

I allow myself a chuckle of my own. "Disgusting."

"Right? So. Yeah. I don't know, dating isn't really something on my radar. But what about with you? How are things going on the Savannah dating front? I bet you're breaking a lot of hearts out there."

There's a slight, unexpected hitch on the word "break." Anyone else probably wouldn't be able to hear it, but years and years' worth of having Lo as my only conversation buddy has trained me to hear any and all emotions she gives off with what she says, and we both look away just at the mention of a heart being broken.

I've been saying ever since Devon died I don't feel anything anymore. Most of the time, I mean it. When bad things happen now, I'm just numb to it all. Drowning in misery got real old, real fast, so I decided I was done. Being a zombie was way better than any of that pain. With Logan, though, she's my kryptonite. She brings all the shoved-down feelings right back to the surface. When she sent that message about maybe meeting up so we could celebrate Devon's birthday properly, just seeing her name sent me into a tailspin. I wasn't expecting it, and I sure as hell wasn't expecting her to want to see me so soon, and when it popped up on my notifications thread, I shut down for the first time in ages. Barely ate for three weeks. Slept only in fitful, exhaustion-filled bursts. Couldn't even look at my phone without feeling like the panic was going to eat me from the inside out.

I do mean it when I say I don't feel anything, but Logan is the true, absolute exception. And, for some reason, hearing that break in her voice, knowing it was her who broke us apart even if I had my part in it, stirs something within me that I can't name and so, so don't want to feel.

To combat it, I end up taking another sip of soda, swallowing hard as I set the can down. "I'm not focused on the dating scene at all." I tell her. "Been too busy. I've got a lot on my plate."

You do? Since when? You're a second-year frickin' college dropout, Sav.

Logan stares right at me—like she can tell I'm lying. I mean, I'm sure she can. If I can tell her emotions in just one word, there's no doubt in my mind she's still got all my dishonesty tells memorized. But she only smiles again, resting her head in the palm of her head.

"Tell me everything," she says. "Please. I've missed this. I've missed you. I should've..." A soft sigh escapes her mouth. "I shouldn't have let things end the way they did. I shouldn't have let us stop talking. I really miss you, Sav. More than I ever thought was even possible."

A *whooshing* sound comes from overhead as she finishes speaking. Predictably, a world-famous Hilton Head afternoon shower, something that only adds to the disdain I already feel. Things are getting heavy right as it's starting to pour?

That's got to be some kind of sign to get the fuck out of Dodge. For now, at least.

"Um..." I place the soda down, digging my nails into my palm. I need to decompress. Gather myself. "Do you... would you... you don't mind if I go and take a nap, do you? It's just, I'm tired. I didn't sleep well last night. Plus, this'd give you time to unpack and whatever."

Logan's gaze lifts slightly, a gesture that tells me right away I've thrown her for a loop. Clearly, she was hoping this would be some sort of door opener.

In true Logan fashion, however, she gives an amicable nod, clearing her throat in an equally-as-puzzled way. "Oh, yeah. I mean, of course." She scoots her chair back from the table. "Yeah. Go on. Rest. I'll, uh... maybe go and sit on the porch. I've actually got this one quick assignment to finish, so this works out super well. Um... maybe we can order a pizza tonight? Or, I don't know. What were you thinking for dinner?"

"You choose." I give her a noncommittal shrug. "I'm too tired to care. See you in a bit?"

“See you in a bit.” She grabs a laptop bag, swinging it over her shoulder and heading towards the covered patio. “You, uh… sleep well, I guess.”

It’s a chore to force this smile, but I do it, anyways. “Thanks. And you… enjoy your homework.”

We both nod this time. One of those intensely awkward, oh-my-God-please-get-me-out-of-here nods. I nearly dart to the guest room afterwards, while she steps out onto the patio.

Once upstairs and safely behind closed doors, I let out a deep, damn near agonizing exhale. I’m already exhausted. I feel like I’ve been goddamned run over from all the stress so far.

And the kicker? I’ve barely been with Lo for fifteen minutes.

Good God.

What the hell did I get myself into with this weekend?

SHE MAKES SPAGHETTI AND MEATBALLS FOR DINNER.

It's the smell that brings me out of my stupor. That same smell I became so accustomed to back in elementary and middle school, the smell that made me want to spend every weekend at her house rather than mine because her mom made such good Italian food. It's a smell that instantly transports me in time. To us. To meeting Devon in freshman year. The first time we all went over to Lo's to study for a group project, her mom made spaghetti and meatballs and we tried to work out whatever the fuck photosynthesis actually means over that and a plate of garlic bread. We ate it before the sophomore spring formal, too. Forever and a day, it's been a dish I've just associated with Lo. Now, waking up to the aroma, it's flooding my mind with everything Devon-related.

The spring formal.

That fucking photosynthesis project.

I think we made it once here, too. Actually, I'm pretty sure it's the first dinner we ate the very first time the Harrington's let us stay here with Devon for the weekend.

The anger raging inside me bubbles over before I can even think about containing it.

"Spaghetti and fucking meatballs?"

A shrill tone sounds from my voice as I stomp into the kitchen, one that I don't recognize and have no idea where it's originating from. Ordinarily when I get mad, I go silent. Screeching like this is not me. Regardless, I don't stop to think before I keep speaking.

"Are you fucking kidding me?" I land at the side of the oven, folding my arms." You had to go and make spaghetti and fucking meatballs? There wasn't anything else we could have for dinner?"

Lo's head snaps up at the sound of my voice. Clearly, she wasn't expecting me to be Off-The-Handle Sav this quickly, and she blinks a couple times as she sets her pasta spoon down. Running a hand through her hair, she stammers, "I don't... Sav, I just..." She swallows. "I wanted to kick off this weekend right. That's all. Just, like... relive memories. Good memories. Our memories. I don't... I wasn't... I'm not trying to upset you."

"Oh, you aren't? Really? You're not trying to upset me, so you made a dinner that has Devon written all over it when I fucking told you I need a fucking trigger warning when it comes to him? How does that make sense, Logan? Please. Tell me."

Her face clouds a little, and I can't tell if it's with regret or anger. If it's the former, she's clearly not as smart as she used to be. If it's the latter, she's got another fucking thing coming.

She shifts the pot off the stove, taking a moment to think through what she wants to say before she responds. Gaze lifting, she says, "Honestly, Sav, I wasn't even thinking about Devon when I started making it. I just... I saw the box, and I thought... I thought it'd be nice. We had our talks over spaghetti way before it was a thing with him. That's all, Savannah. I promise."

Tears rush to my eyes. I don't want them to, but there they are, and I bite down on my lip so they don't make too noticeable an appearance. "So, you're seriously telling me you forgot we had spaghetti the first fucking time we all hung out at your house? The smell didn't immediately transport you back? Is that what you're saying?"

The clouding becomes more prominent, and as it does, there's no question about the underlying emotion: that's all anger. "Jesus Christ," she mutters, pinching the bridge of her nose. "Here we go again."

I raise an eyebrow. "Excuse me?"

Pointedly, she ignores the question, instead jumping into the argument full-force. "That was seven years ago, Savannah." Her tone becomes noticeably colder. "Seven years is a long time, in case you haven't noticed. So, yeah. Yeah, I did forget that. Excuse me for not having a perfect memory. Are you really going to jump down my throat for not remembering one night seven years ago?"

"Are you really this shit at reading a room?"

She snorts. "Oh, that's rich. You're talking to me about reading the room? Seriously?"

I can feel my eyebrows scrunch together. "What the fuck are you talking about?"

"Um, maybe the fact that you *suck* at reading the room?" She narrows her eyes. "How can you even say something like that when you started posting all this depressing crap on social media the instant we became friends again? You hadn't posted anything for two months before my request. The second you accepted it? Sad meme this, and depressing quote that, and wow-my-life-sucks everything in between. You really want to talk about reading a room when you go and do that kind of stuff?"

I mimic her snort, louder and colder. "It's my account. What, do I need to text you before I post something new? In case you forgot, we aren't exactly in each other's lives anymore."

"And whose fault is that, Savannah? It wasn't me who made it impossible to be your friend anymore. It wasn't me who was snarky and mean about every single word that came out of my mouth. It wasn't me who went on rampages every night. It wasn't. All of that crap was you. *You* were the one who became a stranger after Devon passed, so don't you dare get all high and mighty about us not being close like we used to be."

The hatred gets a million times more powerful when she says this. My fists clench without my having realizing it's happened until I look down, and I stare at Logan for a moment, honestly wondering if I have to spell it all out for her. And it's not that I don't want to, either. I'd be more than happy. She just won't like the way I say it, and for a celebration that's only involving the two of us, that'd be a real shitty way to spend our first night.

Allow me to take a trip down memory lane for a moment, though. Allow me to remember exactly what happened, exactly why I became a *stranger*, as Logan so nicely put it.

Two weeks after the car accident, Aunt Claire decided it was for the best if I did school from home for the rest of the year. There was only a month left until graduation, and since being in a place that reminded me so strongly of Devon was one of the worst ideas in the world, it was more or less necessary if I didn't want to fail out. So, when that happened, I basically became a hermit. Didn't want to see anyone. Didn't want to talk to anyone. Didn't even want to leave bed most days.

The only exception to all that? Logan. Because of course it was Logan.

I was even planning to suck it up and go to our senior banquet dinner for her. I was so ready for it, too, because I needed a night where I could forget everything and let the world vanish. I even made a special trip to the mall with Claire, all so I could have the perfect dress.

Two days before the dinner, Lo called me up out of the blue and said we needed to talk.

An hour later, she'd broken up with me.

I was left a mess after that. So devastated I didn't even want to walk in my own goddamned graduation ceremony, let alone go to the banquet dinner. And, again, this was all right after Devon died. Right after I'd spiraled into the most intense depression I'd ever, ever known.

Who the fuck wouldn't have turned into a stranger?

"Okay, fine," I snap. "You really want to know why I keep posting depressing shit?"

As though to truly drive home how pissed I am, I raise an eyebrow as I slide onto one of the super ugly, but super fancy barstools the Harrington's have before their granite counter. "You want the truth?" I continue. "The God-honest truth? Why I'm sad? Why I don't want to talk about Devon? Why I took so damn long to answer your message about this stupid weekend?"

She folds her arms. "It's stupid now?"

"It's a fucking birthday party for a dead person, Logan. What do you think? Who the fuck gathers around and bakes a cake and blows out candles for someone who isn't even here anymore? It's such bullshit. And, God, you know what? Here's the fucking truth. I honestly don't care if you want it or not—you're getting it. You're a shitty fucking person. Maybe I turned into a stranger after Devon, but you turned into a monster. How can you be such a good friend to him, someone who's six fucking feet under, while you say 'fuck you' every time you look at my face? What, am I not important because I'm not dead?"

"What are you going on about now?" She lets out a sigh, like listening to me is a chore.

"You left me all alone after he died!" My voice raises an octave, and I don't even fucking care enough to try and stop myself. "You were like, 'Sorry, bye, let me go traipse off to New York and make fancy new friends and leave Savannah all alone.' I needed you, Logan. I needed you to be the one thing in my life that didn't change. But I guess I'm not as important as a corpse, right? Let's celebrate Devon, sure, but fuck Savannah."

She stares at me for a moment. As though she can't believe the words coming out of my mouth. Then, with a scoff, she steps closer to me, lips pursing. "Can you really blame me for leaving? Like, honestly? Savannah, what was I supposed to do? The only time you said anything to me was when you were yelling. Why would I have stayed when I was having you throw insults at me every single time I tried starting even the simplest of conversations?"

"Because that's what best friends do, Logan. That's what they're supposed to do, anyways. I wouldn't have left. I would've stayed back in Charlotte, given you exactly what you needed."

"Oh, yeah? And what would that have been? Please tell me, oh wise one."

It's my turn to give an eye-roll. "What, do they make you a sarcastic jackass in New York?"

"Better than a miserable social leper."

I have to admit—this fucking stings. If Seventeen-Year-Old Sav were here, she'd probably pause the arguing to try and maintain composure so tears wouldn't sting her eyes. But I don't cry anymore, and I'm sure as hell not going to let Lo take these cheap shots, either.

I dig my elbows into the island, giving her as intense a look as she's giving me. "So, why'd you invite me all the way out here, then? If I'm a miserable leper, why didn't you just come and celebrate Devon on your own? I mean, it's not like you need me. You've made that pretty damn clear with all your hoity-toity New York friends."

"Oh, God, Savannah." She rubs a hand down the length of her face. "So, are you saying I should've never left home? Is that it? You needed me, so I was supposed to put my whole education plan off-track? For one person?"

"It's what I would've done."

"Well, good for you. I'm glad. But we aren't the same person. We never have been. I don't cope with stuff the way you do. I don't even think about stuff the way you do. I couldn't stay back in Charlotte. And especially not for you, not the way you were back then. Do you even remember what you said to me? How much it stung?"

I can't help but roll my eyes. She's talking to *me* about something stinging?

"What did I say, Logan? Please tell me. *How* did I hurt you?"

Her eyes start to water, which throws me off track. Okay, that's so not what I was expecting. Did I... seriously just make her cry?

What the fuck?

"You called me a bitch, Savannah," she whispers, shaking her head. "You called me a bitch every time we argued. And you said I was selfish, that you hated me, and that you wished it was me who died in the accident. Then, five seconds later, you'd act like you had no idea why I was so angry. Do you even know how hard it is to *think* about that? Never mind the fact I had to hear it. Every time I see your face now, it floods back in. I can't help it. It's there in an instant."

This fully stops me for a moment, kind of sucker-punching me in the gut when I hear it.

Stupid as it sounds, I actually don't remember that. Everything she's recalling, it's a total blank in my head. There's so much of that time I've blocked out. It all hurt too much, so I literally forced myself to forget. There's not a single part of me that thinks she's lying, though. I've heard all those words before, played on a near-constant loop and directed towards myself.

Oh, fuck.

I took what I was feeling out on Lo, didn't I?

"I don't... I..." I hug my arms tighter over my chest, having no clue how to respond. I'm not good at confrontation. Never have been. Throwing stones? I rock at that. Actually taking the hits? I'd rather lay down and die.

I clear my throat. "Logan, you know that wasn't true. I'm... you know I was just..." I shake my head. "I was hurting. Devon had just died. I didn't know what to do. We all say things we don't mean when we're hurting, right? And you... I still needed you. I've never been strong like you are. I... that's when you should've known I needed you, Logan. All those things I said, I was thinking them about me, not you. I just... I took it out on you. And I didn't mean to. I'm sorry I did. But... couldn't you have said that before you went and broke up with me and gone off to New York? It hurt so much to lose Devon, Logan. Losing you... I don't think you even know how much it hurt to lose you so soon after the accident."

"What, like you were the only one who lost a friend that day?" Lo's eyebrows furrow together. "That's the issue with you, Sav. It's always about you. Never once do you think about how anyone else is affected—it's just Savannah, Savannah, Savannah. Who hurt *me*? Who left *me*? But here's a newsflash: yeah, I do know. Devon was my best friend, too. It tore me up, too. And have you ever stopped to think about how I couldn't just stay home because every single place I went made me think of him? The bakery. The grocery store. Hell, even the stupid dog groomer. He was the one who told me where to take Magnolia. So, yeah, I know how much it hurt. I had the same exact hurt. And that's why I needed to leave. I couldn't stand being in the same exact place my whole life. Especially not after all that. I wanted to travel. I wanted to explore. I wanted to find myself."

"Well, why the hell couldn't find yourself with me?" I shoot up from the barstool, hearing a quiver I hate enter my voice. "We could've moved together. Gone to some school in the middle of nowhere, found some place that we could've made all our own. You didn't have to go to New York. You *shouldn't* have gone to New York. When your best friend needs you, when something major's going on and you know that not being at their side would crush them, you don't go. That's what being a best friend is all about. You should've known the moment I said what I said how much I was hurting. You should've been there. And it was a dick move not to be."

"Oh, my God. Do you even know how hypocritical you sound right now? Y---"

"*I'm* the hypocrite? Did you really just say that?"

"And how the hell am I the hypocrite, Savannah? For wanting my own life?" Lo scoffs. "God. I wish I could record this, somehow. Show you how much of an asshole you're really being right now. It's not a crime not to want to be attached to your hip. That's not what being a best friend is. And, sorry, but 'I thought those things about myself'? That's not an excuse. You were so out of line, and it hurt me for longer than you'll ever even realize. But I decided I didn't want to be mad forever. I buried the hatchet. I wasn't going to keep letting that make me think of you differently, and I'm not going to now. It's not fair. But I need you to understand I had to leave. There was no choice. I was suffocating. I—"

"So was I!" I throw my arms up. "We were in the same boat. You didn't have to leave. We could've sorted through it together."

"No, Savannah." Her voice grows even colder, and for a moment, she stops herself short, like this is all she's going to say.

The look on her face is completely unrecognizable. I've never seen her this pissed. Ever.

Finally, she steps back, hugging her arms tighter over her chest. "I just... I almost don't even know what to say to you right now." Her voice drops another octave, and she runs a hand through her hair, looking like I'm some huge task she has to take on. "There was no way I could've sorted through all the shit I was feeling with you there. You dragged me down, Savannah. I don't care if that's what you felt about yourself. I don't care if you didn't mean it. Bottom line, you still said it, over and over again, and it still hurt like crazy every single time. So, if you seriously think I'm in the wrong for doing what literally anyone else would've done, you've got a scarily warped view of all of this. I needed out. I needed to get away. And, also, that's what you're friggin' supposed to do at the start of college. God, every teen movie we watched told us that. I—"

"But we were best friends, Logan. You don't jus—"

"Jesus Christ, do you ever know how to stop talking? Like, even for five seconds?" She gives me a look that says, without question, 'you're the scum of the fucking earth'. "I was barely eighteen when we graduated. I'd just lost my best friend. I'd had to celebrate my birthday without him, for the first time in four years. I needed to leave. And I didn't do anything wrong—except maybe become your friend in the first place."

This one cuts fucking deep. Even deeper than the 'leper' comment from earlier. Way down in the pit of my gut, a place I didn't even know was accessible. For a moment, it feels like everything around me stops, and I can't say anything, instead feeling like I've swallowed a golf ball.

When I do look up, I stare fucking daggers into her. "I guess I was right, then." I say, almost as though I'm declaring the sky is blue. "You are a bitch."

She scoffs again. "I am, am I? Fine."

Heading over to the opposite side of the room, she grabs her knapsack from where it's haphazardly been thrown on the beige pleather couch. She hangs one of the straps over her shoulder and turns to face me, eyebrow raised. "It took me a lot of fucking courage to send you that message," she says. "I didn't want to come back here. I didn't ever want to go back to the last place I hung with Devon. But I knew I owed him a birthday, and I missed you, and I wanted to make up. But all of this? So not worth it. I'm out of here. I'll celebrate Devon on my own."

I'm almost not even given opportunity to reply to this—she's that quick to move, and by the time her words finally register in my brain, she's already halfway out the door. I have to dart to follow her at an acceptable pace, an intensely confusing panic rising in my chest as I do. This makes no sense. If I'm so mad at her, why don't I want her to leave? Why am I not jumping for joy like I would've been when I first got here?

I don't understand it, but I chase her, anyways, grabbing onto her wrist right before she steps out the door. "Logan, wait." I shake my head, my voice cracking unexpectedly. "Please... please don't. We said we'd do this. For Devon."

"Yeah, and then you started dredging up all this fucking shit." Her eyes narrow at me. "I'm not doing it. I won't. Get out of my way."

"Lo, I'm so—"

"Oh, save it. You weren't sorry then, you're not sorry now, and I'm not dealing with this. Move." She bumps herself against my shoulder, successfully moving me from her path and stepping out onto the Harrington's front porch.

The moment the door opens, rain starts assaulting us. It's still a monsoon outside, storming harder than I've ever seen on the island and painting the sky an angry dark grey that seems to match the argument perfectly. All the palm trees lining the driveway are swaying as though they're damn near about to fall, tilting this way and that in a rapid fashion. Lo barely takes another look at me as she pulls her hood over her head, the familiar chirp of her Sedan's unlock sound following only a second later. A sinking feeling washes over me.

I just fucking did it, didn't I?

She's about to leave.

I fully expect her to race out of here like we're at a NASCAR event, leaving so fast I won't even know what's hit me. As she nears where she parked, though, all I see is her crouching, lifting a hand to shield her face from the wind and the storm. Sunny (yes, Logan's one of those weirdos who names their car) chirps again, but the headlights aren't visible, and as I take a closer inspection, I realize I can't see anything but a huge mass of pine needles and leaves.

Sunny chirps a third time.

"Uh, Logan?" I cup my hands around my mouth, trying to amplify myself as she disappears into the whirlwind. "Everything... everything okay?"

No response comes for a good thirty or so seconds. It's like she's completely disappeared, somehow melding right into the swirl of wind and God knows what else. A pit of concern grows in my stomach, but like an idiot (and a coward), I just stand frozen, waiting for her to show back up.

A minute goes by. I still don't see or hear anything.

Groaning, I wrap my sweatshirt tighter around my body. Well, that's great.

Guess I'm going out into a massive fucking rain storm.

"Logan?" I raise my voice as I move closer to the driveway. "Hey, are you alright? I can't see you. Tell me where you a—"

Thankfully, Logan reappears just as I'm about to step off the porch. Completely drenched and wearing a most un-Logan-like scowl, she gets back under shelter, scowling at me as she does. The anger's so intense it practically radiates off her, but more prominent than that is the exhaustion now etched all over her face, like every remaining ounce of energy she had was just sucked right out.

I wait as she shrugs off her sweatshirt.

"Damn tree's fallen on Sunny." She runs a hand down the length of her face, making it clear this is the last thing she wants to deal with. "It's totally smashed. I can't go anywhere. I'll have to call AAA, and I'm sure they're not going to want to come all the way out here in the middle of the storm. Looks like..." She lets out a groan, not at all dissimilar to the one that just escaped from me. "Shit. Looks like I'm spending the night here, after all."

I reach out to grab her knapsack for her. "Sorry. That sucks." I shake my head, awkwardly stepping to the side so she can come back in the house.

Rubbing the back of my neck once I've shut the door, I cough a little. Shit. Now, I've got to prepare myself for an apology I don't know how to phrase, but need to give, desperately. Even if I don't remember being such a bitch, and even if I didn't mean it, she's absolutely right. The words still came out of my mouth. Worse, they hurt her.

One way or another, I've got to make up for that.

"Uh..." I cough again as she turns towards the staircase. "Logan. I'm... I'm really sorry for... for being so selfish. And such a bitch. I'm... it wasn't fair to you. I'm sorry. And I do want to catch up properly. But I just... I dunno. All of this, it's so har—"

"Okay, so this is what we're not doing." She cuts me off, shaking her head and whirling around on her heels. "Don't think that just because I can't leave, I'm going to forget about all this. You think I'm a bitch. Awesome. Great. I'll be in the guest room all night, then. You won't have to deal with me. And you know what? I'll stay in the room on the other side of the house. You can have the big one. Have your own fucking wing. Just, when my pizza comes later? Leave it outside my door for me, will you?"

I sigh. "Logan, don't do that. Don't shut yourself in your room."

"No, actually, I think that's the perfect thing to do." She shakes her head. "Goodnight, Savannah. And, in case I leave before you wake up in the morning..."

Her eyes line up directly with mine. "Goodbye."

And, with that, she's just up and disappeared.

Again.

IT'S MIDNIGHT WHEN I HEAD TO HER ROOM.

Midnight's an early hour for me. Ordinarily, I don't sleep until around two or three, so I'm kind of surprised when her light's off and the door's locked. I honestly forgot this is around the time most people turn in for the night.

Either way, I knock. I've been going back and forth for hours about whether I should bother her again, and now that I've worked up the courage, I'm not going to chicken out. More importantly, I owe her so much more explanation for everything that happened in high school.

I can't believe how insufferable I was earlier. How I literally attacked her for doing the same exact thing I've done every single day for three years: try to get through the day by any fucking means possible. I mean, God, of course she left for New York. For starters, Charlotte has Devon written all over it. Two, I was such an asshole afterwards. All night long, memories of that time in my life have been flooding back in, and I don't at all come off in an appealing light in them. I didn't just call her a bitch. It wasn't just the name calling, or the arguing, or the disappearing. It was picking fights over petty, petty shit, like the pens she used for her art. It was blaming my bad moods on her. It was bringing up fights we'd gotten over long ago, just so I could prove I'd been in the right all along.

I was a selfish, cold, heartless bitch after Devon. Plain and simple. And when you throw in the kicker? How I told my best friend since the fourth grade I'd have fucking preferred her to die?

I mean, fuck. Who the hell *wouldn't* have left after that?

Coming here makes me feel like the perfect idiot. Inside, I'm screaming, telling myself to quit while I'm ahead, to save myself the heartache of knowing I'm never going to know my best friend again.

Externally, however, I knock again. "Hey, Logan?"

No answer comes for a moment. Obviously, this is what I'm expecting, and though it is kind of disheartening, I stick my hands in my sweatshirt pockets, trying so hard not to let it get to me.

She's pissed, Savannah. You would be, too. You've just got to suck it the fuck up.

"Can, um..." A lump lodges itself in my throat, one that quickly threatens to suffocate me. "Will you come out here? Please? I just... I know there's a lot I need to say. And I get it if you don't want to listen. But you deserve an explanation, and I want to give it to you, and I... fuck, Logan. I'm sorry. I'm really, really sorry. And if you'll let me... I'd love to talk."

Again, I get nothing. The silence becomes deafening, just like it did back in fourth grade, and my chest seems to become infinitely heavier. I really fucking fucked things over, didn't I?

Claire kept warning me this'd happen. That my anger would get out of hand one day, and I'd go too far and say something I couldn't ever come back from. In my head, I always imagined it happening with someone I don't have that close a relationship with, someone dispensable.

The thought of driving Logan away forever is unimaginable

Still, though, I turn to leave. If there's one right move I can make, it's that. I've hurt her enough already. Been enough of a bitch. She needs the space, and by God, will I give it to—

"Sa... Savannah?"

She sniffles loudly from within the room. It's a noise that has me alert in an instant, because I just know it's one that accompanies crying. I take a cautious step forward.

"Are you, um..." I rub my forehead, awkwardness taking over every inch of my body. "Are you alright, Lo?"

This time, the response is almost immediate. She swings the door right open, revealing a tearstained face and a quivering lip. Then, shocking me halfway to death, she wraps me in a tight hug, making the move before I can even process what's going on. With another sniffle, she buries her face in my shoulder.

"It's his birthday," she whispers. "He should be here, Savannah. He should be alive. It's such crap. All it took was one drunk driver. One stupid decision, and he was gone. How is that right?"

I'm still not ready for the Devon talk. Truthfully, I don't know if I'll ever be. But as though my body isn't one with my brain anymore, I find myself hugging back all the same, rubbing my hands up and down her back. "It's fucking bull. I'm so pissed. Still." A small, bitter chuckle sounds from me. "All this time later, and I'm still just as mad as I was when I first found out. Honestly, I don't think I'll ever stop. I'd do fucking anything to kill that fucker."

She lets out a bitter laugh of her own. "Me too."

A shuddery breath escapes me, and as I pull away from Lo, I brush my hair away from my face, looking right at her. "I'm so sorry, Logan. For what I said to you. For how awful I was. For all of it. I..." I shake my head. "God. There's no excuse. I was an asshole, and I'm sorry, and you deserved so much better. Never in a million years would I have wanted you to be in that accident over him. That's a choice I could never make. I just... it's like I said—I was taking a lot of the bullshit I was feeling about myself out on you. And I'm so sorry."

She gives me a small smile. "Maybe I shouldn't have been trying so hard to reminisce with dinner. I promise it wasn't supposed to be Devon related. It just felt... wrong, not having our usual meal. Like, we were messing this up somehow. So, I... I don't know. I'm sorry I dredged up those feelings so soon."

I give a very slight shrug. "I need to face them, anyways." Looking to my feet, I hold back another shuddery breath. "I've, uh... I've been hiding from that for way too long. From a lot of shit, really. I... what you said tonight... when you told me what *I* said..." This time, I scoff. "I'm the bitch, Logan. Not you. I'm sorry."

She glances down. "I never meant for you to feel like I abandoned you. I didn't want to hurt you more. Swear. I just couldn't handle being in Charlotte after he was gone. I was drowning, and I needed to get out. But breaking up with you the way I did... I should've gone easier with the whole thing. It's like you said. I should've known you were hurting. I should've been nic—"

"No. No, don't you dare try to apologize for me being selfish and a needy little shit." I squeeze her wrist. "We were eighteen. You'd lost Devon, too. You did the right thing. For both of us. I'm just..."

Another golf-ball-sized lump rises in my throat. "It scares the shit out of me to think about losing people," I say, blinking as tears start to drip down my cheeks. "It's what scares me the most since Mom and Dad. It's, like, something is closing in on me if the thought even enters my mind. And you know me when I'm scared—I don't get sad; I get angry. So, I... that's what I was doing. I was mad because I felt like I was losing you. I knew I was. But I went too far, and I was a huge bitch, and I never should've said what I said. And I'm so fucking sorry that's what you think when you see my face."

She squeezes *my* wrist now. "It was a really, really bad time. For all of us.

And even if you don't think I need to be sorry... I do. Because, yeah, maybe you didn't say the nicest things. But that was senior year. We met in the fourth grade. It shouldn't have been so abrupt. And I should've at least left the door open to talk. It shouldn't have been three years later, and only for Devon."

I look at her properly. "You were suffocating. And I was insufferable."

"But I loved you." She lets out a bitter, slightly incredulous chuckle. "That's the stupidest part of all of this. Even when everything went down, I was so in love with you. That's when you're supposed to be the most dedicated to making it work—when you love someone. And I almost did, too. I almost didn't call you that night. I went back and forth so many times before I picked up my phone. But, in the end, it just seemed... easier. If I broke things off, it wouldn't hurt anymore. Only, I was so wrong. Even as I said what I said, I knew it was wrong. I just knew I couldn't go back."

I rub the back of my neck. "You... you loved me?"

She laughs again. "Is that really what you got from all that?"

"Sorry. Sorry. I just... we never said it. Not in that way. It was always... I-love-you-because-we're-best-friends love."

"Of course I loved you, Savannah." Her eyes glimmer with tears. "I still do. But it was all so damn hard."

I smile a little—a super sad smile. "You can say that again. And, um..." Clearing my throat, I drop my voice an octave. "I still love you, too. Even if I know for sure I've been too much of a bitch to deserve it."

We stare at each other for a moment now. Apparently, we've run out of things to say, and once the heaviness between us becomes way too prominent, Lo gestures to the bag of these peanut butter/chocolate squares I've got in hand—our favorite candy since forever.

"You, uh... want to go call a truce?" She asks. "Talk all this out? Because, um... eating my feelings... it sounds like the exact kind of thing I need right now."

I hold the chocolate up almost as though it's a trophy, feeling my grin widen slightly. "Sure as hell didn't bring it up here for nothing. C'mon. Deck chat?"

She grins back—a grin I haven't seen since high school. "Yeah. Deck chat."

WE START THE TRUCE BENEATH A STAR-FILLED, GORGEOUS, NAVY BLUE SKY.

Hilton Head's storm has cleared up just for the two of us, it seems.

"I failed out this year." My voice drops to a whisper as Lo settles down beneath me, and I avoid looking at her, instead opting to tug at a loose string hanging off my sweatshirt sleeve. "At Winthrop. Spring semester came, and I... I dropped the ball. I don't know. Part of me didn't want to do anything anymore. That's, uh... that's a really big problem for me these days. Claire says it's depression. I don't want to do anything, so I don't. And this semester... I don't know. It caught up with me. A little too late, probably."

"Oh, Sav." Logan reaches for the chocolate bag, unwrapping a piece and sticking it in her mouth. Tossing the wrapper back in, she looks at me. "Wait. Spring semester? But when I sent you that message, you said—"

"Yeah, I know what I said." I shake my head, internally kicking myself for going on and on about how I was happily a member of Winthrop's LGBTQ/ally association, and their choral group had never sounded better until I came along. My gaze travels to my feet. "You seem so happy back in New York. I guess I felt like I had to pretend I was, too. To, like, make it seem like I could still get along fine on my own. I don't know. It was stupid. I'm sorry."

She surprises me by reaching for and squeezing my hand. Again, it's one of those gestures I became accustomed to in high school—this was how we always comforted each other back then—but that feels so different tonight. We're in different places. We're different people. It's hard to connect something so familiar to a life that now feels so damn foreign.

But I smile a little at Logan, anyways. "I'm glad you got out of Charlotte," I say. "You seem so much happier in New York. And, hey, one of us actually did what we said we'd do. That's a fifty-percent success rate. Go us."

A sad expression comes to her face. "Savannah... it's not like you're not successful. You know that, right? Depression, it sucks. It's a mental illness. Emphasis on *illness*. It totally changes you. The way you think. The way you do stuff."

I take my own piece of chocolate. "Claire thinks I should go to therapy. She keeps pushing me. And I know I should. It's not just being sad that's my problem—it's all the anger, too. You've seen that side of me more than anyone else. But I just... I don't know. I should, but it's scary."

She squeezes my hand tighter. "I get that. I should probably see one myself. Trust me, I'm no stranger to depression."

I swivel so I'm facing her better. "You? But you're... Perky Asshat Logan."

She laughs. It's soft, it's brief, and I almost don't catch it, but at the last moment, I do. Out of the corner of my eye, I watch her rub a hand down the length of her face, lips curling into a slight grin. "You want to know the truth about New York?"

"You actually do have a Mr. or Mrs. Logan and you just didn't want to tell me?"

"God, no." She snorts, straightening up and taking the bag from me again. Taking two pieces this time, she pops them both in and says through a mouthful of chocolate, "I've got nobody even close to the realm of a Mr. or Mrs. Logan. I told you; I'm trying to fast-track my degree. Get out of there as soon as possible. Besides my roommate, I talk to maybe three other people, and that's on a super limited basis. And even when I do talk to Hayley—that's my roommate—we talk about the most basic things. Rent. Bills. How her waitressing job is going, or if I want to maybe order a pizza on Friday. Stupid, small stuff like that. It's lonely in New York, Sav. Really, really lonely."

I feel my eyebrows furrow. "But, on all your social media—"

"Sav. That's social media." She gives me a pointed look. "All the stuff I post, I post to make Mom less nervous. You know how she was when I got in—the moment I told her, she started giving me all these reasons why New York is the worst place on earth to go to college. I had to spend months convincing her I'd be fine. Then, when I got there... it wasn't anything it was cracked up to be. Like, the people are cool, and the classes are awesome, but for someone like me, it's so lonely. I'm not eclectic like any of the people in my major. I didn't have this awesome life before New York. I'm just average, and over there, 'average' gets you nothing but wishing you'd have read up a little more on what social life is like at your new school so you didn't spend every night in your apartment, wishing you could talk to someone who probably hates your guts."

The hair on the back of my neck stands up. What she's saying, it's way too familiar for my liking. I know that loneliness. I know that yearning. I know it so well, I'm probably more used to it than the sight of the back of my own damn hand. It's what I've felt on a pretty much constant basis ever since Devon passed and everything with Lo and me went down.

It's painful in a way I'd never want anyone else to ever, ever have to feel.

And here Lo is, describing it more perfectly than I ever could.

"But..." I hug my legs tighter. "Wait. You've really been missing me that much? The whole... 'wishing you could talk to someone who probably hates your guts' thing—that's how you've been feeling about me? Even after what I said? Even after how... shitty I was?"

"Come on." She nudges me. "Of course I've been missing you that much. I meant what I said about regretting breaking up the moment it happened. You were only like that after Devon died. It's not like you're some terrible person—you were hurting. And so was I. And like I said, I ran. But it was the stupidest thing I could've done. You're the best friend I've ever had. Kind of the only friend besides Devon. I've wanted to pick up the phone and call you so many times since graduation. I just... I don't know. I always psyched myself out."

More tears drip down my cheeks. "I wish you would've called."

"God. Me too."

We stare at each other again. This time, it seems like a million unspoken words and feelings are passing between us. Like we're caught in our own continuum and nothing else even matters. The trance seems to last forever.

"Sav?" Logan scoots a little closer, brushing her knees against mine. She turns to face me, reaching out to tuck a strand of hair behind my ear. "It's been hell not having you around. It's been hell always having to think about what it could be like if you were. All of it, it's been hell. I'm so sorry I let things end the way they did."

The bastard tears make a comeback. I don't even realize it, either—not until Lo's got her thumb on my cheek, brushing one of them away before she leans in and places a soft kiss to my temple. All in an instant, my body goes into overdrive. A tingling sensation runs from the bottom of my spine all the way to my fingers and toes. Flutters go haywire in my stomach. The smell of her strawberry shampoo reminds me so much of our past that I lose all inhibition just like that. My hands take on a life of their own, and I cup her face in my hands, pressing a soft kiss directly to her lips.

She sinks into it. I do, too. We don't pull away for at least a minute—maybe longer—and the entire time, the world around us seems to fade into some kind of background realm. The wind previously breezing against us can't be felt anymore. I don't notice how it's grown chilly anymore. All that's in front of me is Lo, and she's the only damn thing I care about.

She starts giggling once we finally do break apart. Those small, girlish titters I heard all the time in high school, accompanied by a wide grin spreading across her lips. "So, am I an asshole for saying the whole reason I made this into a weekend celebration instead of just one night was because I was hoping this'd happen?"

I can't help but join in with the giggling. "Oh, you did? It had nothing to do with Devon always wanting a huge celebration for his twenty-first? Is that what I'm supposed to believe?"

"Okay, so part of it was that. But the other part? The more major part?" Her eyes soften. "You. This. You don't know how much I wished this would be a thing."

"Yeah? You mean that?"

Lo leans in for another kiss. Briefer, this time, but somehow filled with something that was missing before. "Of course I mean it. We're Sav and Lo. We belong together. Even if we're both idiots from time to time."

The tingling spreads throughout my whole body. Something about hearing this—something about her being the one to say it—means more to me than the fact I thought the same things all on my own God only knows how many times before. When we were younger, Lo and I always said we lived on the same wavelength. The things she thought about the world, I thought, too, and every so often, we'd be able to finish each other's sentences even if we were talking about the most random subject ever. It was like we just fit together, like meeting in fourth grade was some predestined sort of shit.

But I thought we lost that after everything that happened. I thought we lost everything we once had—we weren't two sides of the same coin anymore, but strangers on different continents.

And, god fucking dammit, I find the tears pushing their boundaries a little more as I try to think of a good response. When I come up empty, though—because of course I come up empty—I just lean into her. Heavily.

"Are you sure you're not just saying this because of the moment?" I glance up at her. "Because… I can't do this if you are."

"No. Absolutely not. Sav, I… I can't say it enough. I *missed* you. I missed you so much, it hurt. Like, there was this physical, awful pang in my heart, and I honestly wanted to stab myself in the chest just to see if maybe that'd make it go away."

Another laugh escapes me. "I'm glad you didn't."

"Me too. Would've been messy. And goddamned expensive. ER trips in New York are no joke. They cost an arm and a leg just to walk through the door." She wraps an arm around me, kissing the top of my head. "I don't know what's been going on with you. You barely know what's been going on with me. But, Sav… I can't stop talking to you again. I can't."

I move away slightly, but only so I can look at her. Grabbing her hand again, I reply, "I don't think I can do that, either."

It's her turn to cup my face this time, and when she leans in for another kiss, it lasts longer, runs deeper, and seems to totally cast aside any and all anger or despair or doubt about me and Lo trying to be the me and Lo of senior year again.

Once more, the world dissipates. Once more, she's the only thing I can focus on.

We start moving back into the house, mouths pressed together like they're two pieces to a puzzle we've been trying and failing to solve for longer than either of us can remember. I don't even realize it's happening until we're in the Harrington's guest room, but just like that, the door is shutting behind us, and Lo and I are suddenly even closer than I could have ever hoped we'd be again.

AFTER A HEAVEN-FILLED, WONDROUS NIGHT, I WAKE TO PANCAKES IN BED.

Golden sunlight streams in through the window. The smell of coffee instantly wafts to my nose. Lo appears in an oversized T-shirt—*my* oversized T-shirt—and her pink hair is disheveled and knotted, but in a way that works for her. She doesn't look like a slob; she looks relaxed.

Setting a tray with food over my lap, she leans in and kisses me again. "I hope you know you were snoring and it annoyed the hell out of me."

I smile, pulling her into the spot at my side and squeezing her shoulder. "Yet, I don't seem to recall you whacking me with a pillow. Which, you know, would've been the thing to do if it really bothered you that much."

"I was too tired. And, besides, shouldn't you be mindful of that sort of thing when you're sleeping next to someone? God, Savannah. How inconsiderate."

Taking a small sip of the coffee, I raise an eyebrow. "Hope you can forgive me."

"Mm. I'll think about it." She reaches and plucks a strawberry off my plate, folding her legs crisscross-applesauce style. "Does that mean you slept good, though?"

I smile. "Yeah, actually. I did. You?"

"I didn't sleep too much. I wanted to look at you instead."

"Ugh, okay, this just went from 'sweet' to 'creepy' real fast." I sit up a little straighter, groaning as I do because there's this weird, awful kink in my neck. Lo's eyebrows furrow slightly.

"You good?"

"Neck cramp."

"Ah, what I was made for fixing." She starts massaging my neck without my even having to ask, and as she does, I set the tray over to the side, sitting even taller and turning my head so we can meet for another kiss. We both lean into it with all we have, Lo somehow managing to keep up with the massage, and she's damn near beaming as we pull away.

"So, uh... this means Savgan is a thing again, right? I'm just trying to make sure I'm not reading into something that's not there."

"Oh, my God. Savgan?"

"You don't like our ship name? I spent a lot of time trying to come up with it." She laughs. "Seriously, though. What does all this... what does it mean? Are we back together? We don't hate each other anymore? Are we going to have to do the long-distance thing that I already know you're going to suck at because you never answered my texts even back in high school?"

"First off? Don't think we ever truly hated each other. We're both just way too stubborn for our own good. Two—"

"Okay, can't argue with that one."

"Well, of course you can't. I'm always right." I smirk. "Two? I'm so not interested in the whole long-distance thing. Mainly because I so don't want you back in New York."

She scoots around so she's sitting in front of me rather than right next to me. "I love all my classes there. I mean, it's lonely, but... I don't think I can leave."

I look down. "I'd be lying if I said I didn't want you to. But... hell, we've been through worse than having to deal with some long distance. If you're up for that headache, I am, too. Because, fuck, Lo... last night was amazing."

Her grin widens. "It was, wasn't it?"

"Better than I could've ever even dreamed of. By a longshot." I take her hands in mine. "Plus, even if it's not something I want, maybe the distance will be good for us at first. Maybe I'll finally listen to Claire—"

"That'd be a first," she mutters.

I roll my eyes. "Don't be an ass. But, I mean it. I need to fix this. Fix myself. So, I will. I'll find a therapist when I get back home. Finally start sorting through all this shit. Because the last thing I want is to turn into Monster Savannah again."

Logan laughs. "Is that what we're calling her? Monster Savannah?"

"Most fitting name, don't you think?" Now, I kiss her hands. "I want to be better. I do. Being such an ass all the time is so exhausting. So... I'll try. Put the distance to good use. I mean, I've kind of got no choice—my only alternative is complaining."

"And, God, would that be in a pain in the ass over the phone."

I laugh. Kiss her hands again. "Don't make me rethink this whole thing."

"Like you'd even dream of it." She mimics my eye roll, sighing a little as she leans back. "Maybe I should put the distance to good use, too. Actually make some genuine friends in New York. Actually do the college thing right."

I raise an eyebrow. "Wouldn't that be a first?"

She just chuckles and leans in to kiss my cheek. I rest my head on her shoulder.

"I've really missed Savgan," I whisper. "Like, way more than I even realized."

"Same here."

A small silence settles between us. She's just staring down at me, and I'm just looking up at her, and it seems like we're both trying to figure out exactly what this all means. But, as she hugs me a little closer, she whispers, "We're wrecks when we don't talk to each other. We can't go back to that."

I laugh. "It's not something we can afford, is it?"

"Not by a longshot." She tucks strands of hair behind both my ears. "So, that means Savgan is back on, right?"

"Is this seriously how you're asking me to be your girlfriend for the second time?"

"What, not romantic enough?"

I only roll my eyes, leaning in for another kiss. This time, it seems to be understood I'm not intending to pull away for quite a while, and we work together to make sure the pancakes and everything else are safely cleared from our path before falling away together once more.

It's pure bliss, the whole entire morning. Me, Logan, and nothing else but the sound of the waves crashing and wind breezing through the open window. The outside world doesn't exist. Everything that hurts doesn't exist. There's no pain, no anger, none of the awful, suffocating feelings that've been consuming me—consuming both of us—for three years straight. In fact, it's almost as though those feelings were never there in the first place.

When we fall back asleep, tangled together in a fuzzy down comforter, I'm freer than ever. Even if nothing is completely fixed yet. Even if it'll be a long time before we get there.

For now, we're together again.

That more than makes up for everything else.

ABOUT ANNA-MARIE LOPEZ

Anna-Marie Lopez has been writing on and off for practically her entire life. As a child, she could be found filling notebook after notebook, and teachers always said she had a passion for storytelling. Now a young adult, she fully intends to put that talent to good use. If you ever meet her, it's all but guaranteed she's thinking about her writing. The only time that's not the case is when she's working towards her psychology degree, and even that's (somewhat) being done with the hopes she'll be inspired for a bestseller.

In her down time, Anna-Marie is a self-proclaimed musical theater "obsessionist", as well as a candle hoarder and incense addict. What can she say? Aromatherapy is one of her favorite things. Born and raised in the beautiful state of North Carolina, she also enjoys nice weather, spending time with her family, and trying not to go crazy in her house filled with three dogs and three cats.

Writer and psychologist in the making, look forward to an Anna-Marie Lopez original coming soon!

EVEN THE WEEDS SAY LET HER GO

BY SAM TRATHEN

Even the Weeds Say Let Her Go is about a young woman, hiding out with her man during a very personal war. Despite the love and care Boru gives her, Myre can't help but dream of someone else-- someone she has never even seen before. Does he dream of her too?

I

The bonny boy in the woods was hunting, Myre dreamt. Chasing the wild deer through the wild wood-- fleet as hound, quiet as a hare. He took his kill with careful ease, shut the deer's eyes, kissed her head like a mother lying her child down for a nap, and dragged her away. She followed him from a distance so he wouldn't see her, wouldn't know that she was watching him.

A fey breeze picked up his muddy-brown curls and tousled them with love. The deer was laid out in the open field, where a bit of sun could peep in and give him the light he needed to butcher her properly. Myre watched as he took out his belt knife-- a simple, iron thing with a single engraving she could read: *May all your wounds be mortal.* The knife licked the deer's white belly from neck to tailand slit her open. Her bonny hunting lad turned his strange eyes her way, his narrow body twisting like a sailor's rope, making her heart swell. The heavy, copper scent of blood turned Myre's stomach, but she knew, instinctively, he wouldn't nick the intestine and release that fouler scent. She trusted him, even as her belly roiled.

"Worry not! I'll leave you your share," he whispered, with a heart-wrenching smile. And then, he went back to his business, sitting on his knees and drawing the knife across the buck's belly.

And Myre? She closed her eyes and went back to her waking life.

2

She woke up to nothing.

Well, there was a cottage, to be sure. There was food in the pantry and thick, heavy furs on the bed. She wore a nightgown made of soft, red linen. No more wool. No, wool was from before. Boru did everything to make her feel comfortable, and that had included getting rid of the wool, which made her hot and itchy. Comfort. The linen was light-weight and comfortable, sure. But it also reminded her that she was here-- far away from home, locked in, sick, perhaps?

No, not sick. Just missing half the time. Sometimes more than half. Last night, she'd wandered the hundreds of miles home, back to the Hunt and the wildwood. She'd seen her bonny hunting lad. Too sweet-faced to be a beguin to her. Not like Boru.

When she thought of Boru, her heart swelled and she brought clean, sharp air into her lungs. But the instant her head began to spin, she had to stop it.

Feel the earth beneath your toes, her father would say. *Don't get lost. Feel your body, listen to what it needs. Food, water, comfort. Then feel your emotions and tend to their needs, too. Small, brief steps back to Myre. Don't go all the way down the path, no matter which way it's going. Don't follow them forever and get lost. Don't get lost.*

Where was Boru?

Hunting, said one train of thought. Not just for meat, either, but the herbs that kept her head from swimming away, more furnishings for the cottage too, probably.

He's fed up with you and left forever, said another. She didn't hear them as voices in her head, no. They were both thoughts that came from her, from somewhere deep inside that she could not control. Myre struggled to figure out which one to listen to, just as the door opened.

"Love," said Boru, seeing her awake. "Alright?"

Tall and handsome, like a sycamore tree was Boru. Neat dark hair, too thick to curl and nearly black. His eyes were so deep a blue, they, too, nearly seemed black. There was a bristling of little hairs on his cheeks and chin, and when he stopped to kiss her, they scratched Myre's lips and brought her, tingling, all the way back to her body. He smelled of the rain and of the world besieged by it. A nice enough smell.

She smiled at him, narrow shoulders deflating carefully. "Yes, alright."

"Good. There's coney drying on the racks outside. And that nice fellow from the town, remember him? Uh," he was always bad with names and he chewed over a few possible ones while she watched his broad face work, "well anyway, he brought us some vegetables in exchange for a few pelts. Reckon I can cook up a stew, keep you nice and warm."

"You know how to cook?" she asked, dumbly. But a look of pain crossed over Boru's face, tightened his wide lips until they were nearly invisible. "What's wrong?"

"You ask me that every day," he said, finally closing the door behind him and waking over to sit on the bed next to her. "I'm not mad. I just wonder what else you are forgetting. And why we can't seem to make it stick." He reached forward and took her tiny, pale, and pointed chin in the crook between his thumb and forefinger, then ran that forefinger on the bottom of her chin, tickling her neck. "My Myrebird."

He always made her feel so small. Not like a little girl, but like something precious and fine. Like a dragonfly's wing. Or the bud of butterfly weed. Too perfect and precious for this world. She curled to his touch like a cat in search of a scratch and shut her cucumber-green eyes.

"I'm trying," she whispered. "I remembered why we're here."

"Oh?"

"Surely you know!"

"Of course I know," he moved his hand to her ear and then ran his long fingers through her tangled hair. When it caught and snagged, embarrassment flared in her heart, but he merely reached over to the bedside table and withdrew the prickly brush. "Come here, little bird." She turned her back obediently and he knelt on the bed, then set to brushing out the snarls with such tender care, she felt nothing. Myre was never this kind to her own hair, knew you had to struggle and fight to get it to the state it was supposed to be. Her mother's blood had blessed her with such thick, curly, copper locks-- the sort that every girl in court once envied, but Myre doubted any had the patience to put up with them. She certainly didn't. "But it seems the more you say things, the more they stick. So, say it, love."

"It's too warm for stew," she whispered, closing her eyes and relishing in his touch. "It's summer, for the sake of the bones beneath the hills! Time for fresh greens and cold bread, butter sitting in ice and salt."

If she could have seen his face, she would realize how sad her love looked. She also might have seen the snowflakes melting from his hair. But she didn't.

3

The next time Myre awoke, Boru was lying next to her, bare-chested and warm. In his hands was one of the old books her father had given him-- one of the ones about war. The book's spine was making an indent on his chest, pushing the thick, dark hair to the side, growing redder and redder. Myre sat up to get a better look at him, and he spared her a glance. The smell of rain was gone, replaced by the musk of man. Once, she'd liked that scent, especially the smell of Boru. But now, it seemed oppressive and dank. Too heavy for her little nose.

"How are you feeling?" he asked, before turning his eyes back to her.

"I dreamt of him."

"Of your bonny lad in the woods?" She nodded and her hair, which she noticed was either still snarled or had gone back to snarling in her sleep, bounced up and down. "Hm. What's he up to now? Staying safe in these trying times, I hope?"

"Oh," she whispered, then nodded, childlike. "I think he's alright, I do. He's smart. I can see it in his eyes. And he's always got a big dog with him." She grinned. "One of your dogs. So you know he's safe."

At the door, a massive, black hound thudded its tail against the wall, pleased to be acknowledged. She looked up at Myre with big, brown eyes and shook her head so that her long, curling horns wobbled back and forth.

"Safer than us. That's something, I guess," Boru turned the page of the book, and Myre felt a strange burst of giddiness at the noise the paper made against his skin. "But how are you, my girl?"

"I'm fine. I feel... happy. Every time I see him. I can't explain it."

Boru set the book down on its front-- a crime that would make her father shit his trews--using his bare chest as a bookmark. "You love him, you do?"

"Yes."

"You want to go to him?" There was no sadness in his voice. Just a query.

"I wish I could. But I think I can only do it in dreams." She sat back on her knobbly legs, the red linen nightdress catching around her belly. She tugged it straight. "It's not like you." *Not like I love you, I mean*, she finished in thought, forgetting he couldn't hear those. "It's different. I want to *hold* him."

"You know we can't leave here, Myrebird," Boru whispered, and now he was taking the book up again. But instead of returning his eyes to the old, yellowed page, he untied the yellow ribbon around his wrist and set it between them, then set the book on the crooked bedside table. Myre had never realized when she was growing up in the Hunt's keep how lucky it was to have nice furniture. She wondered if Boru'd made that crooked little table, or if it was a relic, left over from the peat farmer who they'd purchased the cottage from. Sure, Boru was never meant to be a carpenter! He was a warrior. A protector! "We can't just up and go, seeking your dream lad, bonny though he might be." He said it so gently, so without jealousy. A lesser man would scowl at the very mention of another. And then there was the *we*, too. Other men wouldn't consider the *we*. They would think the very mention of another, handsome love meant that *we* became *she* and *I*. But Myre thought nothing of it, either.

"I know. I have to get better."

"We have to keep you safe," Boru whispered his careful correction. He reached over and took her hands, pulling her onto his lap. "There's big things going on out there right now."

"There's a war," she whispered. He sighed and nodded. "Because of me?"

"Your sister--" no, that wasn't the right word for her. Myre saw it in his eyes, "--the Queen. She wanted to sell you off to Carren. Remember? And take me as her champion." Jealousy. That's why there was no hint of it in Boru. The emotion now turned his stomach, made him as nauseous as she'd been, back in the beginning.

"She wanted to make me a bride," Myre filled in, sliding her bare thighs around his hips. She felt the heat of his body beneath the blankets. "But not to you."

"If you want to go back to that, my bird, my ghost, I'll take you. In a heartbeat. But it wasn't what you wanted. Not then. Say the word, if it is now. If it's changed."

"No," she whispered. "I want to be here with you." Her voice cracked.

Boru and his dark, stag's eyes. He was incapable of even thinking of a lie. She trusted him with every ounce of her being. And yet, why did the bonny hunting lad speak to her so? "People are going to die for that."

"Yes. But not you. They're choosing to die. Your father wouldn't march them if they didn't. He'd storm the Hold all by himself if he had to." Myre reached up and touched Boru's thin line of a mouth. He wanted to be there with him, she could see. Didn't want to be stuck here with her-- but someone had to keep her safe, didn't they? She couldn't do it by herself anymore. She thought again of the touseling breeze that rustled the bonny hunting lad's hair. Thought of his fey eyes, the dappling of freckles all over his cheeks and nose.

"I don't want him to die," she whimpered.

"He's strong, your father," Boru whispered, putting their heads together. Dark blue met silvery green. "You know he's far too clever for Death to catch."

4

He was sleeping beneath the stars. His long, graceful fingers curled into the fur of his massive, black dog. His bow and hunting knife were within arm's reach. But even as Myre tiptoed through his little camp, her bonny hunting lad didn't startle, wake, and attack. He slept on, peaceful as a baby. Around him, even in the moonless night, she saw little red flowers growing like a wreath around him. Butterfly weed. That's what they were called. She recalled it like she might have recalled her name in a previous life. Butterfly weed.

This was as close as she'd ever gotten to him. Usually, she'd stand on a bluff or plateau and watch him and the hound (almost shoulder-height to him and he was far from small!), wind their way along the hills and highlands, bow in hand in case a coney managed to dart along, or a lone witch's horse stalked out to threaten them with teeth.

Myre's red, linen nightdress was gone. In place of it, she wore a stark, white sheet, wound about her body as if it were a curtain rail. Her red hair, long and freshly washed and brushed as it never was in life, lay over her shoulders like a cape. Her feet were bare, but the bracken hurt them not. She seemed to know just how to step to avoid their prickers and stickers. The hem of the shroud didn't even catch them as she approached at a near-run.

"I just want to see your face," she whispered to the sleeping lad. "I want to see it up close. I have this silly notion, you see, that your freckles match the stars above. I want to see if I can find the hunting cat constellation. Then I might find my way home. Or at least, to you."

The boy didn't move nor respond. She took that as permission to get close.

She approached his side, searching out the heat of his body with her small hands, as she often did when trying to find Boru in the dark after a nightmare. But this one, he was so pale, his skin seemed to absorb the starlight and reflect it, like a mirror hit by a sunbeam, almost too blinding to look upon. But she found the girth of his ropey arms, found the smell of his leather and wool kit, and beneath it, nearly hidden beneath the smell of the wild that clung to him, that alluring scent of man. She found the sigil of the one-horned stag, pinning his woolen cloak like a blanket around him. Funny. There'd never been a one-horned stag in the Hunt. Not that she knew of.

"Are you one of my father's warriors?" she asked the sleeping boy, reaching down to touch the copper emblem. Sure enough, it was cold with the night air. "Did you earn this merit in some battle recently, for me? Do you not have a mother to tell you, there's no use going to war over a woman who will never hold you nor kiss you?" The sleeping lad said nothing. She touched the wool then, felt its tiny fingers cling to her own.

And then she saw it. He turned his head and where there ought to be a left ear, there was nothing but a hole and the tiny, pink, worm of a scar.

The black dog rolled over and kicked its long, powerful legs, chasing an invisible grimalkin, no doubt. The boy gave a sleeper's hum and went with his pup, snuggling down closer into her ruff, pressing a cheek to her fur.

"Is this how you got your sigil?" she asked, brushing his hair (warm and kitten-soft) aside to get a better look at it. "Did this happen to you because of me?" Grief overcame her, that so rare a lad should suffer in her stead! All because she didn't want to go over the sea and be a bride? Because she didn't want to surrender her Boru to the Queen, who demanded his loyalty and love? As was her right, as Queen?

"A champion's contract is but three years," she told the sleeping lad, in a cracking voice. "He could be home before long. But I..." a marriage contract, whether to Boru or to some unknown, foreign face in Carren, was forever. Just like a missing ear. "You've given this up in sacrifice to me," she told her sleeping friend, "and yet I am no goddess, no force of nature deserving of it." Her voice hitched in her throat and she began to weep, not as a woman grown weeps but as a bairn weeps, for want of a mother. Desire for the comfort that comes in being set down in a crib, to sleep the night through with the worries of tomorrow left to just that-- tomorrow.

Her tears speckled his upturned cheek, adding texture to his freckles. The boy hummed again in his sleep and brought a hand to his cheek, brushing away her tears without any concern, then went back to his own dreaming.

Just like the months in the cottage, time passed without count. And eventually, Myre's sobs subsided. Strength came to her again, and she drew herself up, puffing out her narrow chest, bringing herself, step-by-step, back to Myre.

"Who are you? And worse, who are you to me?" she warned him. "I love Boru more than I love my own skin. But you're enchanting me. Like one of the folk from the hollow hills. Why must you haunt me? Am I not tormented enough?"

The sleeper murmured a wordless agreement.

If he were a ghost, she thought she'd heard somewhere, he wouldn't have a heartbeat. He might be able to hum and murmur in his sleep, but he'd have no heart beat, surely? Myre drew her hand back, then set her own glowing, pale hand on the middle of his chest, on his sternum, searching out the heavy and comforting thuds beneath the wool.

Several things happened then, and all at once:

She saw herself, from the boy's eyes. Felt his wakening, the clasping of his hands down on her own, saw her own stricken face; her wide, green eyes; her stringy, lank hair. She felt the punch to the chest that knocked him, sitting, into a breathless wheeze.

Then, she saw the two of them from the point of a mysterious third party-- felt the kindling in his arms, felt the heart-stopping terror at the sight before them. She felt the kindling fall to the ground, hit his knee on the way down, felt herself spread his legs into a run across the little camp. She even heard the thoughts of this interloper: *get away from him!* And, *we'll deal with your kind no longer! Haunt him no more!*

And Myre, for her part? She turned into a barn owl and flew away.

5

After that, Myre didn't dream of her bonny hunting lad for some time. How long, she knew not, for the days no longer had any meaning. Time no longer had any meaning nor measurement, save in the form of a beard. Boru's chin scruff came and went. For a while, it grew into a full beard-- not as it'd been when they were younger, patchy and stringy like sprouts, but full and thick and beautiful. When they made love, she tangled her fingers in it, kissed his sweat away from it.

And then, one day, it was gone. He was fresh-faced and beautiful, and she kissed the bare chin over and over, like a friend she hadn't seen in a long, long time.

But that was all Myre knew of the passing of time in the cottage.

6

One day, in some unknown season, Boru came home from his daily rovings with a package for her. He'd been gone all day. Lately, he'd been able to do that. She no longer thought he'd left her, gone home to the Hunt empty-handed, to tell her father she was no longer worth the effort of a war. He'd eased those thoughts away from her with careful love, contented her with his long looks and warm hands. Sometimes, she might hear her own voice in the back of her head, warning that he was gone. And yet, somehow, as if it just wasn't loud enough anymore, she was able to dismiss it without so much as a wave of her hand.

And that was a far better gift than any that could come wrapped in parchment paper and a silk, woven bag. Still-- she beamed when he brought the gift out and tore at the paper like a wolverine.

"Paints," he said. "Keep your mind busy. I didn't even think it, but you must be going stir-crazy in here while I'm out. Maybe you could make something nice and pretty for our little home here."

Home. This wasn't a home. It was barely a house. Myre fingered the small, clay pots and the handful of brushes he'd managed to scrounge out of the nearby town. And she smiled. "Aye, I could do that then."

"There wasn't much," Boru said, taking off his boots and pausing while down there to ruffle the dog's ears. "But you're creative. I think you can manage just fine, right, Myrebird?"

"Right," she said, closing the pots and setting them aside, then led him to the bed for a proper thank-you.

She didn't start until the next day, when he was off chasing coney. Myre unwrapped the pigments from each of their parchment wrappings and set them in a line on the ruddy, wooden table, then realigned them according to the limited rainbow-- red, yellow, blue, black, and white. Enough to get along with, sure. They smelled of egg yolk, charcoal, beeswax, and more. And though the smell was powerful, it didn't turn her guts. And that was something.

And that's when she realized the problem.

He hadn't bought her anything to paint on.

No vellum, pot, or tile. The parchment paper was too ripped to be of use. Instead, she turned her eyes around the cottage. The shoddy bowls and cups they used for their sup were creamy with glaze. No paint would stick to them. The furniture was made of rough, uneven wood. It would tear her precious brushes to pieces.

There were the walls, of course-- for a moment, she saw the flowers and greenery she longed to cover them in growing and crawling all over, filling them with color. A hazy memory of the butterfly weed crowded around the bonny hunting lad's sleeping form came to mind. That made her smile, made her heart swell all over again. She had always loved growing things.

She'd always loved creating things, too. There was a time when she may have even called herself an artist. Her father would say she could turn a turd into a sculpture, were she bored enough. All she had to do was apply her little, clever hands like swooping birds and even the lowliest place would flare with light and beauty. The Hunt's keep was covered with her work, from floor to ceiling. Paintings, woodcarvings, leatherwork, engravings on their drinking horns. All of it growing with the flora and fauna she loved so much, she had to preserve it forever.

One summer, long before she'd ever had to go meet her sister at the Hold, Myre took it upon herself and her pottery wheel to re-do all of the dinnerware in the keep. What had been boring but utilitarian clay plates and bowls became sweeping works of art-- green, white, and even a touch of gold. A memory of when the Hunt's folk had ruled all the isle. Father sent special, all the way to the Stone, for that gold. And he'd only done it, not because he knew her skilled hands would make it stunning, but because he knew the joy of simply crafting it would make her smile. Yes, that was right. She'd been in a funk too-- bad dreams and spitting fits-- and the pottery project raised her above it.

When she'd get into these creative fits, Boru would simply sit back and watch her. He was clumsy with anything that wasn't a dog or a bow. No matter how she encouraged him to dig into the paints or the clay, to try his hand at bringing something to life, his confidence defeated him every single time. "*You can make beauty enough for the two of us,*" he'd say, after every failed attempt. *"Maybe,"* she'd reply, *"but I wanted to make it together."*

There had been a time when every inch of Myre's life was covered by that which she created. And that was when she had been happiest. To be of use. To bring color to the red stone walls of Fallowfall Keep. Her home. To make her people smile, and her father scruff her hair and say, *"My my, my Myre! What's it you've done now?"*

Why hadn't she done so in so long? Where had she been all this time, wasting away without paints and clay? Maybe that was why the dreams came? And the fits? Maybe it was simply all that creative energy rotting inside of her, forcing itself out through spit and bile?

Either way, it was time. Excited, Myre put the pigments into a wooden box, ladled some water from the basin into one of the misshapen clay cups, and crawled, barefooted, over to the bed. She found her spot against the wall, made a back brace out of pillows, and surveyed her surface.

Where to start?

Trees. You always started with the green, she knew. Even flowers knew that. For they, too, started off as green shoots, springing from the ground, eager for sunlight to bring to life their true colors.

Small pines sprang up first, their long, narrow trunks buffeted with arms in hunter green, shamrock, asparagus. All mixed by her loving hand. When they dried, she tipped them with sweet whites and blues. Around the bases of her trees sprang up moss; from that moss, the long, skinny necks that would become flowers.

But what color for those?

The butterfly weed!

Now, near gleeful, she mixed red and yellow, pulled the reddest bits out first, then the orange, then the yellow highlights on top of that. Her little scene was soon speckled in those dream buds.

When she drew away, she found she'd painted herself into a corner. Just like in her dream, there was a wreath of little red buds. But the middle was empty. Perhaps, Myre yawned as she thought it, she could put a little fawn lying there.

Maybe later.

7

The bonny hunting lad whistled a song Myre swore she'd heard before. A jaunty, little festival tune, one of those ones that everyone knew. She mouthed the words alongside his whistling, but didn't dare speak up. Not after what happened last time.

"She set out milk for me, my brother,
Thought I'd grow wheat in her field,
Once glance, I'd not love another,
More than wheat, this love will't yield."

He wasn't hunting today. Not for meat, at least. If he was, the whistling would've scared away any catch. Instead, he sat and waited upon a bluff, with the big dog behind him to brace his back. Myre watched from above this time, lurking in the trees. A voyeur perhaps, but she didn't have the time to feel ashamed. Her focus was as narrow as his hips.

In his hands he held a whittling knife and a hunk of wood. Half the hunk was already coming to life-- an owl with wings spread wide. And his hands were skilled-- the artist within her recognized and appreciated. She could make out every perfect feather.

"And when she laughs she rings like bells,
And when she sings, my heart beats red,
No home there'll be for us to dwell,

The road's our house, the earth our bed."

Someone was coming up the hill.

"You know I loathe that song," said the stranger, coming into sight. Myre couldn't seem to register his face-- and then she realized why. *You're not here for him.*

"Too bad. It makes me think of you," said the bonny hunting lad, with a clever grin. He got to his feet, abandoned his whittling, and crossed the scant space between them to embrace the newcomer, kissing him fully on the mouth.

For all the cinders in her chest, Myre couldn't look away. And yet, it wasn't jealousy that burned in her heart. A fierce joy. An infectious pride.

8

"Did you fall asleep painting, Myrebird?" Boru's deep voice set her dream to wings, and she opened her eyes, finding herself in the bed at the cottage, with the four close walls all around her, standing guard. As they always did.

"Maybe," she said, blearily, locating the brush. It had dried against her cheek, sticking there, thanks to the paint. She tugged it loose, then used it to gesture to her face. Boru chuckled. He set his own things down-- more food from the village, it seemed, as well as his bow. If there was meat, it'd be in the smoking shack outside. Her stomach grumbled.

"Well, you deserve it. Looks like you wore yourself right out." He took off his coat and kicked snow from his boots, then took those off as well. "You haven't been this busy in quite some time."

"Come, have a look," Myre said. She eased herself up from the bed and went over to wash the stiff brushes in the basin. Boru hummed agreement, then finished taking off his outdoor clothes. He pulled his hair up into a ribbon behind his ears-- it was getting long-- and went to inspect. Myre busied herself, making roses blossom and fade in the water with the brushes, until his voice called her back

"Is that him?"

"Hm? Who?"

"Your bonny hunting lad?" He tapped the wooden plank with his hard fingernail. She set down her brushes and crossed the cottage to join him on the bed.

"I was going to paint a fawn?" The question was more for herself than for Boru. And yet, there he was, nestled between the butterfly weeds, just as he'd been in her dream. Neat and simple was her style for painting people-- and neat and simple, he was. No brush stroke ever wasted. She knew it was her brush that had made him, brought him to life-- from his strange eyes, to his splattered freckles, to his long fingers clasped over his chest, like a corpse waiting patiently upon its pyre. Even his missing ear. All there.

"Don't look like a fawn," Boru mused. "I mean, don't get me wrong, love. It's very pretty. But kind of strange to have him watching us, don't you think?"

"I don't..." she stopped. There was no sense in telling him she didn't remember painting her bonny hunting lad. He wouldn't understand. Boru tried and tried, but he never did. "...I'm sorry," she whispered. "I can paint over it."

"No need. If seeing him makes you happy, then I'm happy with him joining us here." He raised an imaginary drinking horn to toast to their new companion. "I mean, seems like he's been here the whole time anyway, doesn't it? Might as well join us in the flesh. Welcome, bonny hunting lad! I've heard so much about you." He chuckled again.

"You're trying to be nice," Myre whispered, disappointed. "But you don't have to. I don't know why I painted him. He's just... stuck in my head."

"Do you love him?"

"Yes." The answer didn't strike Boru as it might have struck another man. His face stayed perfectly still, but in the shining depths of his eyes, Myre sensed his grief the same way an aching bone augurs a coming storm. "Not like I love you. It's different; I told you. I don't know how."

"Do you wish you were with him?" He asked the question so carefully, so measured this time. "With him instead of me?" Few men are brave enough to break their own hearts in a whisper, but Boru was one of them.

"I wish we both were with him." At this, Boru snorted. "Not like that!" Myre tittered at him. "It's just, I feel peaceful when I dream of him. I know you're not at peace. I don't... I don't know all of it. But I mean, *of course* I can tell, my love, that your heart is breaking every single day, cracking more and more like a baby bird hatching." She took his large, callused hand in her own and wound her fingers around it. "I wish he could give you the peace he gives me. That's all."

"But... I'm the only one in your heart? In that way?" He clarified, just to be certain. He had never been the jealous sort, not Boru. For the way they both saw it, they had chosen each other so young. Who would waste those years spent longing and loving? They had defied a queen to be together, for the sake of the bones beneath the hills!

But then, too-- they were young. And the young tend to think that way. That things will always be as they are.

"Of course!" Now it was her turn to snort, indignant. "How could there ever be anyone else?"

"Prove it."

She grinned at him like a little cat eyeing the cream, and brought her nose up close to his. "I'm sorry sir, but I don't know what you mean."

Boru nuzzled her. "A simple kiss. If my lady would permit, would do just the trick."

"Only a kiss?"

"Well..." She smiled at this, then gave him what he so desired-- a kiss, but far from simple. The memory of her bonny hunting lad and his faceless stranger shot briefly into her mind, but she shoo'd them both away with her hand, then turned it and lifted her linen nightgown above her head. *You have your kisses, one-eared stag, and I have mine.*

"*Whoa*!"

"What?" *More paint*, was Myre's first thought. But Boru pushed her back, surveyed her lithe, nude form. His eyes focused on her middle.

"You're showing so much!" he said, in surprise. "I... you've been wearing naught but that gown for so long, it was hard to tell. I guess," he laughed again, and Myre sensed tremors of excitement and nerves in that laugh, "I guess it's actually happening, isn't it?"

"Oh!" she giggled and set a hand on her belly. "I haven't even thought of it in so long, it seems." A memory, from some other life. *We're going to have a child,* she'd told him. *She'll have to let us marry now!*

"I was worried," Boru admitted, a breathy sigh easing itself into his shoulders, "with all the stress going on, and your breaks and fits, I thought maybe--"

"--I didn't lose it," Myre said. She reached over and took his hand, then set it on her belly. Inside of her, the baby kicked at the warm weight of its father's hand. She had grown used to the kicking-- it didn't seem novel anymore, just seemed to be a part of her, the same as her heart beating. Tears sprang into Boru's eyes, and he laughed, throwing his head back. He reached forward and grabbed her and baby both and pulled them into a bear hug, wrestling them into the blankets. She shrieked a giggle and struggled to get away, but he engulfed her, held her down, and kissed every inch of her, until she was so overcome with the tickling of his chin hair, she could barely breathe. "S-S-Stop! *Boru*!" He did, at long last. "You thought I'd lost it and was hiding it from you?"

"Dogs do that, sometimes. Bury it in the yard. Eat it."

She was overcome with giggling again. "Yuck! I'm not a dog, Boru!"

"I know, Myrebird. But you've given me not a single complaint this whole time. And... things being what they are, I figured you had more to worry about." He laced their fingers together and kissed her neck. "My mother always said it was a nightmare, carrying me. Even after having my brothers. Said she couldn't sit up straight without yakking all nine months. Said it was the most painful thing."

"That's because *you're* a pain," Myre teased.

"Excuse *you*, my lady. I just thought if I was such a struggle, surely I'd bring that to you. I was worried."

"Well, this one isn't a pain. They'll be sweet as a honey and calm as a sunny day."

"It's yours, so, maybe I could see sweet. But calm? Nay, lady. You're brewing a wild child in there." Their smirks met one another over her bare shoulder, and he kissed that, too, just to be certain. "I may not be a seer. But even I can see that."

"Oh *hush*!"

But neither one of them could hush.

9

This time, it was Myre who waited at the top of the hill. Her white, winding sheet billowed in the wind behind her. On her shoulders, her heavy hair tried to restrain it like ties holding back curtains.

"There you are," whispered a voice she knew. She turned.

Her bonny hunting lad stood there, tall and beautiful, dressed in the copper-red and white of the Hunt. Not a soldier's leathers. His dark hair played in the wind. From how he stood above her, he was powerful-- not the meek, little creature she'd seen creeping through the brush and bracken so many times. No-- this was the kit and fly, the gait and glower of a prince. Fear trembled through her heart. Instinctively, she touched her belly, but found it flat. And that? That amplified her fear, told her bones to run, run and never look back. He knew she was his voyeur, and he'd come for justice. She tried to rise, but found she couldn't.

But then, he sat down, cross-legged, right next to her. Their shoulders nearly brushed. There was a red gladiolus behind his remaining ear, blooming like a wound. And behind that, a lover's braid tucked, hidden. Both he wore without care. Boru would've blushed and shied like a nervous pony if she'd tried to do that to his thick locks!

"I've been waiting for this," he said, with a shy smile. He was older than she was. Not by much. How strange! His smile was broad, as though he'd just grown into his teeth.

"You knew it would happen? That you and I would meet?" His face faltered and that smile faded. But she reached out and took his hand. "I didn't even know you knew I've been dreaming of you." A question darted into his mismatched eyes. "It's alright if you did! You don't have to tell me how you knew. Not if you don't want to. You don't have to tell me anything about what happens." A darkness came into his eyes. "In fact, I think I already know, but the thought is too heavy. It's not like silence-- saying it aloud won't banish it, will it?"

They were quiet together for a long time, each simply daring themselves to look at the other. Eventually, after several passes, their eyes finally met and Myre realized what made his gaze seem so strange to her: one of his eyes was a deep, dark blue, nearing black. The other was silver-green.

"It was a painting," he said, in his surprisingly deep voice. "A painting of me you did on a pine chest. Sleeping in the flowers." He smiled sheepishly. "He told me that you did it on a wall. After you went back, he took an axe to the whole place, burnt it down. But he couldn't do it to your painting. He brought it to the Hunt and my *athair,*" an old word, from the treason-tongue, the one the Queen banished. But Myre knew what it meant. *Grandfather*, "made it into a chest for me. For me to place the things I love."

The things he loves.

"Who is he? The one who rings like bells to your ear?" her voice cracked as she grinned at him, like two children sharing a secret.

"My heart," said the bonny hunting lad, and a pink blush crept over his freckled cheeks and his pert, fox's nose. "My healing salve. The one they must look to if they wish to see the whole of me." He looked away. "He's funny and tough. And when he's mad, he bites down like a bullhound and doesn't let go. Boru says you and he have that in common. Says you're both half storm. I think you'd like him."

"I think so," she agreed, laying her cheek on his shoulder. He turned and set his own cheek atop her head, then, with a careful hand, reached out and touched her hair, combing the snarls away with his long fingers. Just like when Boru did it, she felt nothing. No pull, no snag.

"Do I have to go to Carren for all of this to pass?" He startled and pulled away, and Myre looked up at him in shock.

There was a desperate, hopeless look in those queer eyes, try as he might hide them from her. His broad lips hung open and she could see the curve of his too-big teeth "No. You don't have to go to Carren. She sends Winnie instead."

"*Winnie*!" Myre's heart nearly shattered in two. She leapt away from her bonny hunting lad, as if he'd struck her. "Why her? She's too young!"

"I..." he faltered, "...I don't know how to answer that. It seems I've spoken too much already." He hung his head and licked his bottom lip. "But how does one tell a hart not to catch the loosed arrow in its breast?" Myre felt as though the breath had been choked out of her. She touched her own throat, as the lad's eyes watched her, too careful to betray anything else.

"You sound like my father when you talk," she said, folding her bottom lip between her teeth.

But the bonny hunting lad continued, for his message was too important to delay. "She makes a promise and she has to keep it. That's what Queens do. For you? No, she has other plans for you, when she finds out that you can do this." He held his hand out flat in front of him, and she met it with her palm. "And she has other plans for me, too." A silvery tear puddled up in the crook of his green eye, then fell in a long line into the earth beneath them both.

Myre could see it now, as easy as if she were floating above the Hunt, looking down at the rivers and roads and laying them out on a map in front of her.

And yet, she found a gentle peace in the acceptance of what her life was going to become.

"Will you suffer without me?" she asked, after another long while. "Don't lie now. I'll know if you're lying!"

He rubbed his eyes, flicking away tears into the soil. "So much." His voice shook in his chest and cracked like a rotten fruit, right down the middle, exposing the pit. "But I survive. All of it. You're going to think I won't, but I do. I promise." She put her small, cold hands on top of his warm ones, and he turned them up to take her palms in his own. The butterfly weed wrapped itself between their fingers. "I survive. And I am happy."

"Good," said Myre. She leaned into him but didn't let go of his hands. The wool of his cloak caught on her dry lips. "That's all I could ever ask for you." They both fell silent again-- the lad to his shameless tears, and Myre, to her peace.

How much longer did they sit there? Again, time had no meaning-- not to Myre, and not to her bonny hunting lad.

"You have to go," said the boy at long last. There were tears in his eyes. "I don't want you to. He doesn't want you to. But that's how it happens, isn't it? You can't not go any more than Boru can not grieve you."

"Yes," Myre whispered. She touched his sad, wet cheek, cupped his face in her hands, the way his mother never would. "I love you. I always will. Isn't that silly? I don't even know you. I don't know if you're kind or cruel, if you're clever or foolish. But I love you more than anything in the whole world."

He took her into his arms, pulled her close to his chest. The effort knocked them both from their sitting position, into the grass, but neither fought their topple. He pressed his lips against her forehead, then her nose, then her own lips. The muscles beneath his red and white kit were ropey and hard. They lacked Boru's bulk. No, he was built more like Myre's father-- lean and long, powerful as a cracked whip. He smelled of aloe, chamomile, and willowbark. *My healing salve.* But what did he need to heal from?

Nevermind. That was not a question for her to know the answer to. *I survive. And I am happy.* That was all Myre needed. That was all that was left for her. She breathed in deeply again, filled herself with him one last time. He smelled of Boru-- of dog, sweat, and grief beyond knowing. He smelled of her-- honey and salt.

"I love you too," he whispered into her hairline, as wakefulness tugged at the edges of her mind, threatening to pull her away. "Now go, and be brave."

She did.

10

Spring was coming to the karst and to the cottage. Boru saw the limited greenery peeking up through the grey stone. Soon enough, the rains would come, and with them, a handful of bright, sunny mornings.

Inspired by the reception of his last gift to her, Boru had spent the morning in the village seeking seeds. Not for flowers, but for food. Myre would like that, he thought. To grow things. To fill their bellies with rutabaga, carrots, peppers, maybe even a fruit tree eventually. Apples, probably. She liked apples. It would be new to her, sure. But everything she did, she did with purpose and skillful cleverness. The art of doing these things brought her back to herself more than anything else Boru had ever tried. How happy she'd been with the paints! The silliness with her strange fawn in the red weeds aside, it made him happy. Why hadn't he thought of that before? But then again, Boru faulted himself, he had never been a clever man. Simply a man in love. And love? It makes all men idiots anyway, so what was the point?

They could be happy here, alone.

Before peeking into the cottage with his new prizes, he stopped outside, took off his furs and his leather kit, stripped down to his linen trews, and began to till the earth with a borrowed hoe. A small garden for her to start off with, sure. That'd be enough for now. He'd never tilled anything before. Starting off small would help him figure it out. That's what Myre always said at least-- *just a little clay, just a little paint. You'll get it, my love.*

But tilling was more difficult than he'd planned. Even though the day was still overcast and grim, he was sweating within minutes. Every few minutes, he had to stop, grab the borrowed pickaxe, and haul it up and down to break the grey stone where it interfered with his plottings.

Finally, he gave up. There was no use hiding it anyway. Myre had probably heard him clunking around out here. In fact, he was a little surprised she hadn't come to take a look. May as well give her her gift. And anyway, a ladleful of water would go a long way to helping him finish this.

Gathering up the package of seeds, he didn't bother reclothing himself before opening the cottage door.

Myre wasn't at her most recent painting-- a series of gladiouses and ospreys twirling in flight beneath the window. But she wasn't huddled up in the bed, either. It took a moment for Boru to realize the totality of what this meant.

She was gone.

"Myrebird?" he asked the empty cottage, dumbly. "*Myre*!" Not under the table. Not under the bed. She'd never left the cottage before, not since they'd gotten here months ago. Still, he burst back out the door, expecting to find her prodding at his lame attempts at a garden. But no, she wasn't there, either.

"Myre!" He shouted to the karst, which answered him only in a mocking echo. *Myremyremyremyre...*

He spent the rest of the day searching to no avail. No, she wasn't walking the road back to the village. She wasn't hiding behind the boulders that lined out their land, nor any of the small tree copses nearby. A million directions, she could have gone, and yet it was as if she'd taken flight-- a little, white and copper owl against the grey sky-- and flown away.

When night fell, Boru, who was too tired to even continue weeping, returned to the cottage. He knew he had to eat, even though he couldn't stomach it. It'd be no use, searching for her without taking care of himself. But while his belly begged, his mind screamed. He knew he had to sleep, otherwise he'd start seeing her in the bracken, the shrubs, the wind-- everywhere she wasn't.

And that's how he found it. The note on the crooked bedside table, written on crumpled parchment paper. When Boru lifted it, several, tiny, orange flowers fell out.

My dear,

I had to leave. I have to go. I have to confront her, and put a stop to this before she can hurt anyone else. She's going to send Winnie in my place. I can't have that. Not my girl. Not my darling niece.

I don't know if you knew this, if you were keeping it from me or not. If you were, then, well, I know you did it because you love me, but Winnie cannot be held responsible for my cowardice. She's just a child. And the rest of them? Of the Huntfolk? My father, and all the others who march and throw themselves against the Queen's walls? It's not their fault. It's time for me to pay my dues. We can't wait any longer.

I'm not angry with you. I know you did it for love. I do. I would have done the same to you, but you need to trust me. Am I so far gone that I don't deserve trust?

Go to my father. Wait there for me. I will settle everything with my sister, and then we can be together again.

Just know these things from me and me alone:

We will survive together. We will be happy together.

We are having a son.

I love you.

Myrebird

He crumpled the note and threw it to the ground, then kicked the leg of the table so hard, the whole damn thing came tumbling down.

ABOUT THE AUTHOR

Sam Trathen is a fantasy author and content creator. Originally from Nine Mile Falls, WA, she has lived everywhere from Honolulu to Connecticut but now hails from Tampa, FL. While attending Columbia College Chicago, Sam won the 2012 Elise duBois scholarship for her short story, The Prodigal. When she isn't writing, she's playing tabletop roleplaying games (she's a wood-elf bard, thanks for asking), brewing mead, and recording her podcast, Sounds Dicey, with her husband Mike, and her English Pointer, Bocephalus. Her story in this anthology is a prequel to her forthcoming novel, The Sons of Witches.

You can follow her on Twitter @SamwiseTrathen or on Instagram @meadwitch. Sounds Dicey is available on Google Play and Spotify.

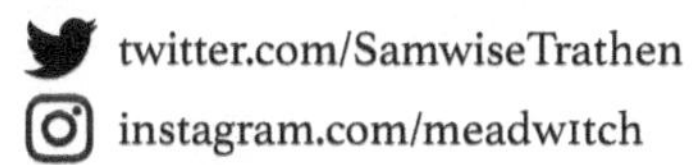

WATER'S EDGE

BY NIKKI LYNN ARCHAMBAULT

Technology.

Coexisting.

War.

Humans and Merpeople used to live in peace and harmony together. Gradually and oh too subtlety things changed after the War. Groups were separated and started to attack each other. Homes were destroyed, families were eradicated, their world burned.

When a young mermaid named Nimue sees an enslaved human man named Finn she feels compelled to buy him and show him what secrets coexist at The Water's Edge.

1

Finn was curled into a ball trying not to be noticed. He was locked in a cage, naked and shaking. Just one of many humans going to the auction block, their fate to be decided by the mermaids and mermen who would buy them. But Finn knew his chance of being purchased by a kind owner were slim-to-none. He wasn't muscular or strong in his appearance. He was beyond thin. Gangly and emaciated, he looked too weak to be useful for manual labor. The only alternative he knew of was to be a pet of sorts.

He almost laughed at that thought. Another option forever lost to him. And all because of his appearance. He was never what one would typically call beautiful, even before his accident. His blonde hair was overgrown, starting to curl a bit on the ends that were almost shoulder length by now. His blue eyes remained his strongest feature.

But the left of his face was forever altered by horrific burn scars. The skin on the left side of his face was marred by peaks and valleys and divots of horribly scarred and marred flesh, discolored in places. The scarring involved his outer ear on the left side which was mangled but still present in its deformed glory and ran around his left eye including his eyelid but left his nose and right side of his face untouched in some kind of act of mercy.

He was no longer aware it was the price he had paid for trying to be brave. His memory was never great, even in the best of circumstances, and now he thought that was a blessing. He didn't remember his name, let alone the circumstances that had brought him to such a sorry state of affairs. His memory was devoid of the knowledge that he had tried to free dozens of captive mermaids and mermen that the humans were holding. Whether they were prisoners intended to be sold or experimented on, he couldn't be sure. He only knew their captivity was wrong. So, he freed them. In doing so, the building they were held in caught fire and he nearly died in the blaze.

Ironic that the act of freeing them led to his captivity at the hands of their kin. Other mermaids and mermen were waiting in the water nearby to ferry the former captives the rest of the way to safety. They took Finn, too. At first, he thought it was a benevolent act to provide him with the medical care to save his life for saving theirs. But once he had recovered enough to be both scarred and stable, he quickly found himself in the same fate as those he nearly died to save.

With his memory unable to recall why he was there or who he had been before, he was assigned the name Finn, as a way to mock him, for being a human, without a tail or fins. He often longed for death as an escape from all this anxiety and suffering. He curled into a tighter ball now with his eyes clenched shut. He began to rock himself, trying to keep the tears from spilling out onto the cold stone floor beneath his bare feet. Then he heard it. The sounds so far-fetched he strained to see if they would be repeated—and they were repeated several times in fact.

"Open that cage."

His door was opened, and a woman approached and tentatively walked into his cage. She gently placed a hand on his right shoulder, trying to calm him. His back was to her and he turned his head to the right to take in her appearance. He kept his scarred left side in the shadows, not wanting to scare her. She was curvy with pale skin and had long wavy brown hair. She was the polar opposite of him in appearance and though she was in human form he could somehow sense she was a mer.

"Nim, we can't waste time looking at each one in turn. Let's make a selection and go. Now." Finn turned his head toward the man, noting that his distinctly Korean features were in stark contrast to those of the woman or mer he called Nim.

Nim waved her hand in his direction effectively silencing her companion. She bent down, almost kneeling but not quite, and whispered into Finn's good ear, "I'm going to help you." She looked back at the man who hadn't even bothered to enter the cage, choosing instead to stand sentry at the door. "Stone, tell them we'll take him."

Finn noticed Stone seemed to balk at the order. He could sense the disdain Stone held for him, especially once his scars became visible to them. But Nim wasn't backing down. Stone was walking away when Nim called out to him "Gown, Stone."

Stone tossed a paper-thin hospital gown over his shoulder in their general direction without so much as a look back at them and continued to stalk away, his displeasure evident in his purposeful stride to make Nim's selection known.

Nim helped Finn to his feet and slid his arms into the gown, despite how dirty he obviously was. She tried to smile at him reassuringly and apologetically. "I know no one likes these things but it's only temporary. I didn't want you to have to leave nude and I thought this would be easiest to smuggle in. You'll get decent clothes once we get you home and you've bathed." When Finn didn't answer she tried again. "Hey, it's okay. A bath or shower. Whichever you prefer. Some new clothes. A decent meal. A good night's rest and you'll feel so much better. Trust me."

Finn was going to nod that he understood, but then he felt like he was falling and then blackness. Nothingness.

2

Nimue was holding Finn's hand as he lay on his back on a cot in the boat Stone was piloting. Boats were their preferred method of travel when not willing or able to transform fully. Nimue was grateful for the boat as a mode of transportation because it provided a cot for the ailing Finn to sleep on during their trip back to Water's Edge.

Water's Edge, the once great resort, that was now a haven to a rogue group of healers, consisting of both Mers and humans. They had high hopes, that their attempt to get back to life as normal before The Wars would be successful. Nimue however had her doubts as The Wars of Sea and Land had made everyone keep to themselves and until tonight Nimue was starting to think that maybe that was the way it ought to be.

There were few Mers left alive that had had only good encounters with humans. Ever since the wars of Sea and Land as the Mers referred to them. most humans were cruel to mers. Even when the Mers were in their human form. Nimue had quickly learned that if you ventured out into the world beyond Water's Edge even in a human form you had to act as human as possible. Any sign that you were a Mer in human form, and you could be killed or suffer one of many fates worse than death. Slavery and or sexual assault were sadly among the possibilities. A Mer wandering about humans must hide their true identity at all costs.

Nimue was so terrified of humans that, as relations between humans and Mers deteriorated, she retreated to the safety of Water's Edge and only left when she absolutely had to. Which as time went by was becoming less and less frequent.

The few humans she had to interact with at Water's Edge were those who had been rescued from slavery and most were brought here near death. Almost all those who elected to stay did so because they had fallen in love with a Mer. As Water's Edge was one of the few places where humans and Mers could intermarry and raise a family together even in secret, most elected to enjoy the freedom they found there behind closed doors. Somehow a human who had chosen to be with a Mer made the few humans there appear less threatening.

Nimue looked at Finn. He wasn't in any position to be a threat to anyone. In truth Nimue doubted he'd make it through the night in his sorry state. She noted his extensive facial scarring and from reading his file she knew what had caused them. Immediately she found him more intriguing and appealing because of them. It gave them something weird to have in common and that amused and comforted her. With a renewed determination she vowed he would live to see the dawn. She'd nurse him herself and he'd make it. She smiled at him and noting the patches of reddish hair in his facial hair so different from the blonde hair on his head it looked almost orangey in the boat's inadequate lighting. Taking his memory issues into account she'd grinned. He would be hers. Her own little Goldfish. She cooed at him "Tell me my Little Goldfish what can I do to make you feel better?"

3

Finn opened his eyes to the sunlight streaming through an endless line of windows. They flooded the room he was in with natural light. He noticed that he was lying on his back on a bed, but when he tried to lift himself to a seated position, he couldn't. Wide straps of a satin-like material wrapped around each wrist, effectively restraining him. He looked down at himself. He was covered with a blue blanket and underneath it he was wearing a dark blue t-shirt with a cartoon goldfish on it and coordinating pajama shorts. He could tell someone had bathed him as his hair was still damp and the dirt on his entire person had been scrubbed away and replaced with a sweet smell like that of salt and seaside lavender with musk.

He looked out the windows again at the surf crashing on the rocks. It reminded him of some TV show with vampires, but he couldn't remember the title or much more about it. He dismissed it and turned his attention to the room he was in. It looked like a hotel room at a resort. There was nothing personal in it but it had everything that one would need. It was painted in a cheery white color that looked yellow when the sunlight poured through the windows, which must be a frequent occurrence. He could see a flat-screen TV near the foot of his bed. But the room was sparsely furnished. Necessities only. Nothing of consequence or that gave him a clue to the owner's preferences.

"Good morning, Finn. Welcome back." A man with Korean features approached his bed on his left side. "You gave us all quite a scare last night. It's good to see you with your eyes open."

A woman entered through the doorway which was on Finn's right side and he turned to look at her. Brunette hair but kept short. Mers did not normally wear their hair short. A human? She had to be. She was thin and tall. Non-threatening. But she immediately spoke to the Asian man. "You didn't undo his restraints yet? Nimue is going to kill you when she finds out."

"I was going to undo them after I took his vitals, Wife. I wanted to make sure he was over the worst of it so when I undid them, I wouldn't have to redo them."

She countered with, "I'd take his vitals quickly then. Besides, he seems fine to me." Turning her attention to Finn, she asked, "Are you feeling better now, Finn?"

Finn was confused. Better as opposed to what exactly? She approached his bed and quickly released the satin bindings so he was free. "Noooo. He said after he takes my vitals," He whispered to her, obviously scared of any negative consequences.

"He doesn't wear the pants in this relationship. Well, not all the time anyway." She smiled at Finn. "I'm being rude, I'm Marina and if you don't remember from yesterday, that's Stone, my husband."

Stone approached the bed then with a thermometer in hand and Finn opened his mouth to comply but almost jumped away when he noticed something about Stone that had not registered earlier. Stone is a Mer. A Mer with a human for a wife? Who did such a thing? He was so confused.

Stone finished taking Finn's vitals and turned to leave. Pausing as he passed Marina, he stated, "Everything looks good, which is a miracle considering how bad off he was last night. My shift is over. Try to get him to eat something before Nim comes back. Granted, that's if he thinks he can keep it down." Stone kissed Marina's forehead and left.

Marina turned back to Finn, beaming. "Do you feel up to eating something? You were so out of it last night, food wasn't an option. I can make pancakes. That might be easy on your stomach."

Incredulous, Finn had to ask, "You're a human yet you're married to a Mer?"

Marina nodded in response. "We don't discriminate in this household. Mers and humans intermarry here the same way people with different color eyes might. Everyone is equal here."

Another woman filled the open doorway and continued what Marina was saying, "We don't discriminate, and we don't wake people up when we're supposed to either." Walking to Finn's bedside, she greeted him. "Good morning Finn, I'm Nimue, if you don't remember me from yesterday."

When she got close, Finn recognized her from the day before and he simply said, "You're a mermaid."

Nimue snorted a bit. "I am."

"Why am I here? If everyone is equal here, then I'm not a slave? I don't understand."

Nimue shot a warning glance in Marina's direction, effectively silencing her. "I don't want you to feel overwhelmed, right now. Last night you were extremely sick as your fever raged on."

Marina interrupted at that. "Stone took his vitals before he left. He says Finn is fine now but it's a miracle considering how bad he was."

"All the more reason not to overwhelm him," Nimue countered and turning her attention back to Finn. She continued, "Your main concern should be to eat and get well. We can discuss why you're here later when you've had some more rest." She turned back to Marina and nodded.

"I'll take that as my cue to leave the two of you. I'll bring back some pancakes then."

Finn nodded his reply and Marina left without another sound or backward glance.

Now alone with Nimue, Finn started to relax. She had saved him, after all. He might not know her motivations, but he knew she wouldn't go through all the trouble of buying him and nursing him through a fever if she was just going to harm him. Hoping to get some answers he asked, "Where are we?"

"My home."

"Here. Above the water? In a human dwelling?"

"This place used to be a resort named Water's Edge before the wars of Sea and Land."

Finn nodded but remained silent otherwise.

Everyone knew about the wars. For hundreds of years, Mers and humans had peacefully coexisted—intermarrying, raising families together, advancing technologies together. But gradually, and so subtlety no one seemed to notice until it was too late, things changed. Various groups encouraged humans to keep their distance. Families that had intermarried were ostracized, if not killed outright. One side started capturing and enslaving the other. So, the other side countered, not with peace but, by likewise capturing and enslaving them on their side. Families died out—literally. Homes were destroyed. The world burned. Neither side emerged victorious. The world was trying to rebuild, but in the rebirth, each side kept to themselves. But slavery and murder to the other side kept on in the rebirth and rebuilding. Most beings, human and mer alike, lamented the lack of progress and destruction. Every human and Mer who could remember how life was before the wars longed for that easy, peaceful existence with an overwhelming nostalgia that only seemed heightened with each passing hour.

"But humans and Mers coexist here? They intermarry? Like before the wars?"

Nimue nodded. "How do you expect things to get back to the peaceful existence we had together before if places like this don't start existing, bit-by-bit? Humans and Mers were meant to coexist. We're stronger together. The children in families that have Mer and human DNA in their lineage are healthier. When we stay apart for too long, our children weaken. Their immune systems are weaker. They are more prone to disease and illnesses. They have an increased likeliness to have all sorts of physical deformities and disabilities. And a heightened predisposition to mental illness as well, even later in life."

Finn gasped as he processed this information. The reality of his situation hitting him full force. "That's why you bought me. Not to rescue me. Not out of kindness, but to breed me?"

Nimue's face fell. She couldn't bring herself to look him in the eye. Thankfully at that moment, Marina reappeared with Finn's breakfast. Nimue prayed he could eat, and she managed a sideways glance to confirm he was in fact eating what Marina brought him. She didn't intend for him to find out the truth for at least a few days—if ever. Ideally, he would have just elected to intermarry on his own. If he had come to that decision on his own, she never would have told him that was her motive for bringing him here.

She shot Marina a sad all-knowing look. Thankfully, Marina seemed to read Nimue's mind and she turned her attention back to Finn and entertained him while he ate his breakfast. Nimue slipped from Finn's room silently, wishing things could have been handled differently.

4

"What's the verdict, Doc?" Finn asked Stone, who took his vitals again, a few hours after he finished his breakfast.

"As I said, your recovery is nothing short of a miracle. I thought that fever would be the end of you given how thin you are and how bad off you seemed. I'm glad I was wrong. Nimue should be thrilled." Stone cringed at his error hoping Finn didn't catch the implication. "I mean, all of us are thrilled that you're doing so well."

Finn waved him off "It's okay Stone, I know."

"Nimue told you?"

"She didn't have to. I figured it out. I suppose my fate could be worse."

"I'm sorry."

"I'm not. Well, except for the fact that Nimue bolted the minute I called her on it."

"That explains why she's been avoiding you."

"She doesn't have to. Like I said it could be worse. Is that how you ended up with Marina?"

Stone cringed again. "Something like that."

"But you guys are happy?"

"Deliriously so. But I didn't force her. I brought her here. That was my choice to bring her here. But she had choices, too. She didn't have to choose me. She could have remained here alone, waited for someone else more to her liking to arrive. But we were meant to be." Stone paused before adding, "Nimue won't force you to do anything, especially to choose her. I can guarantee you that at least. And you won't be cast out if you don't choose her."

Finn nodded his understanding. "So, you bought Marina from the same place you bought me?"

Stone shook his head. "No. Nimue and I had never been there before. I found Marina someplace else." Stone looked at Finn and knew he owed him more details, but he hesitated to say too much. He wanted to reassure Finn that he wouldn't be pressured to do anything he didn't want to do, but he didn't want to betray Marina either by saying things about his wife that she may not want to make common knowledge. He wrestled with his decision in silence for a few minutes before deciding to walk a tightrope between both options. "She was being held by a man. A merman. A bad man. He did things to her. Bad things." He turned to see Finn nod before he continued, "Things so bad, I could never elaborate on specifics without feeling like I was betraying her and her fragile trust in me. He didn't give her any choices. He had heard things about how magical things could be with a human female. He experimented quite a bit. When I found her, she was lying outside on a deserted beach. Covered in blood. Her will to live was gone. She didn't even have the strength, mental or physical, to end it quick, after what he had done to her that night."

Stone shivered, both at the memory and at the thought of what might have happened if he hadn't been at the right place at the right time. "When I approached her in human form, she didn't react at all. Her plan was to just lie there until she died. Maybe she thought I'd help finish her off. I brought her here instead. My pod, or as you would say family, have always been great healers. I had no designs on her romantically. I just wanted to help. I wanted her to survive. To see that not all Mers were like her tormentor. For the first few weeks, if not months, no male human or Mer could get near her. But obviously, that changed."

Finn's curiosity was heightened to a near fever pitch at this point. "What changed?"

A man who resembled a mall Santa Claus appeared in the doorway to Finn's room, "Me." He turned to Stone and said, "Your wife is waiting for you. Go on. I'll stay with him."

Stone nearly bolted at that. "I'll be back, Finn, try to get some rest before lunch." He walked past the older man and was clapped on his shoulder as he exited.

The older man turned to Finn and extended a hand in a greeting. Finn guessed his identity right before he spoke to confirm it. "Marina. She's my daughter."

5

Stone found Marina in their private pool, waiting for him. Naked as the day she was born. When he entered, she smiled at him with the smile she reserved only for him. Words weren't necessary. Stone stripped naked and dove in. Within moments scales appeared in swirls of orange and white and small amounts of black. His tail grew, resembling a koi fish in pattern. Marina splashed him playfully. He closed the distance between them and swooped her up into his arms. Brazenly, she kissed him, her intent obvious. But Stone held himself back a bit. He covered her with playful kisses all over her face. She kissed him with more and more passionate fervor. But he didn't seem able to match her intensity. Realizing something was wrong, she stopped and asked him flat out.

"Finn. He asked about us?"

"Oh."

"I mean, how we ended up together. He assumed I bought you."

Marina pulled him into a tight hug, the water lapping at both of their waists. "It brought everything back. And now you're worried that I don't want you or this."

"Not exactly but close."

"Nothing could be further from the truth. I choose you. I've always chosen you. You're not the Merman who hurt me. You never were. You're nothing like him."

"How can you be okay with this? With us?"

"Love, silly. I think it all comes down to love. You didn't take advantage of me. You didn't force me. You waited for me to heal first. And that thoughtfulness only made me love you more."

Stone started to pull away from her. He still had his doubts, even now after all their many, many years together. He never told Marina the truth. He had felt a pull toward her even in the early days. He had forced himself to deny it, tried desperately to suppress it. He watched her being cared for from a safe distance. He'd stay in the doorway of her room while the women healers, Mers and humans alike, hovered over Marina shielding him from her view. He watched with tears of sadness and frustration pooling in his eyes. He wanted nothing more than to tear into her room and sit at her bedside, holding her hand and murmuring and cooing to her. But he knew if he pushed things, she would never heal and never choose him, so he waited. In the end, Nimue had intervened and helped Marina get used to Stone's presence and helped her to see him as non-threatening. It took time, but eventually Marina was able to be alone with him.

"I never told you. I did love you. Maybe even from the night I rescued you. You were too vulnerable, and I tried to fight it. I only stayed away because I knew that's what you needed. But it killed me to be away from you. So, I went in search of your dad. I brought him back to cheer you up and help you heal. But I think I did it too to earn favor with you."

Marina pulled him back into her arms. "I already knew that. All of it. Without you saying a word. I knew. It's like they warned me. Sex between a human and a Mer is intense. Not just physically, but emotionally and spiritually. It really does feel like a bridge opens up in your heart and soul and connects with yours. It's like everything about you—every experience, every emotion, every everything. It feels like it downloads into your consciousness and you just know. "

Reassured, Stone kissed Marina passionately for the first time since entering the pool. His penis jackknifed out from his tail and Marina wrapped her legs around his waist the coolness of the water urging them to connect in stark contrast. Encouragement neither needed. Stone began thrusting, in and out. The two connected in a dance as old as time itself. Marina panted and he increased his thrusts to meet her frenzied pace. Marina reached her peak moments before Stone did and they rode the high together back down to the water. Marina knew what was coming and took a deep breath before Stone pulled them both down beneath the water to finish spilling his seed inside her. Sated, they rose up above the waterline and still joined—neither knowing the life they had created in that simple, ancient act of love.

6

Nimue was pacing back and forth in a private pool in her quarters. Her pink tail sparkled in the sunlight that shone through the windows. She was trying to keep herself busy in an activity she usually found soothing. But today, she couldn't find any solace for her troubled mind. She was struggling with wanting to be with Finn and wanting to give him space. She couldn't stand seeing horror in his face as he came to terms with the fact that she brought him to the house because she wanted him. She couldn't bring herself to tell him the truth that she needed him. She worried he'd never understand. How could he?

The door to her quarters swung open, startling her. Finn strode in, surprising her further. He had no idea how to get to her quarters. Her question was answered when Joel, Marina's father entered behind him. She shot an accusatory look at Joel.

"You haven't spent any time with Finn today and as a healer myself, I thought he could use some exercise. Thankfully, your pool isn't far from his room and I knew you were hiding out here." Joel stated, standing his ground.

"I knew Finn needed to rest." Nimue had to reign it in to keep from glaring at Joel. He was always meddling in something but overall, he was too lovable to be annoying. Most of the time anyway. "Fine, Joel. Thank you for escorting him here. Leave us."

"Stone and Marina are unavailable for a while, but I'll be nearby if Finn needs anything." The old man winked at Finn and left closing the door behind him.

Alone with Nimue, Finn decided to make his move. He removed his shirt and grabbed his shorts, sending them down with the boxers underneath them and then he stepped out of them.

Nimue immediately placed her hand over her eyes in a comical attempt to preserve Finn's modesty.

He just chuckled in response and lowered himself into the pool. "Sorry, Nim, I don't have a bathing suit. And if we're going to be together anyway, you'll see me eventually." He shrugged. "How does a mermaid make love anyway?"

Nimue pulled her hand away from her face and made sure to keep her eyes on him from the neck up as he splashed in waist-high water. "Much like humans. I have all the same equipment as a human woman. You just have to get used to it being on my tail."

"Oh, I see. Or rather I understand, but I don't see." He reached toward her then. And she easily evaded capture. He gave chase.

Splishing and splashing together like little children. Finally, Nimue caught him and pulled him against her tight. They were both panting and out of breath. Finn smiled at her. Then he splashed her playfully and swam away across the pool. She caught up to him easily enough and it was her turn to swim away. This cat and mouse game with a mermaid twist went on forever, it seemed.

Finally, Nimue decided to end it and extended a hand out to Finn and shook her head toward the exit. She pulled herself across the landing, sliding until only her fluke fins remained in the water. Finn joined her. He matched her by keeping his feet submerged and he became acutely aware of his nudity and lowered his hands to try to shield himself.

"It's okay, Finn. I've seen naked men before. If you like, my bedroom is through that door to your left. I have some extra clothes for you in there that I was going to bring to you later. You can help yourself to some towels in the bathroom too, and get dressed. I'll transform back to human and join you and we can talk.

Finn shrugged. "I'm fine. Or I will be. Just takes some getting used to. I can talk for a bit here, and then you won't have to transform. We can go right back to swimming after."

"If you're sure."

"It's kind of nice being able to talk to a Mermaid. It's not often that I've had the chance to simply talk to one."

"You don't have to be nervous. And just so you know, I can mate in either human or Mermaid form. I unfortunately know for a fact that Stone and Marina go back and forth. Not that I actually witnessed it. I just know. So, if you're more comfortable with humans, that's doable."

"It's not that. Actually, I've heard sex with a Mermaid can be quite magical. We should at least try each one."

"We don't have to though. I still mean to give you time. I want to make sure you feel like you're choosing me. And in the end if you don't choose me, you don't have to worry about being cast out. You'll always have a home here. Always."

"Why did you choose me? I was worried in that cage. Dirty and cold and depressed. I thought no one would choose me. I knew I looked too scrawny for any kind of manual labor. But I also knew my scars would keep me from being chosen as a pet, so I had no idea what would happen to me. Then you said, 'Open that cage,' and I couldn't believe that someone was choosing me. Why?"

"I saw your file. I knew about your scars before I made them open your cage door. I knew how you got them. The fire. Saving Mermaids and Mermen. How it was because of your poor memory that you got the job at that lab in the first place. How it put you at the right place and the right time to save so many Mers. They'd probably all be dead if it weren't for you. How you were given the nickname Finn when the Mers you almost died to save realized you couldn't remember your name after the fire. How much you had suffered at their hands when after they saved your life for saving theirs but betrayed you by imprisoning you and trying to sell you to the highest bidder. They did that instead of freeing you. That was unforgivable. To repay your kindness with such malice."

Finn reached for Nimue's hand and applied a gentle pressure, squeezing it so softly. "It was pity that motivated you."

"No!" Nimue vehemently denied that. "It was heroics. And the misguided hope that after all you had been through you might relate to my past. That was what I ultimately wanted in a mate."

"Your past?' Finn looked at her incredulously. "What does that mean? Tell me, please?"

Nimue sighed "I lived here as a child. The resort was thriving then. No one cared about who was a Mer or a human, or if your family consisted of both. But Mers were often put on a pedestal by humans back then. Most were expected to be the definition of physical beauty. And I wasn't, to say the least. Even as a child, I was always a bit curvier than the others and the worst news was still to come: I was born with a facial deformity. I was taken to every healer, Mer and human alike. No one knew what to do for me and I endured years of senseless bullying."

Finally, as a teenager, my parents took me to a human man who was an expert healer in such cases. He healed me. It was a complete success. My recovery took all summer but once I healed, I was no longer deformed. I couldn't wait to go back to school and make lots of new friends."

But that autumn, the wars started. Bad things happened to pretty, young Mermaids. My parents finally had a pretty, if somewhat still too curvy, young Mermaid at the worst time to be a parent to such a creature. Right as I was ready to rejoin society, it was society itself that fell apart. There was nothing to go back to—not safely, anyway. So, I was hidden away. What I had longed to be for most of my life was now a liability that could lead me to a fate worse than death if not death itself."

I grew up in seclusion in what was left of the resort solely for the purpose of ensuring that I did live to grow up. But I had no life experiences with others aside from family and a select few friends of my parents who were trusted to be around me. I was never allowed to meet new people—Mer or otherwise. I was never able to fall in love. Things were better when my dad found Stone. Ironically enough, humans were about to stone him. My father was a human. He brought Stone here for healing. And I was smitten."

Of course, part of it may be that Stone was the first non-relative Merman my age that I had seen in far too long. But when he, in turn, brought Marina here for healing, I knew it was never meant to be. I loved her too. I would not interfere in the love and happiness they found together. For a while, it was enough to live here with them. But eventually I wanted some of that for myself too. So, Stone took me to look at some humans. I think he thought a sex slave or pet would satisfy me in the short term, but I knew it wouldn't. If I brought someone back with us, it would have to be someone special and I would never demean them by making them some kind of sexual slave or pet either. Your backstory was special, and I had hoped maybe compatible with mine."

Finn turned toward her and leaned in to kiss her on the lips. It was a chaste kiss, but he wanted to make his intentions clear.

Nimue blushed, "Thank you. That was my first kiss."

"I know," he smiled against her lips and then kissed her again.

Nimue pulled away long enough to say, "And that was my second kiss."

"We should get back in the water and see what other firsts we can accomplish."

"Finn...."

"What?"

"If you're serious... if you choose me... then there is something else I'd rather do first."

Finn was beaming. He knew where this was going.

7

Finn fidgeted with the contraption Stone brought him. It was a merman tail in ceremonial white. They were gathering at a centralized pool in the resort. All humans were expected to at least dress like Mers for the duration of the wedding ceremony. But for Finn, the anticipation of what he would be teaching Nimue that night was eating away at him. At least until he saw her swimming down the pool in a sparkling virginal white tail of her own. Maybe, he thought, he could wait a little while longer.

The marriage ceremony was quick and the reception and meal afterward even quicker. The household seemed to know that Finn and Nimue were overeager to have their alone time. Marina came to their rescue, effectively dismissing them and allowing the party to go on without them until the next dawn. They were so happy, that they didn't even notice Marina was refusing all alcoholic drinks at the reception. Too grateful for her assistance, they retreated to what Marina had deemed and decorated as their honeymoon suite.

Nimue's reaction was priceless. She couldn't believe Marina had done this all herself. There were flowers and seashells decorating the space in every shape and color. Fragrance was coming from somewhere and the water in the pool seemed heated.

Finn smiled his signature grin that allowed his dimples to show even through his scars. He reached for her and, shyly, she removed the white tail coverings that left her pink tail visible to view as well as baring her breasts to him.

"Now, Husband, where did we leave off the other day?"

"We'll figure it out," Finn answered, still beaming.

He took one nipple in his mouth. Innocent Nimue threw her head back, thrilling to the sensations filling her as he gently nibbled at it, before giving the other breast the same treatment. He slid his hand past her belly button and thrilled to the sensations of his fingers on her scales. Then he felt the scales shift as if they parted in the water and he realized more of Nimue's intimate secrets were being revealed to him.

He thrust his fingers inside, slowly at first, but then faster and harder encouraged by Nimue's responses to his gentle invasion. Gently, he eased himself inside her, wanting her first time to be in Mermaid form as his penis replaced his fingers and breached her virginal passage. He met resistance but took it slow, retreating a bit and reentering a few times until he could finally pierce her maidenhead and sheath himself fully in her. He continued his thrusts harder and faster at Nimue's urging, and made sure that she reached her peak before he did. Finally, he spilled his seed in her while in waist deep water. They stayed in the pool for a while after, each lost together in post-orgasmic bliss.

Finally, Nimue encouraged Finn to follow her out of the pool. She was eager now to experience sex as a human. Once she had dried and transformed into a human, Finn found himself rendered speechless. He hadn't considered the possibility that in human form, Mers would naturally be hairless below their chin. Nimue was so hairless she had to be born that way it was the only explanation. He decided immediately that, shocking though it was, he liked it as he studied her pubic area and then led the blushing Nimue to their human bed.

He laid her down on satin bed sheets. Marina's attention to detail left them both amused by her care. Finn then gently guided Nimue's human legs apart and kissed around her belly button before entering her. The situation seemed oddly foreign without the presence of scales and water. Even so, they had no trouble achieving a near-simultaneous orgasm this way. After they were sated again, Nimue gave into a fit of giggles.

"Something funny, Wife?"

"Just trying to decide which form I like better—Mer or human."

"I think each has their merits. In any event, we have the rest of our lives to figure it out."

ABOUT NIKKI LYNN ARCHAMBAULT

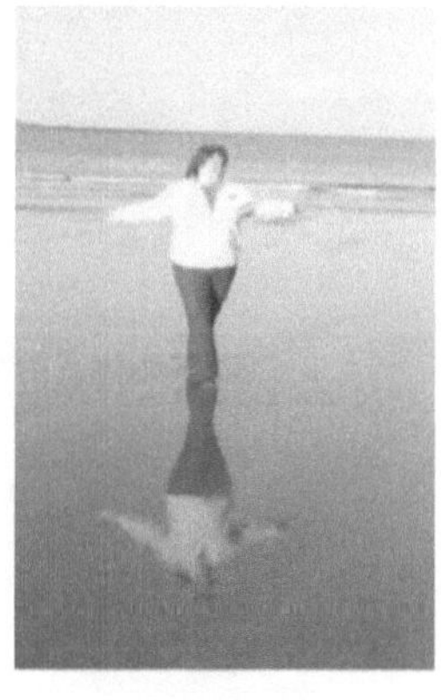

Nikki Lynn Archambault is the Queen of Mermaid and Mermen fiction. She has been dreaming of an alternative universe where Mermaids and Mermen are real and making up stories even when she was too young to literally write them down. Escaping to her fantasy realm helped her cope with growing up with a facial deformity known clinically as a class III Malocclusion or a severe underbite. Her facial deformity was corrected via reconstructive surgery when she was 16 years old but by then the years of endless bullying from classmates had left psychological scars that would never fully heal. At approximately 26 years old she was diagnosed with Asperger's Autism and while the diagnosis brought some relief it brought with it an anxiety that she could never write again without unintentionally infecting all of her characters with Asperger's Autism. That anxiety was eased when she was encouraged to write a short story for a competition at a Fanfiction Facebook Group and she won on her first try. She decided to devote her writing to Fanfiction going forward. As the years passed however her tender affections for the character associated with that Fanfiction Facebook Group had cooled and she was forced to leave as she developed feelings for that character's enemy (who is her muse for her character Finn). She credits being forced out of that Fanfiction Facebook group with giving her the courage to pursue her writing career outside of Fanfiction and leading her toward participating in this Anthology.

She Owns Mermaid Fiction—the Premiere Facebook group for all things relating to Mermaid and Mermen Literature:

https://www.facebook.com/groups/581352852025953/

She also Owns Dwight's Secret Society for Writers—her own Fanfiction Facebook group especially for Fans of the character Dwight Parker and his portrayer Actor Austin Amelio as well as all things from The Walking Dead and Fear The Walking Dead fandoms: https://www.facebook.com/groups/2320698634875307

facebook.com/authornikkilynn.archambault

 instagram.com/nikkilynnarchambault

ACCIDENTAL FUTURE

BY TAMMY GOODWIN

Rachael knew her love of history and science would bring her fame, but she never imagined it would also bring her love! When Rachael saves Thomas the sparks fly as they fall in love and heal each other.

1

To say that the day was going badly would be an understatement. Rachael paced in her cell, testing the walls, looking for a weakness. *Nothing*, she thought, *nothing!* Why would there be a way out? She was the one who designed the cells, and she never made mistakes! Rachael finally slumped down on the small, bare cot nestled against the wall of the cell. Deep inside she knew she didn't really want to get out, she just didn't like being controlled. Getting out would endange more than just her life. She slammed her fist on the mattress. "Why didn't I make these cells nicer!" she muttered to herself, sinking down five inches toward the floor.

2

The Burkin-Keller Institute for Historical and Cultural Research, BKI for short, was founded by Rachael's late grandfather Rayce Burkin and his college roommate Zachary Keller the year after they graduated Rutgers University in 1958. Zachary never married (some believe he found his soulmate in Rayce) and left his share in BKI to Rayce upon his demise.

When Rayce and Zachary started BKI, their intention was to create a living history museum. A place where historic reenactments were interactive and visitors were able to ask questions of the performers, who were all experts in their chosen timeframe of history. Over the years, many of the reenactors left to start festivals, faires, dinner theater, and games throughout the world. BKI would help by providing start-up funding and receive a percentage of the profits to continue their historical work.

Rachael's father was less interested in history and more interested in the magic of science. Growing up at BKI was a treat for young Zack and allowed him to explore his interests in Galileo, Jonas Salk, and his newest interest Marie Curie; on a deeper level. Zack and Marie (real name Adeline) were married a short time later, and within a few months Rachael came along. The small family lived in Adeline's native France where they studied. Adeline studied biology and medical breakthroughs while Zach studied physics and quantum mechanics, a new field he helped pioneer.

On a rainy day in August 1995 while driving to meet friends for a late dinner, their car hit a barrier and flipped; both were killed instantly, and

Rachael was an orphan. Rayce flew to Paris immediately and brought ten-year-old Rachael home to the BKI.

Rachael was a curious child but withdrawn. She often spent hours just staring at one exhibitie or the other. She had no interest in interacting with the reenactors, it was as if through sheer will and observation she could learn everything she needed to know and then move on. Rachael's grandmother had long since passed away so Rayce took on the role of both mother and father and did everything he could to give Rachael a good life.

While Rayce hoped his namesake, Rachael, would choose a career in history and eventually take over the running of the BKI, he was sorely disappointed when she chose the path of her parents—science. Rachael graduated with a double doctorate in astrophysics and quantum mechanics then went on to receive a double masters in pathology and infectious disease control. While offered positions with NASA and the CDC, she chose to return to BKI and help her grandfather run things.

Rayce was delighted to have Rachael at work with him, and his hopes of Rachael taking over BKI upon his retirement became more possible. Rachael spent her days giving tours and planning exhibitions and her nights sleeping in her office and doing research. Rayce chose to ignore his granddaughter's secretiveness and unavailability. He was just happy to have her there with him at BKI.

Rachael had her own motivations for working at BKI and "throwing away" her education. Rachael was a genius and she had her own plans for the future of the Institute. Her plan was to make the institute even more realistic.

3

"How's that new timeline working out?" yelled Mike, Rachael's eager assistant, as she hurried by.

"Almost done," she shouted over the din of the D-Day reenactment occurring above her. In fact, it was done, and Rachael could not wait to test it out. Only a few close confidents knew what Rachael was doing in her basement suite. Her grandfather thought she was designing plans for a new exhibit, performing Skype interviews with candidates and meeting with costume designers. But not today; today was something different, something exciting! Today, Rachael was going to try out her new timeline!

Rachael had done something amazing that no one had ever done before; she had discovered a way to travel in time. Rachael designed a device that could create a controlled wormhole allowing Rachael to go back to any point in recorded history and return safely. The first time Rachael tried the device she played it safe and only brought back a flower she stole from Queen Victoria's Rose Garden, just to make sure she could. The second time, Rachael brought back a chicken, one of many on the farm owned by Laura Ingalls Wilder. But this time was different—Rachael was going to bring back a living human.

Rachael's big picture goal was to bring forward in time men and women with significant knowledge of their time period. With the internet generation in full swing, Rachael was able to easily research her time periods and find men and women she believed would help bring history alive to a new generation. She was not interested in hiring plain, old reenactors for the museum. She wanted something better, she wanted people who lived the experiences they were portraying.

Rachael understood that changing the timeline would have dire effects on the present and had done enough research to know that a breech in the space time continuum could be deadly. Rachael's solution to this quandary was brilliant. She would only bring people who were on their deathbeds, dying of some disease that was a death sentence in their time, but easily curable in the present.

The target for today's timeline was Thomas Wyatt. Wyatt died Oct. 6, 1542, in Sherborne, Dorset, England shortly after meeting with Charles the VII of Frances' ambassador. Thomas was only thirty-nine at his death but had experienced several lifetimes of intrigue at the court of Henry VIII. Wyatt was a well-known poet of the time and introduced the sonnet to England long before William Shakespeare made it famous.

History records that Wyatt died of hypothermia, something virtually incurable at the time but now easily treated. To Rachael, Wyatt was a perfect candidate. Who better to teach museum patrons about the Tudor period than someone who had been imprisoned in the Tower of London twice for treason while also being one of Henry's close friends and a lover to Anne Boelyn?

Mike helped Rachael to design the lower levels where the magic happened. The levels consisted of a control room where Mike would program the timeline into the quantum bridge unit; a travel room, where Rachael would step into the wormhole and come back through when the mission was over; and a research library consisting of every book, article, and crazy idea ever written about time travel, including all episodes of Star Trek and the Outlander series. While Rachael didn't think a slingshot around the sun or some magic rocks would help with the journey itself, she believed that these resources were helpful in other ways. Learning the custom of a more primitive society, adapting to different cultures, and seeing the consequences of mistakes. An entire floor was dedicated to medical care, including all the latest diagnostic equipment, a full lab, and a surgery suite. Also in these levels were two cells in case any of the participants exhibited symptoms of temporal displacement and had to be contained.

At six in the evening Rachael was eager and ready to start the process. She was waiting in the traveling room, and Mike was in control. Rachael had chosen a simple outfit she took from the racks of the reenactors' wardrobe. She made sure there was no modern tech on her body, except of course for the return trip transmitter she had implanted in her arm, just down from her wrist. All she needed to do was tap a simple code through her skin onto the transmitter and she and anyone she was touching would be transported back to the future.

Mike tapped the microphone, making it squeal, and asked Rachael for a countdown. Looking directly into Mike's eyes, she calmly said, "T-minus twenty," and began counting down. Mike's hands flew over the keyboard, and light began to swirl in front of Rachael's eyes. Slowly, over the twenty seconds, the light began to form what looked like a whirlpool, full of beautiful colors from across the spectrum drifting around a center point of indescribable, ever-changing color. When the countdown got to "one," Rachael looked over at Mike and smiled as Mike nodded. She stepped into the colors.

4

It took Rachael a minute for her eyes to adjust to the bright, brisk air. She was standing on the bank of the River Yeo. Rachael looked around and noticed once again how clear the sky was, not an ounce of haze, just clear, beautiful air. *There's something to be said about those emissions controls put in place in the seventies,* she thought. Based on the sun's position in the sky, Rachael knew that time was short. She wanted to speak to Wyatt before it was too late, having consent was important to Rachael.

Trudging on the river bank, Rachael saw a small house in a meadow at a crossroads and a tall church up the dirt road a little father. *This is it,* she thought, *that's the house where Wyatt is staying!* Walking toward the house, Rachael went through her plan one more time in her head. Knock on the door, tell whoever answers that the doctor sent her, meet Wyatt, convince him to go, and get Wyatt to the river—no problem!

As Rachael approached the house, a large man emerged and scurried away toward the church. *I hope that wasn't the doctor,* Rachael thought. Knowing that the English language had changed much in the last five hundred years, Rachael knew she should keep with French. Most nobility and their staff of the time knew both languages, and French had not changed nearly as much as English had. Knocking at the door, Rachael was happy to see a young woman open up and stare shyly at Rachael.

"Bonjour!" Rachael intoned, looking sternly at the girl. "I have been sent by the doctor to get Monsieur Wyatt into the fresh air for his recovery." Rachael breezed past the girl and into the great room. Not waiting to press her luck, Rachael quickly turned to the girl, pretending to be in a rush. "And where is Monsieur Wyatt? Come, come, I do not have all day!"

The girl was shy and in over her head, so she looked away and pointed at a door to the right. Rachael jumped at the chance and briskly walked to the door.

Entering, Rachael saw lying on the bed one of the best looking men she had ever seen in her life! *Oh my*, she thought, *history told me he was good looking, but I had no idea he was THAT good looking*!

Tall for the time, Thomas Wyatt's lower legs dangled over the foot of the bed, his once lush, dark hair lay limp on the pillow, and his normally tan features had a bluish tint to them. Wyatt opened his eyes as Rachael sat next to him on the bed.

Speaking in French, Rachael asked Wyatt if he understood her. It took effort for him to nod his head yes. Rachael quickly told her story, not sure if he was fully understanding everything, but eager to get the words out. Thomas Wyatt's only reaction as Rachael spoke was when she talked of his death, only hours from now. A tremor ran through him from head to toe and he looked a way for a second, only to quickly turn back and meet Rachael's gaze. In the end, Thomas nodded, which Rachael took to mean that he'd accepted and wanted to go. Rachal could hardly contain her delight. Her first "real-actor" was joining the museum. But first, Rachael had to get him out of that house and away from the girl.

"Mademoiselle," Rachael cried out, "come help me bring Monsieur Wyatt outside!" The girl crept in, fearful of many things. Fearful of the man whose house this was, who'd hired her to look after Wyatt in his sickness, and fearful of the loud, pushy woman standing in front of her. At last the girl gave in, taking the path of least resistance. Walking toward the two, the girl was directed to take Wyatt's arm and help Rachael walk him outside. Wyatt was a tall, strong man, but with his sickness he had withered, so getting him outside was not a very difficult task. Once outside, Rachael directed Thomas and the girl to the river bank where they sat Wyatt down in the sun.

"Off with you," Rachael tossed words at the girl like a stone, making her scurry away, back to the house.

Once Rachael saw that the girl was out of site, she turned to Wyatt. He was smiling, enjoying the sun on his body. "Ready?" she asked, and he turned his brilliant smile at Rachael. Even in his sickened state he made her heart flutter and her lady bits tingle. *Yikes*, she thought, *I may just be in trouble here.*

Not wanting to waste any more time, Rachael tapped the code into her arm, and in an instant they were back at the facility. Wyatt was dazed and near collapse so Rachael set out on her task of treating his hypothermia. Mike looked on from the large observation windows. Seeing how nervous he was, he made a note to himself not to let Wyatt and Rachael do anything stupid.

First thing on the agenda was to get Wyatt on a saline drip to give him the hydration he was sorely lacking. Then Rachael began to run tests on Wyatt, needing to know some baseline information to ensure proper treatment.

Strange, she thought, *this doesn't look like any hypothermia I've ever seen.* First, Rachael took blood samples, then moved on to collect mucus and saliva. As she ran her tests, things started to look even stranger. His temperature was fine! *Oh God*, she thought, *this is not hypothermia! What have I done?* Quickly running the rest of the tests, Rachael remembered the girl. She had been sweaty. Rachael had assumed it was from doing housework in a home kept warm to help Wyatt, but no, that wasn't it. *No*, Rachael thought, *no, no, no! I know what this is! And I don't have a cure!*

Rachael ran over and banged on the glass, getting Mike's attention. "It's the Sweat," she yelled through the glass. "The English Sweating Sickness."

Terror came to Mike's eyes as the reality of what she was saying sunk in. *The Sweat*, he thought, *the disease that ravaged England several times during the Renaissance.* Pressing the lockdown button, Mike made the first step in containment. The next step happened as a cloud of gas came down into the lab, causing Rachael to drop to the ground unconscious. Donning his hazmat suit, Mike began the task of moving Rachael and Wyatt into the cells, where they would have to stay until a cure could be found.

5

Rachael woke up not quite sure what had happened and where she was. The first thing she did notice was a blasting headache and a bad taste in her mouth. Moving her tongue around, she started to remember the feel of the gas in her mouth, and it all came back to her. *No*, she thought, *I've really fucked up this time!* No one knew what The Sweat was, what caused it, or how to treat it. Her first foray into bringing people back to the future and she may have ended the world. Ugh!

Rachael began to pace around the cell and make lists.

- 1 — I feel fine!
- 2 — I am not sweaty!
- 3 — I don't feel like I have a fever!
- 4 — My hands and legs work!
- 5 — My heart rate and breathing are normal (or at least normal for someone who is having a panic attack)!
- 6 — Thomas is ...

"Thomas," she yelled. "I forgot about Thomas!" Looking around her cell and approaching the glass wall, she could see Thomas in the adjacent cell, lying on a hospital bed and snoring. She yelled his name again, and he stirred. Banging on the glass, she saw Thomas's eyes start to open.

"Thomas, over here," she shouted through the glass as he slowly met her gaze. A small smile came to his lips. He slowly sat up while continuing to stare at her. Trying his voice slowly, he cleared his throat, looking into her eyes, and began:

Stand whoso list upon the slipper top
Of court's estates, and let me here rejoice;
And use me quiet without let or stop,
Unknown in court, that hath such brackish joys:
In hidden place, so let my days forth pass,
That when my years be done, withouten noise,
I may die agèd after the common trace,
For him death gripeth right hard by the crope
That is much known of other; and of himself alas,
Doth die unknown, dazed with dreadful face.

"You have saved me from death's grip, beautiful angel," he said as he smiled at Rachael. "You have saved me and brought me forth to live again, lost in the beauty of your eyes."

Once a poet, always a poet, Rachael thought, meeting his gaze. Trying to fight it, Rachael had been moved by his words. They had a flow that reached into her heart and pulled at the strings. *Yep, I'm in trouble.*

6

A few restless hours later, Mike contacted Rachael through the intercom system. "Rachael, I have a team of epidemiologists working on this. I paid them well and told them it was a project for the museum, they're hopeful they can figure this out soon. Hang in there."

Each day, separated only by glass, Rachael and Wyatt spoke—Rachael teaching Wyatt about all the technological breakthroughs in the last five hundred years, and Wyatt speaking of poetry and courtly love. What Rachael loved best was when Wyatt spoke of Anne Boelyn and his love for her. Theirs had been a romance for the ages, but they were both married to others, and Anne had caught the eye of the King. Wyatt was heartbroken when Henry ordered her execution. Wyatt knew that the favor of the King was a fickle thing and could change like the wind. Wyatt had known the Catherines as well—Catherine of Aragon the first wife, divorced and left to die with her daughter at her side, and Catherine Howard, the tawdry child bride who had more lovers than the King and showed no fear when walking to the executioner's block. He also knew Jane, Jane who could have saved them all. Jane who birthed the King's long awaited son. Jane's death, a tragedy, but also a time of joy. There was an heir to the throne. Mary and Elizabeth no longer a threat.

Their conversations grew long into the night, their hands placed on the panes of glass between them, so close but unable to touch. Rachael felt something growing inside her that she'd never felt before: a longing, a trusting, a peace. She was falling in love with this man, out of his own time and into hers.

Rachael told Thomas of her parents, a subject she had never felt comfortable discussing. Of her idyllic day in Paris, the love she saw between her mother and father, the passion that brightened their eyes when discussing science, history, and medicine. She told him of their death and the aftermath, explaining that personal history was just as important as the history written in scholarly texts. The history made by her parents and their impact on the world around them.

Looking Thomas in the eye, she could see his fascination. Finally, he understood why she did what she did. Why she'd figured out time travel and wanted so desperately to save people. She couldn't save her parents, not without messing with the space time continuum, but people from history who were as good as dead at the time of rescue, that she could do.

Thomas smiled at her gratefully. She chose to save him, not just because he was a famous poet, but because of what he knew, what he saw firsthand. What secrets to the past he could unlock. She was as brilliant as Anne Boelyn, as cunning as Catherine Howard, and as strong willed as Catherine of Aragon. He had finally found a woman that would have endured Henry! And who would make him very happy.

"What was it about Anne Boelyn that made men destroy kingdoms for her," Rachael asked one day? "I read that she wasn't even that pretty." "What Anne lacked in traditional physical beauty she more than made up for with her charm. She could look into your eyes and see through to your soul. She was always one step ahead of everyone. Brilliant and cunning. She knew what someone wanted without asking, she was attentive and loving and made everyone fall in love with her-both men and women. When you were near Anne, you felt like it was just the two of you, no one else mattered." Thomas looked at Rachael, smiling "You are Anne reborn but with extreme physical beauty." Rachael blushed, caught up in Thomas's gaze. *Oh,* she thought, *he loves me! And I think...I think I love him!* It was a strange sensation being in love. Rachael couldn't remember ever being this happy in her adult life.

Thomas grew stronger every day, and Rachael never fell ill. After a few weeks, Mike announced they had discovered what the Sweating Sickness really was—a tick borne illness that could not be transmitted from human to human. It wasn't a virus after all. Rachael did not cause the end of the world.

Signing with relief as Mike opened the glass doors to their cells, Rachael turned toward Wyatt. She reached out a tentative hand and was met quickly by his. He pulled her in closer and they kissed. A kiss that quelled all the longing and frustration of the last few weeks, a kiss filled with promise of a new world and a life together to explore it.

The End

ABOUT THE AUTHOR

I'm starting my new journey into fiction. I've been published in scholarly texts before but now I have my first short story coming out August 1.

www.ingramcontent.com/pod-product-compliance
Lightning Source LLC
Chambersburg PA
CBHW030842030726
47495CB00005B/1338